DYING TO RIDE

Babe by Jennifer, artist & graphic designer, February 3, 1973 - August 1, 2020

Fractured Families, Shocking Secrets

DYING
to
RIDE

Everything Equine Mystery Series, Book One

Lenore Mitchell

EQUISETUM BOOKS

For my beloved daughters

Jennifer, with love and longing, I miss you,
your hugs, your support

Michele, equestrian extraordinare, you inspire me,
I love watching you ride

And For

Babe my 'one in a million mare'

Babe by Jennifer, artist & graphic designer, February 3, 1973 - August 1, 2020

LESSONS FROM HORSES

There are those of us
who are mysteriously drawn to horses
as if in some ancient time or place
we've experienced their true nature.

We recognize horses at some deep level of our consciousness.
We hearken to horses as a beacon, a homecoming,
an unspoken longing for something we can't define.

As we bond with a horse,
attempting to understand and interpret,
we are learning to nurture another,
to face our fears, and move beyond boundaries…
essential lessons in any relationship.

In this new, quiet communication
of touch and thought,
intuition and expression
we find, at last,
ourselves.

~ KIM MCELROY
Spirit of Horse Gallery

COMING TOGETHER, FALLING APART

THE MORNING SUN PLAYED hide and seek through tall ponderosas, tickling our necks, bouncing over horses' silky manes. A solitary cloud puffed across Colorado's blue sky, the only sounds rhythmic hoofbeats. She looked good on her horse, clearly loved it. Loved them all, had gone on and on about foals that didn't survive. Cared more about animals already dead and buried than anything.

Or anyone.

This ride was a chance to finally be real, honest. At least that was the plan. But conversation fluttered, failed.

If only she'd tried.

But no. This ride began with sunshine and promise, but by the time Rim Rock Cliff appeared, clouds shattered the day. We tied the horses, scrambled up to a ledge in light rain which quickened into a deluge as the world faded to gray. No words now. Too much said, yet not enough.

The angry sky swirled overhead, as dark as her soul. Thunder roared, as loud as her silence.

Her damned silence.

She could've saved herself, saved us both. But again, no. She huddled inside a poncho, lips sealed.

Wet glistened against her cheeks, maybe rain pelting against her guilt, maybe tears. But no matter.

Too late.

Lightning savaged the sky.

She stood, moved toward the ledge, looked down.

One scream, just one. Maybe hers.

Then, silence.

CHAPTER ONE

THE HOT AIR HELD the scent of alfalfa, and occasional whinnies punctuated the hum of human voices. The list of competitions on Colorado's Western Slope grew longer every year. Making my living around horses satisfied a thirst that insisted on being quenched. I almost considered it a compliment when friends said I smelled like the barns where I spent most waking hours. My business card said it all: Margo Richards, Everything Equine. Sure, I sometimes felt like an outcast right where I grew up for preferring breeches and English saddles to the Levi's and western tack favored by most locals. But training horses and riders is basically the same no matter what equipment is used.

Only spring, and already the second time I'd trailered half a dozen horses and their owners seventy miles from the cool forests of home to these showgrounds on the outskirts of Grand Junction. I enjoyed the excitement and camaraderie of horse shows, but all the problems back at the ranch made me feel guilty about leaving this time. I couldn't let my riding students down, though. They got all worked up about winning. Sometimes it took a while for them to realize that the reward for understanding horses goes beyond ribbons.

Except for one cute but ornery pony named Pickles, the other mares and geldings had patient eyes and willing hearts. White bands highlighted braided manes, black polish accented hooves. I busied myself checking tack and doling out last minute advice. My adult students were almost too serious, but the kids were more prone to giggles than frowns. Hugging away an occasional tear was part of the deal, even for some of the adults.

Half past two on the show's final day, and I positioned myself alongside the arena railing to watch Charley, a chestnut gelding with a steady gait and a forgiving attitude. My only student in this English Pleasure class was little Nicole Jensen. The judge called for a trot, and Nicole got Charley moving and began posting, but her up and down movements weren't in sync with her horse's two-beat diagonal gait. I raised a hand to my chin. She noticed right away and sat two beats to correct her rhythm. I gave her a nod; she gave me a sweet smile.

Somebody tapped my shoulder.

"She doing okay, Margo?" A whisper, anxious.

"Not bad, not bad," I said, turning to smile at Beth Jensen. Despite the day's scorching heat and billows of dust rising behind all those hooves, Nicole's mom always looked like she'd stepped out of some magazine. Perfect hair, sandals color-coordinated with a frou-frou sundress, wide-brimmed hat. I teased her sometimes, saying all that perfection made my teeth itch. In response, she said fashion was a foreign country to me, one I should visit. We laughed about it, but she had me pegged. I wasted little time in front of mirrors, lived in breeches and paddock boots, twisted blonde hair into a long braid. Despite our differences, Beth and I were friends, both of us fond of her gutsy and talented ten-year-old daughter.

The judge called for a canter. Nicole cued Charley and off they went, looking smart.

"Good girl," I whispered, just loud enough for Beth to hear.

The weekend, almost over now, was a success. I closed my eyes and sighed. I'd just resumed watching Nicole when another hand touched my shoulder. A large hand. Followed by a deep voice.

"Margo."

Roy Holden loved horses but avoided most shows. More importantly, there was something about his tone, about that way he said my name. I whirled around.

Typical cowboy looks, tall, lean, poker-faced beneath an ever-present Stetson. Not my type, usually. But after three years together, we shared a closeness that had surprised us both at first. He'd proposed, sort of; I hedged, always. Now his lip twitched to one side in the way that meant he'd rather not say something.

"What? What're you doing here?"

His hand tightened on my shoulder.

"It's Bow," he said, looking down at me, then away. "I... Sheriff Plackmon called. I drove straight here."

"The sheriff? Why?"

He looked at me some more, silent, then took hold of my hand and tried to lead me away.

His palm felt sweaty.

"What! Tell me," I said, swallowing around a lump that galloped in out of nowhere and slid to a halt inside my throat.

"She... She's dead," he said finally, his voice low.

"No," I whispered. "No."

Beth gasped and clamped a hand over her mouth, but I only shook my head, hard, squeezing my eyes shut, that lump in my throat ballooning.

Ever since I was twelve, Elizabeth "Bow" Bowan had been like a mother to me. Not that she'd been a hugger or a cookie-baker, but she taught me everything about horses, about common sense. She'd always been there.

Always.

"She can't be dead," I mumbled. "No way."

She was only forty-nine, only fifteen years older than me. She was strong, capable.

Roy drew me close and I burrowed my face into his chest. But then I opened my eyes, stepped back, whispered, "What happened?"

"Someone found her out in the Flat Tops, Rim Rock Cliffs. Sheriff Plackmon said she'd been there, uh, for at least a day."

"No. No," I said again, attempting to swallow but not managing it, choking against images of her in pain before one final breath. Lying there for a day. At least. "Oh my God," I moaned in a voice that didn't sound like mine.

Beth grabbed my hand. "Oh, Margo, I'm so sorry."

I looked at her, bit my lip, turned to Roy.

"How did they... Who found her?"

"Sheriff didn't say. He flew out with the helicopter crew to... bring her back."

I shivered, though only seconds ago I'd been sweating under the baking sun. And then my mind began playing tricks, whisking me all the way back to when my parents died. I couldn't go there, couldn't stand reliving that heaviness, that disbelief I'd clung to after the plane crash and all that followed.

"Not again," I said, without realizing I'd spoken out loud.

Roy's arms encircled me. Death had stolen my parents years ago and now it'd come for Bow, taunting me, snatching those I loved one after another.

"Come on," Roy whispered. "Let's get out of here."

I wanted to tell him and Beth everything would be all right. I wanted to say something to make them stop with the sad eyes. Sympathy made this real, inescapable.

"By the Cliffs?" I mumbled.

"Sheriff said it appears she may've fallen."

I imagined her standing on top of those tall rocks, slipping and scrambling, falling, falling.

It wasn't like her. The area was several hours away by horseback, the trail benign under the forest's shady canopy before crossing streams and curving up hillsides. Bow and her gelding were inseparable. She must've ridden out there.

"Where's Bandit?"

Roy frowned. "I don't know."

I glanced to the east, toward the distant mountains of home, toward forests thick with ponderosa and Douglas fir. Arid Grand Junction nurtured few trees, was by comparison a desert.

"She never rode all the way to those cliffs when it was just her and Bandit. Besides, she wouldn't have let the remaining foals out of her sight for long, not so soon after—"

The only time I'd seen her cry was when she stood by those three graves behind the barn. I shouldn't have come to this show, should've stayed with her because of what'd happened.

Roy put an arm around my shoulders. "Let's go, Margo."

I turned back toward the arena, saw riders lining up to await ribbons.

"What about the final classes?" I mumbled. "The horses?"

Several of my students who'd driven their own rigs stood nearby, and the looks on their faces said they'd heard everything.

"I'll drive your rig if you want," one said.

"Between us, we have extra room for all the horses," another said.

I looked at them, tried to smile. Couldn't.

"I'll help get everyone home, too, Margo," Beth said, sounding like she was about to cry.

"Thanks," I murmured, wishing I could soothe her, soothe myself. But reality had shifted into a nightmare, a dark swirl cooling the summer sun with a swiftness that left me breathless. Three foals were dead, and now, so was Bow.

Roy pointed to his red truck, the one we called the Beast. He'd brought the border collies, of course. He loved Zap and Fetch as much as I did.

"C'mon, ride with me."

I wanted to climb in beside him, snuggle close. But I felt an inexplicable need to be alone, to act stronger than I felt.

"I'll drive my rig, but let the dogs come with me," I said, trying to sound normal without much success.

He nodded, didn't try to change my mind. I busied myself checking the latches and the hitch on my six-horse trailer, clinging to routine, as if that'd help. Once the dogs jumped into the cab, I settled behind the wheel of my one-ton dually, shifted my mind into neutral and forced myself to concentrate on traffic, the highway, the yellow lines. Anything to keep tears from escaping.

Roy's Beast followed, hovering in my rearview mirror.

Halfway home, the drone of a small plane startled me. Wings dipped as the thing circled overhead and, although I tried not to pay attention, it stayed visible far too long, forcing memories to resurface. The single-engine Cessna Dad was flying went down in Colorado peaks so remote and rugged that once searchers spotted the wreckage, it took several days to get there.

Someone said my parents had surely died on impact, as if that should comfort. I had nightmares about crumpled metal and splattered blood for months. I'd worried about pain, how it felt to die.

But that happened twenty-two years ago.

Time twists and then freezes when death comes, though, and images best forgotten never leave. My parents' closed caskets rested at the mortuary that awful summer, the shiny exteriors smooth and cold against my hand. The only way I got through the funeral was by trying to believe they weren't really inside those long boxes. Now there'd be another sad ceremony and it wouldn't help to be older. Maturity wouldn't make grieving easier. I fumbled for the radio, turned up the volume and made myself take deep breaths. But my thoughts drifted back in time.

So many memories.

CHAPTER TWO

JUST ONE WISH, MAYBE two. I knew it was too much to ask, even back then. Still, I needed Mom's arms around me once more, needed to breathe in her warmth. And if I could just hear Dad's steps on the back porch one last time, followed by his voice, his laugh.

But I was twelve then, old enough to know the truth about wishes and dreams, old enough to know death lasts forever. Mom's blue sweater, her favorite, would soon lose the scent of her. Dad's boots would sit unused, gathering dust. I wanted to be left alone to cry, to close my eyes and embrace the dreaded nightmares as the plane crash replayed in the theatre of my mind with silent screams from me or, worse, from my dying parents.

I'd taken riding lessons from Bow, loved hanging around her barn, which was right next to our place, but I couldn't imagine living with her or anyone else. My parents' wills designated her as my godmother and preferred guardian, though, and Bow said she'd be happy to take me in. The only alternative, other than sickly grandparents in Denver, was Aunt Gina, a single airline pilot based in Chicago who looked relieved when I begged the social worker to let me stay in Colorado. The court officially named Bow as my guardian and verified the trust fund that left my parents' ranch to me when I came of age. It was hard to accept that the only home I'd ever known would be leased until I was old enough to take it over, and it was excruciating to see someone else living there.

When I stepped onto Bow's porch all those years ago, I was clutching a tear-moistened tissue and dragging an overstuffed duffle. The first thing I saw was a chicken with its beak tucked inside one red-feathered wing, roosting on the back of a wooden chair that'd seen too many winters.

"This is Henrietta," Bow said, as though introducing a friend.

"Oh," I said.

She leaned down close to the chair. The little hen rose, ruffling feathers, and hopped onto Bow's shoulder, clucking softly.

"She's a Red Bantam. Isn't she sweet?"

"Uh, yeah, guess so."

"You've never been in my cabin. C'mon, Margo, we'll do the tour."

Bow lifted my heavy duffle as though it was a feather and waved me inside. A faded couch that might've started out brown and a huge purple chair dominated the living room, while a stack of dirty dishes rose from the kitchen sink. A box of cereal and a mound of papers decorated a wooden table surrounded by half a dozen chairs, each one different. Bow breezed past those rooms as if they were of scant importance and proceeded down a narrow hall, with Henrietta still attached to her shoulder. The hen lifted one leg and then the other in slow motion, long toes curling on the upstroke and splaying out down, rotating to face me, cocking her head to one side, blinking round chicken eyes.

Henrietta and I stared at each other, and I found myself wanting to reach out and touch her feathers and the squiggly red comb that looked like it might slide right off her head. I was so intent on watching the hen that I almost tripped over two dogs stretched out in the doorway.

"This is my bedroom and these are the guards," Bow said, plopping my stuff onto a chair in the corner. "You've seen them around. The yellow is Bubbles, the brown is Buttons."

Tails thumped the floor and both dogs sniffed me, tongues lolling, tails working. To my surprise, they ignored the chicken. Bow patted them, and then scratched the hen's neck. A small feather loosened and fluttered to the floor.

"Henrietta likes coming inside, but only for a few minutes. She'll want to go back to the chicken coop by the barn soon."

I wondered how a chicken made its preferences known.

Seeing the dogs reminded me of my own animals, both waiting out in Bow's truck. Pinecone, the Labrador that Mom and Dad gave me one Christmas, was my constant companion. When Pinecone napped, Jiminy, my calico cat, cozied herself between the big dog's paws. They'd been part of the family, and now they were all I had left.

"We'll introduce your pets in a bit," Bow said, as if reading my mind. "They'll get along just fine here, and you will too."

I wasn't so sure. My parents grew timothy hay and ran some cattle on their small ranch next to Bow's but living here would be as strange for Pinecone and Jiminy as for me.

Clothes spilled from Bow's closet floor, a jumble of breeches and shirts and boots. Books and horse magazines overwhelmed the nightstand. The dresser top held a mound of lustrous fur, each strand tipped black, sliding into brown, fluffy tan deeper inside. A coat, maybe, or a big blanket.

But then the thing moved. Dark eyes peeked out.

My mouth opened; no words came out.

Those eyes shone like bits of coal. Before I decided whether to be frightened, one leathery black paw poked out, a black-and-tan ringed tail appeared, and the thing unwound into a large raccoon.

Bow moved toward the dresser. "Did we wake you, Ralph?"

The raccoon made a whirring noise and stretched dark paws toward Bow, watching me all the while. The animal wrapped front legs around Bow's neck and hind legs around her waist, clinging there, tail dangling. It nuzzled her, sniffed the chicken, and again turned a comically masked face in my direction.

Bow laughed. "Come say hello, Margo. Ralph is friendly, even to Henrietta. His mama met an untimely end a while back, so he joined my family."

I hesitated, then hurried over. Ralph stretched out a paw, patting first my chin, my cheeks, finally the tip of my nose. He whirred again, but in a different pitch than before.

"He likes you," Bow said, motioning for me to sit on the bed. She transferred the raccoon onto my lap.

Ralph touched my neck with his soft pointed nose.

My fingers sank into dense fur, and I knew right then that living there might work.

Bow handed me bone-shaped biscuits for Ralph and the dogs. The raccoon slouched back on his haunches, hind legs splayed around ample belly, rolling his biscuit back and forth in his paws before munching.

Bow converted a storage area into my bedroom, and it wasn't long before Ralph slept there too, on the bed next to Pinecone and Jiminy. Mom's blue sweater made a reassuring lump under my pillow. Dad's boots stood guard beside my bed. When the nightmares came, Pinecone and Jiminy snuggled closer, but Ralph was the one who hugged me. He read my moods, knowing when to comfort, when to entertain. For a long time, he was the only one who could make me laugh.

Bow's raccoon led me through the nights.

Her horses led me through the days.

When I needed to cry, those horses stood patiently, eyes soft, swishing silky tails, understanding everything.

The ranch entrance had a wooden arch with a sign naming the place Bowan's Backwoods. She gave favored horses names starting with the letter "B," often dogs, too. When I moved in, Bubbles and Buttons were the dogs, Butch, Boo, and Babe among the many horses. That tradition continued and we had fun coming up with new names.

Now, Bandit the palomino gelding would be the last horse in a long and memorable line.

Several months after I moved in, we spread sleeping bags next to a stall where a mare was foaling. That struggle made me think about how little control anyone has over life or death.

The colt didn't choose when to be born.

My parents didn't choose when to die.

After that slippery baby emerged, I cuddled it and traced the softness of its muzzle with one finger. And then my throat closed, things went all blurry, and the sobbing began without my consent. I thought I'd gotten over the worst sadness, and I'd been careful not to cry around Bow. She put her arms around me, lightly. She didn't say everything would be all right, didn't say a word. She just waited. When I finally wiped my eyes and looked at her, I realized how much she meant to me. When I tried to tell her, though, the words sounded hollow and she seemed embarrassed.

Communication between us evolved into something deeper than talking. A kind of telepathy, I suppose, like the way animals communicate with each other, and with humans who take the time to listen. The love Bow and I shared was felt and shown more than spoken.

Bow treated me like her own flesh and blood, like her daughter.

She was only twenty-seven when I went to live with her, but I was just twelve, so I didn't realize how young she was, how pretty. She seldom wore makeup, kept thick auburn hair in a ponytail, lived in breeches, plaid shirts with rolled-up sleeves. Bits of manure clung to the bottoms of boots she sometimes forgot to shed at the back door.

Men hung around, flirting, and she flirted right back. In summer, especially, there were parties with people crowding the cabin and spilling outdoors. Sometimes Bow would disappear for a day or two, leaving a friend in charge of me and the ranch.

One man, Rick Williams, hung around more than most, proposing to her repeatedly. I think she loved him, but for some reason she always turned him down. One time, he found her in bed with another man. He stopped coming around after that.

Back when Roy and I got serious, I told her that neither of us felt ready to commit to more than living together. Bow said she'd wanted to settle down at one time, but she'd gotten over it. She said that although she'd be happy for me if I decided to marry, she considered it boring to live with just one man. Then her tone changed and she added that she'd never felt worthy of true love anyway. She'd done some things, she said, things she'd tell me when the time was right.

But that time had never come. Now it never would.

CHAPTER THREE

MOIST AIR LINGERED FROM the recent rain. The day had slid towards evening by the time I reached Pinedale Springs, a small town dwarfed by mountains rising in three directions. I followed Main Street past the feed store, the lumber yard, and the car dealers to open fields and onto ten miles of dirt road, slowing by my front pasture.

Most of the horses didn't raise their heads from lush grass, except for Babe, my dear old chestnut, and Phantom, my black mustang. Both mares looked up as if welcoming me home, but I drove on while Roy turned into my place.

Bow's ranch, next to mine, covered several hundred acres of rolling meadows interspersed with aspen groves and ponderosa forests. Trails behind her land led into the White River National Forest and eventually to Flat Tops Wilderness. Penstemons poked blue flower stalks above grasses in the pasture where survivors of this year's crop of Quarter Horse foals cantered on wobbly legs around patient mares. Those babies' antics used to make me laugh. In the past few weeks, though, every foal seemed fragile, as if their toothpick legs might shatter. But defective conformation wasn't the cause of losing so many foals this year.

A miscarriage in early spring was followed by two foals who appeared healthy, but died shortly after birth. So distraught she could barely speak, Bow switched the remaining mares and offspring to a different pasture and arranged for toxicology tests on tissue samples from the dead newborns and the mares' milk. She had lost foals before, it happened in any breeding operation. Never this many, though. She was so upset that I'd started canceling plans for the show, but she insisted I go, said everything hinged on final test results that weren't yet available from Colorado State University over in Fort Collins.

Now the cabin door opened and I wished Bow was coming out. But it was Boss, Bow's golden retriever, who appeared, followed closely by Audrey Langford. A tangle of long mahogany-brown curls framed Audrey's usually serene face, but now tears sputtered from reddened eyes. She was the same age as me, but she'd weathered less on her way to thirty-four than I had. Manicured nails and casually elegant clothing might've marked her as the type who make other women feel inadequate, but Audrey was like my friend, Beth. Both carried beauty without pretense.

She claimed to be a biology professor at CSU and didn't look like the outdoors type. Still, in the month since Bow had hired her for seasonal help, she'd proved herself by riding like a natural and shoveling horseshit alongside us without complaint. She'd seemed fond of Bow from the start, but they'd barely had time to get to know each other. Audrey fit right in here. She seemed perfect. Too perfect.

I hugged her, feeling awkward. Bow's dog crowded close, tail low.

It wasn't until we sat down on the porch with Boss, Zap and Fetch close to me, that I noticed two cars parked beside the cabin. First was Audrey's blue Nissan, serviceable but less elegant than its owner. Second was a silver BMW, one I'd enjoyed some time ago, snug in leather seats.

I glanced at the front door. "Where's Dawn?"

"Inside. She arrived this morning."

"How about the others?"

Audrey's eyebrows lifted. "Others?"

"Dawn's mother and sister."

"I have no idea."

Before she could say more, the door opened again. The oldest of Bow's two nieces, Dawn Curtis, lived in Denver with her investment banker husband and two young boys. An accomplished artist, her watercolors graced galleries from Aspen to London. Much of her work featured flowers, but her painting of Babe, my all-time favorite mare, hung in my bedroom and was the first thing I saw every morning, the last image before my eyes shut at night.

"Margo," Dawn said, shaking her head as tears streamed over softly rounded cheeks.

We met in a tight hug and I patted her back. She was only two years younger than me, but I'd always felt protective of her. The bond between us began during childhood summers spent riding ponies, climbing haystacks, and playing hide-and-seek in Bow's barn. We'd seldom gotten together in recent years, but as kids we used to weave each other's hair into braids and pretend we were sisters.

"Can't believe it," she mumbled, sniffling. Boss crowded against her and she patted the dog's head.

"Me neither," I said, swallowing hard. I was close to tears myself, but I would let Dawn cry for the two of us, for now. "You just got here?"

"Needed to see Bow, but..." She shook her head, more tears coming. Boss licked her hand.

I bit my lip. "How did you hear?"

Audrey answered. "I told her. Ruth called this morning; said she contacted the sheriff's office when Bow didn't show up at the store. The dispatcher told her."

Ruth Dunn and Bow had co-owned the B&D Tack shop in Pinedale Springs for years. Small towns spread news faster than Facebook and Ruth reigned supreme as the local know-it-all. But Audrey lived right here in Bow's cabin, helped with morning chores. I looked at her, frowned.

"Bow's truck was here," Audrey said, her voice shaky, "so I thought she was staying overnight with Doc Wilson again. I took care of the horses."

I didn't say anything, but I didn't stop frowning, either.

"I called JJ," Dawn said. "She's bringing Mother over from Denver. But Jason and the boys—" She stopped, began sobbing again.

"What? What's going on?"

"He," she began, "The boys, just..." She shook her head, took a deep breath. "They're fishing in Montana again." She paused, blew her nose. "Jason's been so distant. He's going to leave me. Everyone leaves."

"Oh, Dawn, I'm so sorry."

"I wanted a family," she said, squeezing her eyes shut. "Now all that is gone."

I grabbed her hand, pulled her close.

"Bow is gone," she continued, then opened her eyes, looked at me. "I used to wish she was my real mom. I loved her."

"Me too," I said. "Come inside, now, Dawn. You look exhausted."

She nodded. "So bad," she muttered, following me in and collapsing on the couch.

I was also exhausted, but sleep wasn't an option, not yet. I took my cell back out to the porch, contacted the sheriff's office. A dispatcher promised to forward my message.

Questions swirled in my mind. Not many people went all the way out to Rim Rock Cliffs, for one thing. Bow often took Bandit on solitary rides, but it was unlike her to go there alone.

Roy was at our place feeding the horses, but maybe he could fill in some blanks.

"What time did you hear from the sheriff?" I asked when he answered my call.

"About mid-morning, he called our landline. He asked for your cell number, but I told him I needed to tell you in person."

I nodded, even though Roy couldn't see me, loved him for coming.

"When did they take the chopper out there to, uh, get her?"

"Must've been early."

"But he didn't say who found her?"

"No. Want me to come over when I finish here?"

"Yes, do."

Audrey came out and sat down just as I ended the call. I glanced at her. I had questions for her, but not yet.

"I need to check the horses, feed them."

"I was about to start chores when you arrived," she said. "I can help."

I shook my head, hurried off with Zap and Fetch racing ahead, Boss by my side.

Bow's world centered on the barn from morning to night. Red and faded, patched here and open to the sky there, the building held a dozen stalls, a hay and feed area, a tack room, a grimy bathroom forever out of TP, and a small indoor arena. During foaling season, Bow threw her sleeping bag in the barn aisle near one laboring mare after another. Now, in early summer, most animals were out on pasture.

I slipped inside and inhaled the sweetness of alfalfa hay. My border collies raced around outside, but Boss clung to my side, tail low. I patted her head and moved into the barn's cool interior, my boots ringing hollow against the concrete aisle in an unnerving way. I sucked in a deep breath, hissing it out against clenched teeth, and kept going to the far end of the building.

The tack room, jammed but orderly, held a faint aroma of well-oiled leather. Saddles, bridles, halters, lead ropes, brushes by the dozen, everything had its place. Packing gear for the wilderness trips Bow and I led several times a year took up one entire wall. Shelves bulged with ointments and supplements.

Boss curled into her usual corner, head between paws.

I stood still, leaning against the door frame, imagining Bow preparing for what turned out to be her last ride. Then I noticed the saddles. Bow always kept her favorite, the Billy Cook she used for trail riding, on the rack nearest the door.

A different saddle sat there now, as glaringly out of place as a pair of fuzzy slippers in a row of cowboy boots. It was a western, like Bow's, but one of those used for the dudes we took on pack trips. Looked like it'd been thrown there by someone in a hurry, someone who either didn't know or care where it belonged. Half slopped off the side of the rack, one of the stirrups dangling onto the saddle below. The seat felt damp, not soaking wet, but not dry either. I scanned the other saddles, running my hand over each. None felt moist.

Bow's saddle was nowhere in sight. She always rode Bandit, and her palomino knew the way home from anywhere, even riderless. Her gelding wouldn't just wander around out in the forest. If he'd shown up, surely Audrey would've unsaddled him, notified someone that Bow was missing. If Audrey herself rode with Bow, she would've taken her usual saddle rather than the one now on Bow's rack.

Nothing made sense.

I moved to the bulletin board. Bow and I were both capable riders and it wasn't unusual for either of us to ride alone, but we always left messages for each other, scribbling notes whenever one of us planned a long solitary ride. Nothing fancy, just the time, which direction we were headed, about how long we'd be gone. Bow never failed to leave one unless she wasn't going out alone.

I knew this because of what happened back when I was seventeen. I had a crush on Greg, a basketball star. After he humiliated me one day in the high school cafeteria, I was torn between wanting to die versus whacking him over the head with my chemistry book. Instead, I ran out to the truck I drove to school, gunned the thing home. There, without telling Bow, I saddled Babe and galloped off into the wilderness. What began as an escape turned into near disaster when my mare had colic out in the middle of nowhere. In the end, I spent a chilly October night beneath pine trees and a sliver of moon, walking Babe and watching over her until her gut finally settled. Bow came looking, but by the time she found us the morning sun had risen in the eastern sky and we were almost within sight of home.

After that, we agreed to always let each other know where we were headed when we rode alone.

Always.

There was no note.

I grabbed a halter, lead rope, and a can of grain, hurried toward the main pasture. That moist saddle on Bow's rack, along with the lack of a note, pointed to a companion. But if that was the case, had Audrey lied? Or why hadn't someone else come forward? The gate latch was secure and before opening it, I stood looking from one to the next of a dozen horses, heads down in lush grass.

And there, grazing alongside the others, was Bandit.

Even now, with the sun low to the west, Bow's gelding was easy to spot in a herd. Some palominos look washed out, pale, but not Bandit. His coat shone like burnished copper, mane snowy white. Not far from him, closer to the gate, was a dark lump on the ground. I squinted, realized it must be a saddle.

I unlatched the gate, ran out and bent over the thing. It was a saddle, all right, and even though it was almost unrecognizable, it had to be Bow's. Wet slime covered the distinctive white rawhide horn. Moisture darkened all the leather, turning the normally reddish color almost black. This was the Billy Cook, Bow's favorite. Soaking wet, filthy with mud. Suspicions simmered, along with thoughts of fingerprints on the leather.

Clouds threatened more rain tonight, though, and any meaningful evidence had surely been washed away. Besides, it seemed like a violation to leave her saddle there for one second more, Bandit's muddy bridle curled on top, reins tangled over the saddle horn. I carried the filthy mess to the barn and ran back out there.

It didn't surprise me that Bandit had found his way home, but the fact that he was inside the pasture meant someone had opened the gate for him. Whoever did that must've undone the bridle and the saddle girth, letting everything drop to the ground.

Infuriating.

Audrey had seldom left the ranch since her arrival, so she must've been around, might've even ridden out with Bow. She knew the basics of horse care, knew how particular Bow was about tack. There'd been enough rain and mud to erase footsteps and hoofprints. Maybe Bandit arrived during a lightning storm and Audrey ran out to unsaddle him and was unnerved by the weather.

But why would she lie?

I'd deal with her later. Now, I approached Bandit, holding out a handful of grain. He remained still, his tangled white mane shining in the low sunlight, letting me approach without bothering to move in my direction. He was Bow's horse, after all, not mine. Classic Quarter Horse conformation, superior disposition. Bow kept his picture on her nightstand.

Finally, he took one slow step toward me, then another.

Dead lame.

From the way he moved his off hind seemed to be the problem, but I couldn't see that side of him. After he took a handful of grain with soft lips, I slipped his halter on and swung around to look him over. Dried blood clung to his rump, up high to one side of his tail. No fresh bleeding as far as I could tell. I felt around the wound edges and he swished his tail, limping one step away. Something underneath that blood was painful. I grabbed the cell from my pocket, called the vet.

Doc Wilson asked questions, said he'd be out.

I inspected the rest of Bandit, from muddy legs to scruffy coat. He could use a good brushing, for one thing, as much to check for other injuries as to clean him. Whoever opened that gate for him hadn't bothered to look him over, which steamed me but good. I led him slowly out of the pasture to cross ties at the wash rack. No sense risking more bleeding, so I left the wound alone. Washing the rest of him didn't reveal any other problems. From what I could tell by the way he moved, the gash on his rump might be deep. He needed stitches if that skin wasn't too dry and damaged. I led him to a stall bedded in thick shavings.

"Damn it, Bow," I muttered, "what's going on? I'll see that Bandit gets taken care of, but what happened out there? What happened to you?" My throat choked up, my vision started blurring, but I took a deep breath, forced myself to focus.

I went back out to her pasture, checked the other horses. One of them might've been ridden out with Bandit and Bow, but even though the sunlight was fading, it was still clear that recent rains had washed away any saddle marks that might've remained. Sometimes, girth marks stay on a horse's belly even when rain washes saddle marks off the back, but all the horses had rolled in the muck so even their bellies were mud-caked.

I walked over to the separate mare and foal enclosure, found them whinnying and jostling for the evening feed. After ladling portions of special mix into low tubs outfitted with grates for accessibility only by foal-sized mouths, I satisfied the mare's larger appetites with their own grain. Only two of the broodmares now had offspring to suckle. The other unlucky mares had rejoined the regular pasture herd. Unused feed tubs served as glaring reminders of dead babies.

As if that weren't enough, Bow was gone forever, her horse injured.

Unless Audrey Langford had some good excuses for acting so damn innocent, I'd kick her ass from here to sunrise.

CHAPTER FOUR

I RAN UP TO the house, fueled by flames of suspicion. I'd had no reason to dislike Audrey, no reason to question her presence or her intent in the month since Bow hired her. Sure, it'd seemed unusual for a college professor to spend an entire summer working with horses when the job usually went to a high-school kid, but anyone could be lured by the scent of alfalfa and the softness of a velvet muzzle.

She still sat alone on the porch. When she got a look at my face, she rushed to the edge of the steps.

"What? What is it?"

Everything. Bow dead, Bandit injured. I felt short of breath and not from running. I was tempted to pounce on her, demand that she revealed who the hell she really was, what the hell she'd done. I bit my lip. What mattered was the truth and a non-confrontational approach was the way to get her to spill whatever she knew. Whatever she'd done.

Yeah, right. If this woman was involved in any way, I'd bludgeon the truth out of her before turning over whatever remained to the sheriff.

"You said you've been down at the barn?"

"Of course. I feed the mares and foals twice daily, and was about to do evening chores when you arrived."

It was an effort to keep the anger out of my voice.

"So have all Bow's horses been okay?"

"I looked at the pasture horses but did not go out there."

I tightened the fingers of one hand into a fist behind my back.

"Have you ridden lately?"

"No, actually, I've had too much on my mind."

"Oh?"

"I'm in the middle of a divorce, a complicated one. He, my ex, is a lawyer using every maneuver possible to ruin me, both financially and professionally. It's part of the reason I came here for the summer, to escape."

"Did Bow know?"

"She knew, yes, because at times he scares me. He changed from the man I once loved into a...a total bastard, made me question myself, my entire life. He called repeatedly, trying to coerce me into meeting him in Denver. I kept refusing, so he drove over to Pinedale Springs with an enormous pile of documents he insisted we must go over immediately."

She sounded sincere. But my focus wasn't on her problems.

"Were you here when Bow rode off?"

Her head moved side to side, a slow negative. "That was yesterday, the day he came. It was early when I drove into town to meet him."

"Where was Bow?"

"Down at the barn."

"Anyone with her?"

"I didn't go down there, but I did not see anyone else."

"Any other cars, trucks around?"

"Not that I saw."

"Was she gone when you returned?"

"Yes. She hadn't left a note and her truck was here, so I assumed she went to town with friends or with Doc Wilson. When she wasn't back by dusk, I fed the horses as usual. She was often out late on weekends, as you know. I went to bed without waiting up for her."

"How about her horse? Did you open the gate for him?"

"Gate? No, he was already out there, grazing with the others."

I frowned. "Did you even look at him, see that he was wounded, lame?"

She clamped a hand over her chest. "Hurt? Bandit is hurt? What happened?"

"I don't know yet."

"I had no idea anything was wrong until Ruth called this morning, said..." She paused, hung her head before whispering, "Bow was dead."

"Bandit apparently came back to the ranch on his own. Someone had to open that pasture gate for him."

"I was not here."

I just looked at her.

She went inside, returned with a piece of paper, handed it to me. "Don Kelsey and his firm."

There was nothing serene about the look on her face now.

"I cannot blame you for being suspicious, but I have no idea if anyone rode with Bow or who opened the gate for Bandit. How bad are his injuries?"

"I'm about to find out," I said, seeing the white pickup turning into the driveway. I asked Audrey to stay inside with Dawn, because I didn't want her at the barn and because I couldn't trust her. Or anyone.

Doc Wilson unfolded out of the truck's cab, stretching to his full height of six foot plus. His slender frame made him appear even taller and I'd always teased him about the way he had to bend down to tend foals. He wore brown overalls, as usual, and this evening his baseball cap was bright yellow.

"So sorry," was all he said.

A lump formed in my throat, so I just nodded until I could finally speak. "Who told you?"

"News travels fast. Hank Reynold's wife heard from Ruth Dunn. What happened to this gelding?"

"Wish I knew." I flipped on the barn lights and led the way to the stall. "I found him lame, caked blood on his rump."

Bandit leaned against one wall as if to ease his hind leg. I slipped the halter on, coaxed the gelding out into the aisle, and Doc Wilson got busy. After cleansing the wound, he glanced at me.

"This is a slice from something sharp. Maybe a knife."

I gasped. "A knife?"

"Can't be certain. But there doesn't appear to be as much ripping of surface tissue as you'd expect if he backed into a branch or something jagged."

"It does seem strange to be wounded on the rump," I said, "but a knife!"

"If this gelding made his way home from out in the forest, who knows what trouble he may've gotten into."

But my thoughts were on Bow. I shut my eyes against images of someone coming at her with a knife, of struggling, bleeding.

Doc put a hand on my arm. "Sorry, Margo."

I opened my eyes, sighed. "Can you tell for sure, about a knife?"

He looked at me, then away. "You're thinking someone might've stabbed Bow too," he finally said.

I bit my lip, shrugged.

He probed the gelding's wound. "With a fresh cut, it'd be easier to assess. By the look of this, it's over a day old. The surrounding tissues are bruised enough to muddy things. All I can say for sure is that the object was sharp."

Even the possibility of a knife made me shudder. And Bandit wasn't one to run off unless there was good reason.

"So can you stitch him up?"

He nodded. "After I debride the edges. Whatever sliced him went in at least an inch."

"Will he be lame for long?"

"Rest him in a stall a few days to start," the vet said, injecting Xylocaine around the wound's edges. "Then we'll see how he moves. Doubt lasting problems, but muscle takes time to heal." He walked to the back of his outfitted truck, returned with two packages. "I'll insert this drain, stitch him up, dose him with antibiotics."

I patted Bandit, thought about knives, about Bow.

"Remaining foals okay?" Doc asked without looking up.

"Seem fine," I replied. "How long before those tests—"

"Toxicology tests take time. CSU does a thorough analysis."

"Think the report will show what went wrong?"

He shrugged. "Hard to say. Sometimes foals aren't meant to live, you know that. Still, Bow lost too many this year."

An understatement. He'd seen them, dead newborn foals curled up as if asleep, one after another, two in the last month. Then came graves, mounds of sorrow, followed by tests and unanswered questions.

I put Bandit in his stall and followed Doc to his truck.

"I'll drop by every morning to check the gelding, change the dressing and make sure the drain stays put." He looked down before adding, "I can't believe she's gone."

"I know. Thanks, Doc."

He and Bow had been good friends, and more. Matter of fact, he'd never married, and he'd remained one of her more frequent lovers. He finished packing supplies into the neat compartments that turn the bed of a pickup into a mobile vet field hospital.

"I'll try to have the sheriff here when you come tomorrow," I said, "so you can tell him about the possibility that Bandit's wound came from a knife."

Just after Doc left, Roy's red Beast arrived at the barn. Roy got out, rushed over, drew me close.

"Things are taken care of at home," he said. "What's happening here?"

The comfort of his familiar arms around me unleashed the numbness, the disbelief that I was trying so hard to suppress. I sighed, shook my head, unable to speak.

After a while, I filled him in, unable to keep my voice from quavering.

"I'm here, Margo, I'm here," he said. "We'll sort it all out."

We left my rig by Bow's barn, took the Beast back to our place, and after eating a few bites of something I didn't even taste, I fell into bed with Roy beside me.

❋   ❋   ❋

Not long after Roy and I finished morning chores the next day, we headed to Bow's barn and got there just as Doc Wilson arrived. A black and white SUV with a red and blue bar on top came next. No lights, no siren, but my own sense of urgency was flashing.

Sheriff Ben Plackmon exited the SUV, adjusted his battered Stetson, and strode over to us. Kind hazel eyes, bushy eyebrows, and a middle-aged potbelly completed the picture of a nice enough guy. He fitted in so readily around Pinedale Springs that it was easy to forget he'd only been here a few years. The word "competent" didn't come to mind at first glance, but he was a lot sharper than he looked.

"Sorry about Ms. Bowan," he began. "I got your message, planned to come speak with everyone in person." He looked at Doc. "Sick horse?"

"Come with me," I said, leading them into the barn. I slid the door to Bandit's stall open. Roy watched from the aisle while the rest of us eased in beside the palomino. Doc Wilson explained about Bandit's wound. Sheriff Plackmon listened, peered at the gelding's wound while Doc lifted the bandage.

"You can't be certain about a knife?" the sheriff asked.

Doc shook his head. "But it was something sharp."

The sheriff asked more questions, produced an iPhone from his pocket, snapped close-ups of the wound. It looked smaller now that it was cleansed and stitched.

"Call, if need be," Doc said before leaving. "I'll be back tomorrow."

"I'm sure Ms. Bowan was a fine rider and all," the sheriff said, "but she might have had some trouble with this gelding. Could've reared or bucked her off."

"I doubt it," Roy said.

"Absolutely no way," I said. "For one thing, horses can't negotiate the steep path to the top of Rim Rock Cliffs, so Bow would've dismounted, left Bandit tied to a tree. But her horse never reared, never bucked." It was an effort to keep my voice calm. Any suggestion of blaming Bow's death on Bandit was intolerable. "This horse knew Bow. They trusted each other. He'd never hurt her."

"They never mean to," the sheriff said.

Roy shrugged. "True."

I'd eaten enough dirt while training horses to agree.

"Horses are like people," I said. "Some are trustworthy, some aren't."

The sheriff nodded.

I'd seen him riding and he wasn't bad, in a Sunday afternoon sort of way.

"This is one of the most trustworthy animals around," I said. "But you went out there, saw her."

Another nod. "Took the chopper out to the Cliffs, checked the scene, brought her back."

"How about her saddlebag?"

"Personal effects will be returned in due time."

"How about her knife? Was it in her saddlebag?"

"I can't say for sure just yet."

"Where, um, where is she now?"

"The town morgue, Margo," he spoke softly.

I imagined a steel table, hard, cold.

"What do you think happened?"

"The investigation has just begun."

"Still, you must have some idea," Roy said.

"Nothing official, not yet. But those rocks would be very slippery after all this rain. Easy to lose footing, just one misstep. Her remains were close to the base of that cliff, like after a long fall."

The word "remains" made me cringe.

"She knew better than to climb around in the rain," I said, trying to envision her on a high ledge, wondering why she'd even gone out there.

"You didn't say who found her," Roy said.

"A person on horseback; covered her as much as possible, then rode in to notify us. Cell phones don't work way out there, of course."

"Did this person recognize her?"

He blinked without replying.

"So, who was it?" I asked.

"Asked us not to say."

I frowned. "But why?"

"It's all under control. The coroner is involved and a full investigation takes time."

"You told me it looked like she'd been...dead for a least a day," Roy said.

"Correct, and the coroner will attempt to determine a more exact time frame."

"Bow didn't ride there alone," I said.

"What makes you say that?"

"She needed solitude every now and then, and she knew how to handle a horse in the wilderness. But she seldom headed in that direction by herself, for one thing."

"That so?"

"Yes, and she left a note if she planned on a lengthy solitary ride. Always. I did too. Just in case."

The sheriff nodded. "Good idea."

"There was no note this time. C'mon, I need to show you some things. Also, I don't know who was here when Bandit showed up and yet somebody opened the pasture gate for him. Whoever it was left Bow's saddle out in the rain."

Roy and the sheriff followed me into the tack room.

"Look at this," I said.

I'd hung Bandit's wet bridle on a peg and placed the muddy mess of Bow's favorite saddle off in a corner.

"And one of the other saddles still feels moist, and it's on the wrong rack, besides."

The sheriff bent down for a close look at the Billy Cook, then ran his hand over the saddle that was draped haphazardly on Bow's exclusive rack. He gazed up. An irregular splotch darkened the ceiling right above.

"That's not wet up there," I said, "it's been that way forever, just stained old wood. This tack room always stays dry. Besides, none of the other saddles feels the least bit moist."

He pushed the rim of his cowboy hat up with one finger and regarded the out-of-place saddle again. He didn't nod, didn't say a word.

Roy was silent, too, but he was taking everything in.

"Bow kept things in order at the barn," I said, "and she was especially careful about her personal tack. And what about her saddle, any possibility of finding fingerprints?"

Sheriff Plackmon bent down over the Billy Cook again.

"This is too rain and mud-soaked to retain useful information. Sometimes leather holds onto fingerprints, and mud can too, but not in this much of a mess."

He snapped more photos, tapped notes into his phone.

"Did the gelding have any other cuts, scratches of any sort that showed before you washed him?"

"His legs were scuffed," I said, "but no more than expected on a trail like that. I checked the other horses, couldn't tell if any had been ridden."

He made more entries on his device.

"Let's head up to the house so I can talk with whoever else is here." He turned to Roy. "You were around the day Ms. Bowan rode off, right?"

Roy nodded. "But I was next door, not over here."

"Did you notice any activity around this barn?"

"No," Roy replied. "I was working in my office on the other side of the house."

"You spend much time over at this barn?"

"Not much. And I travel for work, so I'm gone a fair amount."

"You two been married long?"

Roy winked at me. "We're not married, yet. But I'm working on it."

"Been together a while?"

"Moved in with her three years ago."

"What line of work you in?"

"Consulting," Roy replied. "I'm a natural resources specialist for large ranches and corporate agriculture operations."

A slight nod was Plackmon's only reply before asking, "You ride?"

"Yup. Cutting horse competitions."

Plackmon's eyebrows rose, which for him was a major show of expression. "That so."

Roy grinned. "Somehow or other, a great horse named Mutt lets me sit on him while he sorts out the cattle. He doesn't even seem to mind his name."

Plackmon couldn't keep from grinning back. "Mutt, huh?"

Anyone who knows much about horses admires the exceptional intelligence and agility of a cutting horse. They're somewhat like a border collie when it comes to herding and controlling cattle. And anyone who knows Roy understands his offbeat sense of humor, which was why he gave a spectacular cutting horse an eyebrow-raising name.

Roy grabbed my hand, squeezed it. "Mutt brought Margo and I together."

"Thanks to Bow," I said. "She owned Mutt's dam, selected the sire."

"Bow is well known in some Quarter Horse circles," Roy said. "I took one look at Mutt, wanted him. Then I saw the trainer, this Margo woman..." He leaned close, stroked my cheek.

We exited the barn, walked toward the house.

Plackmon turned to me. "How was your horse show?"

"Mostly fine," I said.

"Some of those kids and their moms think you're the greatest woman to walk the earth."

I stopped, looked at him. "You called my students?"

"Only a few, so far. You're gone a lot."

I couldn't tell if that was a question or a statement.

"Not really. My schedule varies, but I'm at the ranch most of the time, except for occasional shows or when Bow and I lead pack trips."

"Those trips profitable?"

"More fun than lucrative. We sometimes offer a spring trip into the Flat Tops Wilderness, and in the fall, we take several groups to see mustangs at Soda Creek. Each trip lasts up to a week and covers up to one hundred miles."

"So, you're both comfortable riding distances."

"Definitely."

"You and Ms. Bowan co-own this horse operation?"

"Yes, although our ranches are separate. Bow handles..." I paused, looked away. "She handled the breeding, Quarter Horses for English or western pleasure, the best for cutting horse prospects. I do most of the training and the riding lessons."

He glanced at my breeches. "You ride only English?"

"No, but I prefer it."

"Either you or Ms. Bowan having financial problems?"

"Horses are expensive, but we manage."

"You and she get along?"

I smiled. "Always."

He turned to Roy. "How about you and Ms. Bowan?"

"I liked her, admired her. She was one of the first people I met when I moved here from Montana."

"Is that where you grew up?"

Roy nodded. "The family ranch is outside Missoula. I got my undergrad degree there, then went on to UC Davis in California. You can call me Doctor Holden if you'd like. But I keep grass healthy, not people."

Plackmon grinned again, rubbed his chin, and turned to me. "Have you and Ms. Bowan known each other a while?"

"Years. I grew up on the same ranch I now own, with Bow's place right next door. I was twelve when my parents died and Bow took me in, raised me."

"You must be in line to inherit."

"She treated me like her daughter," I said, my voice cracking, "but she never adopted me. Her sister and her two nieces are next of kin."

We'd stood outside the barn for quite a while, but we were almost back to Bow's cabin now.

The sheriff paused under the shade of a ponderosa and pulled out his phone.

"Speaking of family," he began, "before we head in, give me the names and known contacts for all Ms. Bowan's relatives and anyone she'd been in contact with recently that you're aware of."

I began with Bow's sister.

"I recall hearing this woman isn't in her right mind now," he said.

"Helen Bowan Jacobs is a lot older than Bow. She and Ruth Dunn were high school classmates. Helen isn't yet seventy, but she has Alzheimer's, doesn't even recognize her daughters."

He nodded. "Go on."

"The only other relatives are Helen's daughters, Julie Jacobs — JJ — and Dawn Curtis. Dawn is here, and JJ is bringing Helen over from Denver, should arrive soon."

I continued with Audrey Langford, then as many recent contacts as I could remember. I pulled out my phone and provided phone numbers and whatever information I had. When I finished, we joined Audrey and Dawn on the porch.

Audrey rose and met us at the bottom of the steps.

"I fed everyone before you arrived, gave Bandit hay, topped off his water. How is he doing?"

"Doc Wilson stitched him up, put in a drain last evening. He needs stall rest for a few days at least," I said.

Dawn gasped. "Will Bandit be okay?

"The vet thinks so," I said.

While the sheriff spoke with Audrey and Dawn, I went inside and called the Clement ranch to find out if one of their boys had noticed Bandit outside the pasture and opened the gate for him. Tom, father of the four boys, said that his youngest, Mike, often rode his bike past Bow's place. Despite Down's syndrome, thirteen-year-old Mike functioned well, but he didn't have the best memory. Mike liked horses but couldn't manage saddling or unsaddling on his own. He could've opened the gate for Bandit, though. Tom said he'd talk to Mike and get back to me if his son remembered anything useful.

Being in the cabin felt comforting, but also strange. I moved down the hallway and stood at the door to Bow's bedroom. She'd never sleep there again. I wanted to crawl into her bed, burrow under the covers.

"She's still here," Dawn whispered, "always will be."

I hadn't heard her approach, but I turned, hugged her.

"How'd Ms. Bowan get along with folks?" the sheriff asked, once we were all back on the porch.

"She was outspoken," Roy said, "didn't hold back from sharing her opinions."

"But she didn't have enemies," I said. "About the only person she didn't get along with was Carla Simpson."

The bushy eyebrows lifted slightly. "Why?"

"Simpson wanted to sink her hooks into Bow's land," I said, "kept pressing her to sell, claimed property values will drop when drilling rigs come to this area."

"Well, she is a realtor and a developer," Roy said, "so it's natural for her to negotiate for land."

"Right," I said, "but she layers on pressure, tries to force a sale. She needs to take her damn dealing and developing back to Denver and leave the Western Slope alone."

"She made an offer on our place," Roy said, "a generous one, in my opinion."

"I'll never sell and neither would Bow." I paused, throwing Roy a look that said if he wanted to leave this ranch, he'd have to do it without me. This was one of the basics that kept us from a permanent commitment. We were happy together, but his work took him all over the US and even abroad. Settling down wasn't in his DNA.

"The Connelly spread on the other side of Bow's place is sold," Roy said.

"True," I said, "but the critical access and water rights are on Bow's property. Simpson comes around regularly, badgering. She's a pit bull!" I added, my voice rising.

Zap sat up and placed a paw on my knee. I've had other border collies but Zap is the sweetest, ever ready to listen, to console. I patted him and his tail waved back and forth. Fetch looked more ready to play than console, as always.

Dawn sat silent, a faraway look in her eyes.

"I can't imagine this ranch being sold," Audrey said.

"I can't either," I said, although I was surprised that Audrey had any opinion about the place after being here only a month.

"I overheard Carla Simpson sounding quite riled once, calling Bow stubborn, saying progress comes no matter what," Audrey said.

"What was Bow's response?" Roy asked.

"Her exact words were, 'Get the hell off my ranch and stay off.'"
Sheriff Plackmon's expression remained unreadable.

"Last fall, when all this development talk started," I said, "Simpson talked Bow and I into taking her on a private pack trip in the Flat Tops, yakking about how much she loved horses, loved the wilderness. She's a decent rider and her gelding is well trained. If she'd just shut up, she might've made friends with us, even though that wouldn't have softened Bow's resolve, mine either. But Simpson dug right in about dividing this land into thirty-five-acre parcels, told us it'd be great for lots of people to move here. Bow nearly decked her."

Development was something Roy and I often discussed. He loved open spaces as much as I did, but he believed that growth was inevitable here. He wanted me to move to Montana with him because he assumed that state wouldn't be hit with as much rampant development.

"Okay, so what now?" I asked.

Plackmon leaned back in his chair, rubbed his chin. "We'll consider everything, see whether or not there's more than meets the eye here."

I frowned. "What do you mean?"

"Now, Margo," he replied, his voice gentle, "grief can be overwhelming. People in your situation want answers, maybe want them so badly that their imaginations get carried away."

I stood up, stared at him.

"Meaning you already think it was an accident?"

"I did not say that, although it is possible."

Bow's death was no accident, I knew that as certainly as if she'd told me so herself. I'd never thought much about ghosts or spirits, had no idea whether the dead might somehow communicate with the living. Maybe her spirit was planting ideas in my head.

"The coroner's report will confirm a cause of death," Plackmon said, "but I assure you, we'll investigate every angle, every detail."

I wanted to believe him.

"Meantime," he added, "I need for someone to identity the body."

CHAPTER FIVE

AFTER DEATH, THE BODY is an inanimate shell. But before that comes the dying, a limbo, no longer fully alive but not yet dead. Identifying Bow's body, her remains, would make death final, real.

Unless this body wasn't hers. Maybe there'd been some mistake. I looked from the sheriff over to Roy, allowing myself a sliver of hope.

"You don't know for sure?"

Roy moved close, put his arm around me.

The sheriff's mouth opened but he said nothing.

Dawn hung her head, groaned, turned pale then went limp.

Roy and I rushed over, caught her just before she slipped to the floor. Her skin felt clammy, her breathing seemed shallow and rapid. I felt her wrist for a pulse, also rapid.

Roy carried Dawn to the couch. The sheriff stood, watching us all.

"Oh my gosh, the poor thing," Audrey said. "She has seemed ill since she arrived."

"Maybe it's stress," I said, "or possibly flu."

Dawn had always been the delicate type; not exactly sickly, but prone to catching whatever bug made the rounds.

Audrey went down the hall and returned with a lightweight blanket. She covered Dawn, murmuring, "Feel better now, sweetie?"

Dawn's eyes fluttered open then closed again. I felt her forehead, checked her pulse, which was nearer to normal now, and noted that her breathing had slowed too.

"I can stay with her," Audrey said.

I nodded. "Thanks. She's exhausted, for sure. And sad, of course."

Roy and I returned to the porch with the sheriff. I sat on the edge of my chair, dreading taking up the conversation where it'd left off, but the sheriff plunged right in.

"Having someone close to the deceased visually identify the body is procedure."

"Oh," was all I could say.

"Sounds like you were the person closest to Ms. Bowan, legal daughter or not. We need to verify identity soon so an autopsy can be done. I'll go with you over to the morgue now if you're up to it. Doubt the niece could stand going there, seems the fragile sort."

I doubted that I could stand going there, but I said nothing.

"Before we go, there's something you need to know."

I looked at him, holding my breath.

"Here's the thing, Margo. Her face was untouched, but the rest of her..."

My mouth dropped open; my heart started thumping as though it might explode. I didn't want to hear this. I would've sprung up, escaped, if I hadn't felt suddenly weak.

"The rest?" I finally managed to whisper.

Roy reached for my hand, squeezed it. Zap looked at me, began whining.

"Something mauled her torso," the sheriff said in a low voice. "Cougar, most likely. Which is why I asked earlier if her gelding had any scratch marks or other injuries."

"Cougar," I said, shutting my eyes but not escaping images of torn and bloody flesh. I winced, sucking air between clenched teeth.

"Her face is untouched," the sheriff repeated.

I closed my eyes, whispered, "Untouched."

Roy tightened his grip on my hand.

"We suspect she was dead before the animal came around. Still, I contacted Ed at Colorado Parks and Wildlife, and his men will investigate." He paused, lowered his voice. "I'm truly sorry, Margo. There is no easy way to tell you this. But all you need to look at is her face. The rest of her will be covered."

I hung my head, unable to think about anything but the rest of her. Bloody. Mauled. I'd already seen too much, in my mind.

Sheriff Plackmon stood. "It won't take but a moment."

"I'll come with you," Roy said.

"Please, yes," I said, trying to keep my voice level. My tongue felt heavy, dry.

"You can follow me into town," the sheriff said.

Roy nodded.

I peeked inside to tell Audrey we were leaving. Dawn appeared to be asleep.

Roy and I climbed into the Beast's cab, along with Zap and Fetch. Boss hung back but came when I called her.

I didn't want to see Bow in a morgue, to remember her body on a cold steel table. I couldn't imagine those eyes devoid of light, that mouth still. After the essence of a person leaves, when the muscles and bones become mere clumps of tissue, then whatever bad things happened to that body cause pain only for those left behind. I told myself this, over and over, to make the task ahead seem tolerable.

It didn't work.

The word "mutilated" replayed in my mind.

Bow's body was an empty shell now, vacated, her spirit gone to some unreachable place. Death would come to me, to each of us, someday. I knew this, on some level. Acceptance was another matter. I didn't want to accept her death, the finality.

We were silent on the way into town, but my dogs climbed over each other, vying to lick my face, to comfort. Boss remained curled by my feet, head between her paws.

Pinedale Springs projected a cozy welcome. It was the type of town where the farmers market was a social event, where kids knew each other, and Whitley's Ice Cream Parlor ran a tab for kids who came in for a double dip without money.

All in all, it was a quiet little town, which always suited me. But every familiar street, every store I'd known my entire life... All of it seemed somehow changed, now, as if an alternate reality had replaced the familiar.

There had to be a morgue somewhere, of course, but I'd never given it any thought. I'd been too young to be asked to identify my parents' bodies after their deaths, too young to be involved in much of anything. That summer, my only role was grieving and attempting to act normal while holding back tears. Now I was an adult, but I felt myself reverting to the age of twelve, surrendering again to grief.

I hadn't let myself cry, not yet. My role now was acting strong, capable.

Roy followed Sheriff Plackmon's SUV down Main past City Market, Nelson's Hardware, Pinedale Bank. As we passed the B&D Tack store I stared at signs in the window, unable to imagine the place without Bow. Ever since I was young, I'd loved being in the store with Bow and Ruth, running my hand over the smooth saddles, smelling the new leather. Ruth was the brains of the place; Bow was the heart. The two of them struggled to keep the business afloat, especially the last few months.

The sheriff turned into a lot behind the municipal building and parked near an unmarked door. Boss howled, possibly because of some distant siren only she could hear, or maybe because Bow's golden retriever understood too much. I stroked her thick coat before we left her there with our border collies. She watched us leave with sad eyes.

Sheriff Plackmon held the door open and led the way down a tunnel-like hallway lined in gray cinderblock, which smelled faintly damp. An eeriness hung about the place, extracting the air. I'd been in the front, more public portions of this building on occasion, but where we were felt alien.

Our footsteps sounded unnaturally loud.

I wished that either Roy or the sheriff would say something, anything. I needed to hear a human voice, but we proceeded in silence. I would've tried speaking myself, but breathing was effort enough. The hall probably wasn't all that long but it seemed like I was on a treadmill, moving but never arriving.

Finally, the sheriff stopped, opened a door, stepped inside. There was no sign, no indication this was a morgue. The room appeared small; not cozy, but rather claustrophobic. Someone else stood there, someone in a white coat. I looked down at the floor, determined not to look at that person's face or the walls, not anything. This was not a room to remember.

I tried to let my mind go blank, to turn off all thought. That wasn't happening, no, of course not. Roy kept an arm around my shoulders as Sheriff Plackmon guided us forward.

Suddenly I was staring at Bow's face. Her eyes were closed, but I didn't even attempt to fool myself into thinking she was only asleep. I avoided even one glance at the sheet that covered the rest of her, not screaming, not crying, only feeling numb.

The sheriff was watching me, so I made myself nod to let him know that it was her, definitely her, definitely dead.

There'd been no mistake.

And then, without warning, Bow's face and my mother's face merged, floating there, disembodied, filling my vision, my mind. I bit my lower lip hard to keep from screaming. I stared, blinked, stared some more.

My mind was playing tricks on me, I knew that. Bow and my mother hadn't looked alike, not at all. Mom was a blue-eyed blonde with delicate features; Bow had dark eyes, auburn hair, angular cheekbones. There was no way one should remind me of the other.

I shut my eyes and slumped against Roy.

His strong arms tightened around me, but I was drifting, floating back in time.

When I looked again Mom's image was gone and I saw only Bow. I caressed her forehead with the tips of my fingers, repulsed and yet drawn to her cold white skin. So cold. I stroked her hair, lightly flecked with gray, memorized her face one last time. It seemed like I stood there for hours before Sheriff Plackmon's hand touched my elbow.

I turned away, turned to leave Bow in that impersonal place, that place where she didn't belong. Goosebumps raced over my limbs, crossed my chest, snaked through the hair at the back of my neck. I began shivering, fluttering like an aspen leaf. At the same time, my legs rooted, reaching under the floor into the soil beneath.

Roy took a firmer hold of my arm, uprooting me, guiding me.

That last indelible glimpse of her face confirmed what I already knew.

Other people had accidents or jumped to their deaths.

But not Bow.

CHAPTER SIX

ON THE DRIVE HOME from the morgue the cloudless summer sky seemed out of place, unreal, as if reality had shifted, shattered. The only thing I knew for certain was that I had to find out how Bow died. I owed her that. Friendships sometimes fizzle, family ties loosen. Even love sometimes wavers. But no one could replace Bow.

Roy kept hold of my hand, understanding that what I needed was silence to let my thoughts wander, to peek into this new reality.

I loved Roy, loved him so much it scared me.

He was here now, yes, but he'd be leaving again soon, back to roaming western states, then across the planet to New Zealand. His expertise in natural resources kept him busy as a consultant for government agencies and private firms. When he was here, his cell rang steadily, his iPad calendar overflowed with commitments. His bay gelding, Mutt, a vastly better-looking animal than the name implied, stayed in my pasture unless there was a cutting horse event within range of wherever Roy was headed. Those two earned trophies and impressive amounts of money.

We began with friendship, moved on to love. He was so caring, so good in bed, so protective. Smart, too. Near perfect. He loved horses as much as I did. But our relationship followed a trail of compromise. We hadn't gotten as far as who should give up what so we could totally commit. I was rooted to my ranch, my steady life. He needed change, movement.

He worried about me whenever he was gone, which both amused and touched me because before we met, I'd managed just fine alone. I keep a gun around, locked away, forgotten. Roy insisted that I bring the thing out and maintain basic skills, so I periodically grabbed the Glock and accompanied him to the local shooting range. I didn't like shooting, even at paper targets, but it turned out I had decent aim. Meant nothing, though. I couldn't imagine aiming a gun at another human being or at any animal either.

I'd always been strong, independent. But the thought of Roy leaving soon for several weeks in New Zealand scared the hell out of me now. What if he never came back? I loved Roy but needing him rattled me.

When we got home, Roy stayed to feed our horses and begin searching for info on Audrey, while I returned to Bow's place to check on Bandit. In addition to Dawn and Audrey's cars, two pickups sat outside the cabin. One, shiny maroon with black mud flaps, belonged to Ruth Dunn; the other was unfamiliar.

Loud voices come from inside the cabin. Audrey and Dawn sat on the porch, Dawn looking fine now. It struck me how alike they seemed in certain ways. Both had a natural elegance, the kind that didn't necessarily come from money. Dawn flew first class, could afford whatever clothes or jewelry she fancied. Audrey looked like the first-class type too, but the car she drove hinted at a thinner bank account. Dawn wore shorts and a color-coordinated top, while Audrey managed to look more elegant in breeches than I ever could.

After I told my friend Beth that Audrey made me feel like a hick, she nudged me into buying a skirt, online. I hadn't worn the thing yet, but it looked impressive on the hanger. It also made Roy laugh. Beth was so proud of me that I promised to wear it. Sometime.

"I fed, did chores," Audrey said.

I smiled at her. She was too easy to like.

"Thanks. What's up inside?"

Stale cigarette smoke drifted out the open window, fouling the early evening air.

"Carla Simpson and Ruth," Audrey said, "and they started right in."

Of course. I should have recognized that woman's throaty voice. Simpson sounded like she sandpapered her vocal cords. Chain-smoking must've been part of it, but even so, her voice sometimes sounded sultry, other times just plain abrasive.

"Ruth accused Simpson of coming by just to find out who might inherit this place, to start with," Audrey said."

"Nasty woman," Dawn said.

"For sure." I didn't want to go in, but I reached for the door anyway.

Coming in on the middle of their heated exchange was like falling into a round pen with a couple mustangs fresh off the range, Ruth Dunn unapproachable, Carla Simpson domineering.

Ruth was much shorter, with choppy grey hair and wrinkled skin. She was just shy of seventy, but there was a strength about her. Blunt and business-like, she was a hard woman weathered by life and an ailing husband. A professional barrel-racer in younger days, she still rode with effortless grace. She managed to know everyone's business but revealed little herself, apart from devout religious beliefs. She lived in Tony Lama boots, Levi's secured with a silver belt buckle, western shirt, and ever-present denim vest lined in red corduroy.

Ruth had a soft side, but seldom displayed it. Today, it was nowhere in sight.

If Carla Simpson had a soft side, it wasn't apparent. A burning cigarette dangled from red lips. She stood average in height, but a gigantic ego made her appear taller. Middle-aged, always impeccably dressed, today's outfit was a tan pantsuit piped in black, shiny buttons marching over prominent boobs, high-heeled boots. Ever since her arrival last fall, she'd preached the gospel of growth. She was here to save Pinedale Springs from stagnating. Her goal as a realtor and developer was to save our sleepy little town, make it a destination for more people from Denver, from where-the-hell-ever. The fact that no one here wanted that didn't faze her.

Neither glanced in my direction nor reacted to my presence.

"Don't tell me what to do!" Ruth's voice was just shy of a shout.

Simpson's tone was level but edgy. "Don't be so damned exasperating, Ruth."

"Stop blowing smoke in my face and stop swearing in my presence. I am a God-fearing Christian. I do not tolerate profanity. And only friends call me Ruth."

"Okay then, Mrs. Dunn. But there's no need to get huffy. I came only to offer condolences for Elizabeth Bowan's death. Bad enough that she lost so many foals. Three this year, right?" She paused, shook her head. "Life's too short, too fucking— Oh, sorry, slipped out. But let's not turn this into a confrontation."

I rolled my eyes at that but kept quiet.

Ruth said nothing, just stood her ground. Simpson took a step back.

"No matter what you think," she said after an uncomfortable silence, "I liked her. I truly liked her."

"It may not be Christian of me to say so, but the truth of the matter is that Elizabeth hated your guts."

Simpson looked down at the floor, knitting her hands together as if in prayer. "We rode together," she said, glancing at me as if for conformation.

No way was I jumping into this.

Simpson sighed, turned back to Ruth.

"Realtors and developers aren't evil. You people in small towns, well."

Ruth's shoulders stiffened; her hands clenched into fists. For a minute there it looked like she was about to throw a punch. But then she threw her head back, laughed.

A funny look crossed Carla Simpson's face and she almost laughed too. But not quite.

I didn't much care for her, but at least you knew where you stood with someone like that. She kept her cards on the table, if not in your face. Then again, who knew how far she'd go to get what she wanted.

Ruth was no saint, either, despite her fundamentalist religious beliefs. She preached lofty ideals, made it sound like she was better than the rest of us, particularly those who didn't spend every Sunday morning in a building with a steeple on top, but I wouldn't put it past her to try and weasel more than her share from Bow's half of the B&D Tack Store. Ever since the cruelties of Parkinson's disease forced her husband, Jim, to give up ranching, landed him in a wheel-chair and robbed him of every dignity, Ruth's responsibilities had mounted along with her debts. She paid private duty caregivers for him around the clock. She paid a foreman to run their cattle. Even so, her own extravagant spending never varied. She drove a newer-model truck, insisted on the best inventory for the tack shop. There was no outward sign of the financial distress that, according to Bow, had long been simmering.

I stepped back out onto the porch and left the two of them still facing each other, but they seemed to be running low on venom. Audrey and Dawn looked up without speaking. I moved away from the open window and sucked in fresh air. Much better than Simpson's stale smoke.

"I'll check on you two tomorrow, then, right?"

They nodded.

I headed to Bow's barn, checked Bandit's bandage, threw another flake of hay in his stall. The gelding watched solemnly, nodding his head like there was something he needed to tell me.

Bow named him Bandit because she said he kidnapped her heart right when he was born.

I rubbed his soft muzzle.

"You're wondering where she is, aren't you? What can I say, huh, fella?"

The gelding seemed as dejected as Boss. I had little doubt that Bow's favorite horse and her favorite dog were aware that something bad had happened. Being here with Bandit was sad and yet comforting in a way. Made me want to stay.

But I had much to do. I patted Bandit again and went to the tack room to move the dude saddle from Bow's rack over to where it belonged. Made me feel better to get that thing off her spot, but the sight of her empty saddle rack choked me up. I grabbed the muddy Billy Cook saddle off the floor and lugged it to the truck so I could clean it, oil it.

When I got home, Roy told me Beth had stopped by with one of her mac and cheese casseroles. And Beth wouldn't stop there. She'd organize people to deliver a steady supply of food. She was a caring friend, sweet, but as organized as a drill sergeant.

Roy heated up the mac and cheese, and it smelled great, but I only ate a few bites.

"It was awful, seeing her face," I said, "and even worse imagining what might've happened out there."

"Hope it was quick, that she didn't suffer," Roy said.

We were silent for a while.

Roy was the first to speak.

"Should we start notifying people, arranging the funeral?"

"Bow didn't want to be buried."

"What do you mean?"

I looked out the window, gazed at the sky. Heaven must be out there somewhere. The thought of Bow floating around on some cloud made me want to laugh. She was hardly the angelic type.

"She wanted to be cremated, have her ashes spread out in Lost Creek Valley."

Roy ran his hand through his hair. "You sure she wasn't just talking? She did tend to exaggerate."

I shook my head. "Bow told me exactly what she wanted and I must make it happen. Lost Creek is even farther than Rim Rock Cliffs, but it's our special place."

"Okay, then. When will you go?"

"It's a two-day ride, out and back. I'll camp, take a pack donkey." As I said that, a calm came over me, a sense of purpose.

"Don't tell me you'd ride that far alone."

"I love that you're protective, but it's easier riding alone than running the pack trips Bow and I lead. Besides, I can't trust anyone, not yet. Phantom and a donkey will be great company."

"I'm good company too. Wait 'til I have time to ride out with you."

I smiled. "You are great company, but you're headed to New Zealand in, what, a week or so?"

"Less than that, unfortunately. But I'll only be gone a few weeks. Please wait, Margo."

"You worry too much."

"She died out there," Roy whispered, taking hold of my hand.

I leaned close, kissed him. "That's the reason I need to go soon, stop at Rim Rock Cliffs on the way, have a look around."

Roy made a face. "How can you be so easy to love when you're so damn stubborn?"

He put his arms around me and kissed me, taking his time.

"Where did you learn to kiss like that?" I said after a while.

"I read a book about it when I was ten."

"Nice."

"Yeah, so back to the stubborn stuff. It might be safer going with other people."

"I don't know who to trust, except for you."

"Good point."

I leaned my head against his chest, calmed by his heartbeat, his arms around me.

"I need to check my horses," I said after a while.

"I did chores earlier, but yeah, okay."

I loved him for knowing that in addition to time with him, what I also needed was time with the horses, to let them console me in their way.

The moon hung low, nearly full, an orb of soft light that blended my log house into the darkness. Once away from the building, I stopped and gazed at the stars, glittery buttons amid endless black. Something about the night sky, the vastness of it, the mystery, reminded me now more than ever how fleeting our lives are, how small our roles.

I could've followed the well-worn path blindfolded. As soon as I jiggled the pasture gate, good old Babe whinnied and meandered over for a handout. Phantom came running, moonlight shimmering over her black coat. There were few horses I didn't like, but Babe and Phantom stood out. In some way that defied explanation we'd traveled that bridge between horse and human, met in the middle, learned to understand each other. I reached into my pocket, withdrew horse cookies, handed them over first to Babe, then Phantom. Yes, they came partly for the food, but we were bound by something deeper than that.

Babe was almost thirty. Bow gave this wonderful mare to me when I was twelve and Babe took over from there, teaching me how to ride, how to live. She was my one-in-a-million mare, my truest friend. She was too old to ride much now even though she still looked darn good for an old girl. And then there was Phantom, the once-wild mustang I valued more than any horse with fancy breeding and high-dollar price. Choosing favorite horses is like choosing friends. It can't be forced, it just happens.

I was tempted to hop on Phantom bareback, just gallop away from emotions, from everything. I enjoyed moonlight rides, but I didn't have energy even for that, not now. So, I fed them the rest of the cookies, promised myself a ride early tomorrow. When my pockets were empty Phantom wandered off, but Babe remained, resting her head on my shoulder, moon shadows playing over her dark chestnut coat. I stroked her, expecting tears to come, but everything stayed inside, my eyes burning dry.

I stopped by the barn on my way back to the house, hurrying toward the sound of soft scratching. The last stall held no horses, but instead served as a semi-permanent home for Ramona, the raccoon. She gave birth to three miniatures of herself several weeks ago, the usual number of offspring she'd had each of the past seven springs. I peeked over the stall door to watch little ones climbing over her, whirring and cooing. I avoided befriending her babies because they were safer avoiding humans. Ramona was an orphan I raised from a tiny furball into adulthood, so she and I bonded permanently. She cuddled with me at times, just like Bow's raccoon, Ralph, had years ago. I opened the stall door enough to reach in and sink my hand into her lush fur. Ramona whirred at me in a way that seemed like a message of comfort.

When I awoke the next morning, for one hazy moment I let myself ignore what I'd seen in that room, what I could not change.

The sun hovered just below the horizon while I slipped into breeches and tiptoed out of the bedroom carrying my paddock boots, so I didn't awaken Roy. I dropped a note for him on the kitchen table, assuring him today's ride was only a short one, and headed for the barn. Since the sheriff hadn't released Bow's saddlebag yet, I'd taken another of her hoof picks out of her extra stash last night. Now I slid it into my pocket. Knowing that she'd used the thing was comforting.

My barn, while adequate, was much smaller than Bow's and although I had my own round pen as well as a decent outdoor arena, I rode in her indoor arena when weather forced us inside and there was training to be done or lessons to be given. Bow's ranch and ours seemed like one, and I spent as much time at her place as at my own. Many of our horses were co-owned, especially the trustworthy animals that clients rode on pack trips. Same for our sure-footed donkeys who served as pack animals. My two favorite long-ears, Maynard, and Mabel, lived in one of my pastures, while the other donkeys stayed mostly at Bow's. Now things would be different in ways I couldn't bear to think about.

She handled the brood mares and foals while I took over older fillies and colts in various stages of training. Potential buyers were scheduled to try out several fully trained mounts this week. One gelding seemed smart and agile enough to make a cutting horse prospect. Even though I preferred English riding, my admiration for horses used for "cutting," or separating one cow from a herd, was the first thing that'd drawn me to Roy.

I'd have to check Bow's records to see who was expected at her place and when. I also needed to continue riding the rough edges off Spook, the latest young mustang I'd acquired from a local wild horse auction.

Right now, everything seemed overwhelming.

But a ride on Phantom sounded not only rejuvenating, but necessary. I saddled the mare and we headed out beyond fences into the forest. I wasn't heading anywhere in particular this time, although I wanted to get out to Rim Rock Cliffs soon.

Ordinarily, I'd rather ride than breathe. I closed my eyes and inhaled the muskiness of horse sweat and leather, relaxing into my favorite English saddle, an old Kieffer. The rhythm of the mare's movements transported me to that place only reachable on the back of a special horse.

I leaned forward, twisting fingers through coarse strands of the mustang's black mane. She walked slower than usual, as though trying not to jar me. In looks and in breeding she was different than Babe, but in temperament the two could've been sisters.

The forest always felt like home. The eastern sky brightened, the rising sun promising a warm morning before clouds blew in the usual afternoon shower. Brilliant red Indian paintbrush and soft blue lupine turned faces to the light, and ponderosas patterned the trail with shade.

When we came to a level area with good footing I cued Phantom into a trot, then leaned forward and let her run. Her legs powered into a smooth all-out gallop, neck extended, mane ruffling. After a while I sat back and she responded by slowing to a canter, then a walk.

A few more hoofbeats down the trail, aspen burls crowded together, white trunks etched by gnawing elk. Blue columbines poked above grasses in the dappled shade. Bow often stopped when we came to columbines, dismounted and bent down to admire her favorite flowers. When I was a kid, she'd told me those long-spurred petals were fairy favorites, and even though I was old enough to doubt the existence of fairies, I imagined filmy creatures the size of butterflies hovering above the flowers, making soft music only audible if you bent way down.

Now, I got off and let Phantom graze while I stood staring at blue petals, mesmerized by the past, by all that was lost. The mare nudged me with velvet lips. I reached into my pocket and fingered Bow's hoof pick, buried my face in Phantom's neck and let the tears come.

CHAPTER SEVEN

THE MUSTANG STOOD, UNMOVING, acknowledging my grief. Phantom understood sorrow. Born wild, she ran free until the chaos of a helicopter-driven roundup thrust her into a crowded pen with other panicked horses. Not long after that, I first saw her as she stood trembling while a BLM man yanked her in front of prospective buyers. She was a scruffy little thing, mud-caked, mane and tail tangled, eyes white with fear. I was the only bidder, more out of pity than perceived potential. To her, I was merely another fearful creature who'd stolen her freedom.

The name Phantom came to me one twilight evening soon after I brought her home. I was watching the mare gallop out in pasture, her black form dissolving into a darkening sky. Like many other horse-crazy kids, one of my favorite books was *Misty of Chincoteague* and when I remembered that Phantom was the name Marguerite Henry gave to that famous little pony's dam, that clinched it. Misty and Phantom survived on a spit of land buffeted by the Atlantic Ocean in much the same way western mustangs survived on ever-shrinking inland spits of land, buffeted by waves of drilling rigs and rampant development.

The often used but barbaric term, "breaking" a horse is as bad as it sounds and should be struck from conversation, the method forbidden. In those first days and weeks, the mare surprised me by being different from any other horse I'd trained, from mustangs to warmbloods. Every horse has something to teach us humans, but right from the start, Phantom had a savvy that's impossible to explain but joyous to experience. No doubt she suffered from the trauma of the roundup, the new confinement in place of her freedom. Even so, she accepted each step in the basics: first touching, then brushing, accepting handouts, standing tied. When the time came for a saddle on her back, she stood still without even the expected tail swishing. The first mounting is best approached with quiet caution, same as every aspect of training a horse.

Within a few months, Phantom had shed the initial impression I had of her, the trembling, the scruffiness, all that gone as she emerged into one of the most trustworthy mounts I'd ever had. Despite my lingering guilt for having denied her the freedom she'd been born into, the mare seemed truly content with her new life, seemed like my friend.

Now, as I wiped my eyes and sighed, Phantom turned her head as if to comfort me as only she could. I stroked her neck; told her I loved her.

By the time we returned home, my grief felt a touch less overwhelming. Riding served as my psychiatric fix, always had. Horses understood, they just got it. No need for pretense, for hollow words. They felt your happiness, accepted your sorrow. I wasn't much for the human version of religion, but I did believe that special horses came into my life for a spiritual reason.

In the kitchen, Roy put down his coffee and looked up from his ever-present iPad.

"Good ride?"

I nodded, didn't say anything, but he knew why I'd gone, knew I'd finally cried. He was almost as perceptive as Phantom, but we humans use words too much when we might be better off listening, feeling.

He came over and we hugged. Felt good. We were a pair, all right. Both of us stubborn, opinionated, so different in some ways, but still bonded together.

"I'm heading to Denver again," he said, "just for a few days, but I'm not leaving for a while. How about an omelet? I picked up some smoked gouda the other day."

I nodded, kissed him. My cooking cowboy. Everybody needs one.

Kitchens are places I've never lingered in, so it was great that Roy not only enjoyed cooking, but also did grocery shopping. Before Roy moved in with me I didn't know what smoked gouda was and my meals consisted of whatever fell out of a cupboard, which was most often cereal. But he was here and I was happily spoiled. Roy was fabulous and so was the omelet.

"How will I survive while you're in New Zealand?"

He laughed. "I've already planned what to fix in advance. I'll know it'll be challenging for you to open the freezer and defrost something."

"You mean I have to use that microwave thing!"

"It's asking a lot, but yeah, afraid so," he said, grinning. "I'll leave sticky notes by the buttons just in case it seems too complicated. I may even show you where the dishwasher is."

I reached across the table, punched his shoulder.

"Ouch! You shouldn't abuse the man that feeds you!"

I was about to reply when Dawn called.

"They're here. Please come," she said.

"Be right over."

Roy put down his fork. "What now?"

"JJ and Helen just arrived." I swallowed the last of my omelet, gave Roy a kiss. Lucky for him, he'd seldom spent time around Bow's crazy relatives.

"I'll start sniffing online for info on Audrey. Anything else I can do?"

"Just wish me luck," I said, picking up my keys. I kissed him again and headed next door with Zap and Fetch.

Several cigarette butts littered the ground beside Bow's porch. Carla Simpson no doubt left them last evening, since she was the only one around who smoked. I bent to pick them up, scowling. The filters had double gold bands, as if a bit of elegance made up for the fact that these do nothing but pollute and kill.

Inside, different voices than last night, even louder. I stuck the gold-banded butts in my pocket, left the dogs outside, and went in.

JJ stood by Bow's purple chair, holding a glass of what looked like water but was likely vodka, straight up. She was too busy glaring at Audrey to notice me. Tall and reed thin, Julie Jacobs had just turned thirty, but something in her face made her appear older. Brown hair bleached white at the tips and clipped short accented her angular jaw; her lips were thin and free of added color. The first time I saw her drunk was her fourteenth birthday and within a year, vodka became her companion. She became a stranger, changed from those years when her long hair flowed around a happier face, when she and Dawn and I spent summer mornings riding together, afternoons scrambling over haystacks, scratching bare legs, giggling our way to supper.

JJ and I never pretended to be sisters like Dawn and I did, but we got along back then. When she turned sixteen she got a driver's license, followed shortly afterward by the first in a series of DUI citations. I was twenty then and in college, so seldom saw her, but when I tried to talk to her about drinking, she just laughed. Somehow, she still managed to function. Now, she held a series of jobs, had a series of boyfriends. She had a horse and was a competent rider, at least over jumps in the confines of an arena.

The bottle hadn't ruined her, not yet.

Right now, she was using her height to try and intimidate Audrey.

It wasn't working.

Audrey sounded unruffled.

"I came here to work on Bow's ranch."

"I already knew that." JJ threw a frown my way before turning back to Audrey. "Saw you when I came over to visit. You're just a hired hand and now here you are, acting like you own the place. What's your deal, anyway?"

Knowing more about Audrey was one trail I planned to follow but leave it to JJ to bust right in with her mouth blazing. Either the booze or just her take on life had erased joy from her world.

Audrey glanced at me, eyebrows raised, before speaking to JJ again.

"I was not here the day she died."

JJ bristled. "You left Aunt Bow alone to ride out there and die?"

"Back off, JJ," I said.

"Butt out," she said.

"Nothing can bring Bow back," I said. "No amount of crying or carrying on."

Truth couldn't be bullied out of someone, either. And truth was all that mattered.

Bow's sister walked into the room, clutching a black patent purse tightly against her thin chest. She and Bow had little in common, partly because Helen was eighteen when Bow was born, but even if they'd been close in age, it wouldn't have made a difference. Helen Bowan Jacobs' carefully curled grey hair and blue tailored pantsuit gave the impression of a well-to-do sixty-seven-year-old matron, but her blank expression revealed a different story. Smiling at something only she could see, Helen headed purposefully toward the front door.

"Wait, Mother," JJ said softly, rushing to block Helen from leaving. "Where are you going?"

Helen waved her arms. "Out of my way, girlie. Who are you, anyway?"

A look of pain crossed JJ's face. "I'm your daughter."

It probably wasn't the first time that day JJ had needed to provide that reminder. I felt a flash of sympathy. It couldn't be easy dealing with a mother free-falling into the confusion of Alzheimer's.

Helen stood still, mouth open.

"Daughter? You're too tall to be mine."

"Daddy was tall. Don't you remember him? You called him Ed."

Helen smiled and swung around. "Ed? Where is my darling? He asked me to marry him, you know."

"But he's—" Dawn began

"Shut up! Where are you when I need help with her, anyway?" JJ stepped closer to Helen. "It's okay, Mother," she cooed, as if talking to a child. "Sit down, now, please sit."

I wouldn't have thought JJ capable of cooing.

Helen frowned. "Don't be telling me what to do. I'm going dancing."

JJ took hold of her mother's hand. "C'mon to the kitchen, let's find some cookies."

I watched them go, demented mother and discontented daughter.

"Alzheimer's?" Audrey asked.

Dawn nodded. "Getting worse. They keep her in a locked ward, at the home. She's the type they call a wanderer." She paused. "She's been at Sunny Acres for a year now. Fancy place but smells like pee and costs a fortune. I should know, I pay for it."

I must've gotten a funny look on my face because Dawn frowned at me.

"What! If you think I don't care about her, you're right. She raised me, but she never loved me. JJ is her favorite."

No point in disputing what I'd noticed over the years. Although Helen clearly favored JJ, she had never shown much warmth to either daughter, or to Bow, her only sister. There'd always been rivalry between JJ and Dawn as they competed for whatever maternal caring Helen doled out. In the end, JJ drowned her insecurities in vodka while Dawn proved her worth in the art world.

Bow and Helen grew up on the ranch that was now Bow's, but according to Ruth, Helen hated the ranch and ran off to Denver soon after high school graduation. When JJ and Dawn visited Bow every summer, Helen either dropped them off and left right away or just sent them alone on the train that wound from Denver through mountain valleys and inside tunnels to Colorado's Western Slope.

"Does Helen understand about Bow?" Audrey asked.

Dawn shrugged. "Doubt it. She doesn't remember anything. JJ might've told her, but there's not much point."

"How would you know?" JJ asked, coming back into the room, holding a glass of what was probably more vodka. "Just because you pay Mother's bills doesn't mean you care. I'll pay myself as soon as I can."

Dawn looked away without responding.

"Find any cookies?" I asked.

"I gave her a bowl of Cheerios," JJ said. She sank into a chair, her head down, fist over her mouth. When she looked up, tears moistened her face. "I can't believe it," she said, reaching for a tissue. "Can't believe Aunt Bow is gone."

I nodded.

"Did she, uh, do they think she jumped?"

I looked at her. "Why? Do you think she might have?"

JJ shrugged. "The last few times I came to visit, those dead foals were all she talked about."

"I thought you were only here once."

"No, several times. You were always at some show. I'd never seen her so depressed."

"She was upset, yes," I said, "but not suicidal."

"I knew she felt awful, but..." JJ paused, took a big swallow from the glass in her hand.

There was a silence, then, all of us following our own thoughts. Dawn and JJ, the nieces. Audrey, the hired hand. Me, the almost-daughter. Maybe Helen was the lucky one, the one who didn't understand enough to grieve.

The discord between JJ and Dawn made me yearn even more for a real family of my own, made memories of my parents more painful. I'm sure they weren't as perfect as I remembered, but as much as I came to love Bow, even she never erased the crater of sadness left by my parents' absence or the yearning for grandparents I'd scarcely known. I minored in psychology in college in hopes of understanding and maybe accepting the turns life takes.

I'd always wanted to include JJ as a pretend sister, right along with Dawn, but it never seemed right. Relatives were high on my wish list, though. I used to daydream about a bunch of sisters and brothers, trying out names for each one. My oldest brother would be Mark, my younger sister would be Kate. And of course, there'd be Grandma, with a soft lap and white cotton hair; Gramps, with bushy eyebrows and a great laugh. As much as I missed my parents, it was too painful to pretend they were alive again.

It still makes me uncomfortable when people talk about family reunions. My pretend family gathered only in dreams.

Although I didn't know yet if Bow had a will, her sister would be first in line for an inheritance. I wished that Helen could answer some questions, but that wasn't possible. The nieces came next, but it felt wrong to even consider that either of them might have anything to do with Bow's death. They both loved her and she'd loved them too.

And then came Audrey Langford, a wild card. She was easy to like, but there was something mysterious about her.

I walked back to Bow's bedroom. Boss was there, curled up on the bed. The dog looked up, her tail thumped, just once. I sat beside her, working my fingers through dense hair, murmuring to her. Boss acted fond of Audrey and I wondered about asking her to stay for the summer, depending on how things worked out.

Back in the living room, Helen perched on the couch next to JJ, smiling blankly.

"You have no business being here," JJ was saying to Audrey. "This is a family time."

Audrey opened her mouth as if to reply but said nothing.

"No need to be nasty," I said.

"You're not real family, either, so just shut the hell up."

Technically, JJ was correct. Bow took me in, treated me like her daughter, but never officially adopted me. Bow loved her nieces, never forgot birthdays, graduations, and all the rest. As far back as I could remember, JJ was the opinionated one. She was two years younger than her sister and four years younger than me, but she acted like she was superior to us both. I'd never known anyone whose moods swung as fast as JJ's. One minute she'd seem normal, but before you knew it, she'd lock herself into some place you couldn't reach. Maybe it was the alcohol, maybe it was just her.

The feeling of peace, of connection to Bow I'd gotten during this morning's ride, withered. I stood up. "Got to get home."

"You could at least tell us what happened," JJ said.

I perched on the arm of a chair close to the door.

"I was at a horse show," I began, and then told JJ what Audrey and Dawn had heard earlier.

"That's an awful story, girlie," Helen said, making *tsk tsk* sounds.

"Audrey already told me all that," JJ said. "What else?"

"I went to identify her yesterday. Her body was, uh, it was mauled before someone found her. Probably by a cougar."

Dawn gasped audibly. Audrey's jaw dropped open.

"Oh, God," JJ said.

"All I saw was her face and it wasn't touched. The rest of her was covered."

I fell silent, those words, "the rest of her" repeating in my mind. No one had anything else to say, so I stepped to the door.

❉   ❉   ❉

Roy was preparing to leave for his trip to Denver, but first he told me everything he'd found out about Audrey so far. Divorce papers had been filed by her ex, the lawyer Don Kelsey, who headed a firm in Fort Collins. Audrey's claim about teaching at CSU also checked out and, as far as Roy could tell, her financial status was somewhat better than debt-ridden but not wealthy. There was no easily accessible info on her youth.

Roy had only rudimentary info on Carla Simpson so far and nothing stood out. Before he drove off to Denver, he promised to search more on Audrey and Simpson in between his scheduled meetings. I know my way around a computer to a certain extent, but I was happier to spend my time with horses and leave the main searching up to my tall cowboy.

I spent the morning catching up on yearlings and two-year-olds that needed my attention, and the entire afternoon sped by with back-to-back riding lessons. I forgot to eat lunch, so I was starving by dinnertime. After chores, I hustled to the kitchen and found a note from Roy taped to the fridge: "I bet you either forgot lunch or just grabbed an apple, am I right? Open this thing, it's called a refrigerator. Inside, you'll find edible stuff, including two bowls of chicken salad. Grab one, take a fork, sit, shovel food in, swallow. Eat the second bowl tomorrow night. I'll be back as soon as I can. Love ya!"

The salad was good. It would've been even better if the cook himself was here.

After dinner, a couple from the Grand Junction area was scheduled to come and check out a few young Quarter Horses. They wanted two quiet horses for trail riding but hadn't revealed much about their abilities. When they arrived, I showed them two five-year-old geldings, for starters.

It turned out that both the husband and wife had experience and seemed knowledgeable. When they told me their goal was to compete in long-distance trail ride competitions, I asked if they'd consider mustangs. They were intrigued. I brought out Phantom first, told them a bit about mustangs and how much I loved this one in particular while I saddled her for myself. The man was tall, so I saddled one of the bigger-boned five-year-old Quarter Horses for him, and a sweet six-year-old chestnut mustang mare for the wife. The three of us and our horses spent a pleasant hour on trails behind the ranch, and in that time, it was clear that they rode well and they liked the horses I'd chosen for them. When the wife asked how much I wanted for Phantom, I just smiled and shook my head. She smiled back, understanding. By the time they loaded their new horses into their trailer for the trip home, I'd made some new friends as well as a sale. My favorite way to do business. Even so, I wished I could shut the business down for a while…but running a horse operation doesn't work that way.

I'd been so busy all day that'd I had little time to think about Bow, about all the questions.

There was much to ponder. Like who'd ridden with her. I needed to see her saddlebag, for starters. As soon as Doc Wilson said Bandit's wound might be from a knife, I had a bad feeling. Bow always carried a knife in her saddlebag. If someone stabbed Bandit with a knife, was it Bow's knife? And then, who opened the gate for him? And what about the foals and the toxicity tests?

Everything circled back to one question: What really happened at Rim Rock Cliffs?

CHAPTER EIGHT

SHERIFF PLACKMON CALLED THE next morning. He said the coroner's autopsy report stated the cause of death was a broken neck consistent with a significant fall, and it appeared that Bow was dead before being mauled. A wildlife consultant verified that paw prints out there belonged to a large cougar. Trackers were searching for the animal.

The sheriff continued, dismissing everything I'd shown him, everything I'd said. He said the lack of a note from Bow didn't prove she'd ridden with company, nor did the out-of-place dude saddle. He agreed that someone had to open the gate for Bandit but said that was inconsequential. He'd seen Bandit's wound, heard directly from Doc Wilson about the possibility of a knife.

He finished by promising to keep everything in mind.

Uh-huh, sure.

"What did you find out at Rim Rock Cliffs?" I asked.

"We are not ready to divulge details."

"Meaning even if you found something, you wouldn't tell me, right?" I said, my voice rising along with my temper.

"You need to let us do our job."

"How about her saddlebag? I assume you have it."

"We've catalogued everything found."

"That isn't an answer! Was her knife in that bag?"

"Now listen here, Margo. I called you to try and explain what we know for sure so far because I thought it might be of some comfort. But as I said before, the investigation is not complete."

"Right, okay. When can I read the coroner's report?"

"Why would you want to? It's very graphic."

"I'm sure it is. I assume there were...teeth marks from the cougar. But Bandit's wound may very well be from a knife. What if Bow was also stabbed before she fell and before the cougar came along?"

"There was a lot of tissue damage, but no mention of stab wounds." He sighed audibly. "Your part in this is difficult enough. You and all her loved ones must deal with the goodbyes, the grief."

"It would help if you stopped treating me like an idiot. I have a good idea what the official conclusion will be, but I know Bow, and I know she wouldn't have fallen. I—"

"There is another possibility."

"Besides murder?"

"Ms. Bowan might have jumped off that cliff on purpose."

My hand tightened around the phone. "No way! Bow wasn't suicidal."

"I spoke to Doc Wilson again and he told me how upset she was about the foals that died. He was there, saw how she cried over each one. She had cause for depression."

"No. I mean, okay, depression, sure. But she wouldn't kill herself."

"I know this is upsetting, but so far it appears that she might have slipped or else even jumped. Sometimes with incidents out in the wilderness, there's no way of telling for certain. Even so, I assure you this case is still open, still active. I'll stop by later and speak with the other niece and see if Bow's sister is lucid enough to answer simple questions."

"Speaking of simple questions, why are you stonewalling about the knife? Bow always had it in her saddlebag. Always."

He sighed again. "I'll keep you informed as details are clarified. As for her saddlebag and other items, all personal effects will be returned—"

I hit the off button with more force than necessary, but cutting him off with an iPhone offered scant satisfaction.

"Well, shit!" I shouted to no one.

Zap responded, rushing over to lick my arm with vigor, intent on washing away whatever was troubling his human. I patted his head, sighing. I'd always liked Sheriff Flackmon, but if he thought I was the type to sit back and just keep quiet, he didn't know me at all. I pay attention to my instincts when training horses and now those instincts were screaming that Bow's knife wasn't in her saddlebag. Meaning it was somewhere it didn't belong.

Soon after the sheriff's call, my doorbell rang.

"Anybody home?" The voice was brusque, female, and loud enough to carry through open windows.

Ruth Dunn stood there, the picture of western dignity, as always. This day's plaid shirt blended into the red lining of her ever-present denim vest. Tony Lama boots glistened; creased Levi's highlighted slender legs.

I swung the door open. "C'mon in," I said, waving her toward the couch. "Care for some lemonade or iced tea?"

"Lemonade, please," she replied.

I filled two glasses, handed her one. She sipped, and then sat close to Emmy, a semi-permanent living-room occupant. The cat, startled out of her morning nap, jumped down and began licking herself, the preferred method for feline self-soothing. I perched on the edge of a chair, swallowed some lemonade, and waited to hear what was on Ruth's mind.

Emmy yawned, considered her options and selected my lap.

"Helen and the girls here?"

Ruth still referred to Dawn and JJ as girls. I nodded, stroking Emmy's soft white hair. She purred in response.

"Dawn came first. JJ drove Helen over this morning."

"How is Helen?"

I shrugged. "Looks okay, but..."

"Such a shame. God's will be done, though. She was so pretty back in high school."

"What was Helen like then?"

Ruth peered into her lemonade as if images from the past floated there.

"Quiet, mostly. All she talked about was leaving Pinedale Springs."

"Was there some sort of trouble at home?"

"Nothing I knew of. Her folks wanted her to stay, of course. Most of us ranch kids considered it our duty to help. But Helen was different."

"Why did she want to leave?"

"Searching for something, I expect." She sipped lemonade. "She just didn't fit here. She seemed much happier in Denver."

"You kept in touch?"

"Occasionally."

"Bow told me that she always favored JJ over Dawn."

Ruth patted short hair with bony fingers. "That's a mother's right, I suppose."

"It was hard on Dawn," I said.

"Life is seldom easy. Helen waited a long time to be blessed with children, longed for them, but she was well into her thirties before they came. Dawn was adopted, you know."

"Really? I had no idea. No one ever mentioned it."

"Helen assumed she'd never get pregnant, but then, as so often happens after adoption, she gave birth to JJ."

I swallowed the last of my lemonade. "Maybe that's why Helen favored JJ over Dawn, why JJ acts so superior."

"Perhaps, but what does that have to do with Elizabeth?"

"I don't know, I just never knew much about Helen. Bow never said a thing about Dawn being adopted, but she loved both nieces."

Ruth nodded. "And they loved her, too. Anyhow, we need to discuss arrangements."

"Bow didn't want a funeral. I was thinking about a memorial."

"Her proper name is Elizabeth and she should return to her God-given name in death. I lit a row of candles at church to show her soul the way to heaven. She needs a proper burial, of course."

Bow considered Ruth a loyal friend and business partner, someone to rely on, but the two couldn't have been more different. I wasn't about to argue over Ruth's religious beliefs, but I did have to stand up for Bow's final wishes.

"She wanted to be cremated," I said.

"May the good Lord help us. Just like Elizabeth to want something offbeat. Christians must be properly buried. Says so in the Bible."

I stroked Emmy harder than I meant to, but her purring only intensified. No point in saying that Bow honored God by honoring nature, that she was spiritual without being religious.

"Bow told me she wanted her ashes taken to Lost Creek Valley."

"Yes, Elizabeth told me about having her ashes scattered, but she said lots of things she didn't really understand."

"She was your business partner, your friend," I said. "Don't you want to honor her final request?"

"Now look here, Margo, I've known Elizabeth since the day she was born, know her better than anyone, including you."

I sat up straighter. Emmy's eyes opened; the purring ceased.

"Know anything about her will?"

"Her will? I haven't the foggiest idea if she even had one. She wasn't the most organized person, as you know, except when it came to her horses, her barn." Ruth paused, glanced out the window. "But I suppose God would understand if we honored her final wishes."

"I'd imagine so," I said.

"I'll ride out to Lost Creek Valley with you, of course."

I'd planned on going there alone, but I wasn't surprised that Ruth would want to go.

"Are you up for that long a ride?" I asked, realizing as soon as the words were out of my mouth that it sounded patronizing.

She smiled, sort of. "I may be twice your age, and yes, it's been a while since I've been on a pack trip, but I most certainly can and will accompany you."

I bit my lip, considered apologizing, but knowing Ruth, that'd irritate her even more.

"What about the Langford woman?" Ruth asked. "Will you ask her to stay on until Elizabeth's affairs are settled?"

"Maybe. Haven't decided yet. What do you think of her?"

"Seems nice enough. Awfully sad last evening."

I nodded.

"It's such a shame that Elizabeth fell," said Ruth. "The sheriff told me she might have slipped on wet rocks."

"Do you believe that's what happened?"

"It's up to the sheriff to decide. He mentioned that she also might've jumped."

I just looked at her.

"She was depressed about the foals, of course," Ruth said. "Elizabeth was a strong woman, but after that last one died, she said she might have to sell the ranch."

I gasped. "What?"

Ruth nodded. "She didn't want you to know, not yet. A second letter came from the university. It upset her terribly."

"Doc Wilson said the final toxicology reports from CSU weren't available yet, but the initial tests came back negative for contaminants."

"I know, Margo. But even Elizabeth wasn't aware that they did further tests until a second letter said they'd gone ahead with something experimental. They weren't expecting to find anything..." Ruth paused.

I held my breath, waiting for the rest.

"The new tests showed arsenic in the mares' milk."

"Arsenic?" I couldn't believe it, especially when the initial tests were clear.

"Elizabeth was shocked too, of course. They assured her it wasn't enough to harm full-grown horses or even yearlings, but it built up in the mares' placentas, poisoning some foals before they were even born."

I frowned. "So that's why Bow moved the mares and foals to a different pasture. But where would arsenic come from?"

"The expert asked Elizabeth if there were any manufacturing plants nearby."

"People were all riled about Titan Lumber's pressure treatment operation a few years ago," I said, "but that's over ten miles away."

"Yes," Ruth said. "Some were convinced that arsenic in preserved wood contaminates the air, the water, the entire world."

"The lumber industry uses a less toxic lumber treatment now."

"Yes, but the CSU woman said that the solvent, complete with arsenic, would have seeped into the underground stream. It isn't far under the surface and it runs from the lumber plant through Elizabeth's property."

"So, the arsenic moves up through the soil into grasses?"

"Apparently."

"Oh, God," I whispered, not in a religious way. Ruth didn't seem to take offense. "No wonder Bow would consider selling. Did anyone else know?"

"No one but me. She hadn't even told Doc Wilson. And she knew how upset you'd be, didn't want to alarm you before she decided for sure what to do."

What could I say to that? On the one hand, Bow tried to spare me, but it hurt my feelings, and my pride, that she'd chosen to confide only in Ruth.

"Where is the letter?"

"No idea, but I assume Elizabeth kept it somewhere. It's in God's hands now."

"You and Bow knew each other a long time. Bow told me there were things she'd done, things she'd tell me about sometime. Any idea what other secrets she was keeping from me?"

"Secrets? How would I know?"

I looked at her. Talk about an evasive answer.

"Was Helen fond of Bow?"

"Oh yes, Helen was very excited when Elizabeth was born. I remember Helen walking the floor with her new sister, singing to her. Her parents were older, you know, and busy with the ranch, so they had little time or inclination to coddle a baby. Helen took Elizabeth with her to Denver for a few months every now and then, partly to make up for leaving her parents, but Helen just seemed to love babies."

"Bow had pictures of Helen and her parents on her dresser," I said, "but I don't remember her ever saying much about any of them."

"That's not surprising. When Elizabeth was a teenager, she lived with Helen and Ed for at least one entire school year because Helen claimed there were more opportunities in big cities than there'd ever be in Pinedale Springs. Helen was glad Elizabeth went to college, but very disappointed when she chose to return to the ranch and raise horses. They stayed in touch, but the closeness evaporated. Helen seemed to grow bitter after that."

"What happened to their parents?"

"You might say they worked themselves to death. Mary Bowan was over forty when Elizabeth came along and she died less than twenty years later. Within a month, Elizabeth's father followed Mary to the grave."

"Did he die of grief?"

"Possibly. When his horse appeared riderless, several men rode out and found his body at the base of a cliff. They thought he either fell or jumped."

I gasped.

"It wasn't at Rim Rock Cliffs," Ruth added. "Somewhere in the wilderness, though."

I swallowed hard. "If he died by suicide —"

"No way to know for sure. But Elizabeth and Helen were inconsolable."

"Bow inherited the ranch. What about Helen?"

"Some of the land was sold," Ruth said, "and money from that went to Helen."

After Ruth left, I thought about families, about what grief could do to a person. Bow was eccentric, for sure, but she seemed as well adjusted as the next person. Then again, how objective was I when it came to her?

I'd never thought of Bow as wealthy. Her cabin was small, her barn in need of repairs. But the ranch that'd been passed down to her included crucial underground and surface water rights Carla Simpson needed for her development project. I didn't know if soil contaminants would hinder Simpson's plans. I'd heard about suburban homes being built over reclaimed landfills, about other homes contaminated by seepage of noxious waste in underground rivers.

Bow's land and her animals would pass to Bow's immediate family, meaning her sister, Helen, and the nieces, Dawn and JJ. Her share of the B&D Tack store might also be valuable and it would be included in Bow's will, if she had one. Greed could make people do strange things, awful things. Maybe greed had made someone anxious to inherit, to see the land sold. But there was still the matter of something evil lurking beneath pastures on land meant to nurture.

When I looked at Bow's face in that morgue, I promised to find out what happened to her. Homicide investigators begin by scrutinizing those closest to the deceased person. Relatives first, then business partners, friends. And in addition, lovers; in Bow's case it was a long list.

A look at Bow's will and then that last letter from CSU might show me the way forward. My inexperience as an investigator was a deficit. Which was putting it mildly. My motivation to uncover the truth, however, was a bonus.

CHAPTER NINE

MICHAEL GOLDBERG'S BALD HEAD glistened in late afternoon sunlight from the enormous west-facing window. His chair was leather, his desk oak, his cuff links probably real gold. He'd been one in a succession of Bow's lovers some years ago.

I sat across from him in a blue velvet chair, gazing at walls which held so many paintings that the place could've been a museum instead of a lawyer's office. He watched me, a faint smile on his face, his hands folded on the desk.

"Which do you favor?"

I took my gaze off a stunning Matisse and looked at him. Pinedale Springs was a casual kind of town, but even the Goldberg and Brown, Esq. receptionist who'd ushered me in oozed elegance. I'd worn my recently acquired skirt and a decent pair of sandals, but still felt like a hick.

Dawn would've appreciated this. Over the years, she'd done several exquisite watercolors for me, including the one of Babe, another of Phantom galloping across a stark white canvas, black mane and tail feathered by imaginary wind.

"They're all wonderful," I finally replied, swiveling in my chair. "The Matisse is fabulous, but that landscape in the corner is great too. A Charles Russell, right?"

"Yes, indeed. Acquired that one in Montana last March. There's an annual sale at the Russell Museum in Great Falls."

"How nice. You certainly have eclectic tastes."

"I enjoy all styles." He unfolded his hands. "So, Ms. Richards, you came here regarding an urgent matter?"

"Yes, and just call me Margo. Thanks for seeing me on short notice. I'm here about Elizabeth Bowan, about her death."

"I heard." He paused, looked at the ceiling. "She'll be missed. I've never known anyone quite like Bow."

Their affair had been over for years, but his lingering affection was plain to see.

"I have reason to believe her death wasn't accidental," I said.

His eyebrows stretched up toward a shiny scalp. "Oh? But I heard she fell."

"Or was pushed."

"What makes you think so?"

"A string of things that don't add up," I replied. "There's not enough to go on yet, though."

"How can I help?"

"For starters, I need to see her will."

"I know she raised you, but are you designated as power of attorney or are you named as an executor?"

"I have no idea what sort of legal papers she had, if any."

"I did advise her on occasion regarding legal matters, but she never came to me to execute a will."

I frowned. "Oh."

He placed his hands palm down on the massive oak desk and leaned forward.

"I presume you intend to see who stands to benefit from her death."

"Yes, although she didn't have much, at least not in cash form. But she had the ranch, half-ownership in the tack store."

"If there is a will, chances are that it'll surface soon. Perhaps she simply composed her own document."

"Would that be legally binding?"

"Yes, of course, if properly done."

"Then all I have to do is find the thing. If she made one."

Goldberg leaned back in his chair. "Correct. You might begin by asking her bank if they have a safe-deposit box in her name. They can't release anything without proper documentation, of course. Then again, Bow was quite unconventional, so maybe she simply hid important papers."

I thought of the clutter in her cabin, winced. Her barn was orderly, her home, not so much.

"I suppose you don't know if she had life insurance, either?"

I shook my head. "No idea."

"Some policies can be worth a fortune."

"Hmmm."

"Do you suspect anyone in particular?"

"Not yet. I'm just gathering information about everyone Bow had dealings with, trying to make sense of things. One person she disliked intensely was Carla Simpson, the realtor. Does she happen to be a client of yours?"

"I'm not at liberty to reveal information about clients."

"I understand. Simpson is anxious to acquire land for her development."

He nodded. "That would make her ambitious."

"And maybe ruthless?" I asked just to get his reaction.

Goldberg blinked, slowly. "How so?"

"Carla Simpson needs to acquire Bow's ranch to secure underground and subsurface water rights. I don't know how far she'd go to get what she wants."

He pursed his lips, blinked again. "Off the record, Margo, she may appear rather brusque, but that doesn't mean ruthless."

"No, of course not," I said. He'd just revealed in a roundabout way that Simpson was his client.

"Even if I were at liberty to divulge information, which I most certainly am not, I can tell you in strictest confidence that I've seen nothing to indicate Ms. Simpson is anything but a legitimate businesswoman."

I stood up, smiled. "I understand."

"You must realize how hard it will be to prove that Bow's death was not accidental," he said, rising also. "Still, bits of information can help in unforeseen ways."

"Please let me know if anything comes to your attention," I said, handing him my business card.

He glanced at the card, placed it on his desk, and extended his hand. "Yes, for Bow's sake, anything I can do, as long as I don't breach confidentiality." Sadness clouded his eyes.

First Doc Wilson, now Michael Goldberg. Bow had captivated each of them and they still remembered her fondly, as did others she'd loved. She said she never wanted to marry, but I wondered if there was more to it.

City Bank stood only three blocks from the lawyer's office, so I left the truck parked and walked. I knew the bank had Bow's accounts, but they denied having any safety-deposit boxes in her name. I was almost back to my truck when JJ appeared.

"Wanna go with you," she began, wobbling as though about to lose her balance. Bright sun lit the white spikey ends of her short brown hair like a head full of candles, but the effect was not angelic.

"Go with me where?" I asked, just to rattle her, even though she was sloshed.

"Ruth said taking Aunt Bow's ashes to Creek Valley. I ride along. And Dawn too."

"Her body hasn't even been released for cremation. But did Ruth tell you we're planning a memorial?"

"She, yes. Dawn and I too."

"Of course. Also, do you happen to know if Bow had a will?"

"What? No. Are you in...in charge?"

"Nope, not me."

She moved closer, towering over me, the wobbling increasing.

"You drink too much, JJ."

"Fuck off."

"Get a life, JJ. And get some help."

She made a fist, pushed it into my rib cage. "Mind your damn busy, or I'll…" She paused, her mouth open. "I...uh…" She blinked, looked like she was about to fall.

I grabbed her arm. "C'mon, JJ, let me take you home."

"I'll take me," she said, but she followed meekly, got in the truck when I opened the door for her, didn't object when I fastened her seat belt.

I had no idea how she'd gotten into town, but she was clearly in no shape to drive now. She slept most of the way home but opened her eyes suddenly and looked at me as if she had no idea who I was.

"What the hell?" she said.

"We're almost back at the ranch," I said.

"Ranch?"

"Your Aunt Bow's place."

"Uh-huh, Captain comes, Royal will here."

"Your horse, Royal Captain."

"Uh-huh. Riding him."

"Okay, sure," I said, out loud. *Not a chance,* I thought, *even if she sobers up.*

I parked close to Bow's cabin, helped JJ out of the truck and onto the porch.

Audrey opened the door, took one look at JJ, grabbed her arm and we both helped her inside.

"I spoke to Doc Wilson when he dropped by this morning," Audrey said. "He says Bandit's wound looks good."

"Thanks," I said. "Keep an eye on JJ, okay?"

"Yes, sure."

"I saw her in town. Not sure how she got there, but here she is."

"She sobers up once she eats something," Audrey said. "I took her vodka bottles, diluted them with water."

"Can't hurt," I said. "But she needs help."

"Yes. Don is an alcoholic too, so..." She shrugged.

"I can't imagine how difficult it'd be to live with someone like that," I said. "I need to go and spend some time with Bandit, then I'll be back, see if everything's okay."

I grabbed two apples from the kitchen and walked down the familiar path to Bow's barn, but before I entered I plucked a big handful of fresh grass to make up for the fact that Bandit couldn't yet get out to graze. After Bow's gelding reached for sweet apple chunks with soft lips and chomped every blade of grass, I went and grabbed a brush and a mane-and-tail comb from the tack room, then spent an hour or so leisurely grooming the palomino while his jaw slackened, head and neck lowered in relaxation. Spending time with Bandit seemed enjoyable for him and it was therapeutic for me. I hoped it wouldn't be long before he could return to pasture.

I slipped back inside the cabin, intending to have a look in Bow's closet, but Ruth and Dawn saw me.

"We have questions about the ride to Lost Creek," Ruth said. "We're all going, of course."

"Me too, maybe," Dawn said.

Oh, great. Ruth would tell the others right away, of course.

"The memorial comes first," I said to divert their attention.

"Right," Ruth said. "The girls and I have started working on that, although Dawn still seems a bit under the weather, and that one..." She paused, frowning at JJ. "I see that you're back, JJ, you're sober again."

JJ tilted her head to one side. "I wasn't... Oh, hell. Whatever."

Audrey came out of the kitchen and told me in a whisper that JJ had eaten a sandwich and downed several glasses of water.

"Anyway," Ruth said, "I started a list of people who still haven't heard about Elizabeth, and we need to decide when and where the memorial will be."

"Do you mean a funeral?" Audrey asked.

The word "funeral" sounded too real, too final. I shook my head to remind myself that was the reality now.

"We won't have her..." The word "body" reminded me of the morgue, of Bow's cold skin. "This is just a time for everyone to come together, celebrate her life."

"Yes, of course," Audrey said, nodding. "Sorry."

"No worries. It'd be best to hold the memorial here at Bow's place, outside. It'll be a large crowd. We can rent chairs and we'll need a few tables for food, I suppose."

Ruth nodded. "Good ideas, Margo. What day?"

I blinked, drew a blank. I could barely remember what time of day it was without my watch. Sunday afternoon was when Roy appeared at the show, and the days had blurred into one another after that.

"Let's plan for Friday or Saturday," I said. "That'll give us time to notify people and get things ready."

Everyone nodded, even JJ.

"Where's Helen?" I asked, thinking maybe she was in the bedroom.

"I figured there'd be so much going on that I couldn't keep track of her, so I arranged for a temporary stay at Pinedale Manor. They have a locked ward." JJ turned toward Dawn, who nodded.

"Of course, have them bill me."

"I'll have folding chairs and some tables delivered," JJ said, sounding clear again. She glanced at Dawn.

"Sure, you arrange the company and I'll take care of it."

JJ might be sober, but she still didn't bother thanking her sister. Audrey's sandwich and lots of water had diluted the booze for now, though.

"All right, when should we plan on leaving for Lost Creek?" Ruth asked.

"It'll be a while," I said. *As in never*, I thought.

"I'm going," JJ declared. "Royal Captain will be here in a few days. My friend is trailering him over."

Her gelding was a high-strung thoroughbred. I'd watched JJ riding him in an arena. The horse wasn't right for her, not in an arena, not anywhere. The gelding certainly wasn't suited to a long tide on challenging trails. JJ wasn't a bad rider, but she wasn't a very good one, either, especially drunk.

Ruth must've been thinking the same things because she frowned and turned toward JJ.

"The trails can be challenging around here, JJ. Why not let Margo fix you up with a seasoned trail horse?"

"I'm riding Royal Captain."

Ruth looked at me as if she wanted me to say something.

But all I did was shrug. I could've told JJ that it took a full day's ride to get to Lost Creek, and that some of the trails are steep and rocky, but what was the point? JJ wouldn't listen, and besides, I was going alone.

"I should go, too," Dawn said, sounding uncertain.

"And I'll ride Gus, of course," Ruth said, referring to her favorite Appaloosa, a gelding who was just as ornery and cranky as his owner. She loved him, though.

"Could I come too?" Audrey asked.

"Why not," I said. Let them all think they were going. But there was no chance I'd take any of them out to Lost Creek Valley. For one thing, I didn't know who to trust, if anyone. But the journey with Bow's ashes was mine alone. Bow and I rode out to the valley every year. The last time we rode there together was early last fall, not that long ago. Neither of us could carry a tune, but that didn't stop us from singing at the top of our lungs once or twice during the ride, just because. We settled into happy silence once we arrived and sat listening to busy chickadees calling to one another from high branches of the enormous ponderosa that was our special tree. It was the kind of place that made talking optional, where nature told us things we needed to know. When Bow asked me to take her ashes out there, I laughed at first, but then I looked at her face, saw that she was serious. So, I promised. I told her I hoped to be a very old woman before she died, but even then, I'd saddle a horse, keep my promise.

Ruth and the others starting planning which saddles they'd use, what clothes to wear. Let them plan and scheme all they wanted to.

I was the only one who knew the way to Lost Creek and my only companions on the ride would be Phantom and Maynard.

I slipped down the hall to Bow's bedroom. Her closet always looked like things were thrown in at random. I rummaged through the mess and found two cardboard boxes that held papers. Partial tax returns were tossed in among a bunch of old horse magazines, but there was nothing resembling a will. JJ, Dawn, and Audrey were all staying in this cabin. Any one of them, or even Ruth for that matter, could've snooped through Bow's things. With or without a will, though, there was legal precedent dictating who inherited what part of the ranch and Bow's portion of the tack store, as well as what would happen to the horses she and I co-owned. I hoped Bow had made a will, but knowing her, I doubted she did.

I was about to give up on finding either a will or the CSU letters, but I opened the second box. Still no will, but there was a folder containing two letters from CSU. Bow had shown me the first one, which stated no contaminants were found in any of the samples submitted but ended by promising a final report soon. The second letter referenced a toxicology research project headed by Mary Ashton, PhD, and emphasized that the methodology was experimental but more specific and potentially much more accurate than other testing methods. There was a list of tests done on tissues, mares' milk, soil, and grasses. Every single result came out strongly positive for arsenic, just as Ruth had told me. No wonder Bow thought she might have to sell the ranch, no wonder she moved mares and foals to an entirely different pasture.

I folded both letters and stuffed them in my pocket, closed the boxes and put them back in Bow's closet. I told Audrey to call me if JJ and Dawn needed me, then went back to my house and checked plans for the next day.

❋   ❋   ❋

After the next morning's chores, I called Doc Wilson to ask about the toxicity tests. He had no way of assessing the type of complex lab analysis that Colorado State University could do and advised calling the university direct.

The name David Folger, DVM, appeared on the letterhead of both reports, but only the second letter included a direct number to the CSU toxicology department. I called it, and a recorded announcement said Folger was doing field research and wouldn't be available for several weeks, but that someone would return calls if requested. I left my name and number, and within minutes, my cell buzzed.

"This is the CSU toxicology department, returning your call."

"Is Doctor Mary Ashton available? I need to speak with her. It's urgent."

"One moment, please."

After a short time on hold, a more authoritative-sounding woman's voice said, "Mary Ashton here. How can I help you?"

I explained about Bow's death, about the two CSU letters.

"I'm sorry to hear about Ms. Bowan," she said. Her tone sounded detached, which I supposed was to be expected. "Are you a relative?"

"She raised me," I said, "and we're also business partners. I'm following up about soil contamination on her property."

"I see. Unfortunately, final results will not be available for several days."

"Is there some way to expedite that?"

"I am afraid not. This is a new and experimental procedure and the time frame is precise."

"When you spoke with Bow, I mean Elizabeth Bowan, what did you tell her about the safety of her land?"

"I've pulled up the report on my computer, and although I don't recall the precise words I used, I do recall speaking with Ms. Bowan. What is apparent is that there is a significant amount of arsenic buildup in certain portions of her property. That serves as a final portion of the report and will not change. What we are confirming now is a predictive amount of arsenic accumulation for the future. That information will conclude the report."

"The first letter said there was no contamination. Why didn't the first test show anything?"

"Doctor Folger's report represents initial testing; it reflects what we've been able to ascertain with current methods. The improved methods, while deemed experimental, will soon be the standard and will increase accurate results."

"I see. So, arsenic was what killed two foals?"

"It appears so, unfortunately, because poisons are sequestered in grasses, consumed by mares, then become highly concentrated in the placenta."

"And why did it show up this year and not before?" I asked, although I thought I knew the answer.

"Contamination of this sort develops slowly, over time, but once the concentration reaches toxicity, the effects spread more rapidly."

"The surviving foals have been moved to a different area. Does that make them safe?"

"Possibly, but we'd have to assess the soil and grasses where they are to know for certain."

Our ranch as well as Bow's was served by well water. The wells were over two hundred feet deep, but my final question centered on the safety of the liquid that we drank, showered in, cooked with.

Doctor Ashton assured me that areas away from underground streams wouldn't likely be contaminated and that wells drilled for household use were so deep that the water decontaminates during percolation down through hundreds of feet of sand and soil.

I hung up and sat drumming my fingers on the table. It was reassuring to know that my own pastures were probably safe, and besides, there were no foals on my land. But just to be sure, I made a mental note to have my well tested.

I could only imagine how Bow must've felt when they told her that the soil on her ranch was toxic. She must've felt betrayed by the very land that had long nurtured foals she carefully planned for each spring. No wonder she'd thought about selling the ranch. No wonder she had been depressed. Unfortunately, it made sense that Sheriff

Plackmon had mentioned suicide. Ruth knew about the arsenic, which explained why she'd agreed that Bow might've been suicidal.

I shook my head. Other people might be defeated by such awful news, but not Bow. At least that's what I wanted to believe, needed to believe.

CHAPTER TEN

THE NEXT MORNING, I made cinnamon toast, filled a mug with tea and headed over to Bow's place to check on things. JJ and Dawn were on the couch with bowls of cereal.

"Is Audrey still doing chores?"

Before either of them answered, a cell phone rang.

JJ picked it up, her expression going from neutral to horrified. "But...no! What are you saying?" She placed the phone on speaker mode, held it out as though it was toxic. "Who did you say you are? How could this happen?"

"I am Barbara Woods, the administrator here at Pinedale Manor," a woman's voice said. "The nurse said your mother seemed fine at dinner last evening and was happy when both you and Dawn came to visit. Unfortunately, she passed sometime during the night."

"But... She's only been there one night."

"Again, Ms. Jacobs, I am so very sorry. The night nurse does make regular rounds, of course. It appeared your mother forgot to call for help and got up on her own. Being in a new setting might have increased her memory problems."

"We were assured that she'd be checked on regularly."

"Oh, my dear, the nurses did check her, of course, but then later she was already gone when the night nurse entered the room."

"How did she...die?"

"The doctors will examine her and they should be able to provide answers. The sheriff has been notified, as well, which is protocol. Meantime, I'm afraid we do need to ask family members to make arrangements."

JJ began sobbing. "Our mother, she's dead."

Dawn's mouth was open, her expression frozen. She stared out the window, shaking her head as if transfixed by something only she could see.

The phone slipped from JJ's hand to the floor. I picked it up. "This is Margo Richards," I said, "and I'll help with...things." I jotted down some numbers the administrator provided.

I wanted to hug JJ and Dawn, but consolation wasn't what they needed, not yet. Both appeared to be so shocked their minds couldn't process this new reality. I knew the feeling. On some level, we know that death hovers, ever near but out of sight, snatching the soul without warning, leaving the body and the grief behind. I thought about everything Ruth had told me about Helen. She may not have been a perfect mother, but she'd had an intense desire for babies when she was young. Her struggles with motherhood didn't make her better or worse as a person, they only made her human.

The fact that both Dawn and JJ had less than perfect relationships with their mother would make grieving complicated. Losing your mother was always traumatic. JJ acted solicitous toward Helen, and while Dawn had appeared less loving, she always agreed to pay for this and previous nursing home care.

I hadn't noticed Audrey slipping inside in the midst of that call. The look on her face confirmed she'd heard enough. She approached me. "I did not think Alzheimer's was usually fatal," she whispered.

"Uh, I don't know," I said. "But now we have two deaths. Two unexplained deaths."

Audrey nodded. "Two sisters, both gone within days of each other."

"Yes, as if Helen wanted to join Bow." I sighed. I took my phone from my pocket, dialed Ruth, asked her to come as soon as she could.

I was making coffee and tea for everyone when Sheriff Plackmon drove up. I let him in the door, then Audrey and I stood silent while he approached JJ and Dawn.

"I'm sorry," he began, sitting down near them, "but I have a few questions. First, please tell me in your own words about yesterday's visit with your mother."

It wasn't a surprise that JJ did all the talking. She always did. Dawn looked pale and shook her head when the sheriff asked her if she had anything to add.

"Did the two of you go together for this visit?"

"I went into town and got to the nursing home before Dawn," JJ said. "She stayed after I left. Both of us took her to the dining room for cookies." JJ paused. "Mother always loved cookies."

"Did your mother walk to the dining room?"

"Of course," JJ said. "She's never had trouble with balance or anything like that. She's never fallen, not once. She has trouble with remembering things, but she doesn't need even a cane."

The sheriff tapped notes into his iPhone, then turned to Dawn. "How long did you stay with your mother after your sister left?"

Dawn shrugged. "Not long," she whispered.

"I know you both want answers about what happened," the sheriff said. "Has the doctor called yet?"

Both JJ and Dawn shook their heads.

"I spoke with the doctor and the nurses. It appeared Mrs. Jacobs slipped and fell on something very sharp. There was a lot of blood."

JJ's mouth fell open. "A lot of blood!"

"So far, it appears that is what happened."

JJ's hands trembled. "How could this be? Why didn't they find her sooner?"

"The autopsy should provide time frames and answers."

"Do you..." JJ paused, frowning. "Why are you questioning us? Are we accused of something?"

"All we need to establish so far is when this happened and how," he said. "The nurse said your mother was instructed to push the call button for help any time she got out of bed."

"Mother forgot things. She didn't even remember me," JJ said, hanging her head. "But she didn't ever really care about me or about Dawn."

Dawn closed her eyes, nodded.

"My deputies searched the bedroom." He paused, glanced at me. "With accidental deaths, like this appears to be so far, it can be very difficult to find answers."

I got his thinly veiled message, kept my expression neutral.

"Do you think someone might've hurt her on purpose?" JJ asked.

"We have no reason at present to believe this was anything other than an unfortunate accident."

Ruth arrived just as the sheriff tapped final notes into his phone and told him she'd accompany JJ to the morgue to identify Helen.

I hugged Dawn and JJ, and told Ruth and Audrey to call me if needed. I'd never known Helen very well, but it did seem like a strange coincidence that Bow and her sister died within days of each other. Then again, Helen was first in line to inherit everything Bow had, which might serve as motive. Dawn and JJ stood next in line, but they already had legal control over Helen and her property. Who else might want Helen out of the way, and why? Even though I felt certain that Bow's death was somehow sinister, I hoped that the sheriff was correct in saying Helen's death appeared to be an unfortunate accident.

❋　　❋　　❋

Back at home, I turned my attention to the foal deaths. I began a computer search of underground water contamination in general and I found enough about a litany of pollutants to know that the planet was in dire need of help.

The local Department of Agriculture website had postings about possible subsurface water contaminants from certain natural gas drilling sites, but there was little about arsenic from previous lumber treating methods or other sources. I called Titan Lumber, on the outskirts of Pinedale Springs, and the manager confirmed that although all lumber companies once used a toxic chemical to preserve wood, there'd never been any long-term toxicities found in repeat tests. The family-owned lumber company had operated for generations and they were known for integrity. I pulled up old newspaper articles but found only speculation, no solid information.

My trusty iPad calendar listed the day's horses to train, riding lessons to give. Before I delved into all of that, though, I thought about the realtor who stood to gain if Bow sold her ranch. I called Simpson's office, arranged to meet her after lunchtime. The secretary didn't ask why I wanted to come, probably assumed it had something to do with real estate. And it did, just not in the usual way.

I did a brief online search about the realtors Simpson worked with in Denver. Her name appeared on a "Realtors of the Year" list twice. The woman knew how to make it rain money.

The question was, how far would she go to get what she wanted? I called one of her co-workers at the large real estate firm she was with for almost ten years. The guy said she was competitive, but he didn't bother asking how she was doing or mention that she was missed. He did tell me her parents and an older brother lived in Chicago. I made notes, then headed for the barn.

While brushing a quiet two-year-old filly I called Angel, I thought about what Ruth had said a while ago when Simpson first moved here. Ruth's news antenna revealed that Simpson had been married twice, divorced twice, no kids. She was on the far side of forty, drove a new truck, boarded her horse at the fancy stable on the edge of Pinedale, and had rented one of the largest houses around prior to her arrival last fall. Either she was wealthy or determined to appear so.

I led the filly to the outside arena, lunged her in a large circle for walk-to-trot transitions. This sweet girl would be ready for a saddle soon.

The next horse scheduled for arena work was a three-year-old mustang gelding I called Spook, for her tendency to shy suddenly from imaginary monsters by either halting abruptly or whirling to one side. Some horses do that out of boredom or just for kicks. Spook wasn't ornery, just high-spirited and smart enough to test the rider. Her gaits were smooth as silk and I enjoyed riding her, but she required my full attention. I spent a few minutes putting her through paces in the arena, then took her out on the trails. No monsters materialized today. She was ready to sell, but only to an experienced rider. As always, being around horses soothed my soul, and provided a break from grief and from acting like an investigator.

The last horse on today's roster was a seven-year-old Dutch Warmblood gelding with fancy papers and the nickname "Happy." He stood 16.3 hands tall, meaning five feet, four inches at the withers, making him taller and larger overall than any other horse on the place right now. Recently arrived from California, he had great conformation and was well trained. His excited new owner, Sue, purchased him as a three-day event prospect, which sounded great, except that Sue was terrified of her new horse. She'd taken lessons from me sporadically on her Quarter Horse and that pair did okay over small jumps, but she wasn't ready yet for galloping across a course and negotiating challenging jumps. When she'd mentioned buying another horse I'd advised her to wait a while, stay with the quiet one she had. That didn't suit her, though, and she could afford any horse she fancied. She wasn't the first person to fall in love with a dream they weren't ready for.

Today was the third time I'd ridden Happy and I worked the big boy on cavalletti, and then over a few jumps. As expected, he did everything I asked. He was just too much horse for Sue. The mismatch had little to do with size, more with ability and confidence. She wasn't here today, but when she'd brought him to me, she'd been in tears. She wanted me to ride the gelding and help her decide what to do, even though she probably already knew.

Dutch Warmbloods were popular for dressage and cross-country eventing, and one other student of mine was wealthy enough to have one. Sue's warmblood would make someone else happy, and Sue would do fine with a different horse.

I groomed the big gelding and put him in a small grassy paddock where he could graze and see other horses in the main pasture. Then I switched gears, cleaned up, brushed my hair, and headed into town.

❊　　❊　　❊

Carla Simpson's secretary didn't seem very fond of her boss, but that wasn't all I learned from Debbie during the half hour I spent in Simpson's front office. On a hunch, I arrived early on purpose for a girl-to-girl. Seemed that the boss was out of the office on the day Bow rode out to the Cliffs. She'd even left her phone in her desk drawer. A realtor without a cell phone is like a horse with an open gate; no boundaries, free to go anywhere, do anything.

Developed portions of the Western Slope were pockmarked with cell phone towers, but in large National Forests and wilderness areas communication with the rest of the world was limited to satellite phones. A place to go if one wanted to be undetectable. Simpson owned a horse and was a competent rider. The odds that she'd ridden out to Rim Rock Cliffs on the day Bow died were remote since there were many other trails around here. Still, playing the odds was why I'd come.

By the time the secretary showed me into Simpson's office, my suspicions had jumped from training level to grand prix. The room was average in size, but an ornate desk swallowed most of the space and a garish landscape on the wall behind her was no doubt meant to impress. It didn't have that effect on me, but I wasn't there to be wowed by a display of affluence.

Carla sat in a high-backed leather chair.

"Have a seat, Margo," she said, without bothering to smile.

Two red velvet chairs on rollers were arranged across from her. I settled into one and crossed my legs.

"Thanks for seeing me." I didn't bother to smile, either.

"I was rather surprised you came."

"Why?" I asked.

"I just hope you're not as close-minded as Ruth Dunn."

When I didn't respond, she squinted and raised one eyebrow.

"Small town mentality," she began, "but of course Mrs. Dunn is from an older generation, less progressive."

"Interesting," I said. I hadn't come to rankle her. At least not right away.

"Well, never mind. At any rate, I am so very sorry about Bow. She'll be missed."

"Yes," I said, wondering how long it'd take her to ask about Bow's property, to find out if I had any control over who inherited what, who might sell.

She managed to trot out those exact issues within minutes and I supplied noncommittal answers to keep her talking. The more she yakked, the hotter I got. Still, let her think she had the upper hand, then slip in some leading questions of my own. Sounded like such a plan that I almost laughed out loud. Part of her business involved manipulating people, getting them to sell or making them want to buy. I handled horses, but no telling if I could handle this woman enough to extract useful information. I soothed horses with a soft voice, so I soothed Carla by complimenting her on attaining Denver Realtor of the Year, twice. Said the plaques looked great. Quite an accomplishment, I gushed, making a big deal of it until she melted under the weight of her enormous ego.

Then, I asked if she'd had many chances to ride recently.

She had.

"There are so many great trails around here," I said.

She agreed.

"I enjoy getting out into the wilderness, don't you?"

She agreed again.

"Ever been out to Rim Rock Cliffs?"

She opened her mouth and I was certain she was about to say yes, but she caught herself before responding in a tight voice.

"Why do you ask?"

I shrugged. "It's an unusual place where not many people go, that's all."

Her arms tightened across her chest. It's amazing how often honest communication bypasses speech, how much a look or a gesture can reveal. Part of the reason I love horses is that, unlike humans, horses never lie. I watched her, hoping my expression was neutral, open.

"Why did you come here?" she asked, after a silence.

"That's my line," I said.

"Pardon me?"

"What I really want to know is why you moved to Pinedale Springs."

"That is common knowledge. This is a land of opportunity. My plan will bring progress to this sleepy little town. Development isn't a dirty word."

I stood up. Time to discard the pretense.

"I know you need Bow's property to proceed with your damn development. Without access to the water on her property, your plan fails. So, how far will you go to get what you want?"

Simpson stood too.

"Look here, Margo, I understand you and others are grieving, but I find your implication quite insulting. You may come back if you're ready to look at the situation logically. Now, get the hell out of my office."

I left, gladly. There was only so much garbage I could tolerate from that woman.

At least before things deteriorated, I saw her unspoken response to my mention of Rim Rock Cliffs. Bow's death opened the door, at least a crack, for Carla Simpson to thunder in and grab hold of the ranch. Could she also be connected somehow with the foals' deaths, the soil contamination that forced Bow to consider selling? Seemed unlikely. But Simpson wouldn't hesitate to benefit from Bow's misfortune. What role did she have in that misfortune, was the question.

I'd gotten her to bite the apple, silently admit dark possibilities.

CHAPTER ELEVEN

NEITHER DEVELOPERS NOR DRILLING companies were strangers in this part of the west, so ranchers held tight to what they had for as long as they could. Topography, prime location, and water availability made Bow's property pivotal for Carla's plan. My smaller ranch, although adjacent to Bow's place, was hilly and more heavily forested. Simpson would still want my land, even though it'd be costlier to bulldoze.

Maybe Simpson was just another developer with big dreams. Maybe she was legit.

She was still on my list of suspects. My suspects! As if I qualified as a real investigator. Not hardly. But I had determination to spare.

The sheriff's SUV stood parked in front of his office, so why not drop in and see if I could sweet-talk him into revealing anything useful? Sweet-talking horses was easy but talking that way to humans never made it onto my skill set.

The sheriff was chewing on a hamburger when a young deputy named Lisa ushered me into his office. Papers littered his desk, lopsided manila folders perched atop a file cabinet. A computer sat on a side table, the screen blank. A pin-cushioned map of the county decorated the beige wall behind him, and the linoleum floor was worn smooth from footsteps predating his three-year tenure.

He swallowed before speaking. "C'mon in, Margo, sit."

I sat. "Sorry to interrupt your lunch."

He pushed the remainder of his meal aside. "How are Julie Jacobs and Dawn Curtis doing?"

I shrugged. "It isn't easy."

"No, sure isn't. The coroner in Grand Junction will be doing the autopsy on Helen Jacobs. That should provide a definite cause of death. Meantime, there was a footprint in blood found at the scene. The deputies checked the nurses' shoes, but of course the entire staff was not present. No matches so far, but they found minute traces of blood elsewhere."

"Do you think she might've been murdered?"

He frowned. "Not necessarily, but we do need to match the footprint to someone's shoe and we're working on that. Too soon even for speculation."

"Bleeding to death must be horrible, but very quick."

"Yes," he said. "So, about Ms. Bowan. I have some reports."

I bit my lip, sucked in a breath.

"Wildlife people observed a young male cougar hanging around Rim Rock Cliffs the other day. They tagged and darted it. Blood samples confirmed human DNA. They returned, tracked the same animal, shot him. Stomach contents also confirmed. The lab has methods for determining that even after a few days." He paused, glanced at me.

I swallowed, nodded.

"The coroner who did the autopsy also sent human tissue on to a lab to check for the presence of feline DNA."

I grimaced, nodded again.

"Tissue damage was extensive. The coroner had already verified teeth marks from the cougar." He paused.

"Go on. I can... I need to hear it all."

"They could not verify knife punctures."

I gripped the arms of the chair, said nothing.

"Those are the facts we're certain of, so I can hand over her personal effects now."

He summoned a deputy and within minutes I was holding a big plastic bag containing some of the last items Bow had ever seen, ever used. I opened my mouth to thank him, intending to leave, but I just sat there, flashing back to seeing her in that morgue.

Plackmon looked at me, spoke softly. "Go ahead, Margo. Take your time."

I opened the bag. There were no clothes, not even the poncho she always kept tied to the saddle's cantle. She would've been wearing it in the rain, though, so it must have been shredded by the cougar. I shook my head. Her boots, encrusted with dried mud, were on top. Next came the saddlebag. It was leather, although it looked and felt like gritty cardboard now. I undid the buckle, reached inside, pulled out a smaller plastic bag containing one orange with the rind going dry, a half-full water bottle, a hoof pick, several lengths of rawhide, and a small first- aid kit.

"No knife," I whispered, looking at Plackmon. "You knew her knife was missing."

He nodded.

"That knife was always in her saddlebag."

"You said that before."

"What if someone took it, killed her with it, then stabbed Bandit?"

"That's speculation. And the autopsy concluded that her neck —"

"But a cervical fracture isn't always fatal."

Plackmon sighed. "Margo, I know this is hard for you to accept."

"So that's it? You're done?"

"The investigation is not complete."

"Where did you find her saddlebag?"

He looked down at his notes. "Close to her body."

"She must've carried it to the top of the cliff, held onto it when she fell...or was pushed."

"The autopsy report is the only definitive thing we have so far, besides the cougar who was found. Bow's death might well be an unfortunate accident and in time, it could bring some comfort to know that."

"Comfort isn't my goal," I said. "I think someone not only stabbed Bandit, but also Bow. She could've been stabbed before she fell."

Plackmon glanced out the window, then turned back to me. "That is only speculation."

I leaned forward in the chair. "She didn't ride out there alone, to begin with, and it's a fact that her knife is missing."

"A missing knife can be anywhere," he said, rubbing his chin.

"Why can't you tell me who found her?"

The sheriff gave me that blank look all lawmen are good at. They must take classes. Facial Masks 101, Blank Eyes 102. I was tempted to ask if the person who found Bow was Carla Simpson, just to try and get a rise out of him. No point, though. He'd been in law enforcement too long to let an amateur like me peel away his mask.

"There are too many things that don't add up, that you're not taking seriously," I said, standing and moving toward the door, holding Bow's boots and saddlebag.

"Wait a minute, Margo. Just hold on, now."

I stopped, turned around.

"This case is not closed. The fact that Elizabeth Bowan died way out in the wilderness makes the investigation challenging but not impossible. I am considering everything you've told me, but my job is separating facts from possibilities."

I nodded. He was just saying stuff. I was too discouraged to be mad at him. I sighed.

"I know you're just doing your job, Sheriff Plackmon."

"In cases like this, we consult a psychologist for an opinion. And as you may know, my wife, Courtney, serves on occasion as the county-approved source for the department." He paused, then added, "It's unusual, but she is the only psychologist in the area."

Courtney was a sensual young blonde on the lean side of thirty, the last person to fit either the position of local shrink or this middle-aged sheriff's wife. Then again, any tendency to stereotype this particular blonde as merely a gorgeous trophy wife shattered after the briefest of conversations. And as for her being young enough to be the sheriff's daughter, that was their business. Still, I could guess what any psychologist might conclude about Bow.

"What did she say?" I finally asked.

"Based on the facts we have so far, she verified that suicide is one possibility."

I nodded. "Understandable. But even if Bow was suicidal, she wouldn't have ridden all the way out there to jump to her death. She wouldn't have left Bandit, either."

"Maybe not," Plackmon said.

I asked when Bow's body would be released for cremation and he said it'd be a while yet. He'd let me know.

I left, settled behind the wheel of my truck, forced a few deep breaths in and out. I cranked up the engine and rumbled out of town. There's no way to arrive or depart quietly in a one-ton diesel, and I wasn't blind to pollution, but there's no way to pull a six-horse rig with a Prius. Since I couldn't afford more than one vehicle, pass the keys to this monster.

Courtney Plackmon had provided what sounded like a solid professional opinion based on what she'd been told. Sheriff Plackmon was an okay guy. I hadn't yelled at him. I was closer to depression than anger.

I got home in time for the three scheduled riding lessons that soaked up the remaining afternoon. After that, I decided to make use of the summer evening by learning more about Audrey Langford, and what better way to do so than by taking her on a little ride.

Lucky me, horses figured into almost everything.

❉　　❉　　❉

Bow and I usually hired a high school or college kid to help during the busy summer season and some of my riding students clamored to be chosen. Taking on a college professor was unusual, to say the least. The job was more about an opportunity to spend time around horses than earning much, but Bow provided meals and a place to sleep while I doled out some cash and offered occasional riding lessons.

Audrey seemed content with the arrangements. The instant rapport between her and Bow didn't seem unusual, since Bow had an easy way with people. She once befriended a guy with a straggly beard who was standing beside his broken-down Harley on a road outside of town. She fed him dinner, let him sleep on her couch, then took him for a horseback ride around her ranch the next morning while his bike was in the shop. Turned out he was a retired architect from San Jose, and he sent her an enormous box of Godiva chocolates every Christmas. Bow's instinct told her who was legit, who wasn't.

That instinct must have failed her at the end.

Audrey drove an older, nondescript Nissan. I had no idea how much money college professors pulled in, but she'd didn't appear wealthy. She was devoid of that snobbish attitude some academics trot out. Men fawned over her, and although she accepted attention with grace, she didn't appear flirtatious. There was an elegance about her. While she didn't avoid questions, she didn't volunteer much, either. She claimed her ex was a lawyer out to ruin her financially and professionally and said he'd driven to Pinedale Springs to meet with her on the day Bow rode off.

I hustled through evening chores, grabbed an apple and a handful of walnuts for dinner, and settled down for a quick computer session. I'm not fond of Facebook, but Roy insists it can be a source of information if you know how to search without the ever-present temptation to check on that college hottie you dated for a while, and so on, until before you know it, you've wasted hours deep diving into the past. Sure, college had its moments. But I stuck to the task at hand, munching the apple and walnuts while I tried without success to verify anything more than Roy had found so far.

Audrey had given me the phone number for Don Kelsey, her ex, so I looked him up online, confirming that he was indeed a lawyer with a splashy firm in Fort Collins, where his specialty was defense litigation. His picture featured an expensive-looking suit, a firmly knotted tie, and a face exuding arrogance.

I logged off and called the firm. A honey-voiced receptionist inquired about the purpose of my call, hesitated when I said, "It's personal," but put me on hold while checking if Mr. Kelsey was available. After mind-numbing minutes on hold with elevator music, a deep voice came on.

"Kelsey here. How may I be of assistance?"

"My name is Margo Richards and I have some questions about Audrey Langford."

His tone turned cool. "And you are?"

"I'm one of the ranchers she's working for here in Pinedale Springs this summer," I said, without mentioning that the rancher who hired Audrey was no longer with us.

"Why call me?"

"I understand you're her ex-husband."

His tone descended from chilled to frozen. "I see no reason to discuss my personal life with you. Nor do I have time."

"Please, Mr. Kelsey. This'll only take a moment. I understand you met with Audrey recently."

"She must've told you this herself. Why do you need verification?"

"Just double-checking, that's all."

"You're withholding information, Margo Richards, and yet you expect answers from me."

I should've expected a comment like that from a litigator.

"Something happened at the ranch," I said, hoping he wouldn't push for details.

"So, my little Audrey messed up, is that it?"

"I just need to know if she was gone on one particular day, that's all."

"She claimed to be too busy falling off horses or whatever she's doing there to drive over to Fort Collins to discuss important aspects of our divorce."

"You met in Pinedale Springs, then?"

"Yes, and I can't stand dusty little towns like that. How the hell does anyone live out there in the middle of nowhere?"

I ignored that. "Do you know why she chose to come here?"

"I've no idea. I can't imagine why she'd want to waste time mucking around in some old barn."

I ignored that too. "What day did you meet her?"

He confirmed that it was the same day Bow died, then, despite his earlier statement about not sharing personal information with me, he rambled on as if talking to himself.

"I did everything for Audrey, bought her a Volvo, a decent wardrobe, kept her safe. She seemed grateful, at first. But she changed. She was the one who asked for a divorce. I should have known she'd turn into such a bitc —"

There was a click, then silence. He'd hung up.

Unless Kelsey was an actor playing a part in some elaborate hoax Audrey cooked up, she'd told the truth about being away from the ranch when Bow died. The guy never raised his voice, but there was something dark about the way he spoke. Audrey implied that he'd gone past yelling at times. He sounded like a jerk, probably a control freak.

❊　　❊　　❊

I grabbed a few carrots and went over to Bow's barn. The sun remained bright even as the hour headed toward evening. Audrey, dressed in jeans and paddock boots, was reaching into Bandit's open stall with a manure fork, flipping turds into a wheelbarrow. I watched her, studying her face. Her expressions.

She smiled at me. "He's a bit restless this evening."

I handed her a carrot, and Bandit nuzzled her, smelling the treat.

Many horses resent confinement in a twelve-by-twelve-foot space no matter how fancy the walls, how deep the bedding. I stepped inside the stall, bent down to press on the gelding's pasterns and alongside the cannon bones, palpating for fill. The pumping action of movement prevents fluids from accumulating in lower extremities of horses. Same basic deal in humans. Bandit's legs felt nice and tight. I slipped him another carrot chunk and turned to Audrey.

"I need to take Phantom for a little ride in the forest, stretch her legs. Why don't you come along and ride Two Bits?"

"Sure! Sounds great."

It was the smoothest way I could think of to accomplish two things at once. I needed to exercise Phantom before my solo journey to Rim Rock Cliffs tomorrow, and having Audrey along this evening would give me a perfect opportunity to ask questions, see what came out.

She saddled Two Bits while I returned to get Phantom ready. Within minutes we were mounted up and walking the horses toward thick ponderosas behind Bow's property. We rode in silence for a while and then Audrey began humming, low. I closed my eyes and thought about Bow. She'd often hummed, too. It calmed everyone, horses and riders alike. There was something about Audrey, something vaguely familiar that I'd noticed before but never quite identified. I opened my eyes and glanced at her. There was an ease about her, a calm. Unlike me, she managed to look elegant in dirty jeans and manure-tinged boots. I tried to picture her lecturing in Biology 101, imagined infatuated freshmen guys.

"I wish I'd known Bow longer," she said after a while, her voice scarcely above a whisper.

"She was special," I said.

"She loved you so much."

"She seemed fond of you too."

"I... I would like to think so." The sadness in her voice was real and it was deep.

She looked at me, opened her mouth as if to say more, but bit her lip and fell silent.

CHAPTER TWELVE

OWERING EVERGREENS SHADED US from the sun. When the
trail narrowed, I motioned for Audrey and Two Bits to go
on ahead. She'd been riding this same Quarter Horse ever
since her arrival. The bay gelding was one of Bow's and the type who
required an experienced rider. He was prone to sudden whirling if
something frightened him and he'd been known to rear a time or two.
Although Two Bits behaved just fine for Bow or me, most people
rode him only once, and often not for long. He never acted up with
Audrey. When she rode him, he turned into a lamb without losing his
spirit. In the beginning, Bow had put Audrey on the bay gelding as
a test of her equestrian skills and her courage. If there'd been grades
involved, Audrey would've galloped to the head of the class. She pos-
sessed a natural ease found only in a few of my best students, like
Beth's little daughter, Nicole, for one.

Although she'd been hired as summer help, when I had time to
fit Audrey in for a riding lesson, she was always enthused. She even
wanted to try three-day eventing, a lofty goal because it involves
dressage, stadium jumping, and rigorous cross-country jumping, all
designed to show flexibility and stamina in both horse and rider. I

figured she and Two Bits might be ready for novice level competitions before long. Both needed more work on the Training Level Dressage test, but they looked solid over jumps.

Most of the time, people just glance at each other. It's considered rude to stare, after all. It's not easy to study someone's face, look into their eyes and see past the public expressions everyone hides behind. Now Audrey rode in front of me on the narrowed uphill trail and staring at the back of her head told me nothing. I needed to study her face, but that would have to wait. The trail widened and Phantom began prancing. My mare knew that the meadow stretched out ahead and was the place where she got to open up, have some fun. Two Bits also sensed what was coming, and so did Audrey.

We trotted the horses a bit, eased them into a canter and then let them run. Phantom can haul ass, partly because she's a mustang and partly because I make sure she stays conditioned. Two Bits wasn't far behind. There's nothing like the exhilarating power and freedom of an all-out gallop. I loosened the reins, balanced forward in the saddle, and felt Phantom's muscles ripple. Her neck stretched taut, black mane fanning. For glorious moments, the world both expanded and shrank. Hooves pounded the earth as horse and rider blended.

At the meadow's far end, we slowed the horses to a trot, and then a slow walk, keeping them moving until their breathing slowed. Audrey's smile was wide, almost as joyous as mine.

"What do you think makes people love horses?" I asked, studying her face.

It was a question I asked my students, partly to give them something to think about, but also because their replies gave me clues about why they wanted to ride.

"That should be easy to answer," Audrey replied, "but it's also complicated. To begin with, horses are beautiful and graceful. If we let them, they transport us into another world, one removed from what humans consider civilized lives. You spend more time around horses than I ever have. What do you think?"

"Well, your words are eloquent, to begin with. And anyone who loves horses is lucky. But you're right. This relationship between people and horses is strange, in a way. Humans are predatory, horses are prey. They should fear us, and sometimes they do, but we're incredibly puny in comparison. And yet, horses allow us to get on their backs, tell them where to go, what to do."

Audrey smiled. "You are also eloquent, Margo. It is beyond reason, but I am so lucky to have found Bow and to be riding her horse now."

I looked at her, really studied her face, trying to figure out why I felt so comfortable around her. Our mutual love of horses was only part of it. So far, the Internet search had verified that she was born in Denver, but nothing else about her childhood. I studied the curve of her cheek, the tilt of her nose, the color of her eyes. And then it stuck me.

Audrey Langford looked a lot like Elizabeth Bow Bowan.

The hair color was somewhat different, but there was a similarity, something deeper than looks, something about their way of being, their essence.

"Who are you?" I asked, holding my breath, not sure what I expected her to say, afraid she might just laugh.

Audrey took a deep breath, gave me a small smile.

"I am Bow's daughter," she whispered.

My jaw dropped. "You... What?"

Had she really said that? A million questions came to mind. I'd expected a connection, a niece maybe, but a daughter?

"I was raised mostly in foster care," Audrey began, as if reading my thoughts, "and for a long time, I never let myself think about my birth mother. It seemed inconsequential. Then, only a short time ago, my life changed. After five years of marriage, I finally got the courage to leave Don. He was...well, he had anger issues. He could be quite charming, but he was hard to please, hit me at times. I tolerated it much longer than I should have. I wanted to get pregnant, early on, but it never happened. A good thing, really. I never took his last name, so after we separated, most traces of our lives together vanished. Being alone reminded me that I had no family, no one at all. One of my friends has an especially close relationship with her mother and I began wondering if I could find my birth mother. Curiosity had as much to do with it as emotional need, at the start."

I nodded, riding silently beside her, seeing even more of Bow in the way she sat a horse, in her smallest gestures. I couldn't believe I hadn't seen them more clearly before.

"It took months of wading through bureaucratic offices and Internet data to discover that Elizabeth Bowan gave birth to me when she was only fifteen."

My mouth fell open again.

Audrey continued, not even looking at me. "I was born in Denver, shuffled from one foster home to another, then adopted by a family in upstate New York when I was almost five. They gave me a pony, fancy clothes, lavish toys, a nanny, and the name Langford. I loved the nanny, adored the pony. When I was ten, the Langfords divorced. I guess it was easier for them to put me back in foster care instead of hassling over child custody. I wasn't allowed to keep the pony, and of course there was no more nanny. The name Langford remained, nagging me about a life I glimpsed then lost."

She took a deep breath and exhaled loudly before continuing.

"They established a trust fund for me, but neither of the Langfords ever contacted me again. They were never abusive, just distant. It never felt like they were truly my parents anyhow.

"They traveled extensively, leaving me at home with the nanny. I barely remember their faces. I would recognize the pony anywhere, though. He was pure white, with some fancy registered name, but I called him Puff. Still have his picture. The nanny kept in touch, in person sometimes, but mainly through letters. Her name is Maria and she is very loving, the closest thing to a mother I ever had. She helped obtain documents proving that Bow is my birth mother.

"I had no idea how Bow would react to meeting me and I have never been so nervous as when I appeared at her door. I didn't tell her who I was when I called about the summer job. Coming here was initially just an excuse to see her face, look into her eyes. I have never had another horse of my own after Puff, but I got back into riding during college, always felt compelled to be around horses. When Don and I first married, he encouraged me to take riding lessons, even rode with me sometimes. He grew up around thoroughbreds, enjoyed riding. I felt so comfortable with horses, starting back when I had my little white pony, that I knew my mother's life would involve horses."

I thought about Tiffany, my young student, and Pickles, her ornery but adorable pony.

"We girls and our ponies," I said. "So, Puff must've looked a bit like Pickles?"

Audrey grinned. "Matter of fact, yes. When I first saw Pickles, he reminded me of him. Except Puff was twice as nice."

"Glad to hear it. But go on, about when you arrived."

"Before I came, I wasn't sure if I should even reveal my identity. Bow barely seemed surprised when I told her who I was, though, which threw me at first. But then I realized that for the first time in my life..." She stopped, began sobbing. "I realized I had come home," she whispered.

"Oh, Audrey," I said, tearing up myself. "No wonder. No wonder I felt so comfortable around you from the start."

She tried to smile, but her chin quivered, more tears flowed.

"Thanks," she whispered, dabbing her eyes with a tissue. "Bow loved you very much and I can understand why."

"Speaking of which..."

She pressed her lips together, sighed. "You wonder why Bow withheld revealing who I really am."

I nodded.

"She said she needed time, said there were other things she had to tell you."

Bow had mentioned the same thing to me not long before she died. But whatever she planned to say had gone unspoken. I looked at Audrey, my eyebrows raised.

She shook her head. "She never got around to telling me, either. She spoke of daughters in the plural, though, said she considered you her daughter too."

"I was twelve when my parents died in a plane crash and Bow took me in, became like a second mother to me." A second mother with secrets.

Phantom jigged sideways, nearly bumping into Two Bits.

"Sorry," I said, steadying the mare and glancing around. The forest seemed quiet, but I'd been so engrossed in listening to Audrey that I could've missed something. Or someone. More likely, though, Phantom was reacting to my tension.

"It was joyous to meet her, my real mother. There was much more to learn about her, much left unsaid."

"She was fifteen when you were born, so you're thirty-four now," I said. "Same age as me." Suddenly I realized this might've been a big part of the reason Bow agreed to be my godmother and then to take me in. She must've been thinking about her own daughter, maybe considered me a sort of substitute. How convoluted life can be.

"What about your father?"

She shrugged. "I asked Bow. There was a name on my birth certificate, Ian McGregor. She said he was sixteen, said his parents kept him away from her after they found out about the pregnancy. So, he contributed sperm and that was all. Bow's parents sent her to Denver to hide the pregnancy and insisted she give me up for adoption. The doctors never even let her hold me, whisked me away from the delivery room. Bow said she felt empty for a long time afterwards."

I imagined an adolescent couple going from sexual intimacy to discovery to denial and fear, with acceptance unreachable. The boy was forced into denial. The girl, as always, paid the heavy price, and was pushed through everything but acceptance. Right now, I felt stuck on shock.

We rode in silence for a while and I had the eerie feeling that Bow's spirit was hovering close. Maybe that's what startled Phantom. I shook my head. I'd never considered myself the type that communed with spirits. Then again, I don't think we humans are meant to understand everything.

"Should I tell the others?"

"Well, that's up to you. I suppose you'll know if it feels right to tell them sometime."

"I will, then, but not right away."

"Why didn't you tell me you were Bow's daughter right after she died?"

"I wanted to, was going to, but when you started talking about murder I thought it best to wait. I was afraid you would think all I wanted was to inherit her ranch."

She was right. Matter of fact, as much as I liked her, I still couldn't afford to trust anyone fully, not yet. Her story about meeting her ex on the day Bow died checked out. She couldn't have ridden out to Rim Rock Cliffs with Bow, but she still could've been involved in a plan of some sort.

Audrey frowned. "*Is* that what you think? That I want to inherit the ranch?"

I looked at her. "If you can prove you're her daughter, you will inherit the place."

She bit her lip. "No! No! That is not what I want. Not at all. I have the documents proving she is my mother and I'll give them to you. But you're the one who should inherit the ranch. You have been her daughter all along."

"Not legally," I said. "She never officially adopted me. At any rate, I haven't found a will yet. My focus now is finding out what really happened to her."

"You cannot believe she fell? Accidents do happen."

I shrugged. "Not to Bow."

"What can I do to help?"

"Keep watching her place, taking care of her horses."

"Of course."

I sighed. "I like you, Audrey, I really do. Liked you from the start without understanding why. I just did and that was enough, at first. Your claim to be Bow's daughter makes sense."

"I'll give you the documents."

"That'd be good."

"My divorce left me broke," Audrey said after a silence. "Don is determined to punish me for leaving him. He's meaner than ever because he feels hurt. Anyway, yes, I am financially distressed, drowning in bills, obligations. But I did not find Bow because I wanted or expected anything from her. I just wanted to know her, spend time with her."

I turned to her, and once again it seemed like I was looking at Bow.

CHAPTER THIRTEEN

EARLY THE NEXT MORNING, Phantom and I were on our way to Rim Rock Cliffs before the first rays of sunshine melted dark shadows. The Cliffs jutted upward, a solitary fluke in the geologically diverse Flat Tops Wilderness. If we kept a steady pace, we'd cover the twenty-mile round trip by early afternoon, well before Roy returned from his Denver business trip, before he had time to worry about me riding alone.

He took long rides himself, so his paternalistic worry about a lone female rider both amused and irked me. Sure, his concern for my safety meant he cared, but I'd never needed or wanted coddling. Male–female relationships were complicated. Another reason I'd never married. I felt comfortable riding alone, in fact often preferred it, but this was no joyride. The Glock sat in my saddlebag and I fervently hoped it could stay there, unused. Carrying a gun bothered me, made me feel even more unsafe because it reminded me that there was a possibility of encountering other humans with guns. It didn't bother me to carry bear spray in case of encountering large hungry predators. Spraying them would likely make them retreat rather than eyeing me as lunch. Humans aren't that straightforward to deal with.

Bow was different. She was a constant presence in my life, predictable. Her absence wounded my soul. My thoughts wandered back to all the times Bow and I rode together, the places we explored.

I leaned forward to pat Phantom's neck, remembering how Bow laughed when I brought this little mare home. I never intended to fall in love with a mustang. But choosing a favorite horse or a favorite human can't be forced. Sometimes that spark of connection happens unexpectedly, like it did between me and Beth Jensen. The two of us peeled away layers of difference before finding a common core. She made me realize that not every friendship had to revolve around horses and riding. True, her daughter Nicole was as horse crazy as I'd been at that age, but while Beth admired horses, she had no desire to ride. I guess in some way, our friendship broadened my viewpoint on life in general and maybe even on horse breeds.

I grew up around Quarter Horses, got stuck on that breed as the most desirable. The first mustangs I acquired were a trio of freshly gelded, underweight two-year-olds with nothing much to admire, in a holding pen full of similarly sad-looking creatures fresh off the Soda Creek Wild Horse Range.

That was almost ten years ago. Bow and I were there together, but we'd gone only to watch the auction, certainly not to buy. But I stared at those horses, feeling sorry for them. Few people were bidding and I raised my hand at one point without even knowing for sure which horse the auctioneer was describing. Bow told me I was crazy, that I'd regret it. I thought she was probably right.

That trio of mustangs challenged me like no coddled, hand-raised-from-birth horse ever could. They made me question my methods, consider new techniques. They showed me how to be a better trainer for every horse that followed. In time, a local rancher paid me handsomely, took all three for stock work, and word spread that I worked wonders on wild horses. People had it backward, though. Those horses worked their magic on me. But mustangs and the Bureau of Land Management which was responsible for many herds remained hotly debated subjects, with some ranchers admiring them while others detested them.

Bow teased me incessantly about admiring mustangs, especially when I took an immediate fancy to this mare I named Phantom. She said the mare was a scraggly little thing, which was true. At first. She predicted this mustang would be even harder to train. Not true. Even after Phantom proved herself, Bow kept teasing, comparing mustangs to Quarter Horses.

"Toy ponies compared to sturdy stock," she'd say, laughing. It was an ongoing mock-rivalry. "Bet my boy Bandit can outrun Princess Phantom across this meadow," was another of her saying, even while she knew the mustang would tromp her heavier gelding's ass. Teasing was fun, but Bow knew a great horse when she saw one, and in serious moments she called my black mustang "Fabulous Phantom."

I glanced at my watch, told myself to quit daydreaming. Once we reached a relatively level stretch, I let Phantom canter, then gallop. She was conditioned and had phenomenal endurance, but I kept tabs on her breathing and level of exertion, slowing her down after a while. Horses are powerful, but they're not machines.

Just short of four hours later, we arrived at Rim Rock Cliffs. Near the base, aspen clustered, casting dappled shade over blue columbines and tall grasses. Beyond the trees, sandstone ledges rose haphazardly as if in homage to the sky.

There'd be no blood, no preserved footprints. Rain would have cleansed all that several times over in the past few days. But I'd come for whatever revelations might remain, and I'd come for a sense of closure. Families of those who've died suddenly and traumatically were often drawn to the place where a loved one's life ended. I'd always thought that was sort of strange, macabre. Now I understood.

I dismounted, loosened Phantom's girth, unbridled her, leaving the halter and lead rope I used on long rides to secure her to a stout aspen. Maybe Bow had tied Bandit to this same tree.

The lowest ledge beckoned and I sat on the hard stone, moving my hand back and forth over the unyielding cold.

"You're here in some sense, aren't you, Bow?" I whispered. "Tell me what I need to know. Tell me if you fell, or someone pushed you."

Her spirit, her essence, seemed almost tangible. I closed my eyes, barely aware of tears seeping over my cheeks.

A sudden chattering interrupted the silence. It was a sound I'd heard before but couldn't identify right away. The hairs at the back of my neck stiffened. I opened my eyes, saw movement in a tall ponderosa. A shadow, dark. I squinted at a black Abert's squirrel. It peered down with bright eyes, squawked once more, then flicked its bushy tail and disappeared. Bow loved these elusive little tufted-ear acrobats who depend on ponderosa cones for a supply of nutritious seeds.

I hadn't come to be startled by forest creatures or just to cry, either. I'd come for answers. I got busy, probing crevices, turning over loose rocks.

The place held tight to its secrets.

A path looped back and forth up the side of the cliff, steep and narrow, nowhere near wide enough for horses. I made my way up to where sparse bits of grass and a few scrawny trees poking out of rock crevices marked the summit. The cliff widened to a small plateau, a miniature version of the flat-topped mountains this wilderness was named for. Taken as a whole, the mesas looked like mountains with their peaks sliced off. Bow and I occasionally brought our packing trip customers up to this cliff on foot, for the view. An impressive portion of the Flat Tops Wilderness rolled out below, pine forests punctuated with more rock outcroppings gave way to groves of aspen, white trunks glistening under blue skies. In the distance, a river splashed over boulders, ribboning through trees into open meadows.

I stood still, breathing in the beauty, wondering why Bow had come here, who had been with her. I was missing something, but what?

Secrets. Bow kept things from me, significant things I had to sort out. According to Ruth, she felt forced to consider selling the ranch. On top of that, she was re-engaging with a long-lost daughter. I thought I knew her, understood her. She'd never been the coy type, always said what was on her mind, or so it seemed.

She had said there were things she'd tell me about when the time was right. Getting pregnant at age fifteen must've been one of those things. Considering selling the ranch was another.

What else, Bow, what else?

Anger didn't seem appropriate at this place, but there was no stopping it. Why the hell had Bow kept so much from me? No one knows everything about another person, but the secrets she kept were huge. And she hadn't kept this stuff to herself. Bow trusted Ruth more than me, probably loved her real daughter more than me. Childish, but there it was. Bow was dead, and even though I would always love her, there was no denying the jealousy, the hurt.

And here was the worst of it. Even as these emotions boiled over inside, there was no way I could admit them out loud. Not to anyone, not even Roy. It was acceptable to shed tears for the dead, to mourn. But I had to suppress everything else, lock it away somewhere out of sight. I was an adult, after all, but my emotional core felt like a kid, twice orphaned.

I walked to the edge of the cliff, looked down.

Bow had done the same, but what was she thinking, what was she feeling? I had no idea if she was desperate or resigned when she took one step and then another, whether she was about to slip. Or be pushed. Did she know she was about to die?

I looked down at Phantom, who seemed suddenly agitated, her head turned toward the forest. I looked in that direction, saw movement. There was no sound that my ears could detect, not even the crushing of pine needles under feet. Phantom was unfazed at the sight of deer or elk.

I squinted, wishing my human vision was more acute, but all I detected was a tan blur moving slowly. And then the light adjusted and I saw that the blur was a cougar, a large one. It was about eighty feet away. Suddenly, the big cat stopped, turned its head toward Phantom and I, then turned and disappeared into the forest.

The animal who'd mauled Bow had been killed, but this area was prime habitat for wildlife of all sorts. Phantom either saw the cat or smelled it. She snorted. I'd brought the Glock and potent bear spray, but both were in my saddlebag. I had to get down off this cliff, had to calm my horse. I swung around, intent on hurrying down, when one foot slipped over the edge of the cliff. I fell hard onto my butt, both legs dangling over the side. It was a long way down. Heights, especially high edges, have always spooked me, but especially here, especially now. My pulse began drumming inside my head. I couldn't catch my breath. I closed my eyes, tried to inhale deeply but couldn't. I was afraid to move.

If I fell, I'd die.

Just like my parents, just like Bow, I would die. One second alive, the next dead. At the sight of my body plunging downward, Phantom would pull back, break away and thunder off. Sooner or later, the cougar I'd seen would approach on large silent paws, would approach with sharp teeth.

My breath came in gulps, my thoughts spun. I had to calm down, stop acting like a helpless child. Maybe Roy was right; I should've waited until he could ride out here with me. I edged myself backward, inch by inch, until finally my legs were on solid rock. By the time I'd pulled myself to a standing position, I felt weak with relief. I stared into the forest, saw no movement. The cougar had gone. Then I thought about Bow and began sobbing. I descended slowly, still sobbing, placing one foot and then the other with care, vision blurred with tears.

Phantom had calmed herself by the time I reached her, but I felt weak with emotion. I leaned close to her, feeling her body expand with slow breaths, borrowing her serenity. Finally, I withdrew a few of Beth's oatmeal cookies from my saddlebag, ate one myself and gave the others to my mare. My butt was sore; otherwise I was physically fine, emotionally better. Ready to search.

There had to be something here, some clue waiting to be found. I hadn't found a thing on top of the cliff. Nothing. Not one damn thing! What did I expect, anyway? If Bow's missing knife was up there, the sheriff would have found it.

But something important was here, at the bottom of the cliffs. I felt it, knew it.

I needed to look harder, smarter. I rechecked crevices, rolled larger rocks aside again, peered under one bush after another. And there it was, a small white oblong under a scraggly wax currant bush. I reached beneath low branches, picked up the thing. A cigarette butt with thin gold bands circling one end.

Carla Simpson had tossed identical butts on the ground in front of Bow's cabin. Fat chance someone else who smoked the same brand had been way out here.

Simpson had come, though, smoked here. What else had she done!

Twisted visions of knives and cougars and blood sucked the air from my lungs.

CHAPTER FOURTEEN

I MARCHED INTO SHERIFF Plackmon's office, brushing past a startled deputy. I hadn't changed out of breeches, hadn't scraped mud off paddock boots. I'd tended to Phantom then sped into town, chased by a plume of dust and rage.

"Simpson was out there."

The sheriff folded arms against his chest, face blank.

"You can't just barge in here."

I threw the cigarette butt on his desk.

He peered at it, then at me. "Lots of folks smoke this brand."

"But few people are brash enough to leave blatant clues. I just came from Rim Rock Cliffs."

He sighed, said nothing.

"Simpson was the one who found Bow. Admit it!"

"There is no solid evidence that Ms. Bowan was murdered. Now calm down—"

"How dare you tell me to calm down! What if Simpson rode out there with Bow, intending to talk her into selling the ranch!" I paused, took a big breath, contemplated the prominent star on Plackmon's shirt. Yelling wouldn't do anything except raise my blood pressure.

Besides, the sheriff had a gun. And handcuffs. The place swarmed with similarly outfitted deputies.

"Maybe Simpson lost her temper," I said, struggling to contain my own anger. "Everyone knows she was after Bow to sell. She needs that ranch. Means and motive."

"Determining that is my job, not yours."

I clenched and unclenched my fingers. Was it a misdemeanor or a felony to punch a sheriff?

"At least check this cigarette butt for fingerprints." As soon as I said that I remembered the rain, the mud, the probability that no matter what I said, what I found, it would never be enough. Never. My eyes began moistening, but no way was I letting myself cry, not now, not here.

"Grief has a powerful hold on you, Margo. We are checking everything, but you need to back away from this, let us do our job."

Yes, he needed to do his damn job. I turned away, turned to leave before I said or did something I'd regret. Those orange jumpsuits aren't very flattering.

"If we uncover more answers, you'll be first to know," he said, as I stormed out.

Speaking of first, wouldn't ya know that the first person I ran into on the sidewalk outside of the sheriff's office was none other than Carla Simpson.

If there is a God, must be a man. A female deity wouldn't have such a twisted sense of humor.

The bitch produced one of her smarmy smiles, muttered something about the weather.

I walked on, intent on ignoring her, but she fell in step beside me.

"Are you okay, Margo? You look upset."

Upset? My fist answered, aiming for her fat face.

She ducked.

I swung again, connecting with her left shoulder.

She stepped back. "What the fuck?"

"You were at Rim Rock Cliffs."

She stood, silent.

I waited, fuming.

"Okay, so I was there. Good thing, too. If I hadn't found her body, that cougar would've kept mauling her. I threw rocks at it... That cat was huge."

I reached for her, latching onto what happened to be a wrist.

She pulled back.

I tightened my grip.

"She was dead when I found her."

I shook my head, made another fist, clocked her square on the chin.

She groaned. "Damn you! Stop it, stop!" She pushed me, hard.

I stumbled backwards, almost falling, my face crashing into a solid lamppost. Simpson had a good fifty pounds on me, and half a foot in height.

The streets of Pinedale Springs are seldom crowded, especially midday, so the only witness to this slugfest I'd started was a woman in shorts pushing a stroller. She stared before hustling her infant across the street.

I had two choices. First was an all-out brawl, and the temptation to smash my fist into Simpson again felt overwhelming. She offered a safer release for frustrations than hitting the sheriff would've. But whoa, hold on. The second option here was a reality check, a maturity reset. Plus, I needed answers more than revenge. I opened my mouth to apologize... But I'd need a higher-level maturity reset for that. I unclenched my fists and arranged my lips into something resembling a smile instead.

"Are you done implying that I'm guilty when I'm not?"

She just had to ask that, didn't she.

I inhaled slowly, blew it out with puffed cheeks.

"I'm after the truth and I don't give up."

Simpson folded her arms tight against her chest. "False accusations don't sit well with me."

I wasn't in the habit of going around hitting people. But either God or fate had planted her in front of me at, shall we say, an inopportune time. That initial punch erupted without approval from my rational self while my irrational self just wouldn't stop cheering.

"I'm watching you."

"Murder is not one of my methods for closing a deal and I'll sue your socks off if you so much as touch me again."

Which was about what I expected her to say. I left, returned to my truck, drove to Bow's place. Audrey, Dawn, and JJ were busy in the tiny kitchen, and Ruth was there too, barking orders.

I'd never seen such a frenzy of cooking, especially not here. Bow would have been amused, but I was in no mood for humor.

Audrey took one look at my face. "What happened to you?"

"I ran into Carla Simpson in town."

"Literally?"

"Turns out Simpson is rather solid."

"Don't tell me the two of you actually fought," Ruth said.

"Okay, I won't tell you."

"You've got a shiner in the making, there," Ruth declared, as though familiar with giving and receiving punches.

Audrey grabbed a bag, filled it with ice, handed it over.

"Thanks," I said, even managed a smile.

"So now that you're finally here," JJ said, "do you plan to help with the memorial, or did you drop by just to stand around?"

Yet again, my fingers curled into fists, but this time my rational side prevailed. Two fistfights in one day might tarnish my ladylike reputation. Besides, Helen had just died. JJ and Dawn had reason to feel sad, angry or any other emotion right now.

JJ looked me up and down, sniffing. "You stink."

"I rolled in horse turds earlier, just for you."

"Bully for you. You can wash your hands and then use a knife to cut those, can't you?" JJ pointed to a pile of carrots on the counter.

No point in letting her get a rise out of me. Besides, I was thinking that anyone can use a knife. But not just anyone can grip the handle of a long blade, hold it over another human being.

Simpson seemed to be holding back when I hit her. But she also seemed like the type capable of losing control, flying into a rage.

"Well, you gonna just stand there, or are you helping?"

"Maybe later," I said, glancing from JJ to the others. Audrey and Ruth nodded. Dawn was at the sink, washing dishes, but she hadn't looked up or said a word.

"Do you need a hug, Dawn?"

"I guess, sure."

But after I pulled her close, she began sobbing.

"I'm sorry about your mother," I said, but she just sobbed harder.

"Her hubby called and she's been moping ever since," JJ said, sneering.

"What's going on?"

Dawn pulled back, wiped her eyes, her nose.

"I think Jason spoke to a lawyer. He and the boys are staying in Montana longer."

I put a hand on her shoulder.

"Nobody loves me."

"Maybe they forget who you are," JJ said. "You might try staying home occasionally."

Ruth shook her head. "That's an unkind thing to say. Both of you have lost your mother. You should be consoling each other."

JJ smirked. "Dawn is gone a lot. I babysit the boys whenever the nanny needs an afternoon off. Meanwhile, she spends most of her time at fancy art things. She was in London a few weeks ago, Paris before that."

"Your sister needs support right now," Ruth said.

"I support her more than you think," JJ said. "Poor little Dawn. Without moneybags Jason, she might have to grow up, get a real job instead of spending so much time smearing paint around."

Audrey gave JJ a look but said nothing.

Dawn didn't react at all, just kept sobbing, softer now.

I could've pointed out that, matter of fact, Dawn regularly sold paintings for thousands. But JJ knew that. She was just being mean. So much for happy siblings. I used to want sisters, but judging from the relationship between these two, I was better off growing up an only child.

"Is there anything I can do to help with things for your mother?" I said.

JJ shook her head. "Ruth helped us make arrangements. When she...we'll have her cremated, then do a memorial when we're back in Denver. Oh, and the sheriff wants to come talk with us again."

"Well, let me know if there's anything I can do," I said. I patted JJ's shoulder, gave her a hug, and wasn't surprised when she began sobbing. Grief was a heavy burden, doubled now for JJ and Dawn. JJ didn't appear to be drinking and I wasn't sure what to think about that. It would be good if it lasted.

Audrey slipped me a packet of documents before I left, and I nodded.

I had more to do than chop carrots. The ranch on the other side of Bow's place belonged to Sam Connolly. I drove over for a quick visit and, possibly, an important answer to a simple question.

Sam's wrinkled face broke into a grin when he saw me at the door. He was pushing ninety, but I couldn't recall him ever wearing what he called spectacles.

"Well, if it ain't Margo, come to pay a call," he said, his grin wide.

I stepped inside, feeling guilty. His wife passed away several years ago and now he spent most of his time indoors with a cat on his lap and an aging border collie at his feet. I meant to visit more often, and when I did, I usually brought one of those carrot cakes he liked. Not that I baked it. Today, I came empty-handed. We exchanged the usual comments on the weather, on horses. He always sat in a chair by the front window. Maybe he'd seen someone driving past, turning into Bow's place on a certain day.

"Nope, don't recall that, but I reckon I do tend to doze off now and agin."

It had been worth a shot. He was the last one I could think of who might have seen a car drive into Bow's place or seen someone opening the pasture gate for Bandit.

I'd always liked Sam. He was the only one so far who'd caved and sold to Carla Simpson. All his animals would be gone soon and he'd be moving on too. According to Ruth, Sam's son was carting him off to a nursing home in Grand Junction. Not only had he lost his wife, now he was losing the ranch he'd lived on his entire life. I hoped Simpson had at least given him a fair price. I promised to visit again soon, carrot cake in hand, and I meant it.

I drove away slowly, recalling riding fences with Bow and Sam each spring, dismounting to repair a busted section here, tighten a wire or two there. Never again. I'd have to find out the name of his nursing home.

My butt was still sore and it would've felt great to lie down for a few minutes, but the day's riding students were about to arrive, so I ducked in my house for an apple, filled a water bottle, and went out to greet Tiffany's mother, Tiffany herself, and Pickles. For once, the white pony behaved himself and carried his pigtailed owner around the arena without mishap. Despite his ornery streak, I liked the little turd. Like many ponies, Pickles was smart enough to know that behaving at least minimally well was connected to the flow of peppermints and to maintaining his rotund belly.

Nicole Jensen was next. Not only was she one of my most talented young riders, the bonus was that Beth always stayed to watch and often brought something for me. This day, she handed over a bag of freshly baked cinnamon muffins. I started in on one right away.

Beth laughed. "Let me guess. No time for lunch again?"

It'd be impolite to talk with my mouth full, so I just nodded. And smiled.

After they left, I lunged three horses on the day's schedule and was putting the last one out to pasture when Roy drove up.

"You're back!" I yelled, running to meet him.

He pulled me close. "Miss me?"

I reached up to touch his cheek, inhaled the scent of him. "Oh, you were gone?"

We hugged some more and then we fed and took care of the horses together.

Having him back filled me with peace, with a touch of normalcy.

"Let me guess," he said as we walked arm in arm up to the house. "Lunch today consisted of an apple and maybe a handful of walnuts."

I grinned. "Wrong! I did have that, but also a mouthful of fresh muffin."

"So, Nicole and Beth were here."

"Yup, and I saved you some. We'll put them on plates, and hey presto...dinner!"

"As adequate as that does not sound, I thought you might like a taste of what I brought home from Denver."

"I'd like a taste, all right," I whispered."

He pulled me close, nibbled my earlobe. Then we kissed, taking our time. As lovers go, no one compared to this guy.

"Hungry?" he asked, after a while.

"Not necessarily for dinner," I replied, feeling breathless.

We ended up taking a long shower. Together. Then came dinner in the form of gourmet sandwiches with fresh cold cuts, brie, avocado, wilted spinach, and something like mayo, only better, all piled high on sourdough bread.

"Don't ever try to escape," I said.

He grinned. "No, I know better. You'd run me down, capture me."

"You bet your ten-size boots."

"We now interrupt this scene for a brief moment of reality."

"No! I've overdosed on reality and it sucks," I said. "However, go ahead, tell me about Denver."

"I went, I did stuff, I missed you, drove home. Your turn."

"Did you miss me the entire time, or just now and then?"

"Quit stalling. You've got that look. What've you been up to?"

"Five-foot four last time I checked."

"Margo!"

"Okay, okay. I've got a list of questions, suspects."

I was already sitting on his lap, but he pulled me even closer.

"Am I on it?"

"Hell yes, at the top." But then I took a deep breath, told him about Audrey.

"Seriously? Bow had a baby at fifteen? Wow. Do you think Audrey is legit?"

"I like her, and she does look like Bow, but...well, I dunno, not for sure." I grabbed the folder of documents Audrey gave me, handed it to Roy.

He flipped through the pages. "Appears official, but we'll have to double check."

I nodded. "She could be a very good actress, I suppose. You verified that she teaches at CSU, the same place Bow relied on for toxicology tests. Her position has nothing to do with veterinary medicine, but there could be some other link, I suppose. Her entire story sounded logical, but..."

"Yeah, a thorough search will tell us one way or the other. What else?"

"Simpson." I told him about meeting Simpson at her office, about the cigarette butt at Rim Rock, about yelling at Sheriff Plackmon. I mentioned seeing a cougar out there, falling, downplayed how scared and sad I'd been.

"This could get dangerous, Margo. Matter of fact," he said, touching my face softly, "I've been waiting to hear how you got the shiner."

"Compliments of my new BFF."

"I assume she came away the worst."

I nodded. "Of course. Clocked her good."

He grinned, shook his head. "You're a fiery little woman, that's for sure. Sometimes I kinda wonder if it's safe to love you." He hugged me again. "Guess I'll take my chances."

I leaned into the hug, loving his arms, loving everything about him. We'd lived together for three years now and I could barely imagine living without him.

"I have a feeling there's more you haven't revealed."

I sighed. "Matter of fact, Helen Jacobs was found dead in the local nursing home."

"This is Dawn and JJ's mother, Bow's sister, right?"

"Yes, the one with Alzheimer's. She was a classmate of Ruth Dunn's in high school." I told him about Helen's fatal fall, the copious blood.

"So, the two sisters died within a short time of each other."

"And it's either a coincidence or somehow related. The sheriff is investigating, but he still thinks Bow's death was accidental. Seems to think Helen's death was an accident too. They did find a bloody footprint near the body."

"One of the nurses, maybe?"

"No matches so far. Plackmon is visiting Dawn and JJ again, partly to have a look at their shoes, I imagine."

"Interesting. You said neither of them felt very close to the mother."

"True, but a person doesn't murder their mother just because they weren't close."

"Speaking of murder, how's the suspect list?"

I shook my head. "Everybody is still on it. In other words, I'm galloping at high speed and getting nowhere. But I'm too stubborn to give up."

Roy smiled. "That's my Margo."

"Uh-huh, but every single person on the list has a motive, a reason they might gain from getting rid of Bow. Greed tops the list. Dawn and JJ stand to inherit; however, if Audrey's claim to be Bow's daughter is legit, she moves ahead in that line. Carla Simpson needs Bow's property for water rights. And then there's Ruth Dunn, who may be after more than her share of the B&D."

"Okay, so what's next?"

"I need to pay a visit to a certain tack store."

"Looking for?"

"Cooked books and it's not even a restaurant."

"That is such a weird term. Anyhow, I presume this won't be a social call."

"I'm the least social person in these here parts. And this visit will occur in the dark of night."

Roy clapped his hands. "Can I come too?"

"If you insist. You can be my bodyguard."

"Ha! As if you need one."

I wiggled my eyebrows, rubbed my hands together, held them up and blew on one, then the other. "Tough, yeah, that's me. Margo the muscle."

Roy chuckled. "More like Margo the menace."

"Watch it, Bud," I growled. "Who're you laughin' at!"

We took his Beast into town, Zap and Fetch riding along. Bow had given me a key to the B&D years ago, so we planned to let ourselves in through the back-alley door. No luck.

"Ruth must've changed the lock, which makes me even more suspicious."

"Hopefully she didn't nail this small window shut," Roy said, fiddling with the window until it slid open.

He hoisted me up and I was about halfway in when we saw a flash of headlights as someone turned into the alley, driving slowly.

"I'm stuck!" I said, wiggling and reaching inside for a handhold, finding zilch. It'd be just our luck if the approaching headlights belonged to a sheriff's deputy. "Push me, push!"

Roy gave one more push; I managed to slither sideways and then plopped inside. Roy slid the window down and I watched as he quickly moved to lean casually against his truck as the headlights arrived. Turned out it was Deputy Nate's patrol car, and he waved to Roy and continued on. Sometimes it helped to live near a small town where everybody knows everybody.

It also helped that Nate was friendly but not all that smart. I had no doubt that Sheriff Plackmon would've stopped, asked questions, pulled out handcuffs. We were, after all, breaking and entering.

The storeroom was windowless, but a flashlight revealed strangely empty shelves that had been bursting with merchandise a week ago. Feeling like an impostor instead of a real investigator, I used my iPhone for pics from the storeroom to the sales floor. Roy delved into computer files, retrieving recently erased info from the depths of the hard drive. He restored and printed copies of spreadsheets showing that the books had been altered, but to make the store look unprofitable. Squirrelling away merchandise lowered the business's worth, resulting in less money to whoever inherited Bow's half of the store.

Maybe Ruth's greed was justified. She and Bow had been close for years, they'd relied on each other. But debt can force people to do things they wouldn't ordinarily consider. Ruth was sixty-seven, old enough to retire, but had far too many responsibilities and financial obligations to stop working. If all she'd done was adjust inventory and records to keep a bigger share of the store, that was wrong, but she hadn't done it to Bow, she'd done it to the inheritors. Digging deeper into the extent of her debt might reveal the level of her desperation and whether she might've also done something to harm Bow.

When we returned home, I sent Roy to bed. He'd been travelling all day and was exhausted.

I sat down with my iPad and a notebook to review what I knew so far, followed by the many unanswered questions.

The coroner put the time of Bow's death about midday last Saturday. Roy arrived at the show to tell me a little over twenty-four hours later, on Sunday. Today was Thursday, and the past few days were a jumble of trouble, of tears.

I'd probably alienated Sheriff Plackmon earlier today, but he still seemed to believe Bow's death was either an accident or suicide, so it didn't matter anyway. He said he was keeping everything I told him in mind, but I found that hard to believe. At least Roy was here to help for a few days before his New Zealand trip.

Bow's missing knife was a major factor, but I had no idea how it went missing or who had it. She didn't have enemies that I knew of. Next came considering who stood to gain from Bow's death. First up were those closest to her. JJ and Dawn, the nieces, loved their Aunt Bow.

JJ let alcohol dominate her life, allowing debts to accumulate. Dawn's successful career as an artist failed to boost her low self-esteem, and her family life now seemed to be deteriorating.

Helen was out of the picture, but her Alzheimer's had made her incapable of plotting anything anyway.

Ruth Dunn, the long-time friend and business partner, had taken steps to lower the value of the tack store, resulting in less for whoever inherited Bow's portion of the business. She'd never shown ill intent toward Bow as far as I knew.

Audrey Langford, the college professor who arrived here only a month ago. Bow took her in immediately as the daughter lost to adoption. Audrey was in the midst of a contentious divorce involving financial difficulties and an abusive ex-husband. I liked her from the start, but the fact that she arrived not long before foal deaths and would stand to gain from Bow's death was troubling.

Carla Simpson, the greedy realtor after Bow's land. I disliked her intensely, so it was especially upsetting when I discovered she was the person who found Bow's body. But I had to put the dislike aside and concentrate on reality.

Bow had lots of lovers through the years, too, although I had no reason so far to believe one of them might've had a hand in her death. None of them should be in line for an inheritance.

Then again, I hadn't found a will.

The only thing I still knew for certain was that I wouldn't quit searching until I found out what happened out at Rim Rock Cliffs. I never gave up when training a horse and I wasn't about to give up on finding justice for Bow.

CHAPTER FIFTEEN

THE MAIN THING ON my mind the next day was Bow's memorial, which had been planned for Saturday, but was moved up a day. After chores, Roy gave me a cup of tea to sip while he made a quick omelet. He could've been a chef, and he enjoyed cooking. The omelet was delicious, as always, but I couldn't eat more than a few bites. After a long embrace, he sent me off to prepare.

First on my agenda was a ride out to a patch of wild blue columbines. For sentimental reasons, only Babe would do this day. Nearly thirty now, the mare still stood out in a herd with her dark chestnut coat accented by four white socks, but her unflappable temperament was the real prize. She was a link between me now and the sad and frightened twelve-year-old I'd been when Bow took me in. The mare was one of Bow's favorites and yet she'd turned her over to me, solemnly "selling" her to me for the sum of twenty dollars, which even back then wasn't enough for a bridle, much less a horse like Babe. Now, I kept wondering if Bow had been thinking about the child she was forced to give up for adoption when she so readily took me in.

Within a few minutes, Babe's slow walk took us to the aspen grove at the far reach of my property. I dismounted and collected an armful of blue columbines, Bow's favorite flowers. Ordinarily, neither Bow nor I picked wildflowers, but today was an exception.

When we got back I untacked Babe, gave her the once-over with a brush, slipped her a cut-up apple and turned her out to pasture. I had just enough time to go over to Bow's place, saddle Bandit with the rejuvenated Billy Cook saddle, secure the bunch of columbines with string, and drape them over the saddle. I led the lame palomino slowly out to where people were gathering in front of Bow's cabin. Boss followed along. I was still in boots and breeches, but then I seldom wore anything else. Besides, Bow would've appeared out of the clouds, laughing, if I'd put on a black dress. The skirt Beth prodded me to buy was the only item of clothing I owned that was anywhere near to a dress.

Beth and Joe Jensen, along with Nicole, of course, were among the first to arrive, and all three hugged me. But when Nicole patted Bandit and then stretched her little arms around his neck and told the gelding that she loved him, I lost it and began sobbing. Beth handed me a tissue and leaned close, whispering that I smelled worse than Bandit and that she'd love to see me wear something fashionable just once, which made me smile.

It looked like every chair was occupied, and many people were standing. Everyone in town, as well as all the area ranchers, knew Bow, and most considered her a friend. Those in tailored black suits and leather loafers sat next to others in jeans, boots, and cowboy hats. Unlike me, Bow loved a crowd, and this might've been one of her legendary parties, except this crowd was murmuring instead of laughing.

I read somewhere that murderers often appear at their victim's funeral, and even though this wasn't a funeral I scanned the faces, wondering who had something to hide. A handful of the men had affairs with Bow over the years, but I couldn't imagine any of them harming her. Michael Goldberg and his blonde trophy wife sat in the third row. The affair between Goldberg and Bow had happened well over a decade ago, somewhere in between trophy wife number two and this third attempt at marital bliss. Doc Wilson, who'd never married, arrived in his outfitted veterinarian's truck and settled on a chair in back. He never hid his affection for Bow and the two of them slipped away for a weekend together occasionally. I knew for a fact that neither the lawyer, Goldberg, nor our reliable and gentle horse vet harbored the slightest ill will toward the woman they still seemed to love.

Sheriff Plackmon and Roy busied themselves adding even more chairs to the neat rows. Bandit stood beside me in front of the crowd, with Boss crowding close. Other people approached, patted Bandit, asked if he'd be okay.

Roy caught my eye several times, touched fingers to his lips, threw kisses.

Then I saw Carla Simpson, dressed in a stunning blue pantsuit and strutting around with her big boobs leading the charge. She waved and began shoving through groups toward me. The woman oozed gall.

"I am so sorry about Bow, Margo," she began.

It wasn't the first time I'd cringed at those words today. People mean well and they don't know what else to say.

"I'm sorry about yesterday, too," she continued. "I know you were just upset, but I told you the truth. Yes, I found Bow, but I didn't harm her."

I didn't say anything.

She frowned. "You don't believe me, do you?"

"Doesn't matter," I said.

"It's true that I wanted to buy her ranch, true that I still—"

"Stop. This isn't the time or place." I turned to stroke Bandit's neck. Simpson irritated the hell out of me. Maybe it was her pushiness, maybe something more. She moved away and took a seat.

I wanted to stop thinking about her, but all during the memorial her words kept intruding on my thoughts. She was easy to dislike, easy to blame, just for being a pushy bitch.

The minister was short and stout with curly black hair. I'd seen him around town, doubted he'd ever spoken to Bow or even known she existed. He looked startled when he realized he'd be addressing the crowd while standing next to a horse. Ruth Dunn must have neglected to mention that Bandit would be present at the memorial. When he introduced himself as "Pastor Heelion," I thought for a minute that he'd said "hellion" and had to bite my tongue to keep from giggling.

Bow wouldn't have chosen a religious person to conduct her memorial. She believed that honoring nature brought people closer to God than singing hymns in brick buildings. Ruth was doing what she thought best, though.

Unfortunately, Pastor Heelion wasn't a great speaker and said almost nothing about Bow herself. Instead, he droned on about heaven and hell. If I'd been sitting down, I might've dozed off. The crowd looked bored, too. This was a memorial, not a sermon. When he finally finished, I almost clapped, but not in appreciation.

Then came the important part; hearing from those who knew Bow, loved her. Ruth talked about the way she and Bow started B&D Tack, how they struggled, how they laughed. Ruth's husband was present, one of the few times I'd seen him out in public for months. Jim Dunn's descent from rancher to invalid proceeded as Parkinson's disease stole all his strength and most of his dignity. A caretaker remained by his wheelchair, bending down every now and then to straighten a limp arm or reposition his sagging head. Despite the underhanded way Ruth had altered store records, I felt a flush of empathy for her and for Jim.

I had things to say, but my words were deep inside, reserved for Bow herself. Besides, I'm fine talking with people one-to-one, but addressing a crowd is not my thing.

Sheriff Plackmon spoke briefly, said that he'd come to know Bow as one of the friendliest people around, that her death was tragic. He didn't use the word "accident," but the implication was there.

Doc Wilson was known by everyone, loved by many. His talent for storytelling was as legendary as his way with horses. The crowd stirred as he walked up and began to speak, taking us back many years. I knew he and Bow had gone off together occasionally through the years but it seemed he and Bow began dating in their late teens.

"Sure thing, lots of people around here lived on ranches and kept livestock," he began, "but even so, Bow stood out because all she ever talked about was horses." He told us how he'd grown tired of small-town life, was thinking about going to college for engineering, but one summer of riding with Bow made him realize how special horses are. She started out by refining his riding skills, teaching him the thrill of cross-country jumping, then reeled him in by dragging him from one ranch to the next to see foals and calves come into the world. If it hadn't been for Bow, he concluded, he might be living in some concrete jungle and working in a cubicle without windows. By the time he finished, everyone, including me, was dabbing moist eyes.

What he didn't say was why he'd never married, but everyone knew it was because the only woman he'd ever really loved was Bow. She had a way with men, but marriage never interested her, or so she'd claimed. I thought about Roy, about why I shied away from a definite answer to his proposals. I wasn't sure how he'd react if I said yes, but maybe I should find out.

Bandit stood like a statue throughout the entire memorial, his empty saddle adorned with those blue columbines Bow loved. Boss remained nearby, never moving her head from her paws.

Audrey sat in the middle of the crowd, her gaze on Bandit. I was the only one who knew she was Bow's daughter.

The last to speak was JJ, and despite the vodka she'd undoubtedly downed instead of morning coffee, she talked about the first summer she and Dawn had spent on Bow's ranch years ago. She'd been nine that year, she said, a skinny city kid from Denver with pigtails and a head full of fear. One hot afternoon, she fell off Noodles, the pony Bow gave her. Only her pride was hurt, but she cried anyway. JJ went on to tell how Bow hugged her and said that every time she fell off, she'd get tougher, until soon it wouldn't bother her anymore.

"Aunt Bow was right," JJ finished, tears streaming down her face. "She taught me to conquer my fears, not only about horses, but about everything life has thrown at me. She taught me to never give up."

I watched her walking unsteadily back to her seat, thinking again about all those summers she and Dawn and I spent together as kids. The nieces loved their Aunt Bow. And now they had lost not only their aunt, but also their mother. I wished there were words to ease their burden of grief.

Dawn didn't get up to speak, but then neither did I. Even when she was the guest of honor at art shows or studio openings, Dawn seldom had much to say. She let her art, or her glorious garden, speak for her. Now, she sat with head down. Not only had she lost her beloved aunt and her mother, but her marriage seemed to be dissolving too. Maybe I could convince her to stay on at Bow's place, at least for a while. She and Audrey were getting along so well that it might benefit them both to spend time together.

Sheriff Plackmon took me aside at one point and said Bow's body would be released for cremation soon. I wanted to ask about the footprint, but I knew he hadn't talked to JJ and Dawn about it yet.

I thanked him and apologized for yelling at him the other day.

He patted my shoulder, said not to worry, that his skin was plenty thick.

The prospect of having Bow's ashes was good news, I supposed, but the word "cremation" made me envision fire, flames. I could think about ashes more easily than I could the process.

Later, I spotted JJ down by Bow's barn, standing close to Carla Simpson. The two were having what appeared to be an intense conversation, and Simpson patted JJ's shoulder. I'd never before seen them together, never suspected that they knew each other.

The day had begun under a cloudless sky and afternoon showers held off, as if in homage to Bow. After most of the food was gone and the crowd drifted away, I led Bandit to a nice patch of grass and let him graze for a bit before returning him to the stall. Then I wandered down to the pasture where Bow's mares grazed in knee-high grass beside rambunctious foals. I ducked inside the fence and a stud colt with a perfect white star on his forehead raced up, lingering near me just long enough to let me touch his velvet muzzle before flicking a comically stubby tail and dashing back to his mama's udder.

No matter who took over this place, things would change. I had no desire to own it, but I hoped someone responsible would take over, someone who knew what they were doing. Audrey might fit the bill, although a shift from teaching college biology to ranching on a full-time basis seemed unlikely. At any rate, if her documents checked out, she'd move to the head of the list to inherit—unless a will surfaced that specified something different.

❄   ❄   ❄

Back at our place, Roy had delved deeper than I'd managed to go in a computer search that verified Audrey's birth certificate was legit. Audrey Langford was Bow's daughter. Her marriage to Don Kelsey and their pending divorce had already been verified.

"Audrey's connection to CSU is the one thing that might still implicate her," I said, "although I'm not sure how."

"Hmmm," Roy began. "She claimed to be in debt due to the divorce, so inheriting the ranch might solve her financial issues."

I nodded. "Yes, if she sold the place. But if she kept it, she'd go even deeper into debt."

"True. Meantime, let's move on to JJ and Dawn."

"Good idea. Ruth told me that Dawn was adopted, but Helen was JJ's birth mother. I need to see how JJ and Simpson are connected. And should we search for Dawn's birth mother?"

Roy shrugged. "No reason to. It's a long and complex process anyhow, but let me pull some stuff on her art."

"I know she's successful, but I don't know details."

It didn't take long for Roy to verify that Dawn's watercolors were on display at galleries in Denver, Aspen, Santa Fe, as well as two places in New York City. Internationally, her work was known in

London and Paris, for starters. All of which meant that even if she was divorced, her financial stability appeared solid.

JJ was different. She wasn't on LinkedIn and her presence on Instagram related to her social life, not her employment status or education. She tended to job-hop, but many others did too.

I told Roy about seeing JJ and Simpson together, but neither of us could guess what they had in common. JJ lived in Denver and that's where Simpson had worked before coming here. But Denver's population was over five million. People could live there for years without ever running into each other.

"Let's jump back to Dawn and Audrey for a minute," Roy said, rubbing his chin. "Dawn said she arrived here on Sunday, the day after Bow died. Audrey was already here, of course. But as you said, the two of them seem very fond of each other. Any chance they could've known each other for a longer time than they admit?"

"Seriously? Meaning, did the two of them plan to kill Bow, take over her ranch?"

Roy shrugged. "Wild, I know, but if we're considering every possibility..."

I sighed. "This is all so...damn complicated. Everyone seems connected in some way, like a huge web, everyone complicit. I thought I could do this, find answers for Bow's sake. But who am I kidding? I'm a horse trainer, not a detective."

"You're doing fine, Margo. It is complicated to consider all the possibilities."

"Yes," I said, rubbing my eyes.

Roy pulled me close. "I bet you didn't eat much of anything all day."

I shrugged. "It wasn't a day to consider food."

Roy guided me to the couch and I stretched out, closed my eyes.

By the time he returned with one of his sandwich creations I was half asleep, but he pulled me into his lap and I ate the entire sandwich.

"What would I ever do without you," I murmured.

"You'll never find out, because I'm yours forever."

It was best thing anyone had said to me all day.

CHAPTER SIXTEEN

For the first time in a long while, I overslept the next morning. I reached over for Roy, but he wasn't in bed. I heard humming, though, and then he was standing in the doorway, grinning.

"Morning, sleepyhead." He came and sat down beside me, gave me a kiss.

"I... What time is it?" I frowned, reached for the nightstand. "Where's my phone?"

"I moved it to the kitchen," he said. "I didn't want it to disturb your nap."

I yawned. "Some nap. I slept for...what, at least eight hours?"

"More like ten."

"No, really?"

"Really. And I fed the horses, told them you'd see them all a bit later than usual. Maynard started to bray, so I had to give him extra grain to shut him up. What a spoiled beast."

I laughed. Maynard had an internal alarm that went off if his servants were the least bit late heading down to feed him. I love donkeys. They're smart and they have a great sense of humor. Mabel and the horses relied on Maynard to take care of signaling for us if necessary.

God help us and all neighbors within miles if we ever neglected to feed at precisely the correct times. Maynard's most purposeful braying carried a long way.

"I've got a special breakfast planned," Roy said, kissing me again.

I closed my eyes, leaned close. "I'm lucky."

"How so?"

"Got myself a tall handsome cowboy, that's how."

"What! Who is he? I thought you was my woman." He kissed me again, a nice lingering smooch.

By the time I was dressed, there were tantalizing smells coming from the kitchen. I stood watching him beat eggs to frothy lemon yellow, stir in something that looked like moist flour with purple dots. Then I noticed a red light on the waffle maker.

I ran over, hugged him. "Blueberry waffles! Oh wow, I love those."

"Huh," he said, grinning, "I never knew. Grab the maple syrup, would ya?"

"You're putting me to work?" I asked, but I opened the fridge, took the syrup out and sat it on the counter, knowing Roy wouldn't serve it cold. No way; he'd heat it.

I closed my eyes. inhaled. "I'm starving."

Within minutes, we were seated at the table, stuffing ourselves with scrambled eggs and blueberry waffles. Nirvana.

"I baked some blueberry muffins earlier and froze most of them, so you can thaw one or two for breakfasts."

"If this continues, I may have to keep you," I said.

"That's the plan."

"But you're leaving soon. I might starve without my cooking cowboy."

"This is a terrible time to leave. And I'm sorry to say I got a call saying I need to go tomorrow."

I knew his New Zealand trip was upcoming, but I'd let myself hope it'd get delayed.

"I'll be okay," I said, trying to sound sincere.

Roy hugged me. "I wish you could come with me."

"I've heard New Zealand is beautiful."

He took hold of my left hand, held it up. "How do you feel about a ring?"

"A doorbell, a ding-a-ling?"

"Don't tease, Margo. I want to be with you forever. We don't have to do the legal thing."

"I love you so much, Roy. Ask me again about the...ring thing when you get back."

He pulled me close, we kissed again. I closed my eyes, memorizing the feel of his arms around me.

"You'd best get packed," I said, reluctantly.

"Uh-huh, but first, tell me your plan. You'll take the satellite phone when you ride out to Lost Valley, right?"

"Yes, I promise. It's the only way to summon help in that wilderness. And I'll carry the damn gun, too."

He smiled. "Loaded?"

I grimaced. Roy knew I hated guns.

"I'll take one bullet, tuck it behind my left ear."

"Fabulous. I had to pick a comedienne to fall in love with. If you get bored with horses, you could do stand-up."

"I'll keep that in mind."

But my thoughts turned to sorting things out here. Something seemed off about the two toxicology tests done at CSU. The first report was signed by David Folger, DVM, while the more recent report was signed by Mary Ashton, PhD. I'd spoken to Ashton and she'd explained that newer methods were the reason the second report showed that arsenic had killed both foals. The first report showed no contamination at all.

I took the reports, laid them side-by-side. Both were on Colorado State University letterhead, both listed a main CSU number, both mentioned David Folger, DVM, as a contact, but only the second one listed a direct number to Folger. When I'd called, someone rang me back and connected me to Ashton because they said Folger was away doing field research. Ashton spoke with authority, but it couldn't hurt to verify what she'd said.

I hadn't paid much attention to the letters themselves, but now I studied them. The differences were subtle, beginning with the paper itself. The first one was a slightly brighter white. The font matched, and the letterhead matched in style and color, but it appeared smaller on the second one. Probably didn't mean a thing, but it made me wonder.

I logged on to the CSU website and scrolled to veterinary medicine. Sure enough, David Folger, DVM, was listed as the veterinary toxicologist, but his direct number online was different than on the letter signed by Ashton. I dialed Folger's number on my cell, keeping my laptop's website open and hoping someone was there on a Saturday. A female who identified herself as Anna confirmed that David Folger, DVM, was doing fieldwork and would be unavailable for several weeks, just as Doctor Ashton had said.

After I explained the urgency of speaking with someone about the report signed by Doctor Folger, I asked to speak with Doctor Ashton, but I was put on hold for such a long time that I was able to surf the CSU veterinarian site. There was no Doctor Mary Ashton listed.

I did see lots about substances toxic to horses. Plants topped the list, including many members of the pea family. I was reading about hay contaminants when a baritone voice came on the line.

"This is Todd Blake, Ms. Richards."

"Yes, please call me Margo."

"Okay, fine. I'm with the toxicology department here in Fort Collins. You have questions about a report requested by an Elizabeth Bowan?"

"I do. The report stated there were no toxic substances in any of the samples submitted," I said.

"Is Ms. Bowan available?"

I explained why I was Bow's representative, that I was her business partner, and now the remaining foals' caretaker.

"The final report is negative."

"Negative! What about the arsenic? So, there's no need for further testing?"

"I'm looking at the report right now and there is no mention of arsenic."

"It's important that I understand this because someone sent a second report signed by Doctor Ashton. I couldn't find her on the CSU website. If the report she signed is falsified, it may have something...a lot to do with Elizabeth Bowan's death."

"This sounds like a matter for official investigation. But first, give me the full Ashton name, please, and spell it as well."

I did so, and then he placed me on hold. I had plenty of time using the CSU website to confirm the man I was speaking with had a string of impressive letters after his name and was, in fact, head of the toxicology department, ranking above David Folger.

When Doctor Blake came back on the line, he said, "We've checked thoroughly in our department and Anna checked with CSU administration as well. I am quite certain that there is no Mary Ashton at CSU, nor has there ever been. There's not even a veterinarian by that name listed anywhere in the entire state of Colorado."

"Oh," was all I managed to say.

"I'm sorry, Ms. Richards. I do suggest you contact law enforcement, as the so-called positive toxicity report did not originate at CSU and must be fraudulent."

"Yes, I will. But can I ask just one or two more questions, Doctor Blake?"

"Certainly."

"Is it feasible that polluted underground water might cause something like arsenic to leach into soil or pasture grass?"

"Possible," Blake said, "but not likely. The water would need to run quite close to the surface and carry a high concentration of any substance for it to reach soil and be taken up by plants."

"There's a lumber yard almost ten miles from where the foals lived, so even a toxic substance from a chemical used to preserve wood couldn't travel through underground water to the mare and foal pasture?"

"Extremely unlikely. One of the aspects we considered when evaluating the sample submitted by Ms. Bowan was the topography of her ranch. Subsurface water in that area is too deep for contaminants to gather in upper soils."

I was busy thinking and made no comment.

"Does that answer your concerns, Ms. Richards?"

"I...yes, thanks for your time."

"Not at all, and I'm sorry about Ms. Bowan. I will, of course, speak with law enforcement and lawyers regarding this matter as well."

"You've been very helpful," I said. "Would it be possible for me to visit you personally at CSU, say Monday afternoon?"

"Yes, of course. My secretary can arrange a time."

He transferred me to Anna and a meeting time was set.

Roy entered the room just as I was hanging up.

"I'm coming with you tomorrow," I said.

"That's great! What's the catch?"

"I can only go as far as Denver."

I filled him in, then called the airline, arranged a seat next to him. Next, I called one of my riding students who'd just graduated high school and asked her to stay here overnight and take care of the animals. Then I called Sheriff Plackmon, arranged to stop by his office.

"What will you tell everyone at Bow's place?" Roy asked.

"That you and I want to spend some time together in Denver before you head to NZ."

We took the Beast into town, accompanied by Zap and Fetch.

"Who do you think is behind the fraudulent tox report?" Roy asked.

"The first one who comes to mind is Simpson, but that sounds too predictable. Audrey has a connection with CSU. I doubt it's her, hope it's not. But something tells me this was more than a one-person deal."

"Agreed," Roy said. "It'd take planning to pull off. Everything seemed legit to Bow and she wasn't easily conned."

"It was enough to rattle her, so she wasn't thinking straight." I sighed. "Ruth was the only one who knew Bow was considering selling her place. Bow told Ruth everything, but it didn't seem likely that Ruth would turn around and partner with Simpson, not for any amount of money."

"Greed is powerful."

I nodded. "And the dead foals were part of it."

Roy scratched his head. "Do you think someone actually killed them?"

"The first one was premature. Doc said it couldn't survive. Bow and I were there, saw the poor thing die. But the next two, I dunno about them, now that we know for sure there was no toxicity involved. I wasn't there, but Doc said the foals weren't premature. He thought they appeared well formed, but each one died a short time after birth."

"And Doc did autopsies, right?"

I nodded. "He told me the other day that the tissues appeared normal, but he asked the lab in Grand Junction to do a final report, sent tissues there because it was quicker than sending all the way to Fort Collins."

*　　*　　*

Plackmon seemed shocked enough to raise both of his bushy eyebrows when we handed over the two CSU reports and explained what Doctor Blake had said.

"This may change things," he said, after comparing the pages. "You are perceptive, Margo. Persistent, too."

I just shrugged, embarrassed. I'd been tempted to hit him the last time I was here. Now he was complimenting me. Who'd have thought!

"My Margo doesn't give up," Roy said.

I cleared my throat. "What about the footprint in Helen's room?"

"Strangely enough, we've found at least five people with shoes that match. Popular tennis shoe. Both JJ and Dawn, to begin with."

"What! Don't tell me they saw Helen bleeding!"

"Now don't go jumping to conclusions, Margo. Neither of their shoes tested positive for blood residue. The other three are employees at the home and each one had reason to be in the room with Helen after her death."

"Now what?"

"We keep investigating," Plackmon said. "That's what we always do. I'm sending all five shoes off to another lab for a more detailed test that shows latent blood, just to be thorough."

I told the sheriff that tomorrow, Roy was headed to New Zealand for a few weeks, and I was going to Denver, just overnight. He said he'd have another look at everything I'd told him, and I promised to inform him about whatever I found out at Denver and Fort Collins.

As we walked back to the truck, Roy put his arm around me.

"Sheriff Plackmon practically hired you on the spot. You've won him over, big time. You could be a detective!"

"Uh-huh, sure," I said. "Now things are looking complicated with Helen, but I'll leave that to the sheriff. All I want to detect are answers to who did what to the foals, and to Bow."

CHAPTER SEVENTEEN

THE FLIGHT WAS SHORT, leaving just enough time for one lingering kiss in the busy DIA terminal before Roy disappeared on his way to New Zealand, leaving me with a rental car and a lot of territory to cover. I began by making plans for the rest of the day. The first thing I discovered about Denver was how much it had grown since my last visit. No wonder I seldom came here. The second thing that became clear was that the car's GPS was indispensable. Without "the voice" telling me which exit to take and where to turn, I'd get lost in the maze of multi-lane highways running past endless chain restaurants and look-alike developments.

Denver seemed like a different planet from the Western Slope, especially sleepy little Pinedale Springs. Dawn's neighborhood was somewhat close to the airport, so a stop there came first. Her house was large, impressive if you're into mansions, but of course no one was home since Dawn's husband had taken the boys fishing in Montana.

Luckily for me, Dawn's next-door neighbor was the chatty type, volunteering right away that their kids played together, that Dawn wasn't home all that much, and neither was Jason. Mrs. Chatty said that they had a nanny, of course, as if no one could possibly raise kids without one. She went on to say that even though Dawn was always the quiet type, she'd seemed upset the past few weeks but she didn't know why. When I asked if Dawn and Jason seemed happy, Mrs. Chatty smirked and said that Jason was the type who got around. She'd seen him in town with a gorgeous blonde more than once. I asked if she'd told Dawn, but she claimed it wasn't her place to stick her nose in other people's business.

Mrs. Chatty seemed like the suburban version of know-it-all Ruth Dunn.

Next stop was a trendy-looking street and a small building with huge windows and a sign proclaiming "Artistic Impressions" in fancy script. A bell connected to the door tinkled as I entered and a slender woman dressed completely in black approached, spikey heels clicking against the dark wooden floor. It didn't take her but a glance to determine that I was not the type who'd come to purchase any of the expensive paintings displayed throughout the space, but when I said I was a good friend of Dawn Curtis, her expression warmed a tad.

Turned out she was also an artist and one of Dawn's closest friends. Once she'd verified that I'd known Dawn since we were kids, her attitude warmed considerably. Within minutes, Cheryl Allen and I were sipping Earl Gray at a back-room table, chatting first about ranch life, which seemed to fascinate her, and then about Dawn.

"She's such a gifted artist, truly," Cheryl said, "but I, like, I've been worried about her."

I dropped another sugar cube into my tea and raised my eyebrows.

She circled both hands around her own mug and sighed.

"I mean, like, she's always been kinda moody. I guess I am too, really. It's like a thing with artists. But Dawn has seemed, like, different lately, I dunno, like troubled."

I nodded, thinking that Dawn had always been emotionally fragile.

"Did she tell you what's bothering her?"

"No. She's been, like, so quiet I can't figure out what's wrong. I've asked her if there's, like, anything I could do, but she just shakes her head. She's always gone, like, inside herself at times, you know?"

"How long has she been quiet this time?"

"About, oh, like two or three weeks. The last painting she did was very, like, unusual for her. Dark colors, purples, reds. She usually works in pastels. I mean, we all switch around sometimes, but like, I've just been worried about her, you know?"

"Did she ever tell you she was adopted?" I asked, since I hadn't been aware of that until Ruth told me recently.

"Sure. She'd talked about that like, years ago. Never seemed particularly bothered by it. I thought she might want to search for her birth mother since she never felt, like, close to her adopted parents or JJ either, but she never seemed interested."

By this time in the conversation, I was tempted to count the times Cheryl said "like." But decided there was, like, no point. Besides, I hadn't come to critique her. Maybe she thought I spoke like a hick. Whatever. Everything she said fitted what I knew about Dawn's place with Helen and JJ.

I told Cheryl that Dawn was worried about Jason leaving her, and she said she didn't know Jason or the boys very well and that Dawn seldom spoke about them. When I told her about Bow's death, Cheryl gasped, saying how Dawn often mentioned Bow and how much she loved visiting the ranch. I asked Cheryl if she knew when Dawn left Denver to go over to the ranch. Cheryl thought about it but wasn't sure which day it was.

On my way out of the gallery I checked several of Dawn's watercolors, mostly large, all pricey. Cheryl had said that Dawn's work sold quite well here and that they drove together to Aspen regularly. Flights to London to show their work happened every few months, and to Paris occasionally. All of which verified that even if Dawn was facing a divorce, she wouldn't face financial difficulties.

Roy had booked a room for me at a hotel not far from the gallery, and once I arrived, I opened my little bag to find that he also had placed two blueberry muffins, an apple, and a small bag of walnuts inside, along with a note.

"Marry me!" it began. "Don't forget me while I'm gone. Don't go sniffing around for hot city-slicker men! Don't forget to eat! And, because I know how you are, I pre-ordered room-service and they'll automatically deliver dinner half an hour after you check in." The note ended with another "Marry me!"

I kept the note, enjoyed the dinner, and wished Roy was there.

❈   ❈   ❈

I slept surprisingly well, ate both muffins the next morning, then checked out and headed to downtown Denver, with the GPS instructing me to turn left here, then right there until it felt like I was driving in circles. Tall buildings crowded together, blocking the sun, the effect striking me as somehow ominous. Finally, I ditched the car in a pricey garage underneath a tall building and rode an elevator to the seventeenth floor, head office of American Realty where Simpson had been a star agent.

I'd worn my one skirt, topping it with a white tailored blouse in a silky sort of fabric, that Beth loaned me. I'd dusted off a pair of black flats from the back of my closet. As expected, though, the receptionist gave me a once-over that would've made a less-determined person cringe. But it takes more than that to bother me, so I produced my best attempt at a sophisticated smile and asked if Kevin Smythe was in, having selected his name from a roster posted by the entrance.

"Is he expecting you?"

"No, actually, I'm only in town quite briefly," I said, peering down at her, enunciating each word as though I was someone important. "He was recommended by an acquaintance." I paused, held up my wrist to peer at my watch as though time was of the essence.

No telling if the receptionist bought what I was pretending to be, but she said, "I'll see if he's available. Please have a seat."

I nodded and sat on the edge of a chair.

Within a few minutes, the receptionist motioned to me. "Mr. Smythe will be with you shortly."

"Thank you, indeed," I said, biting my lip to keep from giggling. This was the first time in my life I'd uttered the word "indeed."

Kevin Smythe turned out to be not only nicer than the receptionist, but also talkative, which was even better. Much to my amusement, he was just as interested in ranch life as Cheryl Allen had been, and he was particularly inquisitive about horses and how I trained them.

City people seemed fascinated with rural living, but I've got to say that for me, it doesn't go both ways. I peered out the window at what I supposed was considered a great view of other downtown Denver high rises, but all I felt was relief that I didn't have to work cooped up in a place like this. Living in any big city would suck the soul out of me.

It took a while to steer Smythe away from ranch life and onto why I'd come, which was for dirt on Carla Simpson. Once he got rolling, he unloaded details about Simpson's competence, competitiveness and proclaimed her a total bitch. About what I'd expected. But what he said next was the shocker.

"Fossil fuel, that's where the real money is on the Western Slope."

"Fossil fuel," I repeated. "As in oil?" I knew there'd been drilling in parts of the Western Slope for years, but Pinedale Springs had been spared.

"Certainly, and natural gas, too, of course. Simpson has been researching the possibilities for some time, supposedly in secret, but I knew. Years ago, oil shale was the big deal over there, but that petered out, wasn't cost-effective. This is different. A potential bonanza."

"Are you saying that Simpson doesn't really care about subdividing land, developing it?"

"That's part of it, sure, but subsurface rights are prime and she's a brilliant bitch."

"How did she learn about the potential for drilling?"

"Some lawyer in Fort Collins. Used to go on about how sharp the guy is."

It took an effort to keep my mouth from dropping open at the mention of a Fort Collins lawyer.

"Do you know this lawyer's name, by any chance?"

"Um, let's see. Keller, something like that."

"Kelsey? Is that it?"

"Yeah, that's it. You know him?"

"Uh, no, but I've heard the name."

As in Audrey's ex-husband, Don Kelsey. Unbelievable. Simpson came to Pinedale Springs seeking a bonanza of cash and now I was here in Denver getting a bonanza of information.

"So, yes," he was saying, "Carla was busy before she pulled up and relocated to Pinedale Springs. Told everyone she'd decided to slow down, step out of the fast lane. But I knew better. She just didn't want to share what she thinks will make her even richer. Took on a young assistant, too, tall woman with spiky hair, disposition to match. Fondness for vodka."

Holy crap! Now my mouth did fall open.

"JJ? You mean Julie Jacobs?"

"Yup, matter of fact. How do you know JJ?"

"I've known her for years. She comes over to visit."

"Huh. Small world."

"You have no idea. So, about JJ..."

"All I know is that she wants to become a real estate agent, so Simpson is mentoring her."

"You mean using her."

He laughed. "You must know Simpson pretty well."

"Have you seen JJ lately?"

"Sure. She was here last weekend. Saturday and Sunday are always busy for realtors, of course."

"JJ was here, in this office?"

"Yeah, she was entering data on the computer. Simpson wasn't around, of course, since she'd moved months ago, but she's still connected with this office. JJ went to lunch with several of us both days. She's a hard worker, but she'd have an easier life if she wasn't such a lush. She manages to function surprisingly well, though, from what I've seen."

"Yes, she does," I said, thinking that he'd just provided a solid alibi for JJ. She might be involved with the foals somehow, but she hadn't been around the day Bow died. JJ might not be as sweet as Dawn, but I couldn't imagine either one of them harming Bow.

"Thanks for your time," I told Smythe.

"I've enjoyed chatting with you," he said.

I moved toward the door. "You've been very helpful."

"Good. Just promise me you'll keep Simpson over there permanently."

"That's asking a lot."

"I was afraid you'd say that."

He handed me his card, said to call if I had more questions. My head was spinning with everything he'd said. Not only were Simpson and JJ connected, but even Don Kelsey was in the mix. Might even loop around Audrey.

This trip to Denver was paying off big time.

My next stop was Prairie Lane Boarding Stable on the north side of town, where JJ said she kept her horse. Fancy place, large indoor arena, two outdoor arenas, endless rows of twelve-by-twelve box stalls with deep bedding and cranky horses. In my opinion, keeping animals confined day after day, year after year, amounts to torture, even if they are let out for an hour or two of daily exercise. Still leaves most of their time spent in boring confinement. Handy for the human, horrid for the horse.

The snobbish feel about this place told me most people were unlikely to be chatty, so I strolled around like I knew where I was going until I saw a teen girl with a pitchfork and a wheelbarrow. No doubt either a hired hand or someone working off part of her horse's board.

"Uh, hi," I began. "I'm a friend of Julie Jacobs and she told me to have a look at her horse's stall, see if maybe I'd like to board my mare here."

The girl glanced at me, wiped a grimy hand across her forehead and pointed behind her. "Royal Captain's there, I'm picking out his stall next."

"Thanks," I said, peering in at JJ's gelding, a tall thoroughbred who was weaving back and forth. Talk about bored. "That stall next to his empty?"

"Yeah. Lady moved. Western Slope."

"Huh. That's where I'm from. What town did she move to?"

The girl shrugged. "Like, Pine something."

"Her horse a gray gelding?"

"Yeah."

So, Carla Simpson had not only boarded her horse at the same stable as JJ, but their horses were right next to each other. This place wasn't cheap. It was a good bet that Simpson paid the board bill for JJ's horse. What had JJ done in return?

It was about sixty miles from the stable to the northern Colorado town of Fort Collins, home of Colorado State University, Don Kelsey's office and, if my luck held, more answers. The GPS guided me onto I-25, and I ate the apple and most of the walnuts Roy had provided while I drove, stopping briefly to fill the gas tank and my water bottle, empty my bladder.

Even though Fort Collins had grown, the town remained somewhat familiar since I'd graduated from CSU a while back with a bachelor's in equine science and a minor in psych. My time away from home had been tolerable only because I'd taken Babe with me and grabbed every opportunity to ride her on the trails west of town, especially Horsetooth Reservoir. Driving on College Avenue today brought back memories, mostly pleasant.

I graduated at twenty-one, the age when my parent's ranch officially became mine. Small towns like Pinedale Springs aren't for everyone, nor are ranches. But for me, there's nothing else. I wished Roy felt the same, because I wasn't sure I could manage if he ever left for good. We loved each other, but the trail ahead held twists and turns without guarantees.

I shook my head. No time for that now. I pulled into a public parking lot on campus and headed for the admin building. A glance at my cell phone confirmed I was only a few minutes early for the first of several appointments I'd arranged. I was soon seated in the office of a Miss Johnston, whose title was "Professional Relations." She verified that Audrey Langford not only taught at CSU, but made what Miss Johnston stated was above the average salary, although of course she wouldn't provide a dollar amount. She did say that Audrey was one of the students' favorite professors for Biology 101 and 203, that she had no known affiliation with the Toxicology Department, which was under Veterinary Medicine in an entirely separate section of campus.

I thanked Miss Johnston, returned to my rental car and drove south to the College of Veterinary medicine to meet with Todd Blake, PhD, DVM, Director of Toxicology. I'd spoken with him by phone to verify that only one official toxicology report had been sent to Bow, and that there'd never been a Mary Ashton, PhD, at CSU or anywhere else, for that matter.

"Nice to meet you, Ms. Richards," he said, showing me into his office. The only decor consisted of multiple diplomas and certifications, all in nondescript frames on one light green wall. A large desktop computer occupied one side of his desk; an iPad and an open laptop sat nearby, while black file cabinets lined up like silent sentries behind him.

"Thanks for seeing me, and just call me Margo," I said.

He seemed young for a department director. Tall, thin, a bookish type, complete with rimless glasses.

"So, Margo, you're here to verify what we discussed by phone."

"Yes, for starters. As your records show, one of our mares miscarried this spring, followed by three foals who died shortly after birth. The first was premature, but the other two appeared healthy at first, according to our veterinarian."

Blake nodded, scrolled to a section on his laptop, turned the screen so I also saw it.

"Yes, that's documented here, and the final report came out this morning, confirming no toxic substances."

I leaned in to scan the report.

"I'll print a copy for you," Blake said, "and we'll send a copy to your veterinarian as well."

I frowned.

"You were expecting something different?"

"Uh, no. I just don't understand why the last two foals died."

"Do you suspect someone may have hastened their death or even killed them outright?"

"I... Yes, it's possible."

"And if this occurred, it would be related in some way to Elizabeth Bowan's death?"

"I think so. But nothing makes sense, not so far. Our vet rushed tissue from the autopsy to a pathologist in Grand Junction."

Blake nodded. "Good idea. Tissues are best examined as soon as possible. It would've taken much longer for tissues to reach us, which might compromise results."

"Is there any possibility that something might've been missed here due to the time it took samples to arrive?"

"Quite doubtful. Our lab repeats every test and checks for an extended list of contaminants. The tissues sent to us were accompanied by other samples, including mares' milk, grasses, soil. Only the tissues are prone to possible incorrect results; the other samples remain stable for longer."

I nodded, couldn't think of anything to say or more to ask.

"Do you believe Ms. Bowan was murdered?"

"Yes, I think it's likely."

"I assume you're working with local law enforcement."

"I am, but the sheriff believes Bow's death could've been accidental. Or a suicide."

"I see."

I thought for a minute. "If someone suffocated the foals, would tissue samples taken to Grand Junction show that?"

"Possibly. Lack of oxygen from any cause results in immediate and irreversible tissue damage. Signs of hypoxia would best be observed soon after death. Anoxia, the complete lack of oxygen, follows."

"I'll talk to our vet when I return, ask what his initial notes said. He wouldn't have reason to suspect suffocation, though."

We spoke for another few minutes, mostly because I think Todd Blake felt bad that he couldn't offer more useful information. He was a nice guy, a caring type. He wished me luck, said to call again if necessary. I thanked him and left.

My final stop of the day was a no-appointment drop-in with a guy who seemed neither nice nor caring.

Don Kelsey's office would surely be pretentious and his secretary would have great legs. I'd debated how to approach him, had considered pretending I was someone else, like a new client searching for a lawyer or maybe a detective from the Western Slope. But this guy was no dummy and I was no actress. Best to play it straight, just barge in and be my meanest self. No way I'd let him get the better of me. I was female, I was on the short side, a lightweight. But I was no pushover.

I pulled up to his office, turned off the engine and sat still, giving myself time to breathe in a lungful of grit. I exited the car, pulled my shoulders back, sucked in my gut, told myself I could outwit this dude while he was busy mistaking me for a fragile female.

Ha!

His secretary was the first obstacle but I ignored her bluster, not even checking to see whether she had lovely legs as I barged right into Kelsey's office.

He looked up, frowned, then sat back in his leather chair and let his eyes do a slow roll up and down the length of my body.

"Take it all in, Kelsey. Doesn't bother me." But the truth was that he creeped me out.

"You must be the little rancher who called a few days ago." He smirked, crossed his arms. "What can I do for you?"

"I'm here for answers."

"Well, do have a seat, little lady. This should be entertaining."

"For me, maybe," I said, easing into a chair. "Call me Margo, and please begin by telling me about your involvement with fossil fuel on the Western Slope."

His eyes widened, but his voice remained smooth.

"Now why should you care about that?"

"Because my ranch is on the Western Slope, to begin with."

"But I doubt you understand much about oil and gas, my dear."

"My name is Margo, and don't bother trying to intimidate."

"Whoa, little Margo. Got a bee in your biscuit today, huh?"

"Stop stalling. You're wasting my time."

He flung his hands in the air. "All righty, then, ma'am. Fossil fuel extraction is one of my specialties, meaning I litigate for favorable outcomes regarding subsurface rights."

"I already knew that. Why the interest in Pinedale Springs area?"

"If you knew so very much, you'd realize the vast potential that underlies much of the subsurface around that shitty little town."

"How'd you get involved with Carla Simpson?"

"As you surely know, she's a real estate agent and a smart one. She's got her sights on potential wells that'll be so productive, they'll knock every bit of your clothes off," he said, staring pointedly at my chest.

"Stare all you want. I'd stare at your dick, but why bother."

"Saucy little chick. C'mon over here and we'll get better acquainted."

"I don't give a damn if you're undressing me with your eyes or what the hell you're thinking. I came here for answers and I won't leave until I get them."

He saluted.

I rolled my eyes, but I was glad there was a large desk between us. This guy was not only nasty, he had also physically abused Audrey more than once.

"What the hell did Audrey ever see in you?" It was a rhetorical question and he knew it.

He shrugged. "I'm good in bed, for starters."

I ignored that. "When did you first meet Elizabeth Bowan?"

"Who said I ever did?"

I sighed. "Answer the question."

"Were you ever a cop?"

"No."

"You act like one."

"Again, about Elizabeth Bowan?"

"I might've met her, once."

"Ever go riding with her?"

"Huh uh, although that might be fun. You probably know that I'm originally from Montana."

I nodded. "Grew up around horses, thoroughbreds."

"What is it you really want to know, little Margo?"

I squinted at him. "Why did you come over to Pinedale Springs? And how often have you been there?"

"Well, again, you must already know that I came over because there were divorce papers which Audrey needed to sign immediately, and she refused to come here."

"When did you meet Elizabeth Bowan?"

He shrugged. "Not long ago. About the time Sam Connolly sold his place. Carla wanted me to see the Bowan property."

"Did either you or Simpson tell Elizabeth why you really wanted to buy her land?"

"Again, you must already know the answer, so why are we wasting time here?"

"Humor me."

He looked to the ceiling, shook his head. "Well, Simpson plans to develop the property into ranchettes, for one thing. The subsurface oil and gas plays into the picture."

I frowned. "Once again, did either of you tell Elizabeth about the subsurface prospects?"

"You'll have to ask Carla. She's the realtor. My part is separate."

I stood up. "You're despicable, Kelsey."

"Leaving so soon? I was about to ask you out to dinner."

"Go to hell."

"That's not nice."

I gave him a look. I'd had more than enough of him.

"So, you're not going to ask the one question you really came here to find out, huh?"

I had my hand on the door but I turned, stared at him.

"You wouldn't tell me the truth, so why bother asking."

"I did not kill Elizabeth Bowan. No matter what Audrey has told you about how awful I am, I am a lawyer, and a good one. I don't go around killing people."

I squinted at him. "You do hit women, you son of a bitch." I left, slamming the door as hard as I could. Seeing Don Kelsey in person confirmed the worst I'd expected. He was a total scumbag lawyer in an expensive suit and a pretentious office. He seemed more than capable of killing anyone who got in his way. Both Kelsey and Simpson were around the day Bow died. I already knew Simpson had been out to Rim Rock Cliffs. She claimed she'd just found Bow, chased a cougar away. Kelsey hadn't met with Audrey until the afternoon of that day, leaving his morning whereabouts open. It wouldn't take long to get out to the cliffs in a four-wheeler.

I should've asked Kelsey if he had Bow's knife, just to see if he'd squirm.

CHAPTER EIGHTEEN

ON THE FLIGHT BACK to the Western Slope, my thoughts
soared from questions to sinister possibilities. I'd left a
check for the teen who'd taken care of things and told her
to go ahead and leave after evening chores. It was late when I finally
arrived home, but Zap and Fetch greeted me with tail-wagging en-
thusiasm and accompanied me to check all the horses before the dogs
and I fell into bed and let Emmy purr us all to sleep.

The next morning, I awoke with a headache. The trip to Denver
had moved Carla Simpson and Don Kelsey to the top of the suspect
list, although no telling who'd done what. I had nothing definite, only
suspicions.

And then there was Julie Jacobs, who'd hooked up with Simpson.
JJ was in Denver the day Bow died, so she was clear there, but she
wanted to become a realtor and had been visiting Bow more than
usual the past few months.

After the animals were taken care of, I defrosted two blueberry
muffins, fixed a thermos of green tea and headed into town, accompanied as usual by Zap and Fetch. Border collies are wicked smart

and consider it their duty to accompany me everywhere, especially when a truck ride is involved.

Doc Wilson's office was right on Main Street, two doors down from the B&D, but he spent more of his time on ranch calls, caring for everything from horses and cattle to the occasional llama. A few years ago, Ed and June Riley got a wild hair and started raising ostriches, so Doc added those to his list, until a neighboring rancher threatened to shoot every single one of the big ornery critters if they kept breaking down his fence and scaring the hell out of his cattle. More than once, they were all found on the road, which fortunately was lightly traveled. Ed sold them off to some guy in Utah, and for a while, everybody kinda missed sharing tales about the latest ostrich caper.

Before I was even seated in Doc's tiny office I launched into an explanation about the fraudulent tox report, the one that'd forced Bow into considering selling the ranch. He listened, then glanced at the report Doctor Blake had printed out for me.

"I heard from Grand Junction, too," he said. "The pathologist over there confirmed that their organs appeared healthy. No sign of intra-uterine injury. Their lungs, however, did point to anoxia, which would've appeared after birth. I attributed everything to probable toxicity."

My eyebrows lifted; my mouth dropped open. "So..."

"Something happened to each of them not long after they were born."

"Bow must've called you right away. How soon after they died did you get there to examine them, take tissue samples?"

"I came right away, both times. The bodies were still warm, couldn't have been dead for long. Bow didn't watch the autopsies, of course. They went to dig the graves."

"Who was there besides Bow?"

"There were two others each time. The hired help, Audrey, and the tall girl with spikey hair."

"JJ."

"They were all crying, Bow too, of course. I was sad, and I remember thinking it was strange because those foals looked so healthy. There were no marks on them, not on their necks or anywhere. But something cut off their intake of air."

"Could someone have strangled them?"

"Possibly, yes, although newborn foals sometimes have a mucous plug in the throat. Usually, they cough it out or dislodge it just by moving around. It's rare for such an obstruction to be lethal."

"Especially for it to happen two times in a row," I said.

He nodded. "It would be hard to prove that someone smothered them."

"How long would it take?" I asked, cringing. I imagined a foal struggling, unable to breathe until there was no more struggle. No more life.

Doc shook his head; no doubt he was imagining the same awful scenario.

"Minutes. Not long if their nose was completely obstructed."

I felt like I was about to throw up.

"Would you explain this possibility to Sheriff Plackmon?"

"Yes, of course. I'll go over now, before I head out on ranch calls."

Sheriff Plackmon's eyebrows raised just a touch when Doc and I entered his office together.

He listened while Doc laid out the possible scenario that'd ended up with the last two graves behind Bow's barn.

"Who was there when the foals were born?" Plackmon asked.

"Other than Bow, only Audrey Langford and Julie Jacobs," I replied.

"Even if it appears both foals might've died of asphyxiation, it'll be hard to prove who did it," he said, poker-faced as always.

I told them both about the connection between Carla Simpson and JJ, and in turn about Simpson and Don Kelsey.

"I need to ask you something," I said, turning to Doc after we left the sheriff's office.

"Sure, go ahead."

"This goes back years, and it's about Bow and men."

He kinda smiled. "Well, I don't mind saying that Bow was special. She had a way about her. And it was no secret that I wanted to marry her." He paused, shook his head. "But she wouldn't have been happy, so we enjoyed what we had."

"I know. And she had lots of lovers through the years."

He nodded. "You could say that, yes. If you're fixing to ask if that bothered me, well sure, but I loved her for who she was."

"Did any of her lovers get mad when she dropped them, angry enough to hold a grudge?"

"Only guy mighta felt that way was Rick Williams, and that was over twenty years ago. He had a temper, but never took it out on Bow."

"I remember him. He found her in bed with another guy. It wasn't long after my parents died, so I was about twelve. Do you think he ever forgave her?"

"Matter of fact, he called me when he heard about Bow. Felt real bad. But he's been married a long time, has a son in vet school over at CSU."

"That's good. Anyone else?"

"Nope, don't think so. Guys realized quick how Bow was, either accepted it or found somebody else."

"Thanks, Doc." I gave him a hug and sent him off to keep animals healthy.

Zap and Fetch had waited patiently in the truck, as always, but before my next stop I let them out at the town park for a frisbee session. Border collies live to herd, and in addition to helping me gather pasture horses on occasion, they considered frisbee-chasing another exercise in herding, still important work to them and not done until they were out of breath, panting happily.

Doc was the only current lover Bow had, and he was as far from a suspect as possible. If there were other jealous guys around, Ruth Dunn would know. I walked to the B&D, accompanied by the dogs.

As I entered, I inhaled the scent of new leather. Ruth was alone and looked up.

"Well, hi, boys," she said, clapping.

Zap and Fetch rushed to her side, sat in front of her, tails working, ears alert. They liked Ruth, but they also knew exactly where she kept a jar of dog biscuits. Ruth handed a few over and was rewarded by wagging that increased in velocity.

Only when the dogs were duly fed and petted did Ruth look at me.

"What brings you into town, Margo?"

"I came to see Doc and the sheriff."

"And?"

I shrugged. "Still piecing things together."

"C'mon in back, I'll give the boys some water. You thirsty too?"

"I'm fine, thanks, Ruth," I said, following her to the back of the store. "I need to cover all angles, so I want to make a list of men who had a fling with Bow, no matter when. I asked Doc, but he said only Rick Williams was angry, and that was a long time ago. But you know more of them."

"Elizabeth did have a lot of affairs, and not all of the men were as nice as Doc Wilson."

"Few people are like Doc."

Ruth nodded. The dogs drank their fill then settled by her feet, and she reached down to pet first one, then the other.

"So, who are the others? I need to know about every single one."

Ruth stared at me a while before saying, "Some things happened years ago."

"Sure, but some people carry grudges a long time."

"Oh, Margo. There are some things better left alone."

"Maybe so, but I'll do anything to find out what happened to Bow."

"Let's eliminate Rick Williams, then. Doc already told you about him, how happy he is now."

"Okay, continue."

"Well, let's start with Bow herself, then. She was a loyal friend to me, devoted to her animals, raised you like her own. But when it came to love, she just…" Ruth sighed. "She fell in love, but only temporarily, loved one man at a time, then took on another. I never understood how she managed. I think she was terrified of commitment and I never understood why."

"She loved Doc Wilson," I said.

"Yes, and he loved her enough to accept her. He understood her in a way few others could. And you probably know about Michael Goldberg."

I nodded.

"There were so many through the years. Let's see, there was Dan Scheckter, and Sam Connolly, both of those years ago."

"But Sam was married!"

"Yes, but that never seemed to matter. God knows it should have." She paused, closed her eyes. "Roger Tolman, oh, and Bob Heely, too."

"I got used to seeing men coming and going. But I get the feeling that you're holding back."

"Uh, well, for some reason, when you were young, eleven or nearly twelve I think, Bow had a period where she became, I don't know, unhinged it seemed. She always loved a party, but she seemed wilder than ever for a while."

"I remember the parties, more when I was younger." It was an adjustment from my parents' quieter place when I first went to live with Bow.

"Yes," Ruth said, then fell silent again.

"Please go on. There's obviously something you don't want to tell me."

"You're right, Margo. I just don't know that I should tell you."

Now I was worried, but also determined to hear whatever it was.

"If you won't tell me, I'll find someone who will."

Ruth looked up at the ceiling, then touched her forehead and made the sign of the cross.

"Then God forgive me. This won't make it any easier to find out how Bow died. But it may devastate you, Margo."

When she said that, I had a feeling I knew what she was about to reveal. I swallowed hard, nodded.

"Elizabeth had an affair with your father."

I'd feared she would say that, but hearing the words made me suddenly dizzy. I grabbed the edge of the table.

"I'm so sorry, Margo."

I managed to nod. It wasn't Ruth's fault. I'd goaded her into revealing this. She'd warned me. My head felt weird, light, and yet heavy at the same time.

Ruth hurried to the bathroom, returned with a glass of water, handed it to me.

"Take a sip, if you can," she said, patting my shoulder.

I sipped. "Bow and Dad," I whispered. Zap put his paw on my knee and looked at me as though he understood.

Ruth stayed silent, her head down.

"Did Mom know?"

Ruth nodded.

"Poor Mom. How could they?"

"Sometimes there are no answers."

We sat in silence for what seemed like a long time.

"I loved Bow," I finally said. "I thought she loved me, too. I thought I knew her, but I didn't, did I?"

"Life is complicated and so are people. But your parents loved you. Elizabeth loved you too."

"She had affairs with other married men, broke other women's hearts too."

"Yes, but she was still a good person. She wasn't perfect. No one is. I know you may not accept that, may not believe it right now, but in some way that I will never understand, Elizabeth meant no harm."

"No harm? How can you even say that!" I stood up, feeling wobbly. "I asked for this, Ruth, and it would've been even worse hearing this from someone else."

I lowered my head, covered my face with both hands. What I thought I understood about life, about everything, was all gone. I was a child when my parents died. I loved them, thought of them as perfect. Then I came to love Bow, to accept her as my foster-mother.

"I've been so stupid," I said.

Ruth put her arms around me. "I'm so sorry, Margo."

"Did the whole damn town know about Bow and Dad? Everyone but me?"

"Not everyone. But some others knew, yes."

I closed my eyes, rubbed my face. This was an emotion beyond tears, something so deep I couldn't reach it. Maybe it was grief for a childhood I thought was perfect, but there was more.

"I'm nothing but a hypocrite, Ruth. I never realized that until now. I accepted Bow's affairs as no big deal all these years until it became personal, hit me, no doubt like it did other children, other wives. This affair with Dad must have been what Bow said she'd tell me about sometime."

"I don't know, Margo. Maybe so."

"And if she'd told me herself, how would I have reacted, what would I have said to her? Would I have asked her questions, yelled at her?"

"Give yourself time. God helps us to accept what cannot be changed. And remember that He forgives, as well."

"Thanks, Ruth. I am glad it was you who told me. I do need time to deal with this."

Time. If I gave myself all the time in the world, it wouldn't change one damn thing.

But there was no point in telling Ruth that, no point in much of anything now.

CHAPTER NINETEEN

I DROVE HOME IN a fog, went inside the house that was now mine, the one I'd grown up in with Mom and Dad. I sank down on the couch, Zap and Fetch crowding close, vying to lick my hands, to comfort. I looked around, let my thoughts drift back in time.

My parents always seemed so content, so good together, at least according to my twelve-year-old self. Perfect family, everyone happy. Nothing wrong, not ever.

Ha! Mom must've cried somewhere here when she found out. In the bathroom with the door locked, maybe. Or in their bedroom, lying on the bed she suddenly hated, pillow muffling her sobs.

But maybe not.

She was a strong woman, not the type to let something like her husband's affair totally derail her. Maybe instead of tears, she got pissed, raging mad. Yelling! Threw stuff at him. In movies, it's usually dishes, one after the another. Whack! Against the wall, shattering in pieces she's not about to pick up. Hell, no! Those pieces represent what's become of their life, a gigantic mess impossible to put together. Then comes grabbing armfuls of the cheater's clothes, tossing them out a window, followed by whatever of his is close at hand, preferably stuff that would shatter into pieces, the noisier and more jagged the better.

Lives breaking apart.

But I don't remember anything remotely like that. Not ever. Maybe Mom held her tears inside when I was around. Maybe they sent me away before the fireworks began. Or they tried a less boisterous settlement, she telling him where the hell he could go in a softly hissing voice while he apologized, over and over, said it'd never happen again, that it meant nothing, was just a huge mistake. He begging forgiveness, she making a fist, waving it in his face.

According to Ruth, I was almost twelve when the affair happened. Almost a teenager.

Not long before they died.

Oh God, no!

What if the affair had something to do with the plane crash? Dad was a recreational pilot, couldn't afford to fly very often. What if they'd been arguing during the flight, accidentally hit something that destabilized the plane? Or, worse, did something on purpose?

No. No. I shook my head, sobbed.

I thought back to their funeral, running my hands over the smooth caskets, telling myself they weren't really in there, that there'd been some mistake. I loved them, loved them both so much. I missed them, always would. My tears now were for the future they'd missed, for the family we had been.

And, no matter what, for Bow.

Thankfully, there were no riding lessons scheduled until tomorrow. I managed to put several young horses through their paces that afternoon, then cleaned up and returned to town for a meeting I was in no shape for. But there was no alternative. I had to keep going, keep searching for answers.

Michael Goldberg was as non-committal about the fraudulent letter as Sheriff Plackmon had been. I guess lawyers also need to erase emotions from their faces at times. Anyhow, Goldberg did have lots of questions, and I supplied as many answers as I could.

"Now, we allow Sheriff Plackmon to investigate and officially verify," Goldberg said. "Then, depending on results, we explore the feasibility of bringing a lawsuit against the perpetrators. Of course, if they are implicated in Elizabeth's death, that takes precedent."

I nodded, envisioning a complex and lengthy process.

"Can I ask you a personal question?"

His eyebrows raised. "Personal? How so?"

"About Bow. I mean, Elizabeth."

"Ah, you're wondering why I'm still fond of her?"

"That's part of it, yes."

"She is — *was* — an extraordinary woman. And yes, you must've guessed Elizabeth and I had a relationship years ago." He paused, looked out the window as if it was a portal to the past. "I loved her, and in her way, she loved me too. We shared a loving and, yes, a sexual relationship for a time. That was well over twenty years ago. I never proposed, though, because she was a butterfly; beautiful to know, even briefly, but impossible to contain."

"Thank you for sharing."

"She had many lovers over the years. Do you think one of them, of us, is somehow implicated in her death?"

"I doubt it, but I'm considering everything."

"You're a bit like her, you know."

I chewed my lip, blinked away tears.

"You're as determined, as focused as she was. You'll find out what happened."

I nodded, dabbing tears. I was tempted to tell him about Bow and my dad, listen to his response. But I didn't trust myself to speak, not after being told I was like her. That felt more like a curse than a compliment.

By the time I got home and finished chores, I felt so wiped out that I didn't even bother with dinner. I needed Roy, his soothing voice, his arms around me. We'd exchanged texts, but it'd be another day or so before he was settled enough in New Zealand to begin Zoom calls. There was a framed photo of the two of us in the dining room. I grabbed it, sat staring at him, at us, looking happy.

What if happiness wasn't possible? Michael Goldberg seemed like a nice guy, successful and settled, but he was on his third marriage. Doc Wilson had never married, lived alone, made do with occasional weekends away with Bow. Was that better than an unhappy marriage? And what about my parents? I had no idea what their marriage was really like from the inside. I was their child, but I wasn't old enough to form much of an objective opinion about them as a couple, about their plans, their dreams.

Roy and I seemed wonderfully happy together, but maybe part of that was due to the fact that we weren't married, that we gave each other options. Married or not, I'd be devastated if Roy had an affair, even if he said it was just casual sex. Maybe he'd meet someone in New Zealand and the two of them would fall in love, decide to marry.

Maybe I was driving myself crazy.

I turned on the iPad, picked something on Hulu, zoned out for a while. It helped a little, but the tears started again when I went to bed. Zap and Fetch snuggled close, licking my arms until they felt raw. Emmy moved to my pillow, just above my head.

I felt like Dawn; depressed, aimless, and lonely, despite my furry friends doing their best.

I slept fitfully and awoke with a drumbeat headache. I rubbed my eyes, tempted to lie back down. But right on cue, Maynard brayed, signaling that it was, for Pete's sake, feeding time. There's nothing like a donkey's call. It's a strange sound, irritating and yet I love it. Makes me laugh. Maynard saves his efforts for important occasions. Like impending starvation. Braying translates easily: "Get your ass down here! Now!"

On my way to the barn, Maynard called out again, softer this time because he saw me and the dogs coming. I smiled, quickened my pace. Maybe Maynard knew I needed cheering up. Babe and Phantom were particularly adept at sensing my moods, too, but after moving close for a few neck scratches when I entered the pasture, they resumed grazing. I gave each animal the usual once-over, topped off water tanks, secured gates. As always, I finished with a stroll down my barn aisle to the last stall for a peek at Ramona, who lifted a black paw as though waving at me as she whirred a greeting. I slipped inside the stall, sat down, and my sweet momma raccoon waddled over and settled on my lap, gently accepting dog biscuits. Her youngsters eyed me with curiosity, but I avoided touching them. After a bit, Ramona patted my cheek and went back to her little ones.

The sun was full by the time Zap and Fetch led me back to the house, where some of the peace I'd felt in the barn melted away as sadness crept back. What I needed was a ride, a wide-open gallop, long enough to make the horse and I blend, a Pegasus racing away from earth, from human worry. As soon as possible, I'd saddle Phantom and off we'd go.

Much of the day ahead was filled with lessons, all adults this time, and the hours sped by first with western riders, then English. I saddled Phantom to join the final group of three women and their horses who were prepping for a one-day event. After I coached each pair through a Training Level Dressage test, we did arena jumps, rested the horses, then finished with a few cross-country fences.

One woman, Michele, was a spectacular rider on an equally impressive Trakehner gelding whose forte was jumping, but the pair did great on dressage too. Carolyn rode a thoroughbred mare that was raced as a youngster but had now transformed into a muscular and reliable eventing prospect. Evelyn was a skillful rider, but her horse was a Hanoverian mare with fancy breeding and disappointing performance, especially over fences.

After Michele and Carolyn loaded their horses and departed, Evelyn stayed behind, looking glum.

"Your little mustang outshines my big fancy warmblood," she said, unsaddling her mare. "I've had this horse for over a year, now, so you've seen us a lot. We're just not getting there."

"Well, to begin with, Phantom is small, for sure, too small to make eventing her main pursuit even though she jumps like a dream. But it's not just a matter of size, it's more a matter of heart, of desire. Phantom has more heart than any horse I've known."

Evelyn nodded. "So, what do you think of my mare?"

"Her conformation is good, and I think it's wonderful that there are more warmbloods around these days. You're a great rider, Evelyn, but your mare doesn't seem to have that spark needed for strenuous eventing."

"That's for sure. She doesn't seem to enjoy much of anything."

"But she looked good during the dressage test. Maybe that's her forte."

"Oh, great. I tolerate the dressage because I know jumping is next."

"The mare is heavy boned, which isn't a bad thing, but she does seem more suited for flat work than jumping."

"So, what should I do? I like her, but she doesn't excite me."

"I can tell. And that happens. It's not easy to pair up with the right horse. Have you considered selling?"

"Yes, I have. But I'd need another horse."

"Um, wait right here. I have someone to show you."

Within ten minutes, I had Happy saddled and in the arena.

"This big guy isn't for sale, yet. But he probably will be."

Evelyn looked the gelding up and down, smiling.

I put Happy through his paces, then took him over a few cavalletti and on to the series of jumps that the women had just used in the arena. Happy cleared everything in fine form, enthusiastic but well in hand. I walked him around to cool him, dismounted, unsaddled the horse, and brought him over to her.

"Nice. Very nice. He's a warmblood for sure, but..."

"Dutch," I said. "Seven years old, 16.3. Imported two years ago. Just purchased several months ago."

She circled him, nodding. "He's fabulous! I've heard great things about Dutch Warmbloods. Let me guess. He's too big, too spirited. She's scared spitless of him."

"That about covers it," I said. "She brought him to me for training and as you can tell, he's doing fine, he just needs an experienced rider. I'm about to tell her that. I can ask if she's ready to sell, then let the two of you talk, arrange for you to ride him."

"He's gorgeous, moves like a dream. Yes, I'd love to meet her, see where it goes from there. If that doesn't work out, how about selling Phantom?"

I laughed. "Not a chance!"

After Evelyn and her Hanoverian left, I took care of chores. By the time I got back to the house, I gave in to a lingering exhaustion and fell into bed shortly after sunset. I was in a deep sleep when my cell rang. I tried pretending it was part of a dream, but finally opened my eyes, saw it was only half past ten.

I grabbed the phone, mumbled, "Hello."

"Audrey doesh not belong." JJ's voice was slow, slurred. "She inshists riding to Lath Creek."

She stopped talking, and I wondered if she'd passed out. She could hold a lot of liquor, but everyone has a limit. After a few more seconds, JJ continued.

"She's hidtink sumshang."

Then Audrey came on the line, said simply, "Please come."

I went.

CHAPTER TWENTY

WHEN THE DOGS AND I arrived, JJ was slumped, eyes closed, on the purple chair that had occupied the same corner of Bow's cabin for as long as I could remember. At first, I thought JJ had finally given in to the booze, but she opened her eyes, tried to stand, couldn't manage it.

"Make her go," she said, sitting back, pointing at Audrey.

Ruth was there too, frowning. She never touched alcohol, not wine with dinner, not a cold beer when it was hot. Dawn and Audrey sat on the couch, both looking like they'd also had a drink or two. It was an emotionally exhausting time, so I couldn't blame them. I've never liked the fuzzy effect alcohol gives me, but whatever works, if the bottle doesn't take over. Dawn had convinced JJ to try rehab once, paid for it, too, of course, but JJ left the program on the fourth day. Probably got the shakes and bailed.

"She's drunk," Dawn said, as if that wasn't obvious.

JJ giggled. "Yup."

"All three of them are drinking," Ruth said, her voice tight, arms snug against her chest. "I came by your place to see if you were all right, Margo. Knocked on your door, but there was no answer. I'd made a stew, so I brought it over here, but they haven't eaten."

"Dawn and I are not drunk," Audrey said, but her eyes were bloodshot, her voice wobbly.

"Why she is still here?" JJ asked.

Audrey rose from the couch. "Maybe I should just go to bed."

"No, don't go," Dawn said, reaching out to grab Audrey's arm. "Stay with me."

Audrey hugged Dawn. "It's hard to understand why bad things happen."

"Speaking of understanding," Ruth said, "I wonder about you, Audrey."

I looked at Audrey, hoped she didn't have so much alcohol on board that she'd start blabbing.

"How about some dinner? And some coffee?" I asked, to divert the conversation. I grabbed Audrey's hand. "C'mon, help me."

Ruth rolled her eyes, then said, "Coffee is a good idea, food too."

Audrey and Ruth followed me to the kitchen. Audrey got the coffee going and Ruth heated the stew she'd brought. I helped JJ stagger to a chair, and soon everyone was too busy eating to say much. After some solid food and a cup of coffee, JJ sobered up. I was beginning to think it was safe to leave them and return to bed when Ruth turned to Audrey.

"Tell us about yourself," Ruth said.

"Yeah, do," JJ agreed.

Audrey hadn't eaten much, and her coffee was untouched. She didn't appear drunk, but her alcohol level remained undiluted. Not good. This wasn't the time for Audrey to reveal anything.

"We're all tired," I said, "let's talk tomorrow."

"It is hard to know ourselves sometimes," Audrey mumbled.

Dawn drained her cup of coffee. "I've done things," she began, then fell silent.

"Everyone has," Ruth said. "I still haven't figured out why I got married, for one thing."

Audrey frowned. "But you've been married for years, right?"

"Our forty-second anniversary was this year, but some days I feel sure that Jim is a stranger who just lives in my house."

"Here's to strangers," JJ said.

"Why do you stay married if you're not happy?" Audrey asked.

"I didn't say I'm unhappy," Ruth said. "I love Jim and I believe in the sanctity of marriage. But God doesn't always allow life to turn out the way you think it will."

"Most of us would change some things if we could," Audrey said.

"No doubt," I said, thinking about Bow, about Dad, about life.

Dawn leaned forward and whispered, "Nobody deserves to be happy."

"Happiness is not the purpose of life," Audrey said, sighing. "I considered majoring in philosophy at one time, before switching to biology."

"So why are you just a hired hand here, then?" JJ asked. "You seem too damn perfect."

Audrey shrugged.

JJ was right. Audrey was one of those women who seem too perfect. She had it all; looks, personality, intelligence. Her one fault was that she had no faults, except for her choice in men. JJ moved from the purple chair to the couch, staring at Audrey.

"She's hiding something."

"You're jealous," Dawn said.

"JJ has a point," Ruth said. "I think Audrey is hiding something too."

I shook my head, yawned. "I was in bed, and I'm ready to go back to sleep. Let's shelve this for now."

"Everyone has secrets," Ruth insisted, "and sometimes it's good to share."

"Some secrets aren't meant to be shared," I said, looking at Audrey, but she just blinked and looked away.

Ruth rambled on. "God has reasons for making each of us the way we are. Bow and I are very different from each other. I've known her since she was a baby, and I came to love her not despite our differences, but because of them."

I stood. "That's interesting, Ruth," I said, yawning again for real. "But it's late, time for bed. Let's talk more tomorrow."

No one paid any attention, so I sat back down, knew what was coming. I couldn't stop the question from being asked, nor from being answered. I sighed, watching Audrey.

"Were you ever proud of Bow?" Dawn asked.

"Why of course," Ruth replied.

"Some people are never proud. Even mothers," Dawn muttered.

Ruth turned toward Audrey. "Speaking of family, who are your parents?"

"Yeah," JJ said. "Great question."

Audrey looked up at the ceiling. Everyone was staring at her. I held my breath, hoping she wouldn't tell them, not tonight.

"All I know about my father is his name," Audrey said finally, almost whispering, "but Bow was my mother."

Everyone gasped, a chorus of disbelief. All I could do was watch their faces. Dawn's jaw fell, her mouth opened wide. JJ's face scrunched up; eyes narrowed to slits. Ruth frowned and shook her head side to side, slowly.

Dawn was the first to speak. "But, you?"

"Bow was only fifteen when I was born," Audrey said, "and her parents forced her to give me up for adoption."

"No," JJ said. "No, I don't believe you."

Audrey looked at me, but this was her show now, not mine.

"Do you have proof?" Ruth asked.

"Yes. Margo has seen the documents."

Now all eyes turned to me. Great, just great.

"You knew?" JJ and Ruth said in unison.

"I just found out a few days ago," I said, without mentioning that Roy and I had verified everything.

JJ shook her head, stood up. "You must be after Aunt Bow's ranch."

"No. Not at all," Audrey said.

"Then why did you come here?" Ruth asked.

"I wanted to meet my birth mother, to know her."

Dawn bit her lip. "She loved you, didn't she."

"I hope so. I wasn't ready to lose her."

"God, you're good, but who are you, really?" JJ asked. "We would've known if Aunt Bow had a daughter. She would've told us."

"This is shocking," Ruth said, "just shocking."

I was still getting over the shock myself. Imagining Bow as a teenager with a swollen belly made me want to laugh, but it also made me want to shake my head like some matron with a patent leather purse and a pillbox hat. And after what Ruth told me about Bow and Dad, I didn't know what to believe about anything, anybody. Official documents said things my mind had trouble accepting.

"Did Aunt Bow know who you claimed to be?" JJ asked.

Audrey nodded. "She knew right away, even before I showed her the official papers."

JJ turned to me. "You bitch! You knew along, didn't you!"

Then she swiveled toward Audrey. "And you! Why didn't you tell us sooner?"

Audrey leaned back in her chair. "Bow was about to tell everyone. After she died, I knew you would think I only came to inherit her ranch, maybe even that I had something to do with her death."

JJ sat back down, frowning. "So, did you? Did you kill her?"

Audrey began to sob. "I was so happy to find her," she said, wiping her eyes. "I didn't even know she had a ranch until I arrived."

"Bullshit!" JJ said. "You sniveling little piece of shit!"

"You saw the documents, Margo?" Ruth asked.

"Yes," I said, without elaborating.

"How old are you, Audrey?" Ruth asked.

When Audrey replied that she was thirty-four, the same age as me, Ruth was silent for a minute before saying, "It's possible."

JJ squinted at Ruth. "Seriously?"

"I've known Elizabeth all her life," Ruth began, "and I remember that she spent a lot of time in Denver with Helen, especially during high school. Her parents said she was going to stay with Helen, her older sister, because the schools were better there. Besides, Elizabeth's parents were older by then, too busy with the ranch to deal with a wild child like Elizabeth."

Now all eyes were on Ruth.

"Everyone thought it was a good idea, that Helen would be a good influence."

"Well, I—" Dawn began, and then coughed and choked as though she'd swallowed wrong.

"Are you all right?" I asked, moving toward her.

She stood, clamped a hand over her chest, face flushed. She muttered something unintelligible and left the room. I watched her leave, frowning, thinking about the way she just checked out physically and mentally whenever something upset her.

JJ stood up too.

"I...I don't know what to say. This is just too much. Besides, my horse is supposed to arrive soon, should've been here by now." She walked down the hall, swaying only slightly now.

Ruth and I sat with Audrey in silence for a while. It struck me as odd that Bow hadn't told Ruth about having a daughter. If I'd been in a better frame of mind I would've asked her about it, since Bow seemed to have confided in Ruth more than she had in me.

It was almost midnight when Ruth rose and headed for the door.

"God bless you both," she said as she left. I was about to follow her out the door when Audrey's cell rang.

"Tonight? Please, not now," she said, frowning. She listened for a minute, then repeated, "No, please, I—" She ended the call, looking pale.

"What's wrong?"

"Don insists on coming right away, and he sounds so angry!"

"Now? What's the rush?"

"Some deadlines, he claims. But he exaggerates when he drinks."

"He won't be here until morning, will he?"

"He said he's already on the road. Maybe he'll stop somewhere, sleep it off."

Since her arrival, Audrey had slept in the back room Bow converted into a bedroom when she took me in, years ago. But now JJ had claimed Bow's bedroom and Audrey gave her bed to Dawn. She slept on the couch without complaint. She was the type who allowed everyone to take advantage of her. Always giving comfort, seldom receiving it.

"Come home with me," I said. "I have an extra bedroom."

"Thanks, but I'm fine here, really," she said. "Don will probably just yell at me. Besides, JJ and Dawn are here too. No worries, Margo. I will call you if need be."

We hugged, and she said I was like her sister now.

I didn't feel like anyone's sister tonight. Nor did I feel like telling her I'd met her ex, so I understood the type. I returned home under thunderclouds that obliterated the stars. I fell into bed, guarded by the dogs, soothed by Emmy's purring.

This had been one hell of a day.

CHAPTER TWENTY-ONE

FRANTIC BARKING DISRUPTED A dream. A good one. Roy was walking toward me, smiling, and we were almost touching. The barking didn't stop. Reluctantly, I opened my eyes, blinked at the nightstand, grabbed my cell, which activated, and the home screen proclaimed 3:35.

I groaned.

The rain had ceased, crickets chirped rhythmically. Border collies don't bother barking unless there's a reason. There's not much traffic on our dirt road, especially at night, but the sound of a fast-moving car followed by a sudden flash of light against my window meant someone turning into Bow's place. Audrey's ex arriving from Fort Collins, no doubt. I stumbled from bed, peered out the window, watched headlights approach the cabin. Bow's place was too far from mine to see clearly, much less hear anything.

I considered going over but JJ and Dawn were there, and Audrey had said she'd call if she needed me. I sat down in the living room, waited. Must've dozed off because the next thing I knew, the dogs were barking again, then growling.

I jumped up, saw headlights moving up my driveway.

It was nearly 4 a.m.

I thought about the Glock, but there was no time to unlock the safe. I grabbed the can of bear spray from under the kitchen sink, went to the front door and turned on the porch light as the vehicle parked. It was a black Escalade and Don Kelsey, tall, sculpted jaw, emerged from it. With the same arrogant manner he'd displayed at his office, he approached the porch.

I opened the door a crack, kept the screen door locked.

"What are you doing here?"

Zap and Fetch alternated with growling and barking.

"Well, shit, it's you," Kelsey said. "I'm looking for Audrey."

"She's not here."

Audrey thought he'd been drinking when he called her earlier, but his speech didn't seem slurred and he registered the same on the nasty meter as he had when I'd been in his office.

Maybe he held his liquor even better than JJ.

"There's a light on inside that shack over there. The junker Audrey drives now is parked out front. I pounded on the damn door, walked around. Dog barking inside. She must be here with you."

"Like I said, she's not here." I held up the bear spray.

"Holy shit," he said, stepping back. He was from Montana. He knew this stuff could stop a grizzly in its tracks.

"This is just for starters," I said. "The Glock comes next. Now, tell me why you're here in the middle of the night."

"I...I miss her."

I rolled my eyes. "You're full of shit."

I knew Audrey didn't miss him, didn't want to see him. She slept on the couch, so she'd heard him knocking.

Zap's growl meant business. Fetch barked non-stop.

"Call off your damn dogs."

"Get the hell off my property," I said, covering his leather loafers with bear spray.

"Fuck! Crazy bitch!" He spun on his heel, muttering, "Drove half the night to this goddamn hole. Just like her to be gone." He got in his car, gunned the thing all the way out to the road and headed toward town.

I picked up the phone, punched in Audrey's number. No answer. I slipped the cell in my pocket, grabbed my gun, my key to Bow's house and ran to the truck, Zap and Fetch at my heels.

Dawn's BMW and Audrey's Nissan were parked side by side in front of Bow's cabin. JJ often parked in back. There was a dim light inside. I unlocked the door, stepped in. Boss greeted me. Bow's golden retriever had the bulk of a watchdog, but she was more greeter than growler. A blanket and pillow were on the couch, but no Audrey. Neither bedroom was occupied.

Nothing looked out of place. I had no idea where Audrey or the others were. There were no passengers in Kelsey's Escalade, at least none sitting upright.

Maybe everyone had hidden somewhere. I hurried down the familiar path to Bow's barn. The only sounds inside the dark building were the muted shuffling of hooves against bedding. Two young geldings, one mare, and Bandit occupied stalls. Moonlight chased soft shadows down the barn aisle, just enough to see by, so I didn't flip on bright overhead lights. The horses stood with necks lowered, except for Bandit, who seemed unusually nervous. He'd never liked being confined to a stall, though. I'd see to him later. I checked the tack room, then the feed room. It was darker in there; I was peering toward the shadowy haystack when something moved.

Something large.

The border collies growled and crowded close to me, sensing my nervousness.

Lots of critters take up residence in barns. Mice, of course, and beautiful barn owls, and raccoons and skunks are common too. One time I found a litter of kit fox near the back of my haystack. They were so cute, all curled together with their miniature fluffy tails that I'd wanted to pick them up and cuddle them. Didn't, of course. The vixen fox had been out hunting, no doubt.

So now I wasn't surprised. This was probably a furry family. Still, I tightened my hold on the Glock.

But then I heard groaning. Human groaning.

I flipped on the light and hurried in the direction of the sound.

It was Dawn, and she was sprawled out over hay bales near the back wall. I scrambled over loose hay to reach her.

"What happened? You okay?"

She groaned again; eyes closed. Bits of hay clung to her hair and clothes. I brushed scratchy bits of alfalfa away, saw no obvious injuries.

"Dawn, open your eyes."

Her eyelids fluttered; her mouth opened but no sound came out. Her breathing seemed normal.

I shook her gently. "It's me, Margo."

Her eyes opened but appeared unfocused.

"Talk to me, Dawn," I said. "What happened?"

She mumbled something unintelligible. I called 911.

"Send an ambulance!"

As I was ending that call, headlights turned into Bow's driveway. What if Kelsey had returned? I still had no idea where Audrey was. The headlights stopped at the cabin. This wasn't the Escalade; it was JJ's car.

"JJ," I shouted. "Down here! Hurry!"

JJ ran all the way to the barn. "What're you doing? Horses okay?"

"It's Dawn. I found her in the feed room."

"What! Why?"

"She's unconscious or drugged, something. Was Audrey with you?"

"No. Isn't she in the cabin? I've been driving. My friend is trailering Royal Captain over here, but got lost, so I went to meet—"

I shook my head. "Stay with Dawn. I called for an ambulance. I need to find Audrey."

I had a bad feeling. What if Audrey's ex had drugged Dawn, kidnapped his ex-wife? Or maybe he'd hurt her, left her here somewhere. And then I recalled how nervous Bandit seemed. Bow's gelding didn't care for stalls, but he wasn't the hyper type. I clicked on the barn lights, raced back to his stall, slid the door open.

And found Audrey.

CHAPTER TWENTY-TWO

AUDREY WAS SPRAWLED FACE down in the shadows near the far wall. No visible blood. Her clothing appeared intact. Maybe she was just unconscious.

Basic first aid was something I kept up on in case someone fell off a horse, so I knew not to roll her over without stabilizing her neck. Her head was turned away from me, so I bent down and pressed two fingers into the soft skin on one side of her trachea. She felt warm, but there was no carotid pulse, at least none I could detect.

I log-rolled her over, carefully, praying she was alive. Please, God. I placed my hands on her chest and began compressions.

"Ambulance!" I shouted to no one. She needed paramedics, and now. Had it been seconds or hours since I called 911 for Dawn?

My hands pressed in, out, in, out.

Keep Audrey alive, make her heart start, her eyes open.

Please, God, please.

The siren approached the barn.

"Here, in here!" I shouted, still doing CPR.

If there was any life left in Audrey, the paramedics were the ones equipped to help. Within seconds, two guys in dark blue uniforms appeared. I stood and hurried Bandit out of the stall and into an empty one while the men secured a collar around Audrey's neck and slid a board under her, all without interrupting CPR. Now that they'd come, I felt suddenly weak, limp. It was an effort to speak, to fill them in on what little I knew. Which wasn't much. I had no idea how long Audrey had been there, no idea what'd happened. I'd entered the barn, gone straight to the tack room and feed room without looking into any stalls. When I found Dawn, I tried to awaken her.

I should have found Audrey sooner.

If she had no pulse it meant cardiac arrest, meant time running out.

The paramedics hooked her up to a monitor and then elevated her chin to insert a breathing tube through her mouth. I heard beeps, hoped that was a good sign. Was afraid to ask. As I watched, feeling useless, guilt lashed out with barbed accusations. I should've come right over when I first saw headlights at the cabin, but I fell asleep. Should've looked for her right away when I got here.

Should have, should have... The words pounded in my mind.

They connected the breathing tube to a portable oxygen mask, started an IV. Conversation between the two was staccato medical shorthand.

Then Audrey groaned.

I almost fainted with relief. She was alive, at least for now.

Thank you, God, thank you.

"We'll transport soon," one of the paramedics told me. "The doc at Valley Medical is reading monitor transmissions."

"Will she be okay?" I whispered, knowing it was too soon to tell.

"Any idea what happened to her?" one guy asked.

"I...no, well, maybe her ex-husband did something to her."

"You saw this guy?"

"He came by my place a while ago, but he was here first."

"The sheriff will want to talk with you, he should be here soon. Meantime, tell us what you know about this woman. Name, age, so on."

"Audrey Langford, age thirty-four," I began, and continued, leaving out the fact that she was Bow's long-lost daughter because that was inconsequential, at least medically. That was the main thing I knew about Audrey, though. She'd seemed healthy in the month she'd been here. My thoughts were jumbled.

Audrey groaned again, softly, but it made me remember she wasn't the only one who'd come down to the barn in the middle of the night, maybe running away from Don Kelsey. Dawn was here too, still in the feed room with JJ.

"There's someone else," I said. "She's awake, but I dunno, there's something wrong. Her sister is with her."

The paramedics exchanged glances. "Go ahead, check it out," one said. "This one is stabilizing."

The other guy followed me to the feed room, accompanied by Zap and Fetch, who'd remained right outside the stall all this time and weren't about to let me out of their sight.

JJ was sitting next to Dawn, holding her hand. Dawn still appeared dazed.

"How's Audrey?" JJ asked.

"She's... I don't know. Alive," I said. I turned to the paramedic. "I found Dawn first. Awake, but out of it, didn't talk, didn't seem to know I was there."

The guy approached Dawn. "Hi. How're you feeling?"

Dawn looked at him, said nothing.

"My name is Tom. What's yours?"

Dawn frowned, remained silent.

"She's my sister," JJ said.

Tom removed the stethoscope hanging around his neck, wrapped a blood pressure cuff around Dawn's upper arm and smiled at her.

"I'm just going to check you out a bit, that okay, Dawn?"

She managed a tiny nod.

"Hurt anywhere?" he asked.

She shrugged and moved her head slowly, side to side.

After checking her over, he stood back and turned to me. "Is she on any medications that you know of?"

"No idea."

"She takes an antidepressant," JJ said.

"Do you know the name of it and how long she's been on it?" Tom asked.

"Zoloft, I think," JJ said. "Just started a few weeks ago. She takes sleeping pills, too, Ambien."

"Okay, good to know. That might be what's making her a bit off."

"Will she be all right?" JJ asked, her voice shaky.

"I'm a paramedic, not a doctor, but likely she'll be fine. I'll check in with the ER doc right now," he said, grabbing his cell. After a short conversation during which he provided Dawn's vital signs, explained that she took Zoloft and Ambien, and gave details about her responsiveness, he hung up and turned to us.

"Doc says she doesn't appear to need hospitalization but does need to see someone tomorrow."

"We're from Denver," JJ said.

"I can give you a local doctor's name."

JJ nodded. "I'll take her in."

"I'm going back to the other woman now," Tom said. "Someone should stay with Dawn for a while, help her back to bed."

"I'll take care of her," JJ said.

By the time Tom and I got back to Audrey her eyes were open, but she couldn't speak because of the breathing tube. The other paramedic was asking her to squeeze his hand. When she did, I smiled and burst into tears.

The paramedic working on Audrey looked at me, eyebrows raised. Tom gave me a little smile and said, "It's been a rough night."

That was nice of him, but the damn tears continued. Flashing red lights signaled another arrival. No siren, unless I was so muddled I didn't hear it.

They lifted Audrey onto a gurney outside the stall; bits of bedding and hay cascaded like snowflakes onto the barn aisle.

It was Sheriff Plackmon himself who appeared, I took one look at him and began openly sobbing. Couldn't stop, even though I felt like an idiot. He looked from me to Audrey, turned to the paramedics.

The paramedic whose name I didn't know said, "She's stable, but needs transport to the hospital."

Plackmon turned back to me. "What happened?"

"I'm not sure," I said, trying my best to sound like a grown woman rather than a sniveling child. I swiped a hand across my face, inhaled deeply. "Audrey's ex was here, might've hit her or I dunno what. Something happened to Bow's niece Dawn, too."

"Know anything about this guy, the ex?"

"Name's Don Kelsey, drives an Escalade."

"You get a license plate number?"

I shook my head. "No, but it's black, looks new. He headed towards town."

Plackmon called for an APB on a black Escalade and an immediate State Patrol roadblock.

He turned back to me. "What else?"

Thankfully, I was done sobbing. I filled him in on the past few hours, including what time I'd gone to bed, when Kelsey arrived at my door, how I'd seen headlights, presumably Kelsey's, over at Bow's first. I even managed not to cry again while describing finding first Dawn and then Audrey.

"We're ready to transport," the paramedic said.

Plackmon nodded, and he and I walked down to the feed room. Dawn was curled up on the hay, eyes closed.

"She's asleep," JJ said. "I'm sure she took a sleeping pill earlier."

"No wonder she seemed out of it," I said.

"Paramedics check her out?" Plackmon asked.

JJ and I both nodded.

"Said to have a doctor see her, so I'll take her in tomorrow," JJ said, sounding truly concerned about her sister. Both JJ and Dawn were full of surprises.

"I'll have a chat with her tomorrow, too," he said. "Best to get her to bed now."

He and JJ half walked; half carried Dawn up to Bow's cabin.

Although going to bed sounded more than enticing, I drove the dogs home then continued to the hospital, a small building a few streets back from Pinedale's main drag. Once inside, I had to wait while they "got the patient settled," whatever that entailed. It was starting to get light outside by the time I got to see Audrey, in room fourteen. The breathing tube was gone. There was a simple oxygen cannula under her nose and an IV line in her arm. She appeared to be sleeping peacefully, so I settled down in a comfy-looking chair next to her bed and dozed off myself.

The next thing I knew, a nurse in green scrubs was standing beside Audrey's bed, chatting about the beautiful sunrise and handing her a glass with a straw poking out. I rubbed my eyes and peered out the window, then squinted at the clock on the wall: 7:10. I was usually finished with morning chores by now.

When the nurse left, Audrey smiled at me.

I was about to ask how she felt when Sheriff Plackmon entered the room. He glanced at me.

"Stayed all night, huh?"

I shrugged. There'd been no "staying all night" anywhere because last night was a mess of worrying, hurrying, then worrying some more. Not much sleep was involved, and the kink in my neck spoke volumes about the chair I'd spent the last few hours in, the comfy part having quickly worn off. The night could've turned out worse, though. Much worse.

"Tell me what you remember about last night," Plackmon was saying to Audrey. "Just take your time, give it some thought."

"I... Well, my ex, Don Kelsey, uh, he is a lawyer. He called last night, said he needed to see me again. He lives in Fort Collins, a long drive."

"What time did he call?"

"Somewhere after eleven, I think."

"Did he say anything to make you fear he might do something to you?"

"No, not that I remember. He sounded like he had been drinking, though."

"Has he hurt you in the past?"

Audrey nodded.

"What time did he arrive last night?"

"I'm not sure. It would have been the middle of the night."

"What happened then?"

"I did not want to see him, I was afraid he would be drunk, and that is when he is mean."

"So, what did you do?"

"I slept a few hours, then got up, dressed, and ran down to the barn about the time I thought he would be arriving."

"You ran to the barn alone?"

"No. Dawn heard me getting up, and she came too."

"Kelsey hadn't arrived yet?"

"Correct."

"What happened when he did arrive?"

"I...can't remember. I saw, uh, I remember lights. Maybe headlights, and I assumed it was him."

Sheriff Plackmon nodded, waiting for her to continue.

Audrey shook her head. "I felt scared. Dawn and I hid...inside the barn. But I just..." She paused, shook her head. "The next thing I recall was being placed in an ambulance. And then a bright room in the hospital, before this one. Lots of people asking questions, but I felt so...confused."

"I spoke to your doctor and she said you had marks on your neck last night, as if someone had tried to strangle you."

Audrey gasped. "Really?"

Plackmon nodded. "I had them take photos. You were uncon-scious when Margo found you in Bandit's stall."

Audrey looked at me, frowned. "A stall?"

"How do you feel now?" he asked.

"No longer confused," she replied, sighing, "but I know I'm missing some of what happened."

"Do you recall seeing Don Kelsey?"

"No. No, I do not. So where is Don? Is he here?"

"At the moment he's in my jail, charged with assaulting you and possibly also Dawn Curtis."

"Dawn? Is she all right?"

"She seems fine, but we're not sure yet exactly what happened. Her memory isn't any better than yours, unfortunately. I spoke with her this morning. Please let me know right away if you remember anything. Sometimes it takes a while, but pieces come back."

He turned to leave, asked me to follow him.

"I've got to take care of things at the ranch," I told Audrey, "but I'll be back as soon as I can."

She smiled, nodded.

The sheriff and I sat on a bench outside the hospital, but I couldn't add much to what I'd already told him last night.

"I've been wondering about something, though," I said. "Kelsey must've been at Bow's place about twenty minutes or so, more than enough time to go down to the barn, do whatever he did to Dawn and Audrey. But why would he come over to my place afterwards claiming to be looking for Audrey?"

The sheriff's eyebrows raised slightly, but he said nothing.

"Maybe because he's thinking like the lawyer he is," I said. "It's unexpected. Makes him look innocent."

"Kelsey kept telling me he was innocent," Plackmon said, "but everybody says that. I spoke with Fort Collins police. He has several domestic abuse charges, string of DUIs. But tell me what's going on with you, Margo. All that crying last night was out of character."

"I know, but I found out something about Bow that threw me, turned me into such a mess I hardly recognize myself."

"You don't have to tell me unless you want to."

"Well, it might have something to do with Bow's death in some way. I thought I knew her, really understood her, but then the surprises started. First, Audrey revealed that Bow is her mother, gave birth to her at age fifteen."

Plackmon's eyebrows registered surprise, but the rest of his face remained law officer blank.

"That's not all," I said. "Ruth said Bow was considering selling the ranch due to arsenic contamination. I never knew that. Of course, she didn't know the toxicity report was false. But Ruth also said that Dawn is adopted, which may not play into anything, but it's one more thing that Bow withheld from me and yet Ruth knew for years.

"What hit me hardest, though, was when I decided it'd be good to check out all Bow's lovers. Ruth knew most about that, too, having known Bow all her life. Anyhow, I insisted Ruth tell me everything, but I wasn't prepared to hear that Bow had an affair with my dad back when I was about twelve." I paused, bit my lower lip. "Not long before the plane crash that killed my mom and dad."

"Hard to hear," he said.

"Very," I agreed. "I've been a slobbering mess ever since. Just can't deal with it."

"I don't blame you, Margo. But I do have a suggestion."

"I'm listening."

"You could have a chat with Courtney. I'd ordinarily avoid recommending my own wife but she's the only psychologist around, and she could help you sort all this out."

"But she's a shrink, and —"

Plackmon smiled. "Sure is, and a damn good one. So, here's what I'm gonna do," he said, pulling out his cell. "I'm making an appointment for you right now."

"Yikes."

"You can decide whether or not to go," he said.

Within ten minutes I was back in my truck, heading home. On the seat beside me was a slip of paper that read: Courtney Plackmon, 2 p.m.; the date was today.

Maynard's braying greeted me, and he gave me a look that registered pure disgust at my lack of punctuality two whole days in a row. I dropped a few carrots in his feed bucket as a peace offering and was grateful that horses don't bray too. If all the animals around here were like Maynard, my eardrums would be in jeopardy. I took care of everyone, looked in on Ramona, and couldn't resist letting her sit on my lap for a minute. Talk about shrinks. Ramona always understood how I was feeling without me saying a word. And so did Babe and Phantom. Matter of fact, what I needed more than a stupid session with Courtney was a ride on Phantom, the best psychiatrist ever. Maybe later.

I fed the dogs and Emmy, then took care of Bow's animals before coming home to pour myself a bowl of cereal. I'd run out of milk because Roy wasn't here to handle the grocery shopping, so I ate it dry. Wasn't the first time. No big deal. But thinking about Roy reminded me how much I missed him. We'd agreed to Zoom chat as soon as we could, and things should be set up by today. I'd have to wait until noon here to call, when it would be 7 a.m. in Wellington.

Meantime, I went back over to Bow's place to check on Dawn. She and JJ were eating breakfast, both still in pajamas. Dawn seemed back to normal but couldn't recall even being in the barn last night. I left them, went home, saddled Phantom, and we headed to the forest.

I closed my eyes for a minute, feeling the sway of her movements, the rhythm immersing me in her world. Bow was the one who taught me that riding is a partnership where the horse and rider learn from each other. The trail leveled out ahead, and Phantom began jigging, wanting to go. I leaned forward, letting her run, absorbing her joy, her energy. It was a short ride, one I didn't really have time for, but one I needed.

After that, I called Audrey. She was in good spirits and thought they'd discharge her later.

"I know you have things to do there," she said, "no need to come back to the hospital until they tell me for sure."

Meantime, I lunged two yearling geldings, then went ahead with a scheduled lesson with fourteen-year-old Dan, whose goal was to ride cutting horses. That was out of my expertise, but I could help him work on solidifying his balance and his seat, then eventually turn him over to Roy. Dan was a great kid, and dedicated, too. He lived on a ranch about twenty miles away, and his dad brought him and his horse for lessons every week or so.

I got back to the house in time to catch Roy for our first long distance Zoom chat.

"Howdy, Margo! Miss me yet?"

"More than I can say," I admitted, holding back tears.

"What's happening?"

I didn't want to waste the entire session with my troubles, so I gave him a condensed version of events, including last night, glossed over the bit about Bow and Dad, omitted the tears.

"Oh, Margo, I'm so sorry. I wish I was there with you."

"Yeah, it's intense right now; but tell me about New Zealand. Are gorgeous women knocking down your door?"

"Constantly, but I'm ignoring them. No one measures up to a spicy little rancher I happen to love."

I touched my lips, then his face on the screen.

"I love you, Margo. I miss you so much."

"I love you, too, Roy. It seems like you've been gone a long time already."

"I know." He paused, looking sad. "I don't want to ever be away from you this long again."

I watched his Adam's apple rise and fall as he swallowed.

"What's going on with the Lost Valley ride?"

"I'll leave as soon as I have the ashes," I said, "and I'm letting the others think they're going, but I still plan to slip away by myself with Phantom and Maynard early one morning."

We talked a while longer, neither of us wanting to say goodbye or stop looking at each other. I touched the screen, imagined we were hugging each other, kissing. It was hard to believe he was halfway around the planet.

When we hung up, there was just enough time for a quick shower and hair wash before my appointment with Courtney Plackmon.

I left the border collies at home because it was too warm for them to stay inside the truck and I doubted dogs were welcome in her office. I'd met her several times, but we'd never talked much. What the hell could she or any other psychologist say that'd resolve the sadness, the regrets, the anger I felt toward Bow? I didn't plan on mentioning how I felt about Dad because I didn't know myself. Maybe I'd find out that I was beyond help, a hopeless case.

CHAPTER TWENTY-THREE

Courtney Plackmon's office looked more like a living room, outfitted with a soft blue rug, a couple of comfy-looking chairs and a couch. The walls held framed scenes of trees, flowers, mountains. Several potted plants completed the homey thing. Another surprise was the lack of a receptionist. Courtney herself greeted me when I entered.

"Hi Margo, c'mon in," she said, smiling.

There was a warmth about her, almost motherly, but at the same time, she looked like a runway model; tall, slender, and stunningly beautiful.

"Have a seat," she was saying. She was wearing black slacks, a white blouse accented with a dangly necklace.

I looked around, selected one of the comfy chairs, glad I'd showered and worn clean jeans. I sat back, crossed my legs and my foot started flapping up and down without my permission, so I planted both feet on the floor.

She sat in the other chair.

"How are your horses?"

The question threw me off. I expected shrink talk.

"They're good, all fine."

"How about something to drink? Lemonade, iced tea?"

"Uh, sure. Iced tea, please." I wondered if she'd offer cookies, too. Maybe later.

After she poured glasses for both of us, she said, "You've never seen a psychologist before, have you?"

"Huh-uh. Never." Nor had my college psych classes prepared me for this session.

She smiled. "What did you expect would happen?"

I shrugged. "Lots of questions, I guess."

"We could do that, sure. But it'd only make you more nervous than you already are."

I kinda laughed. She must've aced Nervous Clients 101.

"Let's start by letting you ask me questions. Anything, okay?"

"All right," I said, leaning forward. "What did the sheriff, I mean your husband, tell you about me?"

"He said you're grieving for Bow, you're determined to find out what happened to her, and you're finding out things you never knew about her, for instance that Bow gave birth to Audrey when she was only fifteen, that she and your dad had an affair years ago."

"That about covers it. So, why am I here?"

"Good question. But I can't answer that one."

I frowned. "Why not?"

"Because if you're not ready to talk, there's no reason to be here."

"Well, the sher... Your husband made the appointment."

"I know, and that's the first obstacle. So, you tell me. Do you want to talk or not?"

I bit my lip, looked down. "I don't know," I whispered.

She waited, silent.

I looked at her, stared at the tree picture, glanced out the window, then back at her.

She smiled again.

I wondered if psychologists took classes in compassion. Or

maybe in faking it. How to look like you care, even if you don't give a damn. She looked caring, but who knew?

"I liked psychology in college," I said, "but it's different when it's personal."

She nodded. "That's for sure."

I thought about college, how sophisticated I'd felt sitting in class, taking notes. I sure didn't feel sophisticated now. I looked at her, tried to smile. Couldn't. Felt my eyes watering.

"Damnit!" I muttered. "Knew this would happen."

She placed a box of tissues on the table near my chair.

"This is embarrassing," I said, louder. I grabbed a tissue, dabbed at my eyes. "I, well, I don't know what to think about anything. I mean, everything I believed got blown to hell. If I'd known half of what I know now about Bow, I'd just, well, things would've been different between us."

Courtney nodded again.

I glanced out the window, continued as though talking to myself.

"Who the hell was Bow, really? I knew she slept around, never thought much about it until I found out about her and Dad. I knew some of the men were married, so I'm a hypocrite at best. And then there's Audrey. Good Lord! Bow was all of fifteen, not much more than a child herself when Audrey was born, taken away. Same age as me. Very same age. Bow probably took me in as a substitute for her real daughter."

"Sounds hurtful."

"I suppose." I noticed that Courtney's iced tea was half-empty, while I'd barely touched mine. I picked up my glass, took a few sips.

"So, how do you feel right now?"

"Mad," I said, "and confused."

"Not easy to sort out."

"I loved her, I really did, but now..."

"You think maybe you should stop loving Bow?"

"Maybe. I don't know."

"If Bow was here right now, what would you say to her?"

"Oh, crap. I don't have any idea." I paused, drank some iced tea. "I mean, sure, I wish I could talk to her, ask a bunch of questions."

"You might consider writing to her, whenever you feel like it, however often you want to. Could be one page or an entire journal. Just put it all down on paper. Your questions, your feelings."

"And then what?"

"You decide. You could keep it, stuff it in a drawer, maybe. Or you could tear it up, throw it away. Maybe burn it. Whatever feels right."

"A catharsis, huh?"

"Exactly."

"I could do that, I guess."

"Okay."

"Then what?" I asked.

"Then comes the even bigger issue."

I shook my head. "Holy shit. Not my dad. No. I can't go there."

"Then don't, not yet. Not until you feel ready."

"Are you saying I should? That I must come to terms with him?"

"What do you think?"

"I think the real point is coming to terms with myself, settling my inner conflicts."

She smiled. "Sounds like something out of a psych book."

I smiled too. "Yeah. It's one thing learning something, another thing applying it." I drank more tea. "Most people carry baggage their entire lives."

"True. And no matter what, some baggage hangs around."

"I'm sure it does. I looked past Bow's faults, wanted her to be perfect. And Dad, he was my hero." I closed my eyes, cried. Again. "Sorry," I mumbled.

"There's nothing wrong with showing emotion."

After a few moments, I took some deep breaths, dried my eyes.

"Can I ask you something about Bow, about how she died?"

Courtney nodded. "You're wondering if she might've killed herself?"

"You were asked to provide a professional opinion."

"Yes, and I said that suicide is logical to consider. Even if Bow was depressed, though, there's no way to know if she jumped off that cliff."

"Maybe not."

"Do you think writing to her seems doable, maybe helpful?"

"Yes. It does."

She asked about the horses again, so I told her about my fervent belief that Babe and Phantom served as psychiatrists. To my surprise, she said she understood, and she sounded sincere. She also said that I could come back to see her again if I wanted to.

The session ended without cookies, but with me feeling better, sort of.

I went over to the hospital and down the corridor to room fourteen. Audrey was sitting up in bed, reading a magazine.

"Hi, Margo," she said, sounding just fine.

"Do you feel as good as you look?"

"They are almost ready to let me out of here."

"That's great."

"Yes. Just waiting for results of this morning's CT scan."

"Good. And Audrey, I'm so sorry I wasn't there last night. I should've stayed with you."

"No, Margo. You might have gotten hurt too if you'd been there."

"But I do feel guilty."

Audrey shook her head. "It is bad enough that Dawn was hurt on account of me."

"I'm anxious to get you home."

A middle-aged woman wearing a red dress and a white lab coat entered the room.

"Did I hear a mention of home?"

Audrey smiled. "Indeed, you did, Doctor Bailey."

"Okay if I provide results in front of your visitor?"

Audrey smiled at me. "Margo is like my sister."

"Well, then, your scan looks fine. You did have a concussion, but no cranial bleed. I am discharging you; however, I want you to avoid strenuous activity for a day or two."

"Does that mean no riding, Doctor?"

"Slow riding is fine if you insist, but no falling off, for sure."

Audrey laughed.

Within a short time, she and I were on the road, headed home.

"I'm so glad you're okay," I told her, tearing up.

"What a night."

"Do you remember anything more?"

"No, strangely. I can't recall seeing Don. All I remember is feeling scared."

"Can't blame you. He came to my door, he seems, well, hot-tempered."

"I know. I often wonder why I married him, stayed for five years."

"On the day Bow died, you were with him, right?"

"Yes."

"Was that all day long?"

"He wanted to meet me in town, told me to be there early, about 9 a.m., so I left the ranch at eight. Bow was already down at the barn, but she knew I planned to leave early."

"He was in town in the morning, then?"

"No. He called me, said he was delayed, that he would meet me about noon instead."

"Did you go back to the ranch?"

"No, I remained in town, had breakfast at that cute cafe on Main, then picked up some groceries and just browsed around. Pinedale Springs is so peaceful, different from Fort Collins and the busy CSU campus. I spent time chatting with Ruth at the B&D, then she and I went back to the same cafe for lunch. Don didn't show up until almost 2 p.m., so I didn't get back to the ranch until almost time for chores."

"So, his morning was unaccounted for."

"Meaning what?"

"Not sure yet."

"Oh! Are you thinking he might have hurt Bow?"

I shrugged. "When I flew over to Denver the other day, I went to Kelsey's office. He admitted Carla Simpson is a client of his and that her real interest in acquiring property here is for subsurface rights related to big profits from oil and gas drilling."

Audrey frowned. "Meaning both of them are involved in wanting Bow's land."

"Looks that way. But I have some questions about JJ. She was around when the last two foals died, right?"

"Yes. She and I dug the graves, helped Bow bury each foal after Doc Wilson did the field autopsies. All of us were crying, even Doc."

"Think back to the day each foal died. Do you remember if JJ was ever alone with one of them?"

Audrey looked off into the distance, frowning.

"I remember the second time more clearly. The mare was in the large birthing stall. We all watched the foal slide out, and Bow caught him. It was a colt, wet, of course. He was bay, just like his mama. Bow and JJ began rubbing him down and they needed more towels, so I ran down to the tack room, didn't find towels right away. I heard Bow tell JJ to keep rubbing the colt. She asked me to fill a bucket with hot water while she ran out to the trailer for extra towels."

"JJ was alone with that foal for several minutes, then," I said.

Audrey nodded, looking horrified.

"The poor thing was dead when Bow and I returned. JJ was holding it, crying. But she would never! No!"

I sighed. "I'm finding out that people are capable of things I'd never imagined."

CHAPTER TWENTY-FOUR

S O, WHERE DOES ALL this leave you and me?" Audrey asked after a silence. "Do you trust me?"

I looked at her, considered her resemblance to Bow, not only in looks but also in the best aspects of personality, and I realized two things. I might stay mad at Bow for a very long time, but I couldn't stop loving her or her daughter.

"I want to trust you, Audrey," I said. "I really do."

She smiled, then cried. "I feel so sad to lose Bow, but glad to still have you. So, tell me the rest. You also went to CSU, partly about me. Right?"

I nodded. "I did. Even though Roy and I had already verified your documents, I stopped by the admin building, did one last check. My last stop in Fort Collins was Kelsey's office. And boy, Audrey, do you ever need help picking men."

"I sure do."

I wanted to tell Audrey everything but I didn't think I should, not yet. I trusted her more than the others, but not enough to let my guard down completely.

"When are you planning to sneak away and ride to Lost Creek?"
I laughed. "You are Bow's daughter!"

"Yes, and I'm glad the others know," she said.

I hugged her. I wanted to say she could join me on the ride to Lost Creek, but I didn't. Maybe I was being too careful. If I was a real investigator, I'd know who to fully trust by now, but I was an amateur, too prone to missteps.

"I'll drop you off, then I need to have a chat with Sam Connolly," I said, "find out if Simpson told him anything about subsurface rights when she drew up the sales contract for his place." I'd also be delivering the carrot cake I'd picked up in town on the way to the hospital.

"Take me with you. Bow introduced me to Sam not long after I arrived. I like him."

"Aren't you tired?"

"Not at all."

❋   ❋   ❋

Sam was delighted with the carrot cake and even though his eyesight wasn't as good as it'd been in his younger years, it didn't take him long to squint at Audrey.

"You're related to Bow, ain't ya?"

She grinned. "Yes, I am."

"Now what brings you two pretty young things to see this old man? Got to be somethin' 'bout selling my place, am I right?"

"You're right, Sam," I said. "We're wondering if Carla Simpson mentioned anything about fossil fuels when she negotiated with you."

"Hell no. She's one of them that's out for her own self. Didn't take but a minute's time to see that. I've known for years that there's a whole lot of energy down below. Fossil fuels, both oil and natural gas. Dinosaurs must've gathered right about here, eons ago. Imagine that."

"Did you and Bow ever discuss subsurface rights?"

"Nope, can't say we did."

"But you knew, huh?"

He nodded. "I may be old and wrinkled, but my brain still fires up ever' now'n agin. When that Simpson woman come around, I figured I knew what she was after. Held out till I got part of what this land is worth." He grinned. "Wanna know how much?"

I shrugged, grinning too.

"Six mill."

"Wow," Audrey and I said in sync.

"Yup. Makes me rich. But I got no use for money. Never did, truth be told. I ain't gonna live enough time to spend even a crumb of that much cash. I drew up a will giving half to my son. He never comes around, and he's gonna stick me in some damn nursing home. But it ain't his fault. His wife's the one I never much liked. She don't like me, either. Anyways, that leaves half unaccounted for, am I right?"

"If you say so," I said.

"Took care a that in my will. Done give it to you, Margo."

"Me? Oh no, Sam, no, that's not right."

"It's mine ta give." He paused. "But if you ain't gonna take it, I'll transfer it over ta Bow's daughter, here."

Audrey's mouth opened, but she looked too startled to speak.

"How did you know Audrey was Bow's daughter?" I asked.

"Bow told me about having a baby years ago. She asked me not to tell anyone, and I never did. When Bow brought Audrey by a few weeks ago, I took Bow aside, asked if this was the one. She nodded."

"Do give the money to Audrey," I said. "I don't need it."

Sam shook his head. "Need ain't the thing. Here's what's gonna happen. I'll have my lawyer split the money between the two a ya." He turned to Audrey. "Now, you two think about Bow. She'd have wanted you to take this money, do something in her honor. You two are young enough and smart enough, I expect, to put three mill to good use."

"Well then," I said, "I've always thought about buying property where some of the mustangs crammed into BLM holding pens can run free."

Audrey, who now had tears spilling down her face, managed a whisper. "A mustang rescue is a great idea."

"Now yer talkin'. I knew you two was not only good lookin' but kinda smart."

I laughed. "Just kinda?"

He grinned. "Let's see how long it takes the two a ya to unravel the Feds' red tape and free some of them mustangs."

We promised Sam that we'd visit him when he landed in a nursing home, carrot cake in hand, and he told us that was fine, but to start looking around for suitable property.

❊   ❊   ❊

Back at Bow's place, loud stomping and kicking came from inside a trailer parked by the barn. The rig had to belong to JJ's friend, the one who'd gotten lost and delayed last night while driving over from Denver. JJ and her friend opened the back of the trailer and a large bay scrambled out, snorting. JJ grabbed the gelding's lead rope and jerked it, hard. In return, the bay stomped on JJ's right foot. JJ let loose with a string of expletives and backhanded the animal across his face, then led him over to me and stood as if waiting for a comment.

"Seems a bit hyper," I said. An understatement. I didn't add anything about JJ's handling or the fact that this thoroughbred spent most of every day confined to a twelve-by-twelve stall, all of which contributed to his disposition. I'd seen Royal Captain on my visit to Denver but wasn't about to tell JJ. I was tempted to launch right into questions about the foals, but this wasn't the time.

"Of course he's hyper," JJ said. "Thoroughbreds are meant to be high-spirited. They're not like the nags around here."

She patted him again. He pulled back. She jerked his lead rope again.

"So, what do you think?"

"He's tall," I said, tempted to add that his disposition seemed about as bad as hers.

"I bet your little nags can't even jump."

She knew I hated the word "nags."

"Matter of fact," I said, my voice casual, "Phantom is doing three-six on cross country and over four in an arena."

"No way. That black runt? Must look ridiculous jumping, much less trying dressage."

"Well, dressage is part of three-day eventing. I'll show you our ribbons sometime, mostly blue. But how much trail riding have you and this ex-racehorse done? It's a long ride out to Lost Creek Valley."

"So?"

"The trails aren't groomed, JJ. This is a wilderness with steep hills, downed logs, wide rivers."

"Royal Captain will do fine."

"You'd be safer on one of our horses," I said, even though I had no intention of taking her to Lost Creek on any horse. She and her royal gelding would be staying right here with the others while I did the riding.

"I wouldn't be caught dead on a mustang."

I managed a slight smile. "I wouldn't trust you on one. I meant one of our Quarter Horses."

"I'm riding Royal Captain," she said, turning to lead her horse into Bow's barn while her friend closed the trailer then drove away.

Audrey moved closer after JJ left.

"What a pair."

I nodded. "Absolutely. Anyhow, you go on in and get some rest."

"I'll help with chores first."

"Not today. The Doc told you to take it easy. No lifting, no stress. I'll take care of things here, then head over to my place before Maynard lets the entire valley know he's starving. After the animals are taken care of, I'll come back and have a chat with JJ."

"Be cautious."

"If she killed those foals, I might have to put her out of my misery."

I was nearly finished distributing hay and grain to Bow's mares and the remaining foals when Doc Wilson arrived to check on Bandit.

He'd removed the drain a few days ago, and now he watched as I walked and then trotted the gelding in hand, nodded and told me it was time to allow him out on pasture.

"He looks fine, Margo," Doc said. "Give him a week or two before he's ridden, though."

I let Bandit join his pasture buddies, went in to check on Audrey, then drove over to my place, greeted immediately by Maynard, who let loose with an ear-splitting bray as soon as he saw my truck. It'd take every carrot at the local grocers to appease him, but for now I brushed him while he was eating, and he wiggled long ears in approval. After everyone was taken care of for the evening, I walked back to Bow's cabin, shadowed by Zap and Fetch.

Boss snoozed on a corner of Bow's old couch. The dog looked up, wagged her tail when I petted her. Dawn was in the kitchen, heating what remained of Ruth's stew for dinner, while Audrey rummaged in the fridge for salad fixings.

"Where's JJ?" I asked.

"She's lying down," Dawn replied.

I walked back to Bow's bedroom, and JJ was sprawled out on the bed.

"I need to talk to you, JJ," I said, hoping she wasn't drunk.

She looked at me, didn't get up. "Why?"

"Just a few questions."

"I'm tired. It was a long night. At least Royal Captain is finally here."

She was right about the night. I was tired, too, but it wasn't time to sleep, not yet. JJ wasn't slurring words, so at least she wasn't on the verge of passing out. A glass half full of something sat on the bedside stand.

"I'm glad everyone is okay," I said.

"Yeah, I guess."

"You've been coming from Denver over to Bow's place more than usual lately," I said, for starters.

"So what?"

"I need to ask you about the foals, the last two that died."

She reached for the glass, gulped half of what remained. "Sad."

"Yes, and hard on Bow."

JJ nodded.

"You were here when each of those last two died."

She closed her eyes, hung her head.

"Did you see them die?"

She sat up straight, glared at me. "What kind of question is that?"

"I'm just trying to understand what happened. Doc Wilson did an autopsy on each of them, said they might have suffocated."

She shrugged.

"Audrey said you were alone with each one for a few minutes."

"So?"

"Doc Wilson said if newborn foals have a lot of mucus, it's sometimes enough to obstruct their windpipe so they can't breathe."

JJ reached for the glass, drained it.

"Is that what happened to one of the foals?"

She hung her head, whispered, "How should I know." She got up, walked unsteadily to the bathroom and was in there so long that I went to the door, knocked.

"JJ. You okay?"

There was no answer, but she opened the door, walked even more unsteadily to the bed, slumped down, closed her eyes.

"So, about the foal with all the mucus," I said.

When JJ spoke, her voice was so soft I had to lean close to hear.

"Fast, no struggle...hardly moved...stopped breathing."

"What about the next one."

"I...had to."

"Had to? What do you mean?"

"My friend, she...said I had to."

"Is this the friend who pretended to be Mary Ashton? There was no contamination, JJ, no Doctor Ashton."

JJ opened her eyes but said nothing.

"Did Carla Simpson help falsify the report so that Bow would think she had to sell the ranch?"

No answer.

JJ's eyes remained open, but unfocused.

"Simpson forced you to hurt the foals, didn't she! Tell me, JJ."

She looked in my direction. "No, I...had to prove."

"You wanted to prove you'd be a good real estate agent," I said, my voice low.

"Fucked up." She sobbed. "Bow...had to sell."

"So instead of clearing the first foal's throat, you let it die," I said. "What about the second one?"

JJ smiled. "Soft ears...velvet." She held up her right hand, stared at it as though it was foreign, whispered, "Kissed baby...soft nose."

"Oh my God," I whispered, but JJ wasn't listening. "JJ, look at me," I said, shaking her.

"So sorry..." she muttered.

She wasn't slurring words like she did when drunk but she wasn't coherent, either. She must've swallowed some kind of drugs, washed it down with vodka. I thought about what JJ said about Dawn being on antidepressants and a sleeping pill.

She lay back, closed her eyes. I had no idea what she'd swallowed or how much, but it didn't seem safe to leave her alone now. I leaned out of the bedroom door, motioned for Audrey. She came, took one look at JJ.

"Any idea what she took?"

"No, possibly something of Dawn's. But she drank something, vodka most likely, started confessing, then checked out."

"So, she did...the foals?"

I nodded. "But I don't know all of it yet, who helped her, for starters. Whatever she took would be enhanced by vodka."

Audrey probed JJ's neck. "Pulse is strong, and her color is normal. Maybe we should watch her, let her sleep it off."

I shrugged. "We need to know what she took to decide if we have to get her to a hospital or not. Let's see if we can find any pills."

Audrey searched JJ's luggage, Bow's drawers, found two bottles of vodka under the bed, otherwise zilch.

I told Dawn that JJ seemed unusually out of it, but not exactly drunk. I didn't mention anything about the foals or JJ's rambling confession. Dawn denied sharing sleeping pills or tranquilizers with JJ but didn't know for sure if any of her pills were missing.

"Are you sure she isn't just drunk again?"

"Not sure," I said. All I knew was that each one of us needed a good night's sleep, but prospects weren't looking good. When I got back to the bedroom, JJ still slept, and Audrey sat on the edge of the bed.

"Her breathing is fine and she appears to just be sleeping," Audrey said.

"Why don't you and Dawn go to bed? I'll stay with JJ for a while."

A while turned into four hours of watching over JJ, making sure she'd survive whatever the hell she'd ingested. I was too tired to feel sorry for her. I needed her to survive so she could tell me everything about the dead foals before I beat the crap out of her.

At half past three JJ stirred, opened her eyes, and frowned.

"What're you doing here?" she asked.

"Making sure you survived whatever the hell you swallowed."

"What do you mean?"

I rolled my eyes. "Never mind."

"Don't tell the others."

"About what?"

"You were asking about the foals last night, the ones who died."

I raised my eyebrows, waiting.

"I...I fucked up."

"Is that all you have to say? You killed them because it was part of the plan to make Bow believe her land was contaminated, that she had to sell the ranch she loved. Yeah, you fucked up, all right."

"I wish...I cried, you know."

I looked away. Everyone does things they regret, but sacrificing the lives of two perfectly healthy foals was beyond regrettable. What JJ had done was pathetic. She was despicable.

"I loved Aunt Bow, Margo," JJ said, "I really did. I didn't want her to die."

I closed my eyes, shook my head. I couldn't bring myself to look at her anymore.

"Are you going to tell everyone?"

"Sheriff Plackmon needs to know," I said.

"What about the others? Does everyone have to know? I need to ride with you to Lost Creek," she said, pleading. "I need to help spread Aunt Bow's ashes."

I said nothing, but there was no way in hell I'd take her out to Lost Creek. Not on that crazy thoroughbred of hers, not even if she crawled all the way on her hands and knees.

She reached under the bed for a bottle, filled a glass with vodka, drained it, lay down on the bed and turned her face to the wall.

I stood there for a long time, angry as hell, but also sad. A part of me had wanted her to deny everything, to say it wasn't her. I didn't have to ask if she'd been drinking when she'd done it, when she'd let one foal die without summoning help and then come back to actively suffocate the other one. I felt torn between punishing versus pitying. JJ was a tormented soul, drowning in vodka, wallowing in self-hatred. She was her own worst enemy. There wasn't enough liquor in the world to erase her memory, her guilt. I'd verified that she was working at the Denver real-estate office the entire day when Bow died. So, she hadn't killed Bow, not directly, but she was far from blameless.

CHAPTER TWENTY-FIVE

ON THE DRIVE INTO town to see Sheriff Plackmon the next morning, Audrey asked about JJ.

"I promised her I'd only tell the sheriff," I said, "but what you have to tell him might make a bigger difference anyhow."

Audrey told Plackmon that her ex had sufficient time to take a motorcycle or four-wheeler out to Rim Rock Cliffs on the day Bow died. He could easily have returned in time to meet Audrey in town. There was no proof he'd done so, but the possibility was alarming. We already knew that Don Kelsey and Carla Simpson were involved with buying land, and Simpson was trying to buy Bow's place. Simpson was out at the Cliffs where Bow died, and Kelsey had possibly been there too.

Audrey waited outside Plackmon's office while I gave the sheriff a quick review of things he'd heard before and dismissed, but that had never added up, from the moist out-of-place saddle in Bow's rack to her missing knife, Bandit's wound, the lack of a note, and on through my list. He knew about the fraudulent toxicity reports and the dead foals, and I finished with JJ's confession.

"This complicates things," he said when I finished. "I'll question Kelsey and consider additional charges, if warranted. JJ is guilty of animal cruelty, to begin with. Those poor little foals. You will want to keep Michael Goldberg informed."

I nodded. "As for Carla Simpson, I know she's guilty of greed, of withholding information about the fossil fuel bonanza. Simpson was out at the Cliffs the day Bow died, and Kelsey might have been there too. At least Kelsey is behind bars, but I sure as hell don't want Simpson following me when I go out to Lost Creek."

"I understand how you feel, Margo. However, since there are no solid charges against Simpson, all I can do is ask her not to follow you into the wilderness. Does she even know where Lost Creek Valley is?"

"I doubt it," I said. "Bow and I were the only ones who ever went there. We considered it our special place. I haven't even mentioned the area to Simpson, but JJ probably has."

"By the way, Ms. Bowan's ashes should be available soon. Check with the mortuary. I'll ask Carla Simpson to leave you alone. I cannot order her to do so. Now, as for Don Kelsey, he's charged with domestic abuse, for starters. He'll remain in my jail until his day in court. If he's guilty of more than that, he will face additional charges."

I nodded.

He looked at me for a moment, then added, "I know you are a skilled rider, but be careful out in that wilderness. I trust you're well prepared?"

"I am. And by the way, my session with Courtney was helpful. Thanks for arranging it."

A genuine smile replaced the sheriff's usual mask. "She's special."

❉　　❉　　❉

We arrived home only minutes before Tiffany and little Pickles appeared for a lesson I'd already rescheduled once. Audrey watched, enjoying herself, and left for Bow's place after that.

I saddled a four-year-old filly to work on canter transitions, then brought out Happy, the Dutch Warmblood, just as one car and one truck drove up my driveway. Happy's owner, Sue, got out of the car and Evelyn emerged from the truck.

Both approached, smiling. I figured I could use some good news for a change.

Evelyn spoke first. "I made a few calls, found someone in Colorado Springs who is interested in my Hanoverian."

"Evelyn and I met the other day," Sue said. "We had a nice chat. It's no secret that Happy is too much horse for me right now."

"And I'm interested in him," Evelyn said. "Looks like you were about to ride him. Could I climb on instead?"

My turn to smile. "If it's okay with Sue, that sounds great."

Sue and I watched Evelyn put Happy through his paces, beginning with a warm-up, followed by trotting and then canter. Next, she took the big warmblood over a few jumps in the arena, walked him to cool down, and brought him over to us.

"Happy makes me happy!" Evelyn said, a big grin on her face.

"You look good on him," I said.

"Yes, you sure do," Sue agreed. "I'll need a lot more lessons before I'm ready for a horse like Happy."

"No worries, Sue," I said. "You just got a little ahead of yourself. That happens a lot. Takes guts to admit it."

"So, you'll take me on for regular lessons?"

"Absolutely."

"Sue and I already discussed a price for this big boy," Evelyn said, "so is your commission fixed or a percentage?"

"No commission. All I did was make a suggestion. I'm glad it'll work out for everyone."

"I already told Evelyn I want to come and watch Happy at shows," Sue said. "I still like him, but just from a distance."

"Good idea," I said. "You can have fun, and also learn from watching others ride."

"We'd like to leave him here for another day or two, until the paperwork is settled," Evelyn said, "and I'd like to ride him during my next lesson with you."

"Well, shucks, that means I don't get to ride him myself, but okay," I said, laughing. I had a feeling these two women might become friends, which felt like another win. Happy the horse was the biggest winner of all.

I had one last horse to ride today, and it was Mutt, Roy's cutting horse. I wouldn't be working cows, but I had promised Roy to keep his horse in shape. Mutt was a classic Quarter Horse, taller than most at sixteen hands, but well balanced and nicely muscled. He looked great and had an attitude that matched. I saddled him and we bypassed the arena, heading for the forest instead to spend an hour with lots of trotting to keep his muscles toned, along with some hill work, topped off by his smooth canter on level stretches. Western riders sometimes use "lope" instead of the word "canter," but the horse moves the same no matter what the gaits are called.

After evening chores, it was all I could do to heat up one of the frozen dinners Roy left for me. I missed him more each hour, each day. Zap and Fetch cuddled close to me every night, and I knew they missed Roy as much as I did.

Two teens and three adults arrived for lessons the next morning, one after the other, the sessions extending past lunch, which I seldom stopped for anyway. The afternoon was busy with yearlings and two-year-olds in various stages of training, followed by a six-year-old mare that a client said was crow-hopping and acting up. She said there'd been no change in tack, and she'd always ridden the mare in the same thick snaffle. I started the horse in the arena and moved out onto trails without a single blip, so maybe the rider needed lessons instead of the mare. Sometimes it was a combination, so I'd have to chat with the woman, ask her to come for a lesson on her horse. Even with a gentle snaffle, the rider might be pulling too much on the reins. Often, it's jittery riders. Horses detect nervous humans and react as though it's contagious.

Audrey joined me for a quick snack of apples and walnuts before we drove into town to collect Bow's ashes. Cremation sounded like a reasonable idea unless I let myself think too much about it. No matter what happened to a body after death, grief was the constant. I'd thought a lot about my parents lately, partly because of Bow and Dad, but also because certain memories from my parent's funeral started coming back to me, odd things. So many people I didn't know hugged me back then, said, "We're so sorry," over and over. There was one lady I'd seen around town but didn't know. She had white hair, and she never said a word, just kept patting me on the head. Her fingers were bent and skeleton-like. Sometimes, back then, I'd dreamt about those hands.

The closer we got to town, the quieter Audrey and I became.

I parked outside the mortuary, a red-brick building with an important look about it, as if trying hard to be a fitting place to receive deceased loved ones and then parades of mourners. Remains and remorse, so to speak.

We sat in the truck for a moment.

"This is all so wrong," I said finally.

"Yes," Audrey said. "I miss her so much."

We got out, pushed through double glass doors, and a woman behind the reception desk gave us a look that conveyed automatic sympathy.

"I'm Margo Richards, and this is Audrey Langford. We're here for Elizabeth Bowan's ashes," I said, swallowing hard.

The woman looked at her computer, then at us. "Elizabeth Bowan?" she repeated, her eyebrows lifted. She turned back to the computer for what seemed like a long time before looking up again, a slight frown creasing her forehead. "Have you spoken to her other family members?"

I shook my head, confused.

She rose from her chair. "Please follow me. Mr. Smidt will speak with you."

She ushered us into a room with half a dozen upholstered chairs. A small table held a pitcher of water and half a dozen glasses on a silver tray. A large box of white tissues looked ready for use. We'd barely sat down when a middle-aged man in a pinstripe suit appeared with an official-looking document in his hands.

"I'm Mr. Smidt," he began, "and I do have a Margo Richards listed here as one contact for Elizabeth Bowan."

"We've come for her ashes," I said.

"I see," Mr. Smit said, "but someone came for them this morning."

"What? Who?" I asked, but I knew the answer.

Smit looked down at the paper he held. "A Miss Julie Jacobs. She is listed as a niece of the deceased. Perhaps Miss Jacobs forgot to tell you she'd already come."

I shook my head.

"But there's a problem?"

Yes, there certainly was, but it had nothing to do with Mr. Smidt or the mortuary. When Audrey and I got outside, she turned to me, frowning.

"Why would JJ take the ashes?"

"To keep me from riding away without her."

*　　*　　*

Back at Bow's cabin, JJ was sitting on the porch. I got out of the truck and slammed the door. She stood and walked unsteadily toward us.

"How could you!" I said.

She didn't bother acting innocent.

"I have to go, Margo," she said, starting to cry. "Please take me."

Her eyes appeared bloodshot; her face flushed. Her liver had to be in a constant state of overdrive to process the vodka flow.

"Haven't you done enough to Bow?"

JJ stumbled closer, exhaling in my face. Her breath didn't smell much, but vodka is less detectable than other hard liquor.

"I have Aunt Bow's ashes. I'll keep them until we get to Losh Creek."

"Please give me the ashes, JJ."

She sneered. "No. I'm Bow's niece, and if you won't take me, I'll go alone."

I sighed. "It's an entire day's ride out, easy to get lost."

"Please, Margo. Please take me."

"Hand over those ashes right now."

"No!"

JJ turned away, walked unsteadily to the barn. We remained standing beside the truck.

"She won't give in," Audrey said.

"Any sympathy I felt for JJ is evaporating."

"Yes, but you can't leave without the ashes."

"All of you think Lost Creek Valley is the place to say a final farewell to Bow, but that has always been our special place, just the two of us," I said, tearing up.

Audrey hugged me. "This is so hard."

"Yes, sure is. I need to go home for a while. Tell the others I'll be back later."

Audrey nodded.

❋   ❋   ❋

Back at my place, I did chores, then grabbed my notebook and sat on the porch with Zap's paw on my knee and Fetch curled nearby. I needed to consider facts, and maybe I needed to rethink my plan. If I rode out to Lost Creek Valley alone it would be emotionally satisfying, but it wouldn't get me any closer to knowing for sure who did what to Bow. I began scribbling, searching for connections that mattered, important details I'd overlooked.

Carla Simpson was at Rim Rock Cliffs and found Bow's body. She and Don Kelsey were business partners who stood to gain from Bow's death, but only if whoever inherited the ranch was more willing to sell. Kelsey was in Pinedale Springs the day Bow died and would've had time to get out and back from Rim Rock Cliffs on something like a four-wheeler before meeting Audrey in town.

Heavy rains could've easily erased tire tracks. He was in prison now, charged with assault on Audrey and possibly Dawn. Charging him for Bow's murder was under consideration.

Julie Jacobs, Bow's younger niece, had admitted suffocating the foals as part of the plan to falsify toxicity reports, almost certainly coerced by Carla Simpson. JJ was working in Denver on the day Bow died. Her alcoholism made her emotionally labile and contributed to her never-ending debts.

Dawn Curtis, the older niece, arrived at the ranch the morning after Bow's death. A possible divorce heightened her always fragile emotional state. Success as an artist led to financial security. She readily paid her mother's expenses and often gave money to JJ. She knew she was adopted but appeared uninterested in finding her birth mother.

Helen Jacobs' sudden death at the nursing home appeared to be an unfortunate accident, but even with the Alzheimer's that was destroying her mind, Helen walked just fine. Still, her confusion could've led to her fatal fall on the sharp object that severed a major artery. Even though both JJ and Dawn's shoes matched a bloody footprint found near Helen's bed, no blood residue had been found on either JJ's or Dawn's shoes so far. Helen and Bow dying within days of each other seemed odd but no link was apparent.

Audrey Langford, Bow's newly revealed daughter, was in debt because of her divorce, but would inherit the ranch and Bow's half of the B&D. She'd spent all day in Pinedale Springs so she couldn't have been at the cliffs when Bow died. The remote chance of connecting her teaching position at CSU with the false toxicity report had fizzled. She arrived only a month before Bow died, but if she harbored resentment for being given up for adoption, she kept this well hidden.

Ruth Dunn had mounting debts due to her ill husband's care needs and their ranch expenses. She'd altered the store's accounts and hid merchandise to keep more than her share of the B&D Tack store from whoever inherited Bow's half of the business. Ruth also knew more than anyone about Bow's life, her secrets, her passions. I'd verified her presence at the store for only the afternoon of the day Bow died.

I finished by writing "lovers" but none of Bow's many men stood to benefit from her death. I drew a line through "lovers" and drummed the pencil against the notebook, considering the five women and one man again.

Bow hadn't much use for Simpson and had never said anything about Kelsey, even though she met him once. There was no doubt that Bow loved Ruth, Audrey, Dawn, and JJ, and they loved her too.

Bottom line was whether I should take the four women with me to Lost Creek. If I did, I'd have to stay alert to subtleties and decipher meanings, all while keeping everyone safe. This was not an easy trail. There were rivers to cross, steep hills to climb and descend. Unexpected hazards popped up when least expected. This could be a test for the women, a time to bring out their inner strength or lack of it. When pushed to the limit, people's true selves emerge.

I sighed. So much for a nice peaceful ride.

I walked back to Bow's place, shadowed by Zap and Fetch. As I arrived, the crunch of tires on gravel announced the arrival of Ruth's truck.

"Well, Margo," she said, "JJ tells me we'll be leaving for Lost Creek Valley soon. When did you plan to tell me?"

"Frankly, Ruth, I was planning on going alone. I've reconsidered, though."

"You don't want the rest of us along?"

"It's a challenging ride, for starters," I said, "and Royal Captain isn't a trail horse, for sure. Then there's Dawn, who seldom rides."

"We loved Bow just as much as you did, Margo, and we deserve to be out there for her final tribute."

"Let's go inside, discuss this with everyone," I said.

Dawn was sitting on the couch, staring off into space.

"Are you feeling okay today?" I asked her.

"I'm all right," she whispered.

Ruth sat next to her. "You want to ride out to Lost Creek, don't you, Dawn?"

"I, well, maybe I shouldn't go."

Ruth looked at me as if I should say something.

"Dawn can make her own decision," I said.

"Do you still think someone killed Elizabeth?"

"It's possible, yes."

Ruth crossed her arms, shook her head. "But you don't know who, so you suspect everyone."

"Several people stand to benefit from her death."

"Like me, for instance? I know that you and Roy snuck into the B&D one night, saw that I altered the books in my favor."

"True, we did. You fixed it so that whoever inherits Bow's part of the store will get less, but I know you loved Bow. Turns out you knew her better than I ever did."

JJ walked in, looked from one person to the next. "What now?"

"We're discussing the ride, deciding who's going and when," Ruth said.

JJ moved close to me. "Well, I'm going, for sure."

"Is that right?" I asked, just to get a rise out of her.

"You think you're such hot shit. Who put you in charge of anything!"

"Stop it, stop it now, both of you," Ruth said, then turned to me. "So, are you taking us or aren't you?"

"It's not up to her!" JJ whined.

"Sit down, JJ," Ruth said. "I wasn't speaking to you."

I closed my eyes, took a deep breath. "If all we can do is yell at each other, there's no way we should go on this ride together."

"You're right, Margo," Ruth said. "We need to keep our solemn purpose in mind. Let's all sit down and treat each other with dignity."

The five of us sat, no one saying a word. I knew it wouldn't last, knew who'd be first to speak.

"When do we leave?" JJ asked.

"Where are Bow's ashes?" I asked, keeping my voice calm.

Ruth frowned. "What do you mean? Don't you have them?"

JJ smiled. "I have them!"

"Before we can plan anything," I said, "I need those ashes in my possession."

Dawn rose from the couch, reached behind it, held up a green duffle bag.

"Put that down, you bitch!" JJ yelled.

"I saw her putting a box in this," Dawn said, handing the duffle to me.

JJ reached for the duffle, but it was Ruth who got to her first, pushed her back into the chair.

"Sit down! You are not a child, JJ."

I opened the duffle, withdrew a box marked "Elizabeth Bowan, Remains."

Everyone stared at the box. No one said anything.

Audrey got up, went into the kitchen and returned with five glasses of lemonade.

We sipped in silence, and I wished she had slipped tranquilizers in selected glasses. Ruth was the first to speak.

"We all loved Elizabeth, and we all want to be there at her final resting place."

Dawn squeezed her eyes shut and began sobbing. Ruth put an arm around Dawn.

"All right," I said. "You can all go, but there are conditions. First of all, I am the leader. You all follow me, and what I say goes. No arguing or yelling on this ride." I paused, looked at JJ.

JJ hung her head. "I do want to go."

"Okay, good," I said. "Now, for horses. Is Gus in shape for this, Ruth?"

"Yes, I've been doing more trotting, muscling him up."

"Great. I'll ride Phantom, and Audrey will be on Two Bits. How about Hawk for you, Dawn? He'll take good care of you."

Dawn chewed her lip, but smiled.

"JJ," I said, "Royal Captain is a great horse, I'm sure, but he may not be used to —"

"He's fine. I'm riding him, and that's final."

"No, JJ," Ruth said. "Margo knows these trails, let her pick a horse for you."

"I'm not interested in one of her nags."

"How about one of Bow's Quarter Horses? I can take you down to the barn, show you a few that are seasoned trail horses, and you can pick one to ride."

"Hell, no."

"Then you are not going," Ruth said.

JJ sneered. "Oh, all right, I'll look at the horses."

I knew JJ well enough to realize it wouldn't be as simple as that to get her on a different horse.

"It's settled then!" Ruth said, smiling. "When do we leave?"

"Well, there is one other thing," I said. "No liquor, none. Riders have to stay alert."

"For what, dragons?" JJ said.

"It's a good twenty miles each way, and it'll take us eight hours in the saddle to get there, allowing for several stops. The trail crosses rivers, goes up steep hills. It's not a groomed trail, it's way out in the wilderness. You can't just sit there on the horse; you must pay attention. And we leave tomorrow morning, 6 a.m."

"Then we'd better get busy," Ruth said.

I nodded. "C'mon, JJ. Let's go. I'll show you a few good trail horses. The rest of you can come, too, because all the gear we need is in Bow's barn. We'll take Maynard and Mabel for carrying tents and everything."

"Who'll feed and take care of things while we're gone?" Audrey asked.

"One of my students stayed while I was in Denver overnight," I said, "and she did a great job. The dogs love her, too. I told her I'd need her again soon, so I'll call her right now."

"You are very organized," Ruth said.

"Thanks, Ruth." I looked around, saw that JJ was out of hearing. "Can you take charge of making sure JJ doesn't drink? We'll need to take a few tranquilizers; in case she gets the shakes from withdrawal."

"I can see to that," Ruth said. "I'll call my doctor now. He'll know what to have on hand."

"Good. Speaking of organized, you're not bad yourself."

I turned around. "C'mon, JJ, I'll grab a can of grain and a halter, and we'll see which horse you like."

"I like Royal Captain."

"I know. But he could get hurt out there."

JJ followed me inside the pasture, turned her nose up at all the horses.

"But that bay over there looks decent, I suppose," she said, finally.

"Good choice. His name is Sky." I gave the bay a handful of grain, haltered him, and we put him in a stall next to Royal Captain.

The next couple of hours were spent assembling everything needed for Bow's last journey. Each of these women had the right to come along, I supposed. And I had the right to keep my guard up. By the time we were done, all the horses for tomorrow were groomed and in stalls, ready to saddle in the morning. Maynard and Mabel shared a stall, and they knew a trip was coming up. Maynard sniffed knowingly at the panniers we filled with tents, food, and supplies, and left on saddle racks near the donkeys' stall. I slipped Maynard and Mabel a few carrots and some extra hay before we left them for the night.

I had Audrey come and sleep in my spare bedroom, so she'd be rested.

The only thing left to do was decide if I was making a huge mistake. No way to know. The women were happy to be going. I was resigned to taking them. I brought my saddlebag in with me, placed the satellite phone, the bear spray, and the Glock inside, laid it on my nightstand. I also brought the box of Bow's ashes, put it on the nightstand too.

I wanted to talk with Roy, but his advice was always to be careful. I wasn't a worrier. But I was careful. That night, I dreamt that a horde of faceless beings, neither man nor beast, were chasing me. I reached for my gun, but fell, struggling, trying to run. I looked down and saw that my legs were encased in concrete.

I awoke panting as though I'd sprinted up a steep hill, legs tangled in the sheet, heart hammering. Zap and Fetch crowded close, Emmy moved onto my pillow and licked my cheek with her sandpaper tongue, purring loudly. I rolled onto my back, watched moon shadows float across the ceiling, thinking about Roy.

I'd assured him I'd be fine. I hadn't told him I now planned to test these women, protect the innocent, reveal the guilty. In a perfect world, Carla Simpson and Don Kelsey would be the only guilty ones.

There was a lot I didn't know, but I knew this wasn't a perfect world.

CHAPTER TWENTY-SIX

HOOFBEAT BY HOOFBEAT, THE outside world faded as Phantom and I led four women riders through Western Colorado's White River National Forest, toward the rugged Flat Tops Wilderness and Lost Creek Valley. Meandering trails instead of highways, granite peaks and towering pines instead of buildings. Red-tailed hawks circling high above nervous cottontails. Elk herds following well-trodden paths. Bow knew and loved these places, these creatures. Almost two weeks now since she took her final breath in this wilderness she knew like the contours of her own body.

The first stop would be Rim Rock Cliffs, then on to the valley, resting place for Bow's ashes. I could've made better time alone, but I was stuck with these women. Pressing close behind Phantom and Maynard, the pack donkey, was Audrey on Two Bits with a lead line to Mable, the other pack donkey. Next came Bow's nieces; Dawn, on Hawk, my little brown and white pinto; then JJ and her bay thoroughbred, Royal Captain. It didn't surprise me that JJ refused to ride the Quarter Horse, and there was no sense wasting energy on anger. Ruth brought up the rear on Gus, her ornery but beloved

Appaloosa. Every horse, apart from Royal Captain, was solid on trails, surefooted and nearly unflappable.

The sky held few clouds to begin with, but what started as a soft breeze was gathering speed, promising a change in the weather that would bring the first test for the ditzy thoroughbred JJ insisted on riding.

This group trip was far from my preference, but these women had strong ties to Bow. All felt compelled to come. I'd packed my Glock and my suspicions, my knowledge of how JJ admitted killing the two foals, how Ruth altered tack store books. Even Audrey and Dawn had cracks in their supposed innocence. I'd checked every-one's saddlebags, even the ponchos tied to their saddles. I wanted to know what each person brought with them, from Dawn's paint-brushes and colored pencils to Ruth's Colt 45.

No way would I let this journey resemble the semi-annual wilderness trips Bow and I led, making sure no one fell off their horse, no one got run away with, coddling, catering. Most people who paid to ride with us were interesting and adventurous. Pleasing them provided a portion of our income. But this trip was not about pleasing. This trip was about saying goodbye, and about guilt versus innocence. The trail ahead held challenges to test each of these women, bring out their best, reveal their worst.

Lightning whipped gray clouds; in the distance, thunder groaned. Before long, ozone filled my nostrils and a raindrop spat at my forehead. The approaching summer storm cast a gloom that matched my mood. Even my black mustang couldn't comfort, though she carried the weight of my grief with solemn grace. Phantom's ebony elegance shone like a cloak of mourning, her raven tail a sorrowful flag. On some level, the mare knew about the ashes bundled into my saddlebag.

It would've been fitting for Bow's beloved palomino gelding to carry her remains. I'd ridden Bandit before, knew his ways and would've taken him instead of Phantom for Bow's sake, but he was out on pasture, resting. He'd heal in time, but since he was in no shape for this trip, I'd slipped locks of his mane into my pocket to spread with Bow's ashes.

Before we left, I promised Bandit I'd find out what happened to him, and take care of him. The gelding had nuzzled me, and I let myself believe he appreciated my good intentions. I left detailed instructions on caring for him and the other animals, especially the mares and foals, with Valerie, my student who'd helped out before. If any of the animals even stumbled, she'd call Doc Wilson. Best of all, Zap, Fetch and Boss loved her.

The word "death" remained foreign. Part of me still refused to accept that Bow was gone. Phantom tossed her head, sensing my mood as always. I leaned forward and patted the mare's neck. We rode in silence, the only sounds besides distant thunder the soft creaking of saddle leather and hoofbeats crunching pine needles.

A crackling flash lit the sky. Thunder rumbled again, closer now. Phantom jigged sideways. I sat deeper into the saddle to steady her. The mare never minded the prospect of getting drenched, but neither humans nor horses relish the sky's all-out fireworks.

I turned in my saddle; still four riders on four horses. Good, so far, but the storm approached faster now, right in our direction. The first test. Audrey and Ruth looked unruffled, but JJ's eyes were squeezed shut, and tension etched Dawn's face.

"Better untie your rain gear," I shouted, loud enough for everyone to hear.

They slipped into yellow slickers, bobbing like windblown sunflowers. None of the horses except Royal Captain minded the commotion. I untied my slicker and shrugged it on, sliding fingers over rubbery fabric to fasten snaps. Raindrops quickened into a deluge just as I poked wisps of unruly long hair inside the hood.

Audrey rode like a natural, no problem there. Ruth Dunn was the oldest, but she felt more comfortable in a saddle than a lounge chair, was as tough as she looked. JJ had a reasonably solid seat, since she'd done jumping competitions, but she rode mainly in arenas. Dawn hadn't ridden much lately, but I was more concerned about her state of mind than her equestrian skills. I'd put her on Hawk because he'd take care of her.

Brisk wind carried the spice of wet pine and slapped wisps of hair into my eyes. I shoved blonde strands behind my ears, squinted against whirling rain. Another crack of lightning, loud as a bullwhip. Phantom's muscles tensed, her ears flickering back and forth.

"Easy, girl, easy," I told her, tightening my hold on Maynard's lead line.

A high-pitched scream rang out from behind me.

I turned.

JJ's bay gelding was rearing straight up, ears flattened, hooves punching raindrops. JJ clung around Royal Captain's neck, pressing herself forward, then she let go and screamed again, louder. She slid over the gelding's rump and smacked her skinny butt into a puddle. Fortunately, she had either the sense or the good luck to roll away from flailing hooves. Ruth hurried off Gus and helped JJ to her feet. She didn't appear to be injured.

I looped the donkey's lead rope over a tree limb and steadied Phantom, then made sure everyone else was okay.

The bay lowered his forelegs, snorted, and galloped up the trail, reins dangling, stirrups slapping his flanks. I had known he and JJ would be troublemakers, though being right brought no comfort.

My mustang had shorter legs, but she was agile as a mountain goat. Phantom and I circled into wet timber to cut off Royal Captain, my mare popping over some downed logs, dodging others, panting audibly. Rain splashed onto my slicker, formed rivulets down Phantom's body, plastering her long mane against her neck.

"Hang on, Bow," I mumbled, even though the ashes were secured.

The sound of a branch breaking not far off the trail drew my attention from the runaway horse. The thoroughbred wouldn't run far, he wasn't confident enough to be off on his own. I slowed Phantom to a trot, then a walk, as I peered through the wet. I saw a rider on a gray horse no more than twenty yards away. The pounding rain blurred things, but whoever it was had hefty saddlebags, substantial enough for a long journey. The light-colored animal looked surreal, blending into the wet. It also looked familiar.

I halted Phantom, but my suspicions kicked into a full gallop. I slipped one hand into my saddlebag, wrapped fingers around the cold steel of my gun.

"You! What the hell!" I hollered, paying close attention to the woman's hands.

Carla Simpson sat silently on the grey gelding. There was a self-assured toughness about her, a rawness more evident now that she'd traded business clothes and wheeler-dealer smiles for jeans and riding boots.

"You're following us," I said. It wasn't a question. I loosened my fingers from the gun but kept a mental hold on it.

"No," she said, frowning. "I come out here for solitude. But be careful, Margo! Watch JJ!"

I frowned. "That's rich, coming from you!"

Solitude was something I understood, something I often sought. Ever since Simpson had moved to Western Colorado, she'd often ridden alone. Still, this wilderness was huge. She turned the gelding around, kicked him, and they moved off, blending fully into the rain and fog.

Her manner and her tone registered red on my paranoia scale. It was almost as if she'd wanted me to see her, which was strange. She could be so talkative when it suited her. She wanted her solitude but didn't think anything about destroying other people's ranches in the name of development and drilling. Anything for money. My distrust of the woman intensified. And why did she tell me to watch JJ? Probably just trying to throw me off guard. Not only was I watching JJ, I was also watching everyone else on this ride.

I turned Phantom away. Royal Captain would be slowing down by now, but he still needed to be caught. When Phantom reached a clearing I balanced up against the mare's neck, urging her into a canter. Her hooves drummed moist earth, her flanks heaving under my saddle.

The torrent of rain had slowed to a trickle by the time we saw the gelding and maneuvered out in front of him. He was still moving, but slower. When he saw my mare, he slid to a halt, splattering mud. His reins had broken but he appeared unblemished.

One of the first things Bow taught me years ago was that the look in a horse's eyes speaks volumes about their state of mind, their intentions. This gelding's eyes were widened to white rims of terror, an animal on edge. He stood quivering, ears twitching, nostrils flared.

Phantom and I kept quiet, not crowding him, giving him time. He might choose to run off again, although he looked exhausted. Besides, he didn't appear the type to relish solitude. Gradually, his head dropped, slightly at first, then more. All the while he studied us, deciding whether we were trustworthy.

He was a striking animal, cannon bones short and dense, just right. A dark bay thoroughbred, black points, good substance. Had to be at least 16.2 hands, eight inches taller at the withers than my 14.2 hand mustang, yet more refined. He'd been bred to race, but it was obvious that he'd never been exposed to so much open space, such endless freedom. I'd seen thoroughbreds who made decent trail horses, but this wasn't one of them.

No turning back now, though. There was little time to waste. To make Rim Rock Cliffs by noon, and then Lost Creek Valley by evening, with one or two stops along the way, our pace had to average about three miles an hour, which for most horses meant a reasonable walk.

Several more moments passed, with the main action occurring between the gelding's ears. Finally, he snorted, tossed his head up and down, then took one step toward us, his eyes softened.

He'd decided.

I urged Phantom closer, reached over, grabbed one of the gelding's reins.

"It's gonna be all right, fella," I said in that low tone horses respond to. I dismounted, loosened first Phantom's saddle girth and next the gelding's, to let both horses breathe deeper. I ran the stirrups up on his English saddle. It was a Kieffer, German-made and elegant. I owned one myself, loved the thing, but my rugged old western saddle was more suitable for packing trips. This horse and his saddle belonged in a show ring, not out in the woods. Here he was, though, a rose in a rock pile. I led the horses back at a slow walk to cool them down. After their breathing returned to normal, I retightened my mare's girth, remounted and rode on, keeping a firm grip on what remained of the gelding's reins.

Bow would've had a good laugh over this escapade.

"You shoulda seen this beast run, Bow," I whispered. "I figured from the start that Royal Captain would be as much of a pain in the butt as his owner, the prissy princess."

Phantom's ears flickered. I patted her. She was listening, of course; for all I knew she even understood I was talking to Bow. We picked our way through the forest while faint thunder rumbled in the distance. By the time we reached the others, sunshine poked through clouds, lighting water droplets perched like jewels on pine needles.

JJ glided toward me on long legs, no injuries apparent. She also seemed sober. Then again, with her it was sometimes hard to tell. No doubt she'd tried to bring a flask. Ruth had eagle eyes, though, and if anyone could keep liquor away from JJ, it was Ruth Dunn.

I dismounted, as always feeling like a midget next to JJ. She never rode in anything but breeches and tall black boots, appropriate for the show ring but out of place here. At least she'd selected dark brown breeches, now mud-splattered. Even her face and her spiky two-tone hair sported clumps of grime. She was filthy, but the fall apparently hadn't injured anything but her pride.

She peered down her nose at me, frowning. "What happened to his reins?"

"Hard to say, JJ. He must've stepped on them. It's lucky he didn't trip and fall."

I would've expected gratitude from anyone but her. She didn't show any concern for the animal, didn't pat his neck, check him for scrapes, nothing.

Her long arms tightened against her chest. "This bridle was expensive."

"You should've thought about that before you lost control of your horse."

JJ glared some more. "I didn't lose control, the stupid beast reared."

I sighed. "At least neither one of you got hurt."

I glanced past her to the others, all silent, all ears. Audrey and Dawn looked concerned, while Ruth was chewing on her cheek and knitting her brows together, trying not to laugh.

JJ's frown deepened. "I've fallen before. But I can't ride him without reins."

"I brought some spares."

"I should hope so. He wouldn't have broken them if you hadn't taken so long to catch him."

I watched steam rise off the gelding's flanks and silently renamed him and his owner the Royal Pains.

"You picked out a Quarter Horse last evening, but you insisted on riding this one. I've had enough of your attitude, and your damn horse."

"I never asked for your help."

"Don't plan on getting it again."

"Just because you know this trail, you think you're such hot shit. Bow was my blood relative. You're only —" She stopped, shrugged.

"Go ahead, JJ, say it."

"You're only a little orphan waif she raised out of pity."

I gritted my teeth so hard that a shooting pain spread through my jaw.

JJ wasn't finished.

"After you moved in with her, our summers at the ranch were never the same. Bow never had time for just us anymore." Jealousy and self-pity dripped like tainted saliva from her sharp tongue.

"Stop it, JJ," Dawn said. "Just shut up."

"You're adopted, so you shut up. This is about blood, about real family."

I opened my mouth to remind JJ that Audrey was Bow's daughter, but there was no point trying to reason with her, no point in one-upmanship either. I glanced at Audrey, but her expression revealed nothing.

Ruth, though, was shaking her head.

"JJ! I don't understand how you can be so unkind!"

"I don't give a shit what you understand. You're just an old biddy."

"God help you, child," Ruth said.

JJ looked around, as if daring someone to reply. When no one even looked at her, JJ turned to me, opened her mouth as if to speak, but even she had nothing more to say. Bickering seemed to be the way she related to everyone except her mother. Now that Helen was dead, JJ might find someone else to feel close to. Then again, she might be even harder to get along with.

I grabbed a pair of spare reins, attached them to Royal Captain's bridle, threw my emotions over my shoulder and turned away.

This trip was about Bow.

CHAPTER TWENTY-SEVEN

THE ROYAL PAINS WENT away.

Ruth and Audrey came over, asked if I was all right. I was tempted to tell them about seeing Carla Simpson, but I gave them a nod and busied myself checking Maynard and Mabel's panniers. Long ears pointed in my direction; big brown eyes widened in expectation. Maynard was the most insistent beggar of all the donkeys, but I'd chosen him and Mabel for this trip because they were easy to handle. Besides, they were my favorites, and they knew it. I fished in my pocket for horse cookies, handed some to Audrey for Mabel, and fed the rest to Maynard, who accepted each piece with soft lips, munching with what passed for a donkey grin.

He was an amusing little guy, wiry black mane, tail and dorsal stripe, black-rimmed ears. The rest of him was grayish-tan, from his ample ears to his flinty hooves. He nuzzled me for more. I laughed.

"Sorry, my man, gotta save some for later."

The pack had remained balanced and snug, so I grabbed his lead line, led him over to Phantom, and swung into the saddle.

I needed to concentrate on the reason for this trip as well as the hazards. The immediate question was why the realtor felt the need to come out here and whether she'd let me see her on purpose. JJ had claimed Simpson had nothing to do with the foals, but I had my doubts. I had a feeling we hadn't seen the last of Carla Simpson. As for JJ, I wished she'd turn around and go back. That wouldn't happen, though. For one thing, her horse wouldn't do well alone. I didn't want either of them to get hurt, but I didn't look forward to dealing with them, either.

"Wait, Margo. Wait."

The voice was Dawn's. Now what? I twisted around in my saddle. Dawn's shoulders pumped back and forth, her legs flapping against her horse's side. Another time, it would've been comical. Now, it was just annoying. She'd ridden a lot as a kid, but her skills were rusty. Hawk, the little pinto I'd selected for her, ignored his rider's antics, poking along amiably, always a perfect gentleman.

"Let me come talk to you," Dawn said, finally managing to bring Hawk up next to me.

She wore new jeans, denim stiff as starch. No doubt she'd be rubbed raw on the soft flesh of her inner knees before the day was out. I didn't expect her to buy leather chaps like I wore, but I had recommended comfy breeches, offered her some of mine to try on. She at least had on low-heeled boots, but of a lustrous leather that seemed more suited to the streets of New York than the stirrups of a western saddle. Ever the artist, she would've looked more at home in flowing chiffon and understated linen.

"I just... I'm sorry JJ was such a bitch," she said.

"Why're you apologizing for her?"

"Not for her sake, for yours. JJ doesn't talk to me much, but I think she's in some kind of trouble. I overheard her telling someone on the phone last night that she'd send the money as soon as she could. She said they'd just have to wait, or else."

"Or else what?" I asked.

She shrugged. "That's all I heard; except she said something about results not mattering anymore. Maybe I didn't hear right."

"Any idea who she was talking to?"

"No."

"Okay, thanks for telling me."

I figured JJ must've been talking to whoever had pretended to be Mary Ashton, the fraudulent CSU toxicologist. Or Carla Simpson, maybe.

"I wish you were my sister," Dawn said, half-smiling.

Sometimes I felt more like her mother. I smiled at her.

"Life used to be so much simpler," she said. "You're so good with horses. Your life seems perfect."

"Hardly," I said, but I was wondering if she'd manage all right on this ride. Dawn had never dealt well with challenges unless it involved art.

She was silent for just a short time, and then asked, "Remember how much I used to love horses? I still love them, at least the thought of them, but some horses scare me. You have a way with them, a gift for understanding."

If there was a gift involved, it was a matter of communication. I rode many horses, some of them smart, most of them pleasurable, trained them for everything from trail riding to cross-country jumping. But except for my beloved Babe, I seldom came close to the level of understanding I had with Phantom. Sure, the rider must be in control, but the goal is communicating rather than forcing.

All I finally said was, "Horses will show you their ways if you take the time to watch them, understand how they perceive their surroundings."

I told my riding students the same thing, the same simple truth. Some heard it, some didn't.

Dawn looked thoughtful, but asked, "How do you get them to do what you want?"

So much for understanding. No sense trying to explain that good riders control their horses without making them into slaves.

"Hawk will take care of you," I told her. "He's one of my steadiest trail horses. That little guy wouldn't bolt unless lightning singed his tail. Maybe not even then."

She let go of her white-knuckle grip on the saddle horn long enough to pat Hawk. When I looked over at her, tears were streaming down her cheeks. Maybe all the antidepressants were having a rebound effect or something. Then again, she'd always been emotional.

We rode on for the rest of the morning, mostly in silence, past the storm and into sunshine, high overhead now and hot enough to bead sweat across my forehead. The trail rounded a bend, opening onto a meadow dotted with blue flag iris and the sound of rushing water. Phantom's walk quickened and Maynard crowded close. After the horses and donkeys drank their fill from the swollen river, we loosened their saddles, replaced bridles with halters and lead ropes, tied them to aspen trunks within reach of tall grass.

I withdrew water canteens and sandwiches for everyone from Maynard's pack. Audrey and I shared a comfortable silence. Dawn took a small tablet and colored pencils from her saddlebag and began sketching, graceful fingers dancing over the paper. I didn't notice her eating much of her sandwich.

JJ folded long legs beneath her on a solitary log away from us, picking at her sandwich like a persnickety cat. She pulled a silver flask from her saddlebag, but Ruth approached her, tasted the contents of the flask, upended it and emptied it out on the ground. JJ's face grew red, but neither she nor Ruth said a word.

Ruth tied her Appy gelding to a tree out of kicking range of the other animals as usual. Gus, stout and Roman-nosed, had watchful eyes and a habit of flattening ears and launching a hind leg at any horse who strayed too close to his spotted white rump. She'd owned the gelding over ten years, and it was obvious she loved him despite his stubborn nature. She strolled toward me, the bottom of her red-lined denim vest brushing her silver belt buckle. Her gray cowboy hat matched silver hair and shaded a wrinkled face. She settled down beside me, munched a sandwich, and sipped from an old-style metal canteen.

"Sorry you had to chase down JJ's runaway," she said. "That girl will never grow up."

I shrugged. "Thanks for keeping track of her flask."

"She won't get a drop of liquor while I'm watching her."

I smiled. In some ways, Ruth was like that ornery Appaloosa of hers; prickly but dependable. I'd grown up around her, but I'd never gotten to really know her.

After a while, I strolled over to Dawn. She was drawing flowers, as usual, but this day's sketch was a departure from her usual pastels. The colors she'd chosen were somber: dark purples, deep blues, grays. The flowers appeared jarring somehow, each petal bumping against the next instead of flowing together, and the bottom of the page held black flowers, crumpled, dead.

"That's, uh, different," I said, remembering that her artist friend at the Denver gallery mentioned that Dawn had recently switched to a darker palette.

She shrugged without looking up, without replying.

Our sadness flowed from us in different ways. Dawn turned to her art, and maybe grief explained JJ's increased sarcasm, while Ruth withdrew from her usual jabbering. Audrey was the most even-keeled of us all.

I was in control, outwardly. But if I had to select one word to describe how I really felt, it would be raw, as if something inside had shattered. Shared grief threw the five of us together, binding us one to the other yet highlighting our vulnerabilities. And sooner or later, our secrets would come to light.

Sunlight pranced across the nearby river, the rushing water mesmerizing while concealing whatever lurked beneath the surface. I wasn't looking forward to seeing Rim Rock Cliffs again, but it did seem fitting to stop a second time at the place where Bow died, and it was on our way. The outline of the Cliffs was visible in the distance from here, but it was another hour's ride to the base of those rocks.

Maynard and Mabel craned their necks in my direction, braying softly for the bits of bread I always handed over after a lunch stop. Ruth slipped horse cookies to Gus before tightening his girth, and JJ managed to get Royal Captain tacked up without finding something to complain about. Dawn walked over to where I was adjusting Hawk's saddle, her sketch crumpled in her hands.

I gave her a leg up. "You, uh, didn't like that drawing?"

"I need to do better," she said, stowing her small sketch pad and pencils away, but keeping the crumpled artwork in one hand.

She didn't need to say that the drawing served as a reflection of the gloom we were all feeling. I thought about the blue columbines that I'd draped across Bandit's saddle for the memorial. Those blooms were faded and dry now, crumpled just like Dawn's drawing.

I kept Maynard's lead line taut as we approached the river. Spring run-off deepened the flow, though not enough to cause problems for any of these animals with the possible exception of Royal Captain. Even he would be fine if he took his time, and if JJ kept calm herself. I'd warned her that there were no bridges in this wilderness. She'd sneered and said her horse wasn't afraid of getting wet. Her chance to prove that was coming right up.

Phantom splashed in, followed closely by Maynard. My mare worked her way over slippery rocks, slow and steady. Water jetted downstream in a deafening roar. Waves lapped the bottoms of my boots, meaning an average depth of several feet in spots. Maynard looked almost bored. In about the middle, I turned to watch the others.

Audrey and Two Bits came next, with Mabel following. I waved them ahead to the other side. No problems there.

JJ and Royal Captain entered the water, and I waited with Phantom and Maynard until the thoroughbred came behind us and glued himself to the donkey's tail. JJ's eyebrows were lifted, her eyes wide, but she sat still and didn't look down into the dizzying current. I allowed myself a sigh of relief, and in a few more yards I leaned forward in the saddle as Phantom dug her hooves into soft mud and scrambled up the opposite bank, Maynard behind her and Royal Captain following.

Dawn and Hawk splashed through the river close to Ruth and Gus. Both horses were seasoned, surefooted, steady.

I turned from them toward the cliffs.

And heard a scream, followed by a splash.

I looked back, saw Ruth, saw Gus, saw Hawk.

No Dawn.

Only water, not all that deep, but fast, churning.

Ruth dove off Gus, disappearing into a whirlpool, surfacing empty-handed. She struggled to stand, slipped, arms stretching for a handhold that wasn't there.

Audrey and I both jumped off our horses, grabbed the ropes coiled near our saddle horns and rushed to water's edge. Gus and Hawk scrambled up onto the bank and sank their noses into belly-high grass along with the others. The animals were too busy munching grass to go anywhere.

Ruth was still standing, and moving toward the bank, but Audrey threw a rope to her just in case.

I ran downstream where another arm appeared, followed by a head. Dawn. She opened her mouth as if to scream, then went under again. I raced along the bank, rope in hand. Dawn surfaced again, spitting water, but managed a yelp. I took a wide stance, holding one end of the rope firmly, throwing the other end upstream so the current would carry it to her.

"Grab it! Get the rope!"

She reached out too soon. Not far from her, that wadded-up flower sketch bobbed on the waves, swirled, then disappeared.

I gathered the rope, threw it again.

She reached, got it.

"Hang on!" I hollered, pulling with everything I had.

A pair of mallards dipped and bobbed on frothy waves between Dawn and the bank. The drake's head shone iridescent blue, the hen drifted nearer to the flailing Dawn, and then both birds startled up and away on frantic wings.

I kept the rope taut, pulling.

The ducks had barely cleared the water when Dawn was freed from the swirling pool she'd been sucked into. She staggered upright, standing in water well below her waist, holding fast to the rope, letting me guide her to the bank, eyes wide, lips a rigid circle.

Meanwhile, Ruth had climbed out of the water with Audrey's help and stood bent over, water puddling beneath her. She looked shrunken and cold, gray hair plastered to her head. Audrey dug through Mabel's pack for towels, hurried them to Ruth.

Once free of the river, Dawn sank down coughing, hands covering her face, dripping, shivering. Audrey tossed more towels over to me.

"It's all right now, Dawn. It's over," I said, rubbing Dawn, cuddling her. It was no surprise when Dawn began sobbing.

JJ smirked, muttering, "Crybaby."

Hard to understand how anyone could be that distant with their own sister.

As soon as Dawn was reasonably dry, I ignored JJ, rushed over to Ruth.

"Are you okay?"

"I'm fine, just cold. Thought I could grab Dawn, but that current was too fast."

"You did your best."

"Wasn't good enough."

"Everyone is safe now," I told her.

We let Ruth and Dawn sit in the sun to warm up before we mounted up again.

I looked back to the river as we left. It didn't appear all that deep, but a person can drown in just a few feet of rushing water. Dawn must've looked down, gotten dizzy and pitched off. Ruth was brave to jump in the water, but her age made her vulnerable. I was the guardian of these women whether I liked it or not. I felt like a mother hen, hoping my chicks wouldn't keep causing trouble, wondering which chick would turn out to have sharp claws and a guilty conscience.

When we arrived at Rim Rock Cliffs, Ruth trotted Gus up beside Phantom, looking visibly shaken.

"I feel her presence here," she said.

Above the aspen that clustered at the base of the rocks, sandstone ledges rose haphazardly to the sky. I felt Bow's presence too, felt it just as powerfully as I had when I came alone. Still, I couldn't recall ever seeing Ruth so upset. She'd looked sad at Bow's memorial, but now she seemed fearful. It wasn't like her.

Audrey was silent, her face etched with sorrow.

"I want to remember this place," JJ said, her voice soft, reverent. Then she surprised me by turning to me. "Thank you for bringing me."

I smiled, nodded.

"No," Dawn whispered. "We shouldn't be here." Her face was ashen, and she still looked cold even though the sun had warmed her and dried her clothes for over an hour.

I felt repulsed by what had happened here and yet this place was one stop on the long trail to closure for us all. I took a deep breath and looked at the women. Perhaps some truths were written on these faces. But the face and soul that bothered me the most was Simpson's. She was out here, might even be following us. Maybe she and JJ had something planned.

I waved a hand toward the top of the Cliff. "I'm going to walk up there."

"Stop pretending to be some stupid Sherlock Holmes," JJ said.

So much for her gratitude.

I dismounted and secured Phantom and Maynard to aspen trunks.

Audrey dismounted and tied Two Bits and Mabel. Ruth got off Gus, but when she tied him too close to Phantom, the sour-eyed gelding looked sideways at my mare and pinned his ears back. Ruth moved him to a different tree, and Gus flipped his head side to side like a defiant toddler.

JJ and Dawn dismounted, but both just stood staring at the cliff.

"Can't," Dawn said.

"Me neither," JJ said. "This place is creepy."

"You two stay down here and keep an eye on the animals. Holler if you see anything or anyone," I said.

Neither JJ nor Dawn liked heights, but that wasn't the scariest thing here. I didn't mention the cougar I'd seen in the forest the last time I was here.

I didn't like high places much, either, but I could manage. This time, I was more careful. Audrey climbed without effort, but Ruth was breathing heavily halfway up, so we stopped to rest before pushing on to the top. There was a breeze on top, a chill. I didn't approach the edge. Such a long way to the bottom, long enough to see death coming, think final thoughts. A shadowy coldness passed through me. It felt even worse to be here this second time even though this time I wasn't about to let myself fall.

Audrey and Ruth came and stood beside me, all of us looking down.

"Dear God, poor Elizabeth," Ruth said.

Audrey began crying first, but Ruth and I soon did the same.

"Do either of you believe in...spirits?" I whispered.

Audrey looked at me, shrugged. "I feel a presence here."

"I believe in God's will," Ruth said.

I turned to Ruth. "Do you think it was Bow's destiny to die so soon after connecting with her daughter?"

Ruth shook her head. "God knows all, understands what we cannot."

"We'd better head back down," I said, after a silence.

"Yes," Ruth said, "but first we should pray."

"Shouldn't we wait until we're with JJ and Dawn?" Audrey asked.

"No," Ruth said. "Those girls shouldn't be afraid to climb this hill. Besides, I'm not sure I trust JJ."

Audrey looked surprised. "What makes you say that?"

"I'm just cautious, and so is Margo."

I looked at her, stayed silent. We picked our way back down, skirting loose rocks, stepping sideways at times, and then rounded a bend onto a shady section. There, off to one side, was a patch of moss. I leaned down close to the soft green mass and saw tiny silver funnels Bow called fairy trumpets. She'd laughed at them, making up silly stories about inch-high fairies who came out at night to play music under the stars.

I had no idea what happens after death, where a person goes, what their spirit does, but now, looking at these tiny trumpets, it made me feel close to Bow. We kept going, rounding the last bend of our descent, and I surprised myself by laughing and crying at the same time.

Audrey and Ruth looked at me, but neither asked for an explanation. Some memories should be kept private, close to the heart.

The rhythms of this wilderness were like melodies to Bow, and she knew every note, every refrain. She knew Bandit the same way. She didn't just ride him, she blended with her horse. And I saw some of those qualities in Audrey, the long-lost daughter who had at least gotten to meet her mother, to know her for a short time before having to mourn her.

This place hummed with sorrow and memories.

JJ's voice broke the spell. "You three were gone long enough!"

Ruth frowned, looking like she wanted to smack JJ.

Dawn was quiet, still appearing shaken from the river-dunking, but her color was no longer ashen.

Audrey took me aside, whispered, "I think we should slip JJ half of a tranquilizer. She may be getting withdrawal symptoms. She looks agitated."

"Doesn't she always?" I asked. "But yes, a small dose isn't a bad idea. I'll have Ruth give her some."

"Let's get the hell outta here," JJ said.

Ruth approached her with a small pill. "Swallow this with some water, JJ, it'll make you feel better."

"Yes, ma'am," JJ said, accepting the pill, washing it down under Ruth's watchful eye.

"We're only about halfway, right?" Ruth asked.

I nodded. "Yes, we need to get moving."

We gathered the horses, mounted up again.

Ruth halted Gus for a moment, bowed her head. "Dear Lord, receive our dearly departed Elizabeth in heaven, we beseech you."

The rest of us listened in silence. Ruth was the only devout churchgoer among us. I prayed in my own way, but despite moments of joy with the tiny trumpets, sinister shadows haunted this place, jabbing with sharp fingers.

CHAPTER TWENTY-EIGHT

THE TRAIL AHEAD IS a gentle climb, up and over that mesa," I said, pointing to the west.

Our pack-trip clients never had problems, but they rode horses handpicked for each one's skill level. We rode in silence to the top of the mesa without incident, crossed the level portion, started down the other side. We'd just rounded the first curve when there was a little rumble, followed by one scream and then another.

It was JJ. A mere handful of small rocks had rolled off the wide trail. No big deal, but Royal Captain was jigging. All four hooves remained on solid ground.

"It's okay, just relax," Audrey was telling JJ.

"It's not okay, so just shut the fuck up."

"What's wrong?" I asked, even though it was obvious that JJ had felt her horse stumble, and then scared her already jittery animal by jerking on his mouth. Reins serve as a two-way communication route between horse and rider, echoing fear as well as confidence.

"This trail is too damn steep for a horse," JJ said.

"Let him have his head, keep those reins loose," I said.

"I don't need riding lessons, especially from you, and if Royal Captain gets injured, you're to blame."

"Now you listen here, JJ," Ruth said. "You insisted on riding that horse, so show us you know how to ride him instead of bitching and blaming."

"Burn in hell, old woman," JJ said.

"You need more than the little tranquilizer I gave you, JJ. You need to find God, to begin with. And if you have anything more to say, I'll answer with this," Ruth said, waving her Colt 45 at a shocked JJ. "Now shut up and ride that horse."

I managed not to laugh, but I did allow my lips to smile a bit.

The rest of the descent was steep in places, but nothing to get excited about. Not a peep was heard from the Royal Pains. Ruth might be older than the rest of us, but she commanded respect.

Maynard appeared bored, ears drooping. Donkeys were smart enough to take it easy whenever they could. Most of our packing clients came with preconceived notions about donkeys being stubborn and hard to work with. After a few hours of watching them, though, everyone realized that donkeys were not only surefooted and reliable, but they were comedians too.

On to Lost Valley, I told myself when we cleared the mesa.

To my surprise, JJ bought Royal Captain beside me when the trail widened.

"I, uh, I'm sorry I was mean back there," JJ said.

"No worries." It wasn't like her to apologize, but it was nice.

"I know I'm not always easy to get along with," she said, looking straight ahead.

If I agreed, it might piss her off. If I disagreed, I'd be lying. Silence seemed safest.

"I don't blame you for wanting to come alone," she said.

"Here we are, though. And we all loved Bow."

"I had to come on this trip, had to ride Royal Captain, too."

"Your horse is a nice thoroughbred, and you are a good rider."

"But what?"

I shook my head. "But nothing."

"I loved Aunt Bow, and I'm so sorry about the foals. I really am."

I just looked at her.

"You've never liked me."

"That's not true, JJ. But you are a little difficult to be around sometimes."

She stuck her chin out, narrowed her eyes. "You just can't meet me halfway, can you! You think you're so damn perfect."

"No one is perfect."

"Aunt Bow was close to perfect." JJ paused, sighed. "I loved her."

"I know you did, JJ."

She turned around, making sure the others were out of hearing range. "Did you...tell them about the foals?"

"I told the sheriff, JJ. He had to know."

"I always fuck things up."

"Mistakes happen. But everyone can change."

"I drink too much. How the hell do I change that?"

"With help, JJ."

"I guess." She looked at me. "Know something? I may not act like it, but I like you, Margo."

"That's great, JJ. And I meant it when I said you're a good rider."

"Yeah, okay. Damn, I better leave you alone before you get all mushy." She turned Royal Captain around, went back near Ruth.

I smiled. Maybe there was hope for the Royal Pains, thanks in part to the pill Ruth gave her. There'd be more challenges before we reached Lost Creek, so JJ would have additional chances to show her softer side and her equestrian skill.

The trail veered more to the west, and the next few miles passed uneventfully. A series of hairpin climbs awaited us, much steeper than what had frightened JJ. The ascent wasn't bad, but the top section had about half a mile on a ledge guaranteed to give both JJ and Dawn the shakes.

Audrey was a very good rider, but even she might be scared on the ledge. I doubted much would bother Ruth. If anything was a test for these women, the upcoming climb and the ledge would at least strip away everyone's veneer, leave them vulnerable. The trail was adequate but narrow, negotiable if horse and rider were careful. No need to get them nervous by mentioning this until I had to. Winding up to the ledge then down the other side was the only way into the valley except for an even higher wildlife trail on top of the cliff, well above where we'd cross and unsuitable for horses.

Part of the reason Bow loved Lost Creek Valley was the isolation. No one else knew about it, for one thing. Enormous mountains hugged the place, sheltering it. The beginning of the trail gave no hint of the beauty waiting at journey's end. We never took our packing-trip clients there, partly because we didn't want to scare them on the steep ledge, but mostly because we were selfish. We saved the valley for ourselves. In all the times Bow and I had camped in Lost Creek, we'd found no evidence of other human visitors, no footprints, no trash, nothing. Animals frequented the place, though, including a large elk herd, scattered mule deer, and cougars who preyed on the ungulates, the grazers. Red-tailed hawks rode the thermals, ospreys fished the stream along the valley floor. Lost Valley sparkled even amid this magnificent wilderness.

No wonder Bow wanted to spend all eternity there. I had little doubt that Audrey would love the place too.

I halted Phantom and Maynard at a level clearing and turned to face the group.

"We have another two hours to go. There's only one trail into the valley and it winds up that mountain ahead," I said, pointing. "There's a steep portion of ledge trail."

JJ, who'd looked away when I started talking, now gasped audibly, and so did Dawn.

"Horses do just fine on the ledge," I said, "but the danger is real."

"This is what we came for," JJ began, "and now you're saying it's dangerous?"

"I just want you to be aware that it's not an easy section, but it's doable. Bow and I have been over this ledge many times."

Dawn winced. "How high?"

"Several hundred feet. The trail is wedged into the middle of the cliff. There's room for a horse, but not much room for error."

Bow and I rode experienced horses and packed with level-headed donkeys. If anyone in this group was going to have trouble, it'd be the Royal Pains. Hawk wouldn't stumble, unless Dawn panicked so much that the little pinto faltered. Ruth and Audrey might be challenged, but they were likely to be fine if they remained calm.

I wanted this entire ride to serve as a test for all the women, and the trail ahead would push them, for sure, but I didn't want anyone to die. If I didn't prepare them ahead of time, they'd surely freak out when the ledge came into view.

Dawn rode beside me while the trail was still wide and level.

"When I was little, I never imagined this was how my life would turn out," she said.

"You mean becoming an artist or a mother? Or are you thinking about the divorce?"

"I mean how I turned out inside. Remember that first summer we spent together?"

"Sure. You and I and JJ, climbing a haystack that seemed like Mount Everest, up and up. I remember the scratches all over my legs. That hay was rough on tender skin. We were real young, I was maybe seven, so you would've only been five."

"We used all the band-aids we could find," she said, "vying to see who could plaster on the most from our skinny knees right down to our toes."

"We did have fun," I said. I wasn't all that interested in talking about our childhoods, not now, but if it calmed her, let her babble.

She was silent for a bit before asking, "Did you like me when we first met?"

Odd question. "Yeah, sure. I think so. Why?"

She smiled. "You were wearing purple polka-dot shorts, and your hair was in pigtails. I liked you, even before I knew your name. I'll never forget that day."

"I don't remember that many details."

"You don't?" Dawn sounded hurt.

"It was a long time ago."

"I should start over, do things right."

"Everybody wishes that sometimes," I said, although I was beginning to wonder about her. She was depressed, yes, but she seemed so wrapped up in the past. Neither she nor JJ had experienced a perfect childhood. Join the club. I had all the patience in the world when it came to horses, not so much with people.

"Do you think horses like us humans?" she asked.

"That's a great question. I don't know for sure, but I think they like us if we're nice to them. They communicate a lot, with the swish of a tail, or movement of their head or ears. A lot of what they tell us is subtle. But horses never lie."

"Will they be scared on this steep part?"

"Not unless the rider communicates fear, which can be contagious."

"How long will it take to cross the ledge?"

"About fifteen minutes, so not long."

She sighed. "It doesn't take long to do the wrong thing."

"Hawk will keep you safe, Dawn. All you need to do is take deep breaths and relax, let him do the work."

When we were about to start climbing, I turned Phantom around and put up a hand for everyone to gather.

"Bow and I have ridden across this steep trail without trouble many times, even in pouring rain. Every horse here will do fine," I continued, though I had my doubts about Royal Captain. "The key is a relaxed rider. Keep in mind that a horse knows you're nervous even before you admit it to yourself."

"Cut the crap," JJ said, but her tone was mellower than her words.

"Nervousness isn't the real problem," I went on, hoping JJ would hear at least some of what I was saying. "It's how you act, what you do that counts. Matter of fact, admitting you're afraid is best. I tell my students to scoop up their fear and stick it in a box to deal with later. That way, you can concentrate on riding."

"That's silly," JJ said, laughing.

"Yeah, it is silly, but it works. You must get nervous before jumping a course at one of your shows. How do you handle it?"

JJ looked startled, but then shrugged, said, "Well, I take deep breaths and count backwards, starting with twenty."

"That sounds good, too. The idea is just to keep your mind too busy to worry, don't you agree, JJ?"

"I guess, yeah."

As we started the ascent, I glanced back at Dawn. "You're doing great," I said, smiling.

"If I had a horse of my own like Hawk, I'd, well, I'd love him."

"You can come ride him anytime you'd like."

I sent the pinto a mental promise for an armful of juicy red apples when this trip was over. The little cutie flickered his ears and nodded his head up and down. No doubt dealing with pesky flies, but why not imagine he was thanking me.

"It'll take us awhile to get up to the ledge. Just let Hawk do the work. Hang onto the saddle horn if you want. Your job is to relax and remember not to pull on the reins, so that Hawk can use his head and neck for balance."

"If I pull, will he fall?"

"No, no," I said. "He's not gonna fall. Hawk is one of the best trail horses of this whole bunch."

"Better than Phantom?"

"He's as sure-footed as my mare, and like I said, Hawk likes you."

"You're kidding, but okay. No wonder I always wanted you to be my big sister."

She was sounding more like the Dawn I knew instead of the nervous wreck that grief and stress had turned her into. We were all on edge, pun intended. The climb continued with a series of gentle switchbacks working the way up through heavy timber. Layers of lodgepole pines marched up one side of the trail and sloped down the other; the higher we went, the steeper the slope.

There was a sudden flash of movement in dense trees above. I stared up into the forest, squinting, trying to see. Whatever moved up there wasn't visible. A faint trail wound upwards, leading to the top of the cliff, probably traveled by nimble bighorn sheep. Most likely, a couple of them were what I'd glimpsed. Next, a whirring noise began overhead.

"What now?" JJ asked.

"Squirrel," I replied.

A black Abert's squirrel scurried up a nearby tree, scolding as it went, tufted ears alert. The little critter stared down at us, whirring displeasure at our presence. We rode on and the little thing kept up the racket to hurry us away.

We rounded another switchback and the trail widened through a profusion of white aspen trunks, many bearing scars from hungry elk. Columbine poked blue petals above low grasses, reminding me of Bow. The next switchback led to an opening with a view stretching over the undulating Flat Tops.

I loved this wilderness most of all for what it lacked: asphalt, skyscrapers, crowds—unless the occasional elk herd counted.

"This is too high," Dawn stammered.

"I'm not fond of heights either," I said, "but look at the great view."

"I didn't think it would be this high, and we're not even to the ledge yet."

"We're almost there, so remember what we talked about. Relax and let Hawk take care of you."

She didn't reply.

"You'll do just fine," I said, hoping I was right.

From up above, the trail ahead would look like a ribbon carved into solid rock. That ribbon was wide enough for one horse to walk with ease, but there was scant room for missteps, no room for passing. The upslope side angled steeply, with bits of vegetation and scraggly pines clinging here and there. The downward slope was steeper yet, a vertical wall of rock, rugged and unforgiving. Golden eagles launched themselves from cliff-side nests to circle below us, their seven-foot wing spans gliding the thermals. Tree tops marched below us into distant rolling hills, like columns of soldiers.

Suddenly, there was a loud gasp behind us.

It wasn't Dawn. I looked past her. Royal Captain seemed okay, but JJ was staring down over the ledge, eyes wide, mouth open. And she was about to do a lot more than gasp. Horses, whether calm or hyper, don't react well to hysterics.

"Hey, JJ, look at me," Audrey said. "C'mon now, look at me."

Slowly, JJ's head turned away from the drop.

"Great," Audrey said. "Okay, but you're breathing like a racehorse. Slow it down, girl, give your lungs a break."

JJ closed her eyes, and her chest expanded like a balloon. I didn't want her to notice me watching, so I turned around and moved Phantom forward.

"You and Hawk doing okay, Dawn?" I asked over my shoulder.

"Uh-huh."

I didn't tell her not to look down, because that only makes a person want to do just that. Negatives reinforce a negative. Sounded like something out of a physics text, but whatever works.

We'd made it halfway across the ledge.

The horses and donkeys continued in single file, hoofbeats drumming a soft rhythm. A few pebbles tumbled down onto the trail. Nothing unusual about that. But then there was a noise from behind. Loud, followed by scrambling and scrapping.

A screech.

Phantom jigged forward. I looked back, past Dawn, past Audrey, past JJ.

A small boulder and a shower of rocks had fallen in the middle of the narrow trail close to Ruth's Appaloosa. Gus scrambled on the far side of the boulder, one front leg sliding off the trail, a back leg teetering on the edge.

Ruth was nowhere in sight.

I grabbed my rope, jumped off Phantom and wedged myself past Maynard, past Dawn and Hawk.

"Oh no, she's dead, she's dead," Dawn whispered, staring back, hand clamped over her mouth.

I kept going, clinging to the uphill side past Audrey's Two Bit and Mabel.

Royal Captain fidgeted, pawing the ground, a bundle of pent-up panic with nowhere to go. JJ sat frozen; eyes clamped shut.

"Talk to your horse, JJ," I said as I passed, "try to calm him. Bail off uphill if you have to."

She didn't answer.

By the time I squeezed around the boulder, Gus had managed to get all four hooves back on solid ground. He stood statue-like but quivering, nostrils flared.

I still couldn't see Ruth. If she'd fallen…I didn't want to look, but I knelt and peered down.

Finally, I saw her, fingers clinging to a rock outcrop at least ten feet below the ledge, her legs dangling. If she lost her grip, there was nothing to stop her fall.

It was a long way to the bottom.

"What hurts most?" I asked, making a quick loop on one end of the rope.

"My leg, can't move it."

I lowered the rope. "Grab it, Ruth, easy now."

She reached out with one arm, missed, fingers scraping against rough rocks.

A cascade of small rocks loosened, tumbling down and down.

I angled the rope closer. "Try again."

I held my breath as she reached again, grabbed it.

"Hang tight." I started pulling. "Push against the rocks with your good leg if you can."

I pulled hard, then harder. By the time Ruth's head finally appeared level with the trail, my arms were trembling. I grabbed one of Ruth's hands, then the other for one last tug and almost had her up when a shower of dirt and pebbles tumbled around us.

"Not again," Ruth said. "Dear God, not again."

"Something's up there!" JJ shouted.

There was no time to consider possibilities.

"Lean on me," I told Ruth after she was finally beside me. Her red-lined denim vest was filthy and ripped down the front.

She glanced at the boulder, squeezed her eyes shut and grimaced.

"If that landed on top of —"

"You're safe now," I said, hoping I was right. "What about your leg? Anything else hurt?"

Ruth leaned against me, standing on her left foot, holding the other up.

"Rock bumped against my shoulder, ankle twisted when I fell," she said. "Is Gus hurt? That thing either hit him or came real close."

I'd looked him over while I squeezed past him on my way to Ruth. "No cuts, but I'll check him thoroughly as soon as I can."

It could've been worse. So much worse. I looked at the boulder that had dropped by without an invitation. Talk about rude. It wasn't all that large, but still heavy enough to cause significant damage. There was no time now to ask JJ if she'd seen anything or anyone up above. The possibility of someone causing a rockslide on purpose was chilling. I looked up, thought about seeing Carla Simpson.

Gus had stopped quivering and appeared almost calm now. There were no obvious injuries but, just to be safe, I'd ordinarily have opted to put Ruth on Phantom. Now, squeezing her past the other horses would be impossible with her injured leg. I figured Audrey was the calmest, hoped JJ and Dawn were managing okay. Phantom and the other animals had moved forward a few yards, but my mare held the head of the line, waiting for me.

I gave Ruth a leg up into her saddle. She groaned, but otherwise struggled in silence. She'd need a splint as soon as I could manage it. First, though, we had to get everyone out of here, off this ledge. I led Gus around the boulder, and then hustled back toward the front of the line. To my relief, JJ's eyes were open and Royal Captain stood quieter, though he wasn't totally calm. Audrey was humming, just loud enough that JJ and Dawn could hear.

I remounted, looked back at Ruth, and she nodded and lifted a hand. We moved on. Finally, the slope began angling downward, the drop-off lessening gradually. I kept an eye on the uphill side, watching for any loose rocks, any movement.

Nothing.

No way to predict or prevent nature's inclination to rearrange itself.

Natural beauty soothed; natural chaos destroyed. People could either love or loathe everything wild. The wilderness kept to its own rhythms, its own ways. People worried me a lot more than nature right now. JJ thought she'd seen something or someone up above. Rockslides usually reflected the random work of Mother Nature, but not always.

Trees finally began hugging the trail again, first a few, then more, until we were cocooned on both side by lodgepole pines. The descent was steeper than the ascent. When the entire group cleared the ledge, I got off Phantom, secured her to a tree, grabbed my first-aid kit and a few other things from Maynard's pack and edged back to check on Ruth and Gus. Ruth sat slumped forward, but when she saw me coming, she raised a hand and gave a thumbs-up.

"How's it going?" I asked.

"I'm alive, and so is Gus. God just meant to scare me, that's all."

"What hurts?"

"I'm sore, but not bad off."

The rest of us were half her age, but she was twice as brave. If I'd been showered with rocks and then tumbled off the ledge, I'd have yelled my head off. If her ankle was broken or even just sprained, she'd be in a lot of pain. There might be other injuries, too, but at least she could move all her limbs and she hadn't lost consciousness. Still, even with the pain pills I'd brought, it was a long ride back home. I might have to call in a helicopter for her with the satellite phone.

Now, I handed her a Tylenol with codeine and grabbed her water bottle.

"You're not allergic to codeine, are you?"

"Nope, I've taken it once or twice."

"That'll ease the pain, and I'll splint your ankle. Wrapping it should help some, too."

She accepted everything stoically, said, "Bless you, Margo," when I finished.

Gus seemed fine as near as I could tell. Another relief.

"We have to go back out by way of that ledge tomorrow?" JJ asked, her voice flat.

"Don't worry about that yet," I said.

She sighed. "How much farther now?"

"An hour, give or take."

I remounted and allowed myself a deep breath, exhaling pent-up tension. Neither Bow nor I had ever thought of the ledge as bad or fearful. To us, it had just been a trail with spectacular views leading to our special place. I sighed, rubbing a hand across my face.

Suddenly, Phantom stumbled. Badly. And the next step my mare took was a lame one. I leaned forward and looked down. Sometimes a horse stumbles on a rock, limps a step or two, and then is fine.

Phantom stayed lame.

I halted her and swung off. I'd been daydreaming rather than paying attention to the trail. Immediate guilt.

I lifted her right front leg, the one she'd favored. Sure enough, a jagged rock had wedged tightly between the frog in the middle of her sole and the rim of her metal shoe. I balanced the hoof between my knees, reached into my pocket for the hoof pick I always carry, and loosened the rock.

Stone bruises range from insignificant to severe, depending on where and how hard the rock strikes the sole of the hoof. The worst impact comes when the horse is trotting or cantering. The actual bruise often doesn't even show up until the horseshoer exposes it layer by layer like an onion as the damaged section grows out. A horse that's only walking seldom gets a serious bruise. It can happen, though. I looped the reins over Phantom's head and led her a few steps down the trail, keeping my eyes on that right front.

She could walk, but she favored that one side.

"Why is she still limping?" Dawn asked.

"Stone bruise," I replied, my voice tight, my mind swirling with possibilities.

"What's going on up there?" Ruth shouted.

"The stupid mustang stumbled on a rock," JJ replied.

"Anything I can do?" Audrey asked.

I shook my head. I reached into Maynard's pack for an Easyboot. I always brought a few in case a horse threw a shoe or for something just like this. I secured the rubber bootie-like contraption over the mare's sore hoof.

"I'm going to just lead her on, keep weight off her legs."

"This is going to take forever," JJ said.

She'd done okay on the ledge and I was proud of her for that. But now, she was back to her ornery self, a Royal Pain once more. If her horse was hurt, she'd be demanding that I do something.

I wanted to get done with this ride at much as anyone, but I'd rather be in pain myself than see Phantom hurting. Other than one very minor bout with colic, she'd had no health issues since we'd been together. Early on, Bow warned me about getting too attached to one horse. Good advice. Bow said it's hard when something happens to any of the horses, but unbearable with those you fall in love with. But Bow also admitted she couldn't help having her own favorites. I lost all objectivity, first with Babe and now with Phantom.

I often wondered why I loved horses more than most humans. Not that I disliked people, exactly, I just preferred spending time around horses rather than some of the people I knew, except for Roy, of course. Bow was more gregarious, she loved people, especially men. My dad, for instance. It'd helped to talk to Courtney about that, helped me see that I could both love Bow and also be mad at her, but the anger I felt toward Dad scared the hell out of me. The future held more sessions with Courtney, no doubt.

I've always believed that you could tell a lot about a person from the way they treat animals, whether it's a hamster or a horse. When I did socialize, I preferred being around animal-lovers, particularly horse people. Most are as crazy as I am. I could pick them out a mile away, and not just because of the dirty boots or the hay in the back of their pickups. The friendship Beth Jensen and I shared was based as much on our differences as our similarities, but we shared a love of animals. She seldom rode herself, lived in town with a dog and three cats, drove a Prius, but both she and her husband fully supported little Nicole's love of horses. Audrey loved animals as much as Bow had, which was one of the reasons I'd liked her even before I fully trusted her.

I brushed a fly off Phantom's face, wondering if her thoughts wandered as much as mine.

"How ya doing, girl?" I murmured. She flicked her ears back and forth, a gesture I took as a sign of understanding.

The campsite was coming into view.

CHAPTER TWENTY-NINE

THE TRAIL STILL SLOPED down, but gently now, lodgepoles giving way to Douglas firs and ponderosas as the elevation lowered into Lost Creek Valley. The top of one enormous ponderosa was visible now.

"Our tree, Bow," I whispered. "We made it."

Soon, it would be her resting place forever.

Phantom jigged sideways, making her limp more pronounced. She tossed her head, arched her neck, snorted.

"What is it, girl?" I led the mare around the last bend. There, right in front of us, the remains of a dead animal sprawled across the trail. An elk calf, torn and bloody. Fresh kill, from the look of it, but already the mound bore scant resemblance to the creature who'd run by a mother's side a short while ago.

I'd seen carcasses before, of course, it was part of survival of the fittest, or the fortunate. There were no grocery stores for carnivores, no meat in cellophane packages out here. But this time, I felt suddenly light-headed, thinking of Bow's remains, of the cougar. Before I could dwell on it, though, someone screeched.

It was JJ, and she wailed again, a siren of sound.

Phantom jigged some more, which couldn't be helping her right front. I turned around in time to see Dawn grow pale, her eyes rolling back. I looped Phantom's lead rope around a stout limb and rushed over, joined by Audrey as Dawn fainted, slumping forward in her saddle. Her arms hung limp, torso down, half off the saddle. Hawk stood, not moving a muscle. By the time we'd eased her to the ground, she was beginning to awaken, looking dazed.

The screaming had stopped but now JJ was sobbing loudly, gasping for breath. Dawn was blinking, still pale.

"What... Who?" she began, pushing herself up onto her elbows.

"You fainted, that's all." I put my hand on her shoulder. "And that's JJ crying."

Dawn sat up, frowned. "Blood," she whispered softly, "blood."

"Stay with her," I told Audrey. "Don't let her stand until she's okay."

"Right."

Even Audrey looked a little peaked, but my mind was on JJ, stopping her from fainting too. I ran back and grabbed hold of her gelding's bridle.

"Calm down, JJ, please calm down." Royal Captain was tossing his head, flicking his tail, but he appeared too tired to put on much of a show.

JJ sniffled. "Oh God," she said, "Aunt Bow —"

"I know, JJ, I know." I glanced back at Dawn.

Audrey was bent over her, murmuring. She helped Dawn to her feet, turned her away from the carcass.

"It's an animal," I told everyone. "Just an animal."

Suddenly, Audrey pressed a hand against her stomach, staggered a few paces away, bent over and threw up.

I ran over to her, but she held up a hand.

"I'm all right, just —"

"I know, Audrey, I know," I said.

Even Ruth had her hand over her mouth.

We were all thinking about Bow. I'd seen dead animals before but it was rare to see a fresh kill like this. More often, a rib or leg bone of an elk turned up, bleached white in the sun. It never bothered me, but now the sheriff's words replayed in my mind.

"Most likely a cougar," he'd said, hastening to add, "her face was untouched, but the rest of her... "

Seeing what was left of this elk calf was even harder on the others. Everyone except Ruth and I lived in big cities, far from nature's reality. Like many people, Dawn and JJ knew and loved the soft side of nature, but were happy to ignore the starkness, the unfiltered truth. Audrey lived in a city, too, but she was Bow's daughter and acted like it.

"Did a cougar—" JJ asked, her voice hoarse.

"Probably. Cougars kill to survive." I couldn't hate the big cats. Nature held no grudges.

"But one of them attacked Bow."

"It did not kill her," Audrey said.

Ruth, still sitting on Gus, cleared her throat.

"Audrey is right. The coroner's report confirmed that Elizabeth was already dead when the cougar found her."

We gave the carcass a wide berth as we followed the last bend in the trail. I'd always thought of Lost Creek as almost cozy even though the valley wasn't all that small. The creek dissecting the meadow provided a soothing trickle. Densely forested hillsides encircled the open stretch of lush grasses accented by wildflowers. Aptly named pink shooting stars clustered near the creek, blue columbines nodded under aspen. Bright golden banner flowers crowded each other in the open, saluting the sun.

Bow and I often camped under what we thought of as our special ponderosa, a solitary sentinel not far from the water. We'd inhaled the bark's butterscotch scent, brushed against sticky sap, and felt that in some way this enormous tree welcomed us. Long graceful branches rose to a rounded top. Sitting under that canopy always felt like coming home.

I helped Ruth dismount close to the ponderosa and guided her to a large log that served as a bench. Next came unsaddling Phantom and removing the coiled length of rope that'd served as a lifeline twice this day, first with Dawn, then with Ruth. Now it became a tie-line for the horses. I secured one end to a small but sturdy tree and stretched the other end to another tree.

After all the animals were unsaddled and the panniers removed from Maynard and Mabel, they got brushed, cooled down, and fed grain. I let Phantom, Hawk, and the donkeys loose to graze. We erected two pop-up tents and started dinner. Campfires have a mystique all their own, but the wildfire danger associated with them led to banning open fires in most of the backcountry. Backpack stoves lack allure. People don't dream of roasting marshmallows and singing songs around little tin stoves. Still, the things were light, efficient, and safe. I ran creek water through a portable purifier, and we washed our hands with some, poured the rest into pots on two small stoves. Pre-cut veggies along with freeze-dried chunks of meat went into one pot, the second one boiled water for coffee and tea.

I thought back to all the food served at Bow's memorial, understood now why it seemed appropriate. Food was comforting, an affirmation that we were among the living, that life goes on.

Ruth hobbled to a log and sat there, chopping apples and oranges with a paring knife. I walked over to ask how she was feeling just when she stopped and held up her hand. Blood trickled down the palm.

"Bad cut?" I asked.

She shook her head. "I'm fine."

"Let's see."

"No need," she insisted, but blood kept oozing.

I rummaged through my first-aid kit for a bandage and ointment, hustled back to her.

"Don't make such a fuss," she said.

"Oh c'mon, I just need to play nurse. Gotta use what little first-aid skills I have."

She laughed at that, finally held out her hand. The cut wasn't bad. Still, cleansing and a bandage wouldn't hurt. I leaned close for a good look. The cut was on the fleshy part of her palm, just below the middle finger. But that wasn't the only wound on Ruth's hand. There was a larger gash, a good two inches long, partly healed but still reddened.

"What's with this other one?"

She jerked her hand away. "Nothing. It's nothing."

I squinted at her. "That's a bigger cut."

"I told you, I'm fine." She sounded nervous. "I butchered a few chickens last week, that's all. The knife slipped."

"I'll put ointment on both."

"Whatever."

"There you go," I said, after I finished. "Keep a little pressure over the bandage for a few minutes."

She nodded. She did raise chickens, and she did butcher them. But that was no reason for her to seem nervous. Or maybe she was just tired and achy. Instead of returning the first-aid supplies to the top of Maynard's pannier I put them in my saddlebag, which was handier in camp. My gun was in there, too, loaded, but the idea of aiming the thing at any living being, human or otherwise, felt impossible. That weapon didn't make me feel powerful, it petrified me. I always brought it on pack trips, but I'd never aimed at anything other than paper targets at a shooting range. I tied a light jacket around my waist and slipped the gun into one of the pockets.

We ate in silence. It'd been a long day, and there'd been too much drama. What we all needed was a good night's sleep, but I had no intention of letting my guard down, no intention of closing my eyes.

"Are we spreading the ashes tonight?" Ruth asked.

"Let's do that first thing in the morning. Is that okay with everyone?"

Heads nodded.

"I know everyone is tired, I am too. I'll tie up the horses who've already grazed, but the others need time to eat."

"Oh, that's right," JJ said. "There's no hay."

"But there's plenty of grass, and it's good stuff."

"I brought hobbles for Gus," Ruth said.

"All right," I nodded at her. "I'll get him all set up. Two Bits and Royal Captain need to be held so they can fill up, too."

Audrey stood, said, "C'mon then, JJ, it'll feel good for us to walk around with them."

"Can't you just take your horse and mine too?"

"I don't think that'd work," I said. "We don't need any more drama." I expected JJ to argue, but she joined Audrey without saying anything more.

After I hobbled Gus and set him free to graze, I gathered Maynard and Mabel, secured them to the tie-line and got Hawk and Phantom. After securing Hawk, I led Phantom to the water to soak her sore foot. I'd removed the Easyboot when we reached camp, since the ground was soft, spongy. She stepped readily into the stream and remained there. When I led her back to the tie-line, her limp was less noticeable; a good sign. I slipped her a few horse cookies from my pocket. When I walked away, she whinnied, low in her throat.

"You spoil that mare," JJ said.

"Sure do."

"She'll take advantage of you."

I just smiled.

By the time all the horses had grazed the sky was losing color as dusk set in, the moon's outline began glowing and stars became visible as though someone had flipped a switch.

"It's peaceful here," JJ said.

"Yes, sure is," Ruth agreed.

"I'm glad we've arrived," JJ said.

"And we have the horses to thank for bringing us," Audrey said.

JJ rolled her eyes. "Oh, for Pete's sake, that's their job, to take us where we tell them to. You're all so sentimental."

"There's nothing wrong with loving your horse," Audrey said.

JJ shook head. "They're animals, not teddy bears."

"So, humans are the only ones deserving of love?" Ruth asked.

"We are superior," JJ replied. "You haven't seen a horse using a computer or a dog driving a car, have you?"

"I love my horse, always will," Ruth said, "but then I've had Gus for years. Maybe you haven't had Royal Captain long enough to appreciate him."

"You're all confusing the real meaning of love," JJ said, "and besides, you've surely heard the term anthropomorphism."

"Of course," I said, "but we're not talking about assigning human qualities to animals. We're talking about loving them for who and what they are. When a horse saves your life a few times, you think of him or her as more than an animal to saddle and dominate. I think of Phantom as a friend, a partner."

JJ slapped her chest. "Gag me. Animals are meant to serve and be used, not cuddled."

Dawn looked up from the sketchpad she'd taken out after dinner. "You're being a bitch for no reason."

I glanced over and watched her fingers move, enlivening the page with feathered greenery. Her intricate sketch depicted each branch, each pine needle of Bow's ponderosa that we were all sitting under.

"That's beautiful," I told her. "Bow would've loved it."

Ruth leaned over to look, too. "Elizabeth always said you were a wonderful artist."

"She did? Said I was wonderful?" Dawn sounded surprised.

JJ sneered. "Oh, sure. Dawn is so damn perfect, makes me puke. All she ever does is sit around with stupid paintbrushes or whatever, showing off."

Dawn slammed the colored pencil she held into the ground, burying half of it in the forest duff.

"You're destined to live alone. No one can stand being around you. I should feel sorry for you."

JJ glared. "Go to hell. You can't even keep that wimpy husband of yours, and your kids don't want to live with you, either."

Dawn jerked back as though JJ had slapped her. "I hate you! I've always hated you!"

"Stop it this instant, both of you!" Ruth said. "Pray to the Lord for guidance. You are sisters, not enemies!"

I was sick of these women. Ruth's holier-than-thou manner, JJ's bitchiness, Dawn's moodiness. So far, they'd all reacted to challenges as expected, nothing standing out to make suspicions focus on one or the other. Audrey remained cooperative and helpful, but too damn perfect. Blatant greed tarnished Ruth's holy halo. Even without liquor, JJ's demeanor seldom varied from demanding and irritable, while Dawn bounced from talkative to withdrawn.

I couldn't imagine any of them killing Bow, but I was hampered by the difficulty of recognizing violence due to familiarity. The only facts so far included JJ's horrid killing of the two foals, and even though I'd verified that she was in Denver on the day Bow died, she and Simpson were partnered in some way. But why had Simpson warned me about JJ, and why was Simpson out here? Then came Ruth's altering of B&D Tack books which pointed to greed and possibly more. I was too fond of Audrey and too protective of Dawn to be objective about either of them. I needed to step back mentally, apply fresh perspectives.

Thunder rumbled in the distance. The sky above was clear, but dark clouds clung low on the horizon.

I leaned toward Ruth, asked if she'd given JJ another tranquilizer. She nodded, whispered that she'd made sure JJ swallowed it. As much as I wished JJ and Dawn would calm down, I felt sorry for them. They could be helping each other, supporting instead of bickering. But the pattern began years ago and seemed unlikely to change.

Ruth ran a finger through her short hair. "We've lost sight of what this trip is about. If we listen to God, He will show us the way." As usual, Ruth's messages were right on, just delivered in a sanctimonious way.

"I don't care what you think, old lady," JJ said.

"Shut up, JJ, just shut up," Dawn said.

"God loves you both, no matter what," Ruth said. "And knowing someone cares is as necessary as breathing."

"Yes," Dawn muttered, "or there's nothing to live for."

"You both need to pray, ask God to forgive you."

"Dawn and I hate each other," JJ said. "Can God forgive us that?"

Audrey had kept quiet, but now she shook her head. "You two are sisters, yet you hate each other? What a shame."

"Speaking of shame," JJ said. "You killed the foals, Audrey."

I couldn't let that one go. "Shut up, JJ."

Dawn's jaw dropped. "Someone killed Bow's foals?"

"Yes, but it wasn't me," JJ said.

"Dear God," Ruth said, turning to me. "Who was it, Margo?"

Everyone stared at me. I shook my head.

"Audrey wouldn't do that. It had to be you, JJ," Dawn said, her voice quiet. "You did it."

Raindrops cut short an admission of guilt that should never have been shared.

I insisted Ruth swallow another pain pill and then Audrey and I helped her into the bigger tent. I gave JJ another tranquilizer, but she'd already said too much. Her sleeping bag was on one side of Ruth, Dawn's on the other. I offered to let Dawn sleep with Audrey, but she said she'd be fine next to Ruth.

Audrey and I pulled on ponchos and ran to cover the horses and donkeys with rain sheets. Finally, she and I ducked into the smaller tent. Usually, I fell asleep the moment I snuggled into a warm sleeping bag. Not tonight, though. I wasn't about to take any chances on something bad happening. I'd slipped the Glock inside my jacket pocket earlier. Now I was both glad and sorry that I had it. The damn thing felt far heavier symbolically then it did in reality.

Audrey appeared to fall asleep right away, while I lay there listening to water pinging off the nylon fabric that kept us dry, hoping the next day would be better. As if in reply, lightning crackled, followed by shadows that roamed over the tent, silently sinister.

CHAPTER THIRTY

N O MATTER WHAT THEY'RE made of or how often they're cleaned, tents always smell faintly of dirty socks and musty cloth. The smells of past trips linger, partly embedded in nylon, partly in memory. If I closed my eyes, I could pretend that Bow slept next to me, pretend everything was back to normal.

But no. There was no going back, no normal, not even if Bow was alive. I knew too much now about Bow, about Dad. Even worse, I knew too much about myself and how poorly equipped I was to deal with this new reality.

Distant thunder rumbled again and again, giving way to the sound of steady rainfall, which usually lulled me to sleep. Audrey remained still, unmoving, her breathing steady. I kept my eyes open, determined not to doze off. I needed to keep watch. Finally, I rose, bleary-eyed, pulled on boots and breeches, then the jacket with the Glock. Covering myself with the poncho, I slipped quietly out into the rain. The ground had turned to mud, and I sloshed over to the next tent, peeked inside. JJ, Dawn, and Ruth all appeared to be sleeping, but I had a bad feeling about both JJ and Dawn. Their relationship had deteriorated from bitter to toxic.

I had to keep an eye on them.

The horses and donkeys stood quiet, necks lowered, rain sheets in place. No point in disturbing them and, if I approached, Maynard might bray loud enough to awaken everyone.

Walking in the muck was unpleasant, and there was nowhere to go, anyhow, so I huddled under Bow's ponderosa and covered myself as best I could with the poncho. It seemed like I sat there forever, but periodic glances at my watch revealed that it was only midnight. The time passed slowly. At 1:43 a.m. I got up, stretched, and moved around a bit before hunkering down again. I thought about Bow and the choices she'd made, but mostly I thought about Roy, about the choices I could make when he returned. I imagined wearing white, looking into Roy's eyes, making promises about forever. By 3:35 a.m. the rain had lessened to a drizzle, but my legs were numb with cold and my back was spasming something fierce. I crept back into the tent beside Audrey and snuggled into my sleeping bag, intending only to warm up.

The next thing I knew, darkness was transitioning into the grey of early morning and dew paraded across the tent walls. It was 5:03 a.m. I rubbed my eyes and rolled over. Audrey remained asleep. It felt so tempting to close my eyes again, but I shouldn't have slept at all.

I grabbed my jacket, exited the tent, and glanced toward the horses.

They were gone.

The rain had ceased, but fog hung low and dense, the storm's aftermath. I blinked, staring into the mist. The tie-line was there, but no horses, no donkeys.

I reached into my jacket, withdrew the Glock, and sloshed through mud to the next tent. The inside looked as orderly as possible for three occupants in close quarters.

But only the middle sleeping bag was occupied.

"Ruth! Wake up!" I shouted.

I hurried back to my tent, calling out to Audrey.

"Wake up! Now!"

"What? What happened?" Audrey said, emerging, rubbing her eyes.

"Horses are gone, JJ and Dawn too," I said. "Check on Ruth, tell her to stay put but get her gun out. Then help search. I'll head left, you go right."

I didn't wait for her reply, just ran out to the tie-line. Pieces of lead rope dangled from each place the five horses and two donkeys had been tied. The animals hadn't pulled free, they'd been cut loose. Mounds of mud-splattered blue nylon marked spots where each had shed loosely secured rain sheets. The ground was a mess of black glop churned by hooves.

"Dawn! JJ!" I called, as loudly as I could.

Where could they be?

My heart was racing, thoughts jumbled. Muddy hoofprints indicated the horses left in a hurry and took off in several directions, into the surrounding forests.

Who cut them free, and why?

Dim sunlight illuminated the fog, but the swirling gray made it impossible to see clearly in any direction. I kept shouting, first for JJ, then Dawn, but the only answer came from a scolding squirrel. Finally, the unmistakable bray of a donkey. I hustled up a hill toward the sound and found Maynard and Mabel, grazing. Maynard lifted his head and called softly to greet me, and then both lowered their heads to the grass.

The forest held tight to its secrets.

I left the donkeys and rushed on, zigzagging around rock outcrops and dense pines until I came upon first one horse, then another, both munching grass in a small clearing. One was Royal Captain, the other, Hawk. Each still wore a halter with short pieces of lead rope dangling. Phantom, Two Bits and Gus must've run in the opposite direction.

Still no sign of JJ or Dawn.

I was gathering the thoroughbred and the pinto when someone screamed once, and then again. I considered climbing on one of the horses. Riding bareback was no problem and even riding in a halter might've worked, but the lead ropes were too short to hang on to. Besides, the screams came from below me, through dense forest. I'd make better time on foot. I let go of the horses.

Clutching my gun and peering into the fog, I moved over logs and around trees, making my way down the hillside.

The screams came from the direction of camp.

"No! Oh my God!" The voice was female, husky, not far away.

Whoever it was sounded familiar, but it wasn't one of the other women in my group. I cocked the gun and crept forward, peering into the fog from behind one tree to the next.

The valley's small stream curved over the forest floor before flowing into the meadow. There, in heavy fog, was a woman bent over a body.

I moved closer, gun out. "Stand up, turn around, slow."

The woman faced me. "She's dead, oh God, she's dead."

"You!" I said, frowning, pointing the Glock at Carla Simpson.

"I just got here, just found her!"

"Like you found Bow! Hands up, move away. Now!"

She did as she was told.

I looked past her to the body, saw short spikey hair. JJ lay face down in the water, her body flattened in mud. Blood darkened her white flannel top, pooled in the water.

I straightened up. I had the gun in one hand, still trained on Simpson. I grabbed the satellite phone from my pocket with the other hand, called the sheriff. He listened, said the helicopter was available, they'd leave right away.

Simpson heard my end of the conversation.

"I didn't kill her, Margo! I didn't!"

Keeping the gun on Simpson, I leaned down, touched JJ's shoulder, gently, half-hoping she would turn her head, look at me.

I knew better.

I pressed two fingers into JJ's neck, feeling for a pulse that wasn't there. Death had claimed her, blanketing her with icy cold. Her eyes, open and glassy, stared into eternity. I got to my feet.

"Turn around, move toward that tree," I said, pushing Simpson ahead of me to where the horses had been. Quickly, I dismantled one end of the tie-line and secured Simpson to the tree.

"This is wrong," she said. "Let me help."

"Shut up," I said, making sure she couldn't break loose.

"I knew you were headed here when I saw you yesterday," she began, pausing to inhale a deep breath. "I was worried that JJ would do something else, but... It was too dark to continue, so I camped, rode in this morning."

I gave her a look, said nothing.

"My gelding is right over there, still hot."

I glanced away, saw her gray horse blending into the fog. He was breathing fast, his coat appeared lathered with sweat.

"Poor JJ," she said, her voice shaky. "Who did this?"

Nothing made sense. She might be telling me the truth, but I wasn't taking chances, especially with her.

If this was some sort of competition, death was winning.

First Bow, then Helen, now JJ.

Julie Jacobs could be a pain in the butt, but she didn't deserve to die. Dawn was as close to a sister as I'd ever gotten, besides possibly Audrey. What if Simpson killed Dawn too? What if Dawn killed her sister? Bile rose in the back of my throat. Was I smart enough to stop yet another murder, or had it already happened? I shouldn't have lain down last night. The Glock remained in my hands, powerful and yet useless. The gun couldn't distinguish the guilty from the innocent. Neither could I, not yet.

Maybe Simpson was telling the truth. Kelsey was in jail. If Simpson was innocent, that left the other women. Ruth was in her tent, barely able to walk, or was she pretending? Preposterous. She fell off the ledge. Audrey appeared to be asleep, but what if she wasn't so perfect after all?

Where was Dawn?

I had to find her.

And the other horses: Gus, Two Bits. And Phantom.

Still holding the gun, I moved back into the forest, looking for Dawn, for the horses. I hadn't gone far when Audrey came trotting up on Two Bits, Gus in tow. She rode bareback and had hold of what remained of the horses' lead ropes.

"Where've you been?" I asked, making sure she saw my gun.

"I found these two grazing not far away, got on and rode in when I heard someone screaming."

"What about the others?"

She shook her head. "Have not seen Dawn or JJ. The fog is too thick to see much. Did you find anyone?"

"Someone killed JJ."

Audrey gasped. "Oh, dear God, no!"

She sounded innocent. I wanted to believe she was.

"Simpson is tied up near camp," I said.

"What is she doing here?"

"No idea. Found her standing over JJ."

Audrey gasped again, hand over her mouth. "Where's Dawn?"

"Don't know. I saw Royal Captain and Hawk grazing in a clearing nearby. I don't know about Phantom." But the main thing I didn't know at this moment was whether I could trust anyone, even Audrey.

Morning sun seared through the fog, lighting both forest and meadow, but beauty felt ominous now. I looked at Audrey, wavered, but said, "Keep looking. Holler if you find Dawn or Phantom."

CHAPTER THIRTY-ONE

I RETRACED MY STEPS, calling out to Dawn, but my voice was the only sound. Finally, Phantom's unmistakable black rump came into view near the top of a small hill. I started running, calling out to my mare. She turned to me, but slowly and without whinnying like usual. I rushed to her side. The mare took one small step toward me.

Blood caked on her neck, splotched over her shoulder.

"No! No!"

The red glob made it impossible to tell where the injury was or how bad it might be. The blood appeared too dark to be arterial. I ripped off my jacket and pressed it against her neck, felt for a pulse under her wide jaw. She snorted and pulled away, her breathing faster than normal.

"No!" Phantom going into shock.

Frantic, I reviewed everything about emergencies, about resuscitation. I always brought first-aid kits, one for humans, the other for horses, knew how to use everything, bandages, wraps, ointments, even suture. But the kits were in Maynard's pannier, not here, not now. Besides, I could only do so much.

"Hang on, girl, hang on," I chanted, unable to keep the panic from my voice.

This felt surreal, dark, a nightmare. I had to stop this, roll back time, something. I rocked back and forth, stroking her.

"I love you, Phantom, I love you," I sobbed.

Crying wouldn't help, neither would panic. But I felt helpless, so helpless.

Part of the mare's mane was matted with dark red. Maybe the wound was up high. I felt around, my hands covered in dark blood, but found no source of bleeding.

I closed my eyes, fighting hysteria, losing to it.

Phantom and I, alone, stranded on a dark island of mist. Angry waves crashed, dissolving everything, coming for us. No hope, no return.

My Phantom, bleeding to death as I stood beside her, powerless.

Someone was moaning; it must've been me.

Suddenly, something hit me from behind. I stumbled, reached out to keep from falling. It was no use. I fell as if in slow motion, my vision blurring, then going dark.

It seemed like only seconds but there was no telling how long I lay there before opening my eyes.

Dawn stood over me, a knife in her hand.

She was smiling in a way that made me gasp. Bright red blood patterned the front of her clothing, her hands, her arms.

"You... What happened?"

She stared at me, then down at oozing cuts on her wrists. "I let the demons out."

I rolled onto my side away from her, sat up.

Dawn kept watching me, not moving, just holding that knife.

I stood up, feeling dizzy. "What? What did you say?"

"The demons, the demons."

I eased myself backward, reached in my pocket for the Glock, left it there, hidden.

"You cut yourself?"

She wobbled, looked like she might fall, but didn't. "They told me to."

"You're hurt, Dawn, you're bleeding."

"Yes, blood."

My jaw dropped. "What about JJ?" I managed to ask, knowing the answer, dreading it.

"That bitch killed the foals."

"Oh, Dawn, no."

"That bitch killed the foals," she repeated, frowning.

"You killed her," I muttered, more to myself than to Dawn. I felt suddenly dizzy. "And Phantom? Did you stab her too? Did you?"

She looked at me. "You sound mad."

"Please tell me!" I said, swaying, afraid of falling deeper into this hell masquerading as reality. "Tell me what you did to Phantom."

Dawn frowned. "You love the horse. No one loves me."

I kept an eye on Dawn, turned just enough to check on Phantom. The mare was grazing now, her tail swishing side to side. The dark blood on her neck appeared clotted, but the injury underneath might be serious.

"Did you stab Phantom?"

"My mother taught me never to hurt an animal."

"Yes, but Helen—"

"Helen is not my mother."

"She raised you."

"I couldn't be her daughter, couldn't be JJ's sister. They were wrong for me. You knew that, knew it just like I did. Twenty days ago, the truth came." She paused, a faraway look in her eyes. "I grew inside of Bow when she was seventeen, but Helen stole me, pretended to be my mother."

I opened my mouth, but no words came. According to Ruth, Bow had been sent over to Denver at the age of fifteen, and again several times later. Ruth told me that Dawn was adopted but didn't know the identity of her birth mother. I could barely breathe.

"You...oh no." I paused, shaking. "What have you done?"

"I do what they tell me," she said, her eyes wide, unfocused. "What they tell me."

"They? Who?"

"They talk. Listen, Margo, listen."

The look on Dawn's face transformed her into someone I no longer knew.

"Oh my God," I said, trembling. I knew she was depressed, that she'd been off kilter, but she'd talked about a divorce. "Oh, you're —"

Dawn threw back her head, waving the knife back and forth like an orchestral conductor, laughing in a way that gave me chills.

I looked, gasped. "You... That is Bow's knife."

"No! My knife. Mine! I do what they tell me."

I glanced at Phantom. "Are they, uh, do you hear them now?"

"I hear when they talk."

"Please tell me what you did to Phantom. Please, Dawn."

She smiled, stepping closer, loosening her grip on the knife but not letting it fall. "I sat on her."

"What about Bow?" I asked, holding my breath.

She frowned. "She didn't want to be my mother."

"You rode out to Rim Rock Cliffs with her, didn't you, Dawn?"

She began to sob. "She didn't want to be my mother. She loved Audrey," she said, her voice rising. "Audrey is my real sister." She staggered forward. "JJ hated me. Bow didn't want to be my mother."

She moved closer, raised the knife.

"The voices love me. They tell me what to do."

"You and I...like sisters," I whispered. But this woman standing in front of me now was a stranger.

"You don't love me; you just love the horse. Bow didn't want to be my mother. She didn't love me. She wanted to fall."

"Oh, Dawn."

"I do what they tell me."

"You've had Bow's knife all this time."

"It is mine. Mine!"

She staggered again, looked pale. She had multiple cuts, still oozing. She looked about to fall, but suddenly straightened up, lunged at me.

I jumped to one side, but not before the knife sliced my upper arm; blood spurted. I grabbed her wrist, squeezed hard.

The knife fell to the ground.

She reached for it, but I kicked it down the hill.

"No!" she screamed, and slugged me in the face, hard.

I stepped back, my nose bleeding. I wavered, almost losing my balance. Before I could recover, she threw herself at me like a battering ram, knocking me into Phantom. I crumpled to my knees, nose dripping red, arm bleeding. The mare tossed her head and trotted a short distance away.

"You don't love me, Margo. Bleed, then, bleed!"

She lunged again, and I couldn't believe her strength. She kicked me and grabbed my hair, yanking so hard my eyes watered.

I'd used my jacket to apply pressure to Phantom's neck, so was only wearing a shirt now. I pulled the hem up, swiped the blood from my nose, jerked back, away from her. Then I fell to my knees before springing up to face her, legs spread and arms out, ready. I still had my gun. I could use it, make her pay for what she'd done.

But this was Dawn. Despite everything, this was still Dawn.

She came at me again, arms flailing, legs kicking like a toy soldier gone berserk. She was out of breath now, sweat beading her forehead. Dawn looked pale, but beyond reasoning with, and nowhere near giving in. Despite all the blood she must have lost, she somehow had the strength of ten women. Subduing her would take everything I had.

I grabbed her hand, reached for the other, but she screamed, bent forward and bit my arm, drawing blood. I gritted my teeth and tightened the hold on her one hand.

"Damn you all, damn you all, damn you all," she chanted, kicking, connecting with my shin. Her face was scarlet, her pupils dilated.

Without warning, she went limp.

I kept hold of her, eased her to the ground and quickly looked over the front of her. Her arms had multiple cuts and so did her abdomen, but as near as I could tell, the bright red blood came only from the right wrist. I removed my belt, snugged it above her wrist until the flow ceased. Her eyes were closed, her pulse rapid. She appeared to be going into shock, either physical or mental. Probably both. She was flat on the ground, so I moved her legs up onto a nearby log to make them higher than her heart.

Suddenly, her eyes opened and focused on me.

"My pretend mother never loved me," she whispered.

"Pretend mother," I repeated. "Helen?"

"They said let her bleed," she said, her voice so soft I could barely hear.

"Oh my God," I said.

She closed her eyes, sighed deeply.

I needed to get back to Phantom, but I couldn't leave Dawn alone. I needed to cover her, keep her warm, but the blankets were back at camp. I called out for Audrey as loud as I could, but there was no reply.

What I did hear in the distance was the steady thumping of helicopter blades. The distinctive whirring was moving closer, bringing the sheriff, bringing help. As the sound grew louder, Phantom moved farther away but remained within sight. There was a clearing nearby and I raced over to it, waving my arms overhead.

The helicopter lowered and I rushed back to Dawn.

Sheriff Plackmon emerged, followed by two paramedics. I took a deep breath, felt tears gathering.

"Pressure bandages, a blanket!" I yelled over the noise.

The sheriff nodded and the paramedics rushed over. They kneeled, began a flurry of bandaging starting with a pressure wrap on the right wrist, started an IV, EKG, oxygen, the full routine. There'd been no chance to check her thoroughly, but now they rolled her over. She groaned, but her back looked clear. Then came a green blanket.

Dawn's eyelids fluttered.

"Margo?" she whispered. "I'm ready."

I leaned close, my hand on her shoulder. "I'm here, Dawn."

"Bring the knife," she said.

Sheriff Plackmon stared at her. "This one? The quiet one?"

I nodded. "Bow, Helen, and JJ too."

His eyes widened; his face lost every trace of his usual cop's "no reaction." He pulled a white handkerchief from his pocket, handed it to me. "You're bleeding too, Margo."

"Not bad," I said, although there'd been no chance to look.

I kept my eyes on Dawn while one of the paramedics saw to my arm, inserted a few stitches.

Dawn didn't seem aware of anyone but me. She reached for my hand. I started to pull back, afraid she'd get wild again, but she grabbed my fingers, her grasp weak.

"I'm ready to die," she whispered.

"You're not going to die," I said, hoping it was true.

"They want you to bring the knife, plunge it into my heart. I've already painted that scene in my mind."

Tears clouded my vision. "Oh, Dawn. No. Shhh."

"They say I must die! I want to die; don't you hear them? I lied too, just like the others."

I was sobbing now, gasping. I looked from the sheriff to the paramedics.

"She... Dawn needs help."

Sheriff Plackmon put his hand on my shoulder.

"I had to, I..." Dawn murmured, barely audible. She tried to throw off the blanket, to sit up, but her eyes closed and once again she went limp.

Audrey rode up on Two Bits, dismounted, rushed over. She and Ruth had heard the chopper, of course.

"Oh no! What happened?"

"Dawn," I began, "she... Oh, Audrey, Bow was Dawn's birth mother too. She felt so unloved."

"She's my sister, then, my real sister. But please no, she didn't—"

I reached for Audrey's hand, couldn't say it, couldn't say out loud what her sister had done.

"JJ too, last night," I finally whispered, "and even Helen."

"Oh, little sister." Audrey sobbed, hugging Dawn, stroking her forehead. "Oh Dawn, oh no."

The paramedics took her blood pressure every few minutes. Dawn remained motionless, eyes closed, skin pale.

"Will she...survive?" I asked.

One of the paramedics looked at me. "She's lost a lot of blood, needs a transfusion. We'll transport soon, directly to Grand Junction."

I nodded.

"I have to check my mare," I told Audrey. I ran back to Phantom. I'd kept my eye on her as much as I could while dealing with Dawn. There was no fresh blood on her neck, only the same dark clotted mess. Maybe, just maybe, this was all Dawn's blood rather than the mare's. If Dawn had sat on Phantom, bleeding from her own cuts, maybe the mare was not injured at all. I pressed two fingers against the carotid artery under my mare's jaw. Her pulse was a normal forty-eight beats per minute, strong and regular. A good sign.

The sheriff came up beside me, frowned at the dark mass on the mare's neck. "What happened?"

"Not sure," I sobbed."

"Where is the deceased woman?"

"Down by the creek, not far," I said, pointing. "And Carla Simpson showed up this morning. I found her standing over JJ's body. Thought she was involved, at first."

"I can understand why," he said.

"She might be indirectly implicated in the foals' deaths."

"I'll keep that in mind," he said, and left to find JJ.

Audrey ran up to me. "Is Phantom hurt?"

"I need to wash her neck," I said. "Please come."

We led Phantom to the creek, not far from where the sheriff bent over JJ's body.

"I don't see any cuts," I said after quickly cleaning as much as I could. "So, the blood is probably all Dawn's."

"Poor Dawn. When did you know she...was the one?"

I bit my lip. "I was more suspicious of JJ. And then Simpson appeared, standing over JJ's body. Dawn acted weird at times, talked about feeling unloved, but I had no idea she heard voices."

I couldn't imagine what would happen to her. She'd probably spend the rest of her days in a psychiatric hospital. I wondered if they'd let her pick up a sketchpad and paints, wondered if Jason and the boys would visit.

Ruth had dressed, hobbled out of the tent, and kept her gun aimed at Carla Simpson until I approached. I told them both about Dawn, about what'd happened to JJ. I untied Simpson just as the paramedics were transporting a now awake but very subdued Dawn on a stretcher toward the chopper. I told the sheriff where to find Bow's knife.

After he photographed JJ's body and the surrounding scene, he enclosed her in a body bag and carried her to the chopper. They offered to take our camping gear, but I wasn't sure yet if we should stay here one more night, and besides, we had the donkeys to carry things. I did give them one of the tents, Dawn's and JJ's sleeping bags, and their saddles and bridles.

They offered to take Ruth, but she insisted on staying and said she was certainly able to ride back, so the paramedics splinted her leg.

"You're all tough women, but be careful on the ride back," the sheriff said, before climbing aboard the chopper. I raced over to Phantom to calm her when the noise began, while Audrey and Ruth watched the other animals. The door closed, engine revved, and the thing hovered just above the ground, then lifted.

"Poor JJ," Simpson said, as the four of us watched the helicopter rise above the treetops, then higher still before turning out of sight. "I'll miss her. She asked me not to tell you, but she was studying to become a real estate agent."

I nodded. "I knew."

"Oh? Well, she did agree that developing her aunt's ranch would be a financially sound decision."

"So, you gave her some sort of incentive to help the process along?"

"I promised her a bonus if she convinced Bow to sell."

I squinted at her. "Did you know that JJ not only let one of the foals die without helping it, but also smothered the next one to death?"

"She told me about doing that just before all of you left for this ride," Simpson said. "That's why I rode out here, to make sure nothing happened. But I was too late. I thought JJ was the one—"

"Did she tell you that she arranged for a bogus toxicity test to make sure Bow felt she had to sell?"

Simpson looked startled. "What are you talking about?"

"The bonus you offered her must've been substantial," I said.

"I didn't expect JJ to do anything but talk to Bow. I had no hand in generating any reports at all, nor did I suggest harming those foals in any way." She paused, looked at me. "You still don't believe me, do you?"

I shrugged. "I know about Don Kelsey's litigation regarding subsurface rights."

"Bow didn't own subsurface rights. Most people don't. Sam Connolly was an exception, so his land was worth much more. Look, Margo, I don't participate in schemes, only legitimate acquisitions. I go after what I want, drive hard bargains, but I'm a businesswoman, not a crook."

"No matter if that's true or not, I still hold you partly responsible for the foals' deaths. And that played a part in Bow's death, even JJ's death."

"Nothing I say will change your mind, but I am sorry about all of this. I'll take Royal Captain, pony him back, leave him in Bow's barn."

"He's a handful."

"My gelding knows him. They were stabled next to each other in Denver, let out to graze together. He'll travel calmer with me."

"I saw him and my pinto in a clearing not far from here."

"I'll go collect them."

I nodded. My mind was still on Phantom. I grabbed a towel, led the mare back to the creek and washed her thoroughly, holding my breath. There were no cuts, not one, and she was no longer limping, either, meaning yesterday's stone bruise was mild. I felt faint with relief.

Before long, Simpson rode up holding onto a new lead line she'd put on Royal Captain's halter. Hawk and the donkeys followed, pausing now and then to snatch mouthfuls of grass.

Audrey and I secured Hawk and the donkeys. We offered to feed Simpson and let the horses rest before they set out for home, but she was anxious to make time and had brought her own food.

She might be innocent after all, but I still disliked her and was glad to see her leave.

Audrey and I sat down near Ruth, who looked like she was in pain. For the first time in all the years I'd known her, she looked fragile, elderly.

"We could stay here one more night, how about that, Ruth?" I wanted to stay here forever and yet not for another minute.

"No, I'm ready to head home."

"Are you really up for a long ride today?"

"Yes, indeed," Ruth replied.

I looked at her, knew that despite her injury and her age, she was tough, capable. I turned to Audrey.

"Let's pack up first, and then we'll do what we came here for."

Audrey nodded, silent, her eyes as red as mine.

I felt sorry for her most of all. Audrey found her birth mother only to lose her. She'd grown close to Dawn in a very short time without knowing she was her sister. I'd thought of Dawn as a sister, too, once. And then there was JJ. She'd done bad things, but she didn't deserve to die. No one is all bad. JJ loved her mother, took care of her despite Helen's lack of maternal warmth. Now Helen was gone, too.

As for Bow, I'd considered her almost perfect, an ideal to strive towards, but I'd been forced to realize that she had faults like the rest of us. Bow was only human. Someday soon, I'd write more to Bow, tell her I would never stop loving her. And later, I'd try to come to terms with Dad. Some day.

First, though, I had myself to contend with. I should've known, should've done something to save Bow, to save JJ, to help Dawn. I'd been so blinded by my own bubble of existence that my eyes were closed to everyone else's realities.

So much to grasp, to believe, to deal with. Which reminded me of Roy Holden. I closed my eyes, imagining his arms around me, holding me close. He was still in New Zealand, of course. But when he returned, I'd hug the stuffing out of him, and then I'd let him know that while I'd never be the type for diamonds, plain gold bands would fit just right on the ring fingers of his hand and mine.

"Margo Holden," I whispered, "Mr. and Mrs. Holden."

Meantime, five of us rode out here, but only three remained to spread Bow's ashes, bid her a final goodbye. I insisted Ruth take a pain pill, and then Audrey and I cleared out the one remaining tent, loaded the panniers on the donkeys, and saddled Two Bits, Gus, and Phantom.

Ruth hobbled around, doing more than she should've.

"I put the ashes under the tree," she said, "so whenever we're ready."

Audrey and I joined Ruth under Bow's ponderosa. The huge branches cast dappled shade over an expanse of meadow. Bow and I had enjoyed this shade many times, sharing picnics and each other's company. If I closed my eyes, I could see Phantom and Bandit nearby, grazing, waiting to carry us home.

But I didn't let my eyes close, not now. I had to face reality.

"Right. Let's do this."

Audrey reached over to hug me, and we both sobbed.

Ruth hugged each of us, crying too.

"You and I haven't been all that close," she told me, "but I know how much Elizabeth loved you. I did things I shouldn't have with the B&D books."

I patted her shoulder. "It's okay, Ruth. Bow would've wanted you to have the entire tack store, and I do too. But it's up to Audrey, Bow's daughter."

"I just wanted to know her better," Audrey sobbed.

"She always loved you, though," I said, "I just know she did."

Ruth nodded. "Yes, Bow surely loved you, Audrey, and Dawn too, right from the time each of you were born."

"Oh, Ruth," Audrey said, sobbing more, "I was so happy to meet her. No wonder I felt drawn to Dawn, and to you too, Margo."

"We're all connected by something stronger than blood. We're a strange family now," I said.

"And we'll do what we can for Dawn," Audrey whispered.

I could only nod. I picked up the box of ashes, opened it.

"Here you are, then, Bow. It hasn't been the peaceful trip we'd intended, but at last you're here."

"We miss you, Elizabeth," Ruth said. "We miss you so much. May God keep you and raise you up to heaven."

I began sprinkling ashes under the tree. It was hard to believe these silvery flakes were really Bow. The remains of her flesh and bones might be here, but not her smile, not her wisdom, her spirit. So much to say, no words sufficient.

"The essence of you lives on," I said, handing the box to Audrey, who sprinkled more, then passed the ashes to Ruth.

"I'm so glad I found you, Bow," Audrey said, tears streaming down her face.

I reached into my pocket, withdrew strands of Bandit's mane, and tossed them into the air, letting them twirl and float down to rest on top of the ashes.

We stood in silence.

There'd been signs about Dawn that I saw but hadn't put together soon enough. The silences, the times I'd thought she was merely depressed. And over in Denver, both Dawn's neighbor and her artist friend indicated that Dawn had changed recently.

I'd tried without success to contact Jason and see if he really was divorcing her, but he and the boys were out of cell phone range in Montana. Maybe he suspected she'd been hearing voices.

There was the way she reacted when Audrey revealed her identity, the drugs that masked what she'd almost certainly done to Audrey down at the barn, meaning Kelsey might be a jerk, but maybe he hadn't tried to strangle Audrey, not that time.

And on this ride, she'd screamed hysterically in the river, fainted at the elk calf's carcass. Then there were the drawings, the purple, gray, and black flowers she'd crumpled, then let float away. I'd attributed it all to her long-standing emotional fragility and an impending divorce, not realizing until too late that it was her disintegrating psyche.

I closed my eyes, imagined Dawn and Bow riding together. Bow knew she was Dawn's mother, of course. The two of them surely discussed it on Bow's last day. All Dawn could listen to was the voices.

What if things had been different? What if Bow had kept her daughters, raised Dawn and Audrey together? What if my parents hadn't died and I'd never gotten to know Bow well enough to consider her my second mother?

Life's trail, ever twisting, ever changing.

"One last thing," I said. I grabbed a small blue bottle from my saddlebag. Bow loved laughter, and she always brought a bottle of bubbles along to entertain us. There was no laughter now, but just for Bow, I dipped the wand and made as many bubbles as I could, filling the air with momentary rainbow orbs that danced and bobbed before disappearing, leaving only memories.

I turned to Audrey and Ruth. "Let's ride."

If we kept moving, we would be home before dark. Audrey and I helped Ruth up onto Gus's saddle. Audrey got on Two Bits and led Hawk. I rode Phantom and led the two donkeys.

In spirit at least, Bow would ride beside us always.

ACKNOWLEDGEMENTS

I thank every single person who has taken the time to comment on any page or portion of my writing.

A huge debt of gratitude goes to every author of the many books that have taken me places, taught me things, and made me want to be a writer. Next comes Dea Parkin of Fiction Feedback in Lancashire, UK, who facilitated a detailed and helpful critique followed by thoughtful copy and line edits. I'm also grateful to graphic designer Kim Sharp-leyba who serves as my webmaster and tech advisor. Thanks goes to Kim McElroy, the talented artist with Spirit Of Horse Gallery who graciously allowed me to present her 'Lessons From Horses' in the front of this book. Glen Edelstein of Hudson Valley Book Design is not only talented but also diligent about the details that make a cover come alive and is a pleasure to work with.

Finally, this book would never have gotten finished much less published if not for my beloved daughter, Jennifer, a talented artist and graphic designer. Throughout her life, she was my strongest supporter, my rock. I never thought her hugs would cease.

ABOUT THE AUTHOR

Lenore Mitchell's debut contemporary mystery, Dying To Ride, is book one of the Everything Equine Mystery Series and centers on a spunky female horse-trainer turned sleuth who manages her Colorado ranch amidst the interplay of human dysfunction and shocking revelations. But this story also promises moments of nature's tranquility and soothes with an abundance of horses, from wild mustangs to warmbloods.

Wild Ride, book two of the series, delves more into mustangs and the controversies surrounding them. Beginning chapters are included in the back of book one. Publication in late summer, 2023.

Although 'Horse Fever' infected Lenore early on, she rode only occasionally as a youngster and was twenty-six years old and the mother of a toddler when she bought her first horse. Most rides on Skipper began with a reluctant walk away from the stable followed by a whirl and gallop back home with her clinging on for dear life. That was a short-lived pairing, followed by many riding lessons on school horses. Then Babe came into Lenore's life, and eventually everything changed. A three-year-old drop-dead gorgeous chestnut Half Arab with four white socks and the sweetest floating trot imaginable. Sounds great, right? Except for the fact that Babe had never been ridden. Yikes! This could've gone, well, badly. But with riding lessons from a strict British horsewoman and an even stricter instructor with a thick German accent, Lenore mostly stayed in the saddle while Babe taught her about riding and about life. Beginning dressage and a little jumping followed. Then came the real riding. NATRC (North American Trail Conference) is all about long-distance competitive trail riding, mostly over challenging terrain. Babe and Lenore earned ribbons and life-long memories during well over a thousand competition miles, each ride sixty-miles over two days. Getting and staying in shape involved endless additional miles. When first one daughter and then the other reached eleven years of age, they joined her for rides. Naturally, they rode Babe and Lenore switched to one of her other horses. Throughout the many years Babe was with us, she earned her status as a 'one in a million mare.'

When not writing or dreaming about horses, Lenore is also an amateur botanist member of Colorado Native Plant Society and teaches Native Plant Master courses for Colorado State University Extension.

https://www.lenoremitchell.com

Coming
Summer 2023!

WILD RIDE

Everything Equine Mystery Series, Book Two

by Lenore Mitchell

CHAPTER ONE

EFORE THE MUSTANGS STARTED disappearing, I tried telling myself it was enough to catch occasional glimpses of them running free as the sky, wild as the wind. I loved horses, made my living giving riding lessons, training stout Quarter horses, leggy warmbloods, cute ponies. Margo Richards, Everything Equine was not only imprinted on my business cards but on my soul. But mustangs were unlike any animal I worked with, often tougher, smarter, surprisingly adaptable.

They deserved lush meadows under a warm sun. Reality spawned drilling rigs instead of grasses, threw fences around water holes. Reality came down to dollars, left out the sense.

The last straw was when the Bureau of Land Management on Colorado's Western slope issued a bulletin declaring that despite decreasing numbers of horses at Soda Creek Cliffs, half of the remaining animals would be removed before July fourth, a mere six weeks away. Drought, grazing rights, and energy extraction were cited as reasons, but the gist was clear. Mustangs made the sky too blue, the moon too bright. They sinned by having no financial reason to exist.

The wild horse refuge I'd long dreamt about finally seemed like a possibility as well as a legacy to several special human beings. After last year's death of my beloved foster mother, Elizabeth 'Bow' Bowan, her remaining daughter, Audrey Langford, inherited Bow's place and wanted the entire ranch used as a refuge. A generous donation from Sam Connolly, an old-time rancher, offered seed money. The plans Audrey and I had to provide a forever home for mustangs progressed from maybe never to maybe now. But stubborn obstacles remained.

Which was why my truck was parked outside the BLM office in Pinedale Springs on a blue-sky spring day, and I was inside confronting obstacle numero uno. Joe Gannon was a big guy, not so much tall as paunchy. A middle-aged, middle management sort with an over-sized plaque in the center of his desk proclaiming his importance: Joseph Herbert Gannon, Field Supervisor, Bureau of Land Management. Ever since his arrival only months ago, he'd taken advantage of every opportunity to whine that this little Colorado town was nothing but an outpost on the edge of civilization. It didn't matter to him that all of us locals considered this edge a fine place to live.

Gannon leaned forward in his impressive leather chair, placed elbows on his impressive desk, and scowled. "Like I said last time, Miz Richards, there's nothing more I can do."

Everyone calls me Margo. Miz sounded weird, like I'd suddenly aged from thirty-five to seventy-five. Whatever. "C'mon, Joe," I said, attempting a smile without much success. "Nothing more you can do or nothing more you will do! The BLM has a mandate to protect mustangs, including those at Soda Creek Cliffs."

His scowl deepened. "BLM land has many uses, and oversight of wild horses is just one aspect, a minor one at that."

I clinched my fists. "So, this enormous next roundup will proceed despite the already low numbers of mustangs. And what about the disappearances?"

"As you know, the next gathering is already scheduled. And you keep insisting horses are disappearing. But animals do die. You said that you've lived here on a ranch all your life. Surely you realize that horses don't live forever. Death is just nature taking it's course."

My turn to scowl. If there's one thing I can't tolerate, it's being lectured to in a condescending way. I may be female, I may be on the short side, and I may be so lacking in style that I hadn't bothered to change out of my usual breeches and paddock boots for this meeting. But surprise, surprise. I've got a brain. I've got a temper, too, but managed to take a deep breath and aim a tight smile that didn't reach my eyes in his direction before responding. "Surely, you realize that nature leaves carcasses, bones. Disappearances leave nothing but questions."

He sighed, putting some effort into it. "Do you even know how many are missing?"

"I do know."

"Well, then, give me a number."

"It's your job to know that number," I said, emphasizing the word job. There were at least six disappearances that I knew about.

"Now see here, Miz Richards, getting all huffy is not necessary."

I was tempted to provide a demo of huffy, but he wasn't worth the effort. I just shook my head. "You hate the mustangs, so why won't you authorize moving some of them to my private refuge?"

"Because those animals are on BLM land and under my jurisdiction."

I was on the verge of letting loose with a mouth-full of unlady-like but I held back. Mostly.

"WTF! The BLM wastes hellacious amounts of money on roundups and then maintaining mustangs in those damn holding pens. I'm offering to save the Feds money. Taking some horses off government hands is a favor to taxpayers, too."

"They say not everyone here agrees with your plans to turn the Bowan ranch into a refuge."

He was right about that. "True, but that doesn't bother me," I said even though it did. A lot. Not only did I have to convince the BLM, I also had to overcome the downright hostility some locals aimed my way. When it came to mustangs, tempers flared. Always had, always would. To some, wild horses symbolized the west, freedom. But others called them feral nags, considered them nothing but nuisances taking up space, depleting grasses needed for cattle, land suited for drilling.

Gannon stroked his chubby chin. "Best listen to those who oppose you. At any rate, you are wasting your time and mine. It is not going to happen, Miz Richards."

"Shit," I muttered, pushing back my chair and storming out. Patience never made it onto my skill set, except when it came to horses. Neither did sweet talking bureaucrats. Not everyone in the BLM hated mustangs, but Gannon was the local head honcho. I needed another plan. I needed allies, both inside and outside of the BLM. And soon. I had to establish the refuge before more mustangs disappeared and before the next huge roundup. Some BLM doodle-brains conjured up the sugar-coated term 'gatherings' instead of roundups, downplayed the use of low-flying helicopters, omitted inevitable injuries and deaths from reports.

I had no firm ideas why mustangs were disappearing without a trace, but that wasn't all. According to trusted sources, three foals died in the last roundup, trampled to death in the chaos as a helicopter stampeded thundering hooves toward catch pens. A mare and a yearling colt fell too, shattering legs. The BLM shot all of the injured on sight, leading to arguably more merciful ends than those destined to wallow in over-crowded holding pens the rest of their lives.

Outside the BLM office, I took a deep breath to attempt lowering my blood pressure and hoisted myself inside the truck. Zap and Fetch delivered the usual tail-wagging greeting. My one-ton dually broadcast my sour mood as we rumbled down Main Street. I considered stopping for a double-dip butter brickle at the corner of Main and 3'rd, but not today. Too riled. Always the happy dog, Fetch stuck his head out the passenger-side window, mouth open, tongue lolling while Zap cuddled beside me, dark eyes registering concern.

Both Border Collies were perceptive, but Zap soothed while Fetch entertained. Despite the dog's efforts, I fumed all through town, on past Morton's Auto Dealership and Smith's Hay & Grain to ten miles of dirt road and home.

The ranch where I grew up served as my hub for the collision of life's highs and lows. Anyone who's ever loved horses relates to that mystical feeling of being transported into their realm. As always, I slowed down while driving past the dozen or so horses in my front pasture. Most ignored me, but Phantom and Babe knew the sound of my truck. Both lifted their heads from lush May grasses and trotted toward the fence, inviting me to come stroke their velvet muzzles. Offering a snack was welcomed too, which was why I kept a bag of crunchy horse cookies in the back. I pulled over, loaded up my pocket and the dogs and I ducked inside the fence to spend a few minutes with my girls. Phantom, the sleek black mustang who'd proven herself way beyond expectations, approached first. Then came Babe, the fabulous Half-Arab chestnut who tolerated me as a kid and even now with greying muzzle, she wasn't yet done tutoring me about the link between horse and human.

A few minutes with these two mares rendered me mellow enough to face the rest of the day. Roy was in Salt Lake City, so he'd be home soon. We were now husband and wife, and the delight of our six-month union hadn't yet worn off. I still caught myself staring at the gold band on my ring finger with shock and amazement. I was a married woman, and Roy Holden was officially my man, not just the guy I lived with.

Keeping my last name seemed simpler for business reasons, and speaking of business, as much as I wanted to concentrate on establishing the refuge, that wouldn't pay the bills. There were horses to train, lessons to give, stalls to clean. I grabbed an apple and a handful of walnuts for lunch, picked up a baseball cap and headed to the barn.

I barely got inside before my cell rang.

"Stop messing with those mustangs or you'll be real sorry."

That was it. Short but not sweet. The voice was muffled, definitely male, but different from a foul-mouth who'd called two days ago and unleashed a string of expletives ending with something unpleasant about the horse I rode in on. I didn't say a word to either one, although I considered telling them to have a jolly good day and drop by soon for tea.

I proceeded to groom a skittish young mustang I'd be mounting for the first time today. This chestnut gelding, appropriately named Hotshot, was brought to me by one of the locals who favored these animals for stock work, once the wild was gentled out of them. The rancher was too smart and too rich to risk his own skin when he could wave a wad of cash under my nose and let me be the first human to get cozy with half a ton of unpredictable horseflesh. It paid to be cautious. I've trained enough horses to know that working with any youngster isn't for those intimidated by mangled muscles or broken pride.

The phone made noise again.

I was more intent on gathering my tack and my courage than on continued interruptions, and one threat per day seemed sufficient. Still, who knew, this might be a buyer for one of my horses or a client scheduling riding lessons.

"Margo Richards here," I said while continuing to groom Hotshot.

"Hi Margo," Jessica Parker said as if we'd spoken yesterday.

My fingers opened and a brush full of horsehair plunked onto the concrete floor. Zap and Fetch sprang up from curled slumber and rushed to my side, brown eyes alert.

The last things on my mind were yesterdays, former friends.

"It's been a long time, Jessica," I finally said.

"Yes, way too long. I've missed you so much. But we're always on the move. And things are... complicated."

Things always were, with Jessica. I lifted my baseball cap, swiped the back of one hand across my forehead, stuffed long hair behind my ears. And waited, silent.

"I need to...uh...this is awkward."

Hearing her voice again twisted the present into the past, a swirl of memories. I shook my head against a breathless inability to stop remembering the bond between us that seemed unbreakable until it shattered from neglect.

"Well, then," she said into the silence, "I can't blame you for being angry."

"It's... I'm not mad."

"You have every right, though. Life just, like, happens. Too busy, you know?"

I opened my mouth, wanted to say something profound. Busy, I understood, but still. From grade school on through college, we'd been besties, a duo. After college, she headed to Nashville and a recording contract while I returned to Pinedale and my ranch. We stayed in touch, for a while, first through calls, then Facebook, Instagram. But even those threads raveled amidst her changing contact info, impermanent addresses. I'd tried telling myself it wasn't a big deal, but it felt like one more loss.

Hotshot raised his head, snorted. Nothing like a spray of horse boogers to convey impatience. "I've got an antsy gelding here," I said, rechecking his crossties and murmuring "Easy now, easy, fella." Roy says I whisper those words in my sleep.

"I won't keep you," Jessica said. "I just...." She made a sound between a laugh and a groan.

I was tempted to groan myself. Time had suspended the ease between us, maybe erased it altogether. But something in her tone jolted me. "Is something wrong? Are you sick?"

"No, no. Nothing physical."

I exhaled, banishing half-formed visions of bandages, nurses with needles. Zap licked my hand and Fetch sat, fluffy tail working. I patted first one hairy head, then the other. Assured that no crisis existed, the dogs yawned and laid back down. "It's good to hear your voice. I just...I'm surprised. Hold on for a minute, let me put this gelding in a stall."

"Why don't I call back later."

"It's okay. Just give me a minute."

Hot shot wasn't yet used to standing tied very long. He was the type prone to sudden panic and the risk of having him pull back and get all hyped up would mean a setback and a delay in today's lesson. Within seconds, he was settled and safe.

"Ok, I'm back. What's up?"

"Well, for starters, I'm coming to Pinedale Springs for a concert."

"That's great! When?"

"Like soon, I hope. The sooner the better. I, well...."

"What? Tell me."

She sighed, loudly. "It's, like, complicated. To begin with, my career has, like, taken a nosedive. And then, well, there's some guy...a crazy fan, I guess. He calls, sends letters, like weird stuff. Didn't bother me at first."

"This guy is stalking you?"

I suppose, but it's under control, at least I think so. I'll tell you all about it when we get there."

I imagined seeing her again, wasn't sure how that might unfold. "Where are you now?"

"Heading for San Antonio, our next gig. We've been on the road for weeks."

"Sounds exciting."

"Used to be, back when it seemed like I might make it big. The bloom rubbed off, though. Now it's just a whole lot of work. I'm looking forward to seeing you, spending a few days in Colorado. I wrote a song about mustangs called 'Running Wild, Running Free.' It needs to debut there. And...I need your help."

"Mustangs can use positive publicity, especially around here, but you know that."

"Yes, of course. Which is why we need wild ones on an outdoor stage. Yours, of course."

"On stage? Mustangs? You can't be serious!"

"This is important, Margo. Might be the last song I'll ever write. I need one final triumph."

"What do you mean? Your songs are still on the radio, you're still on stage."

"Yeah, but like I said, it's complicated. My career isn't, well, it needs a boost." She paused. "Besides, I'm homesick, thought we could pick up where we left off."

I wasn't sure where we left off, what fragments of friendship remained.

"So, provide a few horses," she continued, "do this for me. You're still dreaming about a wild horse refuge, right?"

"It's more than a dream now, but not yet a reality. And my goal is to save mustangs, not jeopardize them."

"Now c'mon, Margo. Yours are, like, trained and all, right?"

"Some. Others haven't been handled much; some may never be. Besides, I have mostly Quarter horses. But even the mellowest breed wouldn't tolerate being on a stage in front of berserk crowds."

She sniffed. "I thought you'd help."

"What you're asking isn't reasonable. Why not show videos instead?"

"We're planning the big screen thing. We need real mustangs too, not some nags who wouldn't prick their ears if the stage burst into flames."

"I hate the word nags."

"I know you do. Sorry. But the audience, especially there, will know if the horses aren't genuine. And so will the press."

"The press?"

"Definitely. Publicity is crucial."

I imagined cameras, chaos. "You know enough about horses to realize what you're asking is, just, crazy."

She produced a dramatic sigh. "Are we friends or what?"

"I...now's not the time for this, Jessica."

"They'll only be on stage five minutes, that's all, and in a secure corral. They'll be fine. My new song is soft, mellow."

"Some people around here hate mustangs more than ever, want them gone."

"Hate them? Why?"

"Money. Drilling, cattle grazing and big game hunting are all profitable. Mustangs aren't."

"All the more reason to show your horses off, make people aware. Having them on stage will remind everyone how beautiful they are, how majestic."

"Being on stage in front of a crowd would scare the hell out of most horses."

"But don't you still train horses for movie producers?"

"Occasionally," I said, "but those are exceptionally quiet animals. Most of my horses have never been around bright lights, sudden noises."

"If anyone could train a few for this, it's you, Margo."

My turn to sigh. "Maybe," I muttered. As soon as I said that one word, I regretted it. I'd just turned absolutely not into something Jessica would run with.

"Make it three, no wait, five. And I'll donate a chunk of the proceeds from my concert toward this refuge of yours. Everyone wins."

"It's not that easy," I said. "The herds out there are in real trouble. Some animals are disappearing."

"What do you mean?"

"As in gone without a trace. No carcasses, no bones, nothing except hoof prints."

"That's horrible! Who's behind it?"

"Certain ranchers, possibly. Certain fossil fuel people, even more likely. BLM isn't helping. All driven by greed. And time is running out. I need to get out there again, check the herds."

"Take me with you. I'd love to come."

"It's a long ride, might be dangerous."

"Don't give me that. One of the reasons I'm coming home is to ride out into the wilderness again. I've ridden at Soda Creek Cliffs with you lots of times."

"That was years ago. Things are different now."

"The right publicity would help the mustangs."

I told her to call back in a few days, let me think about the mustang proposal. She had a point about the need for publicity. She also had the same old way of manipulating me. Even so, her idea had some merit. The world was full of horse-lovers, and the more of them who knew about the mustangs' plight, the better.

Then again, what the hell was I thinking.

No way would I jeopardize any horse no matter how much publicity resulted. But I'd let myself fall right into Jessica's trap. Her singing career might be wavering, but her talent for dramatic flair and for playing an old friend remained unchanged. I looked forward to seeing her again, but I wanted her visit to be low drama, for once.

Fat chance.

I saddled Hotshot, led the gelding to the round pen, put one foot and a bit of weight into a stirrup. He allowed it. I stroked his neck, murmuring low, and eased myself onto his back. Born wild, some mustangs adjusted surprisingly well to domestication. But Hotshot was the type who smoldered with resentment at the loss of freedom, this association with puny two-legged creatures. My job was to change his mind. A few circles around the perimeter would complete the chestnut's first mounted lesson.

Someone had other plans.

Halfway around, a yellow ball landed in the middle of the pen, scattering dust, bouncing high. Any horse would've been startled, but the gelding got downright pissed. He snorted, sidestepped, thrust his neck down despite my efforts to rebalance him. First two bucks weren't bad.

Then the little turd got serious. I landed face down, the ball inches from my dirt-encrusted eyes. The thing was the size of a basketball, but smooth and shiny. Someone had gone to the effort of writing a message on it to clarify that this wasn't some random bounce.

Good to know.

The scrawl suggested I should "Eat Shit and DIE." That final word was enlarged and rendered in red.

The penmanship was atrocious.

CHAPTER TWO

THERE'S NOTHING LIKE THE sound of a loud noise followed by cascading glass to jolt a person out of sound sleep at 2am. My feet hit the floor before my brain fully activated. I shuffled into slippers, half-running, half-stumbling in the dark out to the living room, shadowed by a pair of barking dogs.

Zap and Fetch earn their keep by herding stray horses every now and then, but mostly by keeping me company. They're loud, they're hairy, but fierce they're not. Intruders might get heavily licked or assaulted with dog breath. I shushed them, gave the sit and stay command. No sense risking cut paws.

I picked my way through glass shards to the window. Nothing to see. No strange vehicles, no movement. Maybe this was accidental, a rifle fired by some idiot hunter with bad eyesight or poor aim. Except this wasn't hunting season, to begin with.

I squinted into the darkness. Stars above, moon shadows below. The house was a good five hundred feet from the road. I turned on a lamp, scanned the room. Most of the front window had relocated onto the couch, glass fragments spilling onto the rug, a glittering unworkable puzzle. My housekeeping was casual at best, but glass shards added nothing to the decor.

I didn't see the rock at first, because the thing had rolled into a corner. I reached down, picked it up, half expecting to see a message written on it. But no, the thing careened through my window without comment. It was small enough to carry a ways, large enough to demolish glass.

I fished the handgun from the bottom of my underwear drawer, shoved a single bullet in, pulled on jeans and raced down to the barn with Zap and Fetch in tow. Nothing out of place, nor did the dogs sniff out anyone to bark at or slobber on. The pasture horses appeared unruffled too. Back at the house, I sent the dogs to the bedroom, swept up the worst of the glass, taped a sheet of plastic over the window and crawled back in bed. Didn't sleep, not that I expected additional visitors, but no guarantees. Just in case, though, I kept the gun within reach on my nightstand. I hated the cold power of it, the idea that something so small could inflict damage so permanent. I fired the thing rarely and only at paper targets because Roy insisted I keep in practice.

Commotions always seemed to happen when my husband was away, but traveling was inherent in his business as a Natural Resources consultant. If I believed in the fairy-tale concept of soul mates, although no, I didn't, Roy Holden would be it for me. First and foremost, he loved riding, held his own in cutting competitions on Mutt, his talented gelding. He was supportive, a great cook, and oh so easy on the eyes. But even if he'd been here, the window would've still shattered, and I already had a suspicion that the perpetrator was the same one who'd caused the yellow ball ruckus.

I spent the rest of the night stewing over escalating enemies and wondering how to present my case at tomorrow's town meeting. Not that I got nervous, not much anyhow, but schmoozing wasn't my style. By morning, I was bleary-eyed from lack of sleep and glad I'd made detailed notes about everything I needed to say about mustangs and why they're worth saving. I arrived early, feeling that facing my fellow citizens would be about as much fun as facing a firing squad.

Millie Dickson came early too, stomped up and spit in my face. I clinched a fist to deck her, but that might hamper my ladylike reputation. She'd arrived agitated to begin with, mostly because that was her normal state but also because on my way into town, I dropped by her place to inquire about her possible part in first the yellow-ball nastygram that precipitated a bucking bronco session with Hotshot, followed by last night's rearranging the glass in my window.

She turned twenty shades of indignant. As expected.

I understood why she and others felt the way they did about mustangs. Didn't agree, but I understood. My parents supplemented their income by raising cattle on the eighty acres of meadows interspersed with hilly Ponderosa forests where Roy and I now lived. They considered animals commodities, means of making a living. Nature was a force to conquer, an obstacle between them and survival. I grew up surrounded by the struggle to make it from snowdrifts in calving season to dried up water holes on summer grazing allotments. After sacrificing a pet calf I named Betty to profit gods at Denver's National Western Stock Show when I was all of a pig-tailed nine, I developed a permanent aversion to red meat, a distaste for rodeo generally and calf roping specifically. All of which kept me out of step with more than a few locals.

Still, I understood the need for livestock, admired real cowboys, the ones who put caring for their animals above their own comfort. I was totally awed by cutting horses and their talented riders. And I understood firsthand the challenges of ranching life.

Drilling rigs were a different matter. I had no desire to see those, although they were sprouting around here like poison mushrooms. Only so much land, too many uses. Only so much money, too many struggles. Which was why Millie and her Dickson clan weren't the only ranchers who might stop at nothing to get rid of wild horses.

I managed to remain upright for my little speech about mustangs. When I finished, the applause was underwhelming, but the usual group of supportive ranchers and town people gathered, and their presence felt like a warm hug.

Sheriff Plackmon approached too, waving me aside. "I hear you've had another commotion last night," he said.

"Someone felt I had too many windows."

At first glance, Ben Plackmon looked like a stereotypical small town sheriff, mediocre in appearance, but he was all business when it counted. "I assume you didn't see anyone."

"Nope."

"Also heard you dropped by the Dickson place this morning."

I nodded.

"Be careful, Margo, and keep me informed."

I was about to leave too when a tall stranger in an expensive suit approached.

"Your love of horses is quite apparent," he began.

"You must be from one of the drilling companies," I said, noticing the Rolex on his wrist.

"I am Juan Gomez, and you are correct. I represent UEF, Unified Energy Federation."

"So, let me guess. You hate mustangs as much if not more than other people around here."

"Not at all, Ms. Richards, not at all. As a matter of fact, I own horses myself."

"Okay, sure. Racing Thoroughbreds, I assume."

He smiled, showing perfectly white teeth. "Why yes. How did you know?"

I shrugged. "You said that you own horses, not that you ride. But enough chit-chat. I assume you have something to say."

His smile disappeared. "I do not wish to be confrontational, not in the least. As you know, the land at Soda Creek Cliffs contains vast stores of not only shale oil but also natural gas. I hope to convince you that energy companies are not the bad guys."

"And I hope to convince energy companies to stop harassing the mustangs."

"We have nothing but respect for those hardy animals, and we are impressed by your efforts to save them."

"Sure," I said. "But as you must know, I'm not in charge of the mustangs at Soda Creek. That land is controlled by the BLM."

"We are quite aware of that. We're also aware that your internet site and your other activities portray energy companies in a bad light. Negative publicity is unfortunate."

I tightened my arms against my chest. "Since when do companies such as yours care about image? I thought accumulating wealth was the goal."

The man's expression remained neutral, but his jaw clinched. "You are mistaken, my dear, but public opinion is important."

"I am not your dear, Mr. Gomez. But you are right regarding public opinion."

"Despite your adversarial posture, Ms. Richards, the UEF is prepared to purchase a tract of land for you to manage as a wild horse refuge."

"And where might this land be?"

"It's an expansive parcel in southern Nevada."

I laughed. "Ah, so a desert, no doubt. Nevada already has more mustangs than any other state. And let's not forget it's the BLM that controls those animals."

"It would be in your best interest to cooperate with us," he said, his tone smooth as his silk tie.

"Is that a threat?"

"Of course not." He reached into a suit pocket, withdrew a card, held it out.

I took it, but not because I planned to play his game. "Survival of the mustangs goes beyond business, and I'll do everything in my power to move the Soda Creek animals to a safe Colorado refuge."

"Do you have a business card?" he asked.

"Yes, but only for clients," I said, turning to leave.

Energy companies had already begun operations in the northernmost portions of the expansive Soda Creek area and were seeking

BLM permits to expand. But I still had to wonder why Gomez proposed moving mustangs to Nevada. I also wondered if they had their sights on drilling Bow's land, the very location I needed to rezone for a refuge which could accommodate a portion of the Soda Creek herds.

"Hey, Margo!"

I turned, smiled. "Hi Beth, thanks for coming."

"So, who's the tall guy?"

I shrugged. "Big shot oil man."

"Thought so. C'mon, you looked stressed. Let's grab a bite to eat."

Hunger was the last thing on my mind but spending time with a friend sounded good about now. Beth Jensen and I were nothing alike. Our friendship began while cheering for her talented young daughter. Nicole was one of those horse-crazy kids who rode with natural grace and accumulated well-deserved showring ribbons.

I tried being reasonable when talking about wild horses, but passion reared up, ran off with logic. As always, Beth listened patiently while we sipped tea and ate grilled cheese. She sent me off with a much-needed hug and a mellower outlook.

It didn't last long.

The morning after the town meeting and the run-ins with Millie Dickson and Juan Gomez, I awoke to find the front pasture empty, a bunch of my young horses meandering down the road. It was the time of year when nutritious spring grass was sprouting all over my land. Although horses sometimes leaned over fences to snatch mouthfuls of grass, none had ever escaped from any of my pastures.

Until someone cut the fence.

Two names came to mind. But maybe it wasn't Millie Dickson or one of her clan. Maybe it wasn't Juan Gomez or one of his minions.

Maybe my name wasn't Margo Richards.

The dirt road was sparsely traveled. The recipe for disaster called for only one vehicle. I sprinted out toward the wanderers, the dogs at my heels. Zap and Fetch demonstrated herding abilities while I got a dose of aerobics. The first group we rounded up were Quarter horse yearlings and two-year-olds, and close inspection revealed no cuts, no ill effects. Three young mustangs were more skittish and cantered off a ways, which was no surprise. When I finally got closer, I saw large red blotches along one side of each animal's rump. I gasped, fearing blood, fearing injuries.

But no. My mustangs had been spray-painted.

Anger and relief ran a race.

Anger won.